LOVER AND FIGHTER EXTRAORDINARY!

Hot-tempered, fearless Patrick Hepburn was leader of the Border Lords and chief supporter of young Jamie Stuart in his revolt against the King. When Jamie won, he granted The Hepburn lands that made Patrick the match of any Lord.

But not even the King could give to this mighty conqueror the one thing he wanted most—the love of Lady Jane Gordon. Her body, yes, and Jamie arranged their marriage. But Patrick Hepburn had to fight alone the battle of conflicting passions that finally tamed her violent pride and earned her tumultuous love.

THE HEPBURN was originally published by Crown Publishers, Inc.

Other books by Jan Westcott

*CAPTAIN BARNEY

**CAPTAIN FOR ELIZABETH

**THE QUEEN'S GRACE

*Published in a POCKET BOOK edition.
**Published in a PERMABOOK edition.

THE HEPBURN

BY JAN WESTCOTT

POCKET BOOKS, INC. • NEW YORK

The Hepburn

Crown edition published March, 1950

POCKET BOOK edition published November, 1951
4th printing..August, 1961

This POCKET BOOK includes every word contained in the original, higher-priced edition. It is printed from brand-new plates made from completely reset, clear, easy-to-read type.

•

POCKET BOOK editions are distributed in the U.S. by Affiliated Publishers, Inc., 630 Fifth Avenue, New York 20, N.Y.

•

L

PRINTED IN THE U.S.A.

For Mother

PART 1

1

IT WAS LATE AFTERNOON. THE HILLS CUT OFF THE SUN and laid shadows over the plain and valley of Sauchieburn.

The burn itself idled along between tree-lined banks. It was only a mile from Stirling, where the pointed towers of the castle rose, only two miles from the river that emptied into the Firth of Forth, on rather high ground that now in June was dressed in the beauty of a Scottish spring. Here, on the banks of Sauchieburn, the battle which had been fought this day was almost over.

North of the field of battle, on a hillside from which he could see the bitter fray, James the Third of Scotland watched. His knights had been with him; he had sent them away. An hour ago there had still been a chance for victory, and he had sent them in to bolster the falling Highland line. But now there was no chance of victory.

He was alone. In his heavy old-fashioned armor, he sat astride his gray horse on the hillside, while below him the rebel armies drank thirstily the victory that was theirs, and the clear water of the burn ran red with the blood of the loyal knights and burghers.

Clumsily he lifted the reins. He must get a good start now, while a few barons fought on. He would escape. There were certain places in which he might find sanctuary. From one of these places he would gather forces enough to meet his son once more in battle. His son, who had betrayed him.

"I call a curse on him," he said evenly, under his breath. He turned his horse. Lord Gordon had told him he had brought him the best horse in Scotland, if he would but sit it well. Even his loyal barons like George Gordon had laughed at his horsemanship.

Escape lay before him. He could of course find it in England, but the border lay between him and England, and he could never pass through. He must go north, to the Highlands.

Gradually he urged his animal into a steady canter and then into a full gallop. The great flying hooves dug into the soft earth, and the steady sound of the rhythmic gallop was the sweet refrain of escape. Escape and newer battles.

He came to an old road. Along the river it wound. He could not cross the river here, but three miles farther up there was a bridge.

There were few houses. The road narrowed again, widened, and in the distance he could see the outline of a large mill. That meant he was coming to Milltown.

The road curved suddenly. It ran past an old fence and Beaton's mill. James thundered on; he rounded the curve and Dame Beaton, who was drawing water from the well, looked up at his approach, startled. The horse was almost upon her. She screamed in terror, flung down her pitcher and fled.

The horse swerved madly; the pitcher rolled right under the flying hooves. And the king, poor horseman that he was, pitched forward in his armor and fell heavily to the ground. His horse galloped on, riderless.

Dame Beaton peered fearfully into the road. The king was lying motionless. She raised her voice to call her husband.

This was unnecessary. He had heard her first scream, and he was coming at a run. "What ails you, dame?" he asked, panting.

"Look." She pointed. She followed him more slowly as he ran to the side of the fallen man. He knelt beside him. So did Dame Beaton.

"Are ye hurt, sir?" she asked.

There was no answer.

"He has swooned," she said to her husband.

Between them, with the dame struggling for breath, they carried the wounded man into the mill and laid him on the floor, flat. Dame Beaton ran for her second-best cordial, for this man was a gentleman. She could see that.

"He was a poor rider," she said to Beaton, as she knelt again beside the hurt man. "The fall has hurt him, I warrant. Only the fall." She held the cup to his lips and poured a little of the liquid into his mouth.

James opened his eyes. He tried to drink, but it was difficult. "Loose this," he muttered, feeling at his chest. "I am dying," he said weakly.

Dame Beaton threw up her hands. "Merciful God," she cried. "No, you are not. Who are you, sir?"

His low voice answered her. "This day at morn, I was your king. Fetch me a priest, dame. I must make confession."

Dame Beaton uttered another loud cry. She gasped to her husband, "Watch your liege! It is he! I know it is!" She ran out of the still open door, clasping and unclasping her hands. She ran out of the mill yard, and into the road that led to the near-by village.

"A priest," she shouted. "A priest, you good people! Hear me!" She picked up her flowing skirts and ran on. "A priest," she called.

There were horsemen coming down the road. She scrambled to one side, but the village was near now, and she kept crying loudly, "A priest! A priest!"

The horsemen were coming fast. They were coming in pursuit of a single man who had fled. The thunder of the hooves almost drowned out Dame Beaton's cries, but not quite. One of the men slowed down, and twenty feet further he checked his horse. He wore the flowing garments and cassock of a man of the church. Dame Beaton saw him.

"Father!" she cried. She picked up her skirts again and rushed toward him. "God has sent you," she panted. "The Almighty has sent you!"

He had halted the men with him. He bent down in the saddle. "What say you, dame?" he asked curtly.

"A man is dying," she burst out. "He is dying, and has asked for you."

"Where?"

She pointed to the mill. "My husband is there. Hurry, Father. Hurry!"

"Why?" asked the priest. "Who is this man?"

She started to speak, but then held her tongue. "I do not know. But go!"

The priest turned away. She watched the men with him ride up to the mill door; she watched in the distance as the priest entered alone. She was out of breath, and she could not hurry.

Inside the dimly lighted mill, James lay. The priest entered, his gown swinging around his heels. He sent Master Beaton away; he went on his knees beside the wounded man. Was it he whom he sought?

The king's helmet had been removed. His thick hair was rumpled and his forehead was beaded with sweat, his eyes hardly open. When the priest knelt beside him, he looked up.

"Father," he whispered, "I die."

"My son," the priest said slowly. "Ah, my son." He bent his head, and from beneath his cassock he drew a long knife. The king's armor was old. Across his chest it was fastened loosely, and there was a big chink in it. The priest, who was called Borthwick, saw the chink plainly.

The armor parted easily. The knife was driven sharply and cleanly, and withdrawn just as swiftly. James's eyes closed; the priest took the helmet, slipped it over the dead man's head, and pulled the visor closed. Then he wrapped the cloak close around the body of his king. He stood up just as Dame Beaton put her head in the door.

"He has passed," he said mournfully. "Will you summon my men?"

The men shouldered their way into the old dark mill. Under the priest's eyes they picked up the dead man and carried him from the mill house and bore him away. In the mill yard some of the men lingered, and the dame went quickly into the house and shut the door.

"Stay away from the window," she cautioned her youngest daughter. She was shaking with fright. "This is naught for poor folks to know," she muttered. She was worried about her husband, out there with that ruffian crew. "That was no priest," she said. "No priest."

There was only one man she could trust to help her. She still breathed fast. "We must tell our lord, the Hepburn."

2

THERE WERE FEW PEOPLE ABROAD IN THE CITY OF EDINburgh. Shops were closed; their owners had gone forth to battle for their king. Houses were shuttered and tight closed against violence; and inside, though darkness would not fall for two hours, the lights were lighted.

The quiet was ominous. Up the gray ramp, the great castle of Edinburgh brooded over the city, its garrison gone and its cannon silent. The massive gates were open, its state chambers, dark and empty and lonely. Only its ghosts walked. And in its guardrooms a handful of men waited grimly for the news of battle. Against an opposing force they could not hold the castle.

In the streets a few people hurried and ran from the safety of one house to the next. Brigands were waiting. In the absence of the law, in the meaner streets that day, in the narrow twisting closes, there were twenty murders, and no one knew how many petty thefts and robberies. Meat was stolen from abandoned butcher shops, and in one linen shop, the thieves set fire to the house and escaped unseen.

In the finer sections of the city, where the great nobles maintained town residences, the heavy doors were shut and bolted well. Within them, women waited for news of their lords. And in an oaken-paneled bedroom, in a house on Castle Hill, Jane Gordon paced back and forth before a brightly burning fire.

Her hair was plaited and wound around her head. Her long

full gown was drawn tight around her hips with a brilliant red kirtle. She paced like a man, and from time to time she glanced at the slender figure sleeping in the big bed. Finally the figure stirred. Mary Gordon raised herself wearily on one elbow. She had been trying to sleep.

"Oh, Jane," she said. "Jane, please stop."

"I cannot," said Jane evenly.

"Lord, you are as restful as a tigress." Mary sat up, pulling the pillows up behind her shoulders. She leaned back and looked across the tumbled bed to the flames. The wind must be strong outside, for even indoors the bedcurtains rustled with the drafts.

"Do not sit up," Jane said suddenly, pulling her thoughts back to this room. "You're not well enough yet."

"I am. I shall be out of bed tomorrow."

"Nonsense. You still have the fever. Can you eat?"

"I'm not hungry."

"For God's sake, be hungry!" Jane cried desperately. "I must have something to do!" She whirled, and anger made her eyes as golden as the molasses shade of her hair. She stamped her foot and pointed to a sword which hung over the mantel. "I wish to God I could use that!"

Mary sighed with great weariness, sinking down deeper into the feather bed. "Fetch me some food, then," she murmured. "Jane, there is nothing we can do save wait."

"I cannot wait!" Jane burst out. "How can you?"

"I have been very ill," Mary said. Her face against the pillows was pale. Her hair was black, and even after sickness she was beautiful.

"I'm sorry," Jane whispered. "Oh, Mary, if I leave you, could you sleep a bit and then mayhap eat a bite of supper?"

Mary tried to smile. "I think I could." She settled herself in the bed and closed her eyes. Jane tiptoed to the door and closed it gently after her.

In her own bedroom, Jane Gordon sat down on the edge of her canopied bed. The room was chilly; there was no fire. Beside her lay her heavy cloak, which she had flung down carelessly. She slipped it over her shoulders for warmth. For a moment she sat there, and then suddenly she rose and went to the window, pulling back the shutters. She looked down into the cobbled street.

It was empty. Jane, with her cloak already on, whirled from the window; remembering, she returned and closed the shutters. Then she left the room, leaving the door open in her haste.

On the ground floor all was silent. With a wake of open doors behind her, she gained the kitchens and stood poised on the threshold of the long narrow room, her cloak flowing behind her. The men in the kitchen looked up, startled.

"We ride now," she said.

One man named Wat struggled to his feet, trying to clasp his doublet over his round stomach. He and the others had come into the kitchen at the command of Lord Gordon. They were a strange army of protectors: stable hands, ten house servants, two cooks, a barber, Lord Gordon's tailor, and four men at arms. Wat, still clutching his doublet, said, "Mistress, you cannot go abroad!"

"Fool," said Jane. "I go now. If you are coming, follow me." She pointed a finger at one stable boy. "Saddle up my mare, lad," she ordered, and started across the kitchen to the smoke-blackened door.

"Mistress Jane!" said Wat desperately, darting between Jane and the door. "This is madness!"

"Lord Gordon may be lying wounded out there!" Jane waved a gloved hand. "Would you sit here?"

"Aye," said Wat. "And we ha' orders to stay here."

"Think you I am leaving Lady Mary unprotected, dolt? I want only six men. Otherwise I go alone."

Wat knew this was arrant nonsense. But he had never in his life won an argument with Mistress Jane. She was worse than ten headstrong men. Wat grinned. "Ye're daft, mistress," he said companionably. He glanced over his hodgepodge company and picked four men and the stable boy. "Follow us," he commanded, having fastened his doublet. He buckled his belt tighter as he walked.

The stables were deep in dusk. There were but six horses

left. It took only three minutes to saddle up, but Jane begrudged those minutes. "Hurry!"

"Hurry into danger?" Wat asked.

"Hold your tongue," Jane whispered. "You'll fright these cooks."

"They're handier with knives than the tailor," said Wat. "At least they ought to be. Here, mistress."

He helped Jane into the saddle. Then he mounted himself. As they galloped out the open doors, he glanced back at the four riders with them.

They wore the livery of the Gordons. Wat was not sure that was wise. Other men envied the power and position of the Highland Gordons. Wat prayed that the loyal forces had won today's battle, else they, all of them, might be killed out of hand. But there was no time for worry, because Jane was galloping ahead, and he spurred his own mount to catch up with her.

"Speed will be needed through the city," Jane cried, her voice muffled by the wind.

"Speed will be needed everywhere," Wat shouted grimly. "I warrant you know these are the poorest nags we have."

That mattered little to Jane. What did matter was that she was out in this wild afternoon. The wind was strong and fitful, blowing in heady gusts that made her half close her thick-lashed eyes. Here, through the city, she could well imagine that the timorous people behind their barred doors were already watching and saying, "Look! There goes Jane Gordon! Only she would ride out on a day like this!"

Jane held her head high and sat straight and easy in the saddle. She pulled ahead of Wat again, to show the city she was leading these men, and that no matter the day or the hour the Gordons rode out, unafraid, and that their wealth and solid political power went with them.

"I'll race you to the gates," Jane called to Wat.

The words were pulled out of her mouth by the wind. Great clouds scudded across the skies, and the red of sunset touched their high-piled tops with pink. The horses' hooves struck fire from the cobblestones, and the city was silent.

"No," Wat roared.

"It's like a dead city," Jane yelled back.

"A lot of people may be deader before the night's over, including us!"

Narrow closes ran off High Street here, and from any of them might come attack. Jane quickened her pace again, and all six of them pounded forward behind her to the city gates which stood open and unattended. It was those open gates that made Jane realize she was going where few would dare.

Jane, who used only one hand on the reins, lifted her right hand and pushed back a long tendril of hair that had come loose. Through the open gates she clattered, heedless; the road lay free before her, and the way to the south was straight ahead. They had gone three miles further and topped a long steady rise when she saw something that gave her pause.

She reined in hastily. Her horse fretted. Jane waited and looked while she made sure that Wat saw too.

"About two thousand horse," Wat said grimly. "Since there are but six of us, not even sixteen, let alone a hundred and sixty . . ."

"Shut your mouth," Jane snapped. "Can you make out the banners?" They were looking west, and the sky was brilliant. "Isn't it magnificent?" Jane asked.

Wat, who had wheeled his horse, said, "Mistress, this is no place for us!"

Jane set her mouth. She could see plainly that the horsemen were riding hard for the city, but she could also see that she had plenty of time before they would reach her own vantage point.

"I think to stop here awhile, Wat," she announced.

"If you think those are his Majesty's forces, ye're daft," Wat said. "They are nae the king's forces."

"How do you know?" asked Jane.

"Because he had no large cavalry. They'll be Border rogues acomin', I warn ye," he added darkly. "I warn ye. Ye go now." His face was more set than hers, and Jane, who had never before seen Wat frightened, realized he was frightened now. "They be Border rogues," he repeated, and he looked around himself. "And this is nae place to stop. There are too many trees."

"Trees?" asked Jane. There was a deep grove of trees to her left.

"Aye, and more horses!" cried Wat. "Oh, God, mistress!" His face was pale, and Jane saw that not more than a mile away a troop of horse had just appeared over the brow of the nearest hill; the valley dipped down twice between her and them, but they would be on them within five minutes. Now she too, fearful, jerked hard on the reins and turned her horse, just as from the trees to the left came the unexpected attack that Wat had feared.

The men who flung themselves upon the five horsemen and Jane were afoot. One of them seized the bridle of Jane's horse.

She could not look for aid from Wat; there was no time and he was beset, too. She heard shouts and curses and cries. She struck vainly at the hands on her bridle. Another man, coming from behind, yanked her from the saddle. Desperate and angry, Jane found herself deposited on the road in a sitting position. She jumped to her feet and ran to Wat's aid.

Wat was still ahorse, and fighting off three men. The other four of Jane's company had already fled, and Jane ran forward, wielding the whip in her hand.

"Rogues, knaves," she cried. "D'ye dare? Get away there. By God, I'll have you punished for this!"

It was at this moment that the troop of horse Jane had first seen were upon them.

Jane was hardly conscious of them. She was conscious of the fact that Wat had killed one man and was raising his long sword to dispose of another, and the third man was backing off from her attack. He was saying, incredibly, "Hold, Jane. Stop!"

Jane stared at him in utter amazement while around her and the speaker and Wat twenty armored men on horseback formed a ring of steel. Alongside Jane a huge brown stallion stood quietly while its master looked down on her bare head.

Jane paid no attention to him or to the horse, She was still staring at the man in front of her. "Sir David," she whispered, "how could you set your knaves on me?"

David Lindsay glanced from Jane to the armed men around him. He said quickly, "We lost today, Jane. We needed horses. How in God's name could I tell it was you, out here?" He raised his eyes to the man on the brown horse. "I am Sir David Lindsay," he said. "May I present you to Lady Jane Gordon." With this he drew his sword and tendered it, hilt first.

The horseman leaned down to take the proffered sword. He handed it to the nearest man. He seemed to pay no attention to Jane or to Wat. "You are under arrest," he said.

"May I ask the charge?" Lindsay inquired.

"Insurrection against the Crown of Scotland," was the answer.

Lindsay said coldly, "An odd charge, since I was fighting with the loyal forces." But he made no motion to resist the two men who led him away.

Jane watched him go. It was incredible that David Lindsay could be arrested. She looked up at the man beside her.

He was wearing the new, light-steel armor. Under his helmet his eyes were gray in a tanned face. Jane had not heard his name. She said,

"I have a brother, Lord Gordon. Is he safe sir?"

"I do not know," came the reply. His gray eyes rested on her. She was flushed and excited and unafraid.

"He was fighting for the king!" cried Jane.

"He has escaped." He slid down to face Jane Gordon, and stood close to her, taller than she by half a head. She could see the beginnings of a stubble on his clean-shaven face, and his eyes were tired. There were deep lines etched from the nostrils to his mouth. Jane looked up at him in the darkening light, conscious of the armed men all around her.

"Who are you, sir?" she said wonderingly.

"Patrick Hepburn," he said.

The name hung between them for a moment. Then Jane's eyes grew wide, and she stared up at him in sudden raging anger. "You!" she cried. "I know you! You are the Hepburn of Hailes!"

"That is what they call me." His eyes were guarded.

Jane blazed, "You traitor! You dirty thief!"

Patrick Hepburn said nothing. He looked over Jane's head to a soldier. "Bring Lady Gordon's mount," he ordered.

Jane, trembling with anger, lashed out again for all to hear. "You put me in mind of a beggar mounting a throne! D'ye dream you'll be allowed to stay there?"

She lifted her whip. Before he realized she would dare, before he raised an arm to stop her, he had only time to close his eyes. The lash crossed his face sideways, catching the edge of his lip in a scar he would always wear. Under the sudden pain of the blow, he did nothing. He opened his eyes as he felt the pain.

It had been a hard blow. The men on either side of Jane seized her arms; the whip still dangled from her gloved fingers. Between the two men, Jane looked up at Hepburn's face, as the blood trickled down from the high cheekbone and across his mouth. She asked, "Does it take two of your miserable dogs to protect you from a woman?"

Captain Knox paid no attention. He lifted the whip from Jane's hand. "D'ye want this, my lord?"

"No," said the Hepburn. "Return it to the lady. And, mistress, as to your question to me, I might say that it takes two of them to protect you from me." He felt tenderly of his cheek and mouth.

Captain Knox laughed. He dropped Jane's arm. "Hear that, lass?" he asked.

"Your horse, Lady Gordon," Hepburn said, offering his hand to assist her.

The dappled mare stood quietly. Jane made no effort at dignity, disdaining help. It was not necessary for Jane Gordon to do anything except exactly what she wished. She seized the high pommel and swung her leg over the horse, her torn cloak blowing in the wind. But before she could spur ahead, twenty helmeted riders clattered past, to form an advance escort, and Jane had to wait. She looked over her shoulder to the Hepburn, saw he was mounted, and, to her slight surprise, that he was going to ride at her side. Captain Knox was dropping behind. The clouds of dust rising from the hillside told her that another large party of horsemen was following them. In the dusk, the city was a shadow of tumbled roofs on the horizon.

The Hepburn did not speak. He set the pace at a hard gallop and Jane, remembering reports on his horsemanship, darted sideways to see whether they were true.

They were. And as far as she knew he did not glance her way at all. Jane swore under her breath, a long satisfactory oath which her brother used frequently. At least George Gordon had not been caught. Jane rode for five minutes in silence, after which she could bear it no longer. Even in the darkness now, she could see the castle walls plainly. They were nearing town.

"Even if we lost today," Jane shouted, "never dream we are done fighting!"

His voice carried back to her, low and strong. "I do not."

"Oh," said Jane. She paused to digest that. "The people hate you!"

"Only some of them," he replied.

"What did you say?" Jane cried, knowing very well what he said.

He didn't answer; he was looking ahead and slowing his pace. Jane realized that the width of the road here was allowing another troop of cavalry to pass them at breakneck speed. Because of the noise of hooves and armor, Jane was forced to be silent until they had gone back. And farther up, where the road forked, they took the turn to the south.

"Where are they going?" she shouted.

"Dunbar," the Hepburn said.

"Oh," said Jane again. She frowned and darted another look at him. "So your men are garrisoning Dunbar?"

He nodded, and their eyes met for a moment, but she knew he had been studying her, that he had been thinking about her and not about the mighty fortress of Dunbar, which he would have taken in a matter of hours. Jane thought his gaze was detached and impersonal, as though he found nothing to distinguish her from the rest of the nobility who had fought him and young James.

"Am I under arrest?" Jane asked mockingly.

He evidently did not hear her. Once more he was looking ahead. The pace was slowed almost to a walk, for they were upon the city.

"The gates are open," Jane said, divining his thoughts. "I came through them." She repeated her question. "Am I under arrest?"

"Possibly you shall be," he answered.

She threw her head back in laughter. "I?" she asked.

"You, mistress," he said evenly and, Jane, surprised, turned to him in real wonderment.

"Nonsense," said Jane.

"Neither his Majesty nor I want trouble," he said.

"You have plenty of trouble already," jeered Jane. She waved her hand behind her. "How many men have we?"

His mouth drew downward in a small smile. "We?" he asked.

"You!" Jane corrected herself instantly.

"About three thousand, now."

"And they are going to Edinburgh?"

"They will be quartered on the city, and in the castle. To keep order."

"You mean that in war, possession of the capital city is imperative! And your men will arm Dunbar?"

"Exactly," he said. He reined in. In the faint light of early evening, silence reigned over the city, and its gates stood open, waiting for the victor in today's battle. The city awaited; a kingdom awaited. Jane turned to look away from it.

All across the plain she saw nothing but orderly cavalry, in formation. Banners flew from the lance ends, and the trotting hooves were like muffled drumbeats. Then came the first blast of the horns; on each side of Jane torches flared suddenly, the first troop wheeled and the first one hundred riders entered the gates of the city of Edinburgh.

"One moment," the Hepburn said, checking Jane as she started to ride again. "We shall let still more precede us."

"I should think you would want to be first," Jane said bitterly.

"No. 'Tis better to have some companies of soldiers first."

"You know the tricks, don't you?" she cried.

"I warrant so," he said.

The next troop moved past them; five more companies went by before the Hepburn said, "You may ride now."

At his signal Jane swung into place behind four horsemen with torches. Jane, who had to ride through the city, felt the hot tears in her eyes as she witnessed this capitulation. "You are taking it so easily," she whispered.

The progress through High Street was orderly. At the first marketplace, the leading troop separated, dividing itself in half, and disappeared into the narrow closes. Jane heard the banging on the doors of the shuttered houses as they were opened to the conquerors.

At the Town Cross, five more companies spread in all directions, and it was here that five hundred men left the rest to take possession of the castle itself.

Along the streets, upper windows opened and the people looked down apprehensively. One by one the doors of the city opened, and into the houses, quartered on them for order and quiet, went the loyal Border forces who obeyed only one man, the man who rode beside her.

Jane found it hard to fathom. "How could you?" she asked. "You?" She wrinkled her nose thoughtfully. "Just a Hepburn from Hailes. Is it true you are able to raise ten thousand men for battle?"

"I did today," he said, his mind going to the heroism and courage his men had displayed, for it had been they who had finally, after five attempts, broken the Highland lines.

"You and Jamie will never hold what you've taken," she said. Then she realized she was climbing the steep Castle Hill. "You brought me all the way home."

"I could scarce leave you abroad in the streets," he said quickly, almost defensively. While she drew rein he studied her. He dismounted, took the bridle, and lifted her down from the saddle; for a moment his hands rested on her waist. She stepped back from him. He waited and Jane hesitated.

"Come," he said, sharply. He had no time to waste.

"But those men," said Jane, pointing.

"I've assigned twenty men to this house."

"Twenty?" repeated Jane. She stopped in her slow walk to face him. "Why?"

He took her arm and started toward the carved doors. "Because the larger houses can quarter more men than the smaller, and because you may need protection."

The doors had opened; frightened servants held them and peered out into the path of light thrown into the street. As Jane stepped in, she heard him follow. She didn't turn until she heard the doors close. Then, in the light from the candles in the sconces, she let her torn cloak slip to the floor, and looked at him insolently.

"Why are you here?" she asked.

He was looking about himself. On the stairway an oil painting of the third Lord Gordon frowned down on him. The shadows in the room to the left of the hall did not conceal the beauty of the fireplace and mantel.

"This is lovely," he said appreciatively.

"Have you ever seen the like?" inquired Jane icily.

"Not very often," he said, and he smiled a little. His gaze returned to her. "Neither you nor your sister are betrothed, are you?" he asked bluntly.

Jane's eyes widened in real amazement. It was her turn to stare, from the big boots to the lean face under the helmet, marked now with blood. Jane whispered, "D'ye hint, Hepburn? D'ye dream?" Then Jane laughed. "Leave," she ordered.

"I shall," he said. "But you may not. You may not leave these walls. There are twenty men here to enforce my orders, and, Lady Gordon, do not try to countermand or cajole because it would be useless."

Jane was so angry she had difficulty finding words.

"I do this for your safety," he ended.

Jane cried passionately, "My safety is not your concern!"

He looked down at her. "I want no man handling you," he said. "I go too fast, mayhap. 'Tis a habit of mine." He went to the door, while Jane, speechless, stood watching. "Remember, lass," he said, as he stood in the open doors, "you are not to go out."

3

THEY WERE BURYING THE DEAD ON SAUCHIE FIELD. THE noble dead had been borne away, but the common burgher's grave would go unmarked.

A mile away, where thirty thousand rebels had camped the night before, a few tents still stood. On the highest part of a hill, one square silken tent flew the royal banner.

Inside a silver lamp burned. A table was piled high with papers. A page dozed on his stool, resting his head in his arms. On a low couch with pillows, James of Scotland slept.

Thick short lashes lay against the brown cheeks. The dark brows were well defined and the hair was deep dark brown. He breathed quietly and slowly, but his sleep was not deep, for the rustle of the silk in the wind roused him and he opened his eyes. Against the dull red of his doublet, he looked exactly what he was—a man born to be a king.

He had slept only twenty minutes. But time seemed to have receded, or gone by very fast, and he recalled himself to the present.

The page slept. The last time James had looked at the page he was sleeping, so that nothing seemed to have changed. But the papers on the table looked—James raised himself on one elbow. He rose wearily to go over and look at them. They had been disturbed.

The sure knowledge that they had been disturbed came like a blow which he had expected but was not quite ready for. His eyes, wary now, looked to the doorway—it was that curtain which must have rustled when the man who came to spy had stolen away unseen. James, leaning on his intuition, was sure then that it must be a man he trusted well, a loyal baron. No one else would dare enter the royal tent. James felt at his belt absently: the long dagger was comfortingly in place.

It had been rather foolhardy to enter this tent just to see the papers lying on the table. James made a note to remember that the man who was spying would take silly risks to know ahead of time what his king was planning. The signed papers were land grants only; they showed the measures James was taking to safeguard the kingdom which he had won today on the field of battle.

James picked up the papers. The page slept. James started to wake him, for he wanted the stool; then he changed his mind. He settled himself on the couch again, head propped up on one hand, and went through the papers, one by one.

A land grant to Patrick Hepburn, including the towns and great castle of Bothwell. Through James's mind went a picture of the map of the Lowlands and the Border. The Hepburn controlled Hailes, of course, on the sea, and he had been given the wardenship of Dunbar, the fortified harbor and key to Scotland. By now his men should be pacing its ramparts. This new grant of Bothwell would balance his power inland and extend his sway to the gates of Glasgow. Thus he would be a match for the most powerful lord of the Border, the Earl of Douglass.

James rubbed his chin. He needed to shave. The Borders and the Lowlands were disposed of temporarily, but of course James could change this. He could take back what he had given by a stroke of the pen or a royal arrest. But he had no wish to take this back. This was important, for it was the Border nobility, with Hepburn as their leader, who were his most trusted supporters. And more than that it was important that he judge well and that no traitorous baron have power here so near an ancient enemy, so near to England.

He got to his feet. By now Patrick Hepburn would have taken the helpless capital city, manned the castle, and disposed of the nobles taken prisoner today, disposed of them in the castle's heavily barred tower and dungeons. That made James realize that even while this was happening, to his good fortune, other riders, spurring weary steeds, would be galloping into England, to bring to Henry VII the news that the Scottish rebels under the young prince had won today, and that instead of a timorous ally on the throne of Scotland, Henry Tudor had an enemy who could not be bribed or threatened.

But it was not yet time to think of England. It was not yet time to venture further afield. That time would come, and when it did, perhaps the gods would place in his hands the instruments for power, as they had today. James said quietly, "Lad, wake now."

The page raised his head, and seeing the king standing, jumped to his feet. "Your pardon, sire."

"Granted," said James. "Now fetch me water for shaving, and fetch Lord Douglass. Quickly."

"Aye, your Grace." The page backed to the silken doorway; he was gone, and James, left alone, began to pace the rude flooring. He was still pacing when Douglass arrived.

Douglass was a man of great brawn and thick beard. With him was Lord Fleming. They would have knelt, but James waved aside the gesture.

"No ceremony, my lords," James said. He paused a moment. Then his question came sharp and urgent. "Have you aught of news for me?"

Lord Fleming stood silent. His eyes flicked past the papers on the table.

Douglass shook his head. "There is no news."

Fleming now spoke softly, spreading out his hands. "The king, your father, has fled, your Grace. He is gone." Then he repeated one word. "Fled."

Fleming had gone too far. His voice, unctuous, had been tinged with contempt for James Stuart's father. Even in the light of the two silver smoky lamps, Fleming was taken aback by the set of James's face. For a brief instant Fleming recalled the sweet and merciful nature of James's father as he looked at the fiery James the Fourth who had himself killed a man, another Douglass. Fleming stepped back.

The page returned with a covered bowl of steaming water. James, his anger controlled, noticed that Fleming was afraid. James's mobile mouth curled in a sardonic smile.

And Douglass interposed, to placate James, "We shall find your father, sire. Your orders went out that he was not to be harmed. On pain of death. We shall find him safe."

Because of the urgency of this night after battle and victory, James forgot Fleming. And he forgot that the man of whom he was speaking was his father. He said harshly, driving a clenched fist against his palm, "The ways of escape are blocked!"

The page had uncovered the water. Tiny curls of steam wisped from it. The lamps swung. Fleming averted his eyes.

"Aye, your Grace," he said.

"Aye, your Grace," big Douglass repeated.

James Stuart surveyed them both. He was still angry, but the anger was softened by the feeling of victory, the bloody seizure of his father's throne. No matter the cost. He had gained a kingdom, and he was going to guard it well. Perhaps his lords didn't know that yet. Perhaps they deemed they might betray him, as they had betrayed his father. But they would learn. They would learn the lessons he was going to teach them very well. In the meantime he himself must take possession of the first royal castle.

"Prepare to ride to Edinburgh within half an hour," he said.

4

SIR MATTHEW CRADDOCK LAY FACE DOWN ON THE DAMP June earth. It was getting dark. When he opened his eyes for the first time in twenty-four hours, he had difficulty remembering where he was. If it had not been that he remembered losing consciousness just at nightfall, he would not have known how many hours he had lain here.

Now he reckoned it must have been a full day. It must be the seventeenth of June, the day after the battle of Sauchieburn, and rather miraculously he seemed to be alive.

Gingerly he felt the top of his head. He did not sit up. He used his right hand, and he felt caked blood and the still open edges of a wound.

Then he experimented with tipping back his head. He wet his dry lips. Yesterday, after nearly getting his head knocked off, he had managed to ride five miles to this thicket where he had crawled in among these bushes. His horse had probably been stolen by one of the marauding rebels who combed the battlefield after dark. He wet his lips again and tried a low whistle.

There was no response. He gave up the idea of finding his horse. He put his head down again. The soft sounds of a few twittering birds and the rustle of leaves overhead was all he heard; except, when he lay very quiet, he thought he caught the sound of running water.

He got to his hands and knees and began to crawl toward the sound. Bushes brushed at him, and then he was beside a tiny stream which ambled its way over a pebbly bed. He crawled to the edge; he could almost have touched the other side of the tiny stream, kneeling there. He cupped his dirty hands and drank deeply. Relishing the water, he put his face down into the clear cold water and began to splash it over his face and onto his matted hair. Absorbed in this task, he heard nothing till he felt the point of a sword prodding the small of his back, and a voice above him said, "Who are you, knave?"

Sir Matthew didn't move. He swallowed what water there was in his mouth, and said only, "Matthew, sir."

He could not see even the shadow of the man whose sword lazily poked at his vulnerable back. He twisted to one side, agilely, and using the strength he hardly knew he still possessed, he jumped to his feet. Blue eyes narrowed, he looked at his antagonist.

"God in heaven!" He spoke with surprise and relief, as

though he were already trying to plan the next steps which this unexpected meeting would make possible. He passed his hand over his head. "Lord Gordon."

George Gordon's expression was one of relief too. "I thought you'd been killed, Matthew. You fought well."

Matthew was silent at this compliment; and Gordon said, with boyish eagerness and a good deal of pleasure in finding a man he could depend on, "I'll rehire you."

Matthew nodded. His wits were busy. Meantime he wiped his still dripping face on his sleeve, feeling with satisfaction the thin knife fastened to his forearm and concealed under the cloth. "It is necessary I find employment," he conceded. "It is also necessary we find food and drink." He wrinkled his brow; he would sound out Gordon. "Where did you wish to go, m'lord?"

Gordon considered this point. "To the city," he said finally.

This also was necessary to Matthew's quickly laid plans. But he felt he should issue a word of caution, even though he was positive Gordon would not heed it. "You may be arrested." These four words of warning were all he intended to say; they salved his conscience.

"Let it be, then," Gordon announced.

Matthew shrugged his shoulders; it made his head pain, and he winced. "This way then," he said.

In about two minutes he emerged onto the road he had left a full twenty-four hours ago. Gordon plunged out of the thick brush, and came to stand beside him. His expression was puzzled.

Matthew inquired lazily. "Had you been lost, sir? The city is there." He intended to waste no more breath talking. He started out at as rapid a pace as his legs would endure.

The road was dusty and stony. Walking was an annoyance to men who were used to being ahorse. Irritable, Matthew increased the length of his stride. It was an irritation too to have to remember to use a crude English Border accent. He knew he would become more adept at it, but now it rankled. It made his tone sharp.

"Grant me a favor, m'lord, and toss away that plumed helmet."

Gordon took off his helmet and tossed it into a ditch at the side of the road. Without saying a word he proceeded in his long-legged walk. The two men kept side by side and Matthew fought back the weariness and the pain that had begun to beat badly through his whole head. A question came at him.

"Where do you come from?" asked Gordon.

This question he answered automatically. "Dorsetshire," he replied, having a fleeting vision of the storied, gabled mansion house set in the gentle hills of home. Yet Matthew Craddock never had time to question the reasons that had sent him forth. At thirty-two, he had few illusions about himself. After Henry Tudor had been victorious, and Matthew had fought for him on the Continent as well as in England, Matthew had gone forth again to serve his king another way, a way with the spice of danger and adventure, and a way that might pay very high—already had, in fact. It was far too peaceful in Dorsetshire.

"Are you never homesick, man?" asked Gordon gently.

"At times," said Matthew truthfully.

"Right now I should give a fortune to see the towers of Strathbogie," said Gordon, referring to the mighty northern castle from which the Gordons, bred from kings, were wont to defy any and all authority which displeased them, and from which they ventured forth, armed, to defend what it pleased them to defend. George Gordon had liked his king; he had been willing to lay down his life for James the Third of Scotland, but had it not been for the respect and love he bore this king and uncle, he might just as easily have sat in his northern stronghold and watched the fray cynically from afar.

They were passing an inn. Matthew moved to the side of the road to escape its mean light. Ahead now was the distant glow that meant Edinburgh. It was this sight that forced Gordon to speak.

"Matthew," he said, and stopped.

Matthew waited. He waited patiently. Gordon was hesitating, but he would finally speak his mind.

He did. His eyes were on the city, plainer now. "Look you, fellow, you are sharp of wit and write a better hand than I do."

Matthew still said nothing. He had his opinion of his own worth, and it was very high.

"I'll offer you ten gold pieces a month."

Unmoved, Matthew said, "That was what you offered me before."

"I know, knave."

Matthew could hardly make out Gordon's face in the deep dusk. But he knew Gordon was struggling with the thought that for the first time in his life he might be in danger and that he probably faced arrest. Gordon was young. Not twenty yet. He was trying to shoulder this new responsibility.

Gordon said aloud, "I can see the castle. If I am placed there, my sisters, the Lady Jane and the Lady Mary—well, you shall be with them as my secretary. You ken, Matthew, I saw you fight, and I know you can be trusted."

Matthew smiled at this naïveté. But he said solemnly, "I thank you, m'lord. I'll do my best."

"It will be a good best," Gordon said, sighing a bit.

"I shall have only your welfare and that of your sisters to spur me," continued Matthew, lying gracefully.

They were at the gates of the city. In a few seconds they would be challenged. Matthew had just finished speaking when the light of the torches broke through the night, and a voice said, "Halt."

There were four soldiers on either side of the open gates. Between them Matthew and Gordon halted. Matthew said, "We are two soldiers returning from Sauchie. I am a butcher's apprentice, and—"

He was cut off. A dark-faced man looked past him to George Gordon, who, with his torn doublet and unshaven face looked little like the earl he was. But the winking jewels in his sword-hilt gave him away.

However, the captain posted especially at the south gate by

Patrick Hepburn knew that it was easy enough to return from a battlefield with looted weapons. He had done it himself. So he waved Matthew and Gordon on, with a negligent wave. But he watched them go. When they were but ten yards away, he beckoned to the nearest soldier.

"Follow them," he commanded, "and report back here to me."

5

MATTHEW KNEW THAT THE FATIGUE AND THE PAIN IN his head had dulled his wits. The mist felt good on his face, and he licked it off his lips gratefully. Now he was following Gordon, because the city was not so familiar to him as it was to the Scot, who knew every mean alley and every narrow close.

And the fog was getting worse, for which Matthew thanked heaven. The pain in his head was now so bad that he began to think he was not awake at all but drifting around in some kind of nightmare. Gordon didn't speak, and Matthew had no idea how far out of their way they had gone when Gordon suddenly whispered, "Matthew, do you think there are soldiers quartered on my house? Because I'm eternally damned if I don't see horses out in the back court, and my stablers would never leave the animals out. On their peril, they would."

Matthew tried to open his eyes wider and to look over the stone wall which enclosed the stables and back court of the Gordon town mansion. Trees brushed against him wetly.

"You are right, my lord," he whispered back. "Where is the best window for us?" He was wondering if he had strength enough to climb in a window.

"Around here," said Gordon. He made his way silently

over the slippery grass. In the right angle made by the end of the wall and the house was a low, many-paned, bellied window. It was dark within.

Matthew said only two words. "Your sword." He took the weapon from Gordon; clumsily he lifted the heavy sword, and using the hilt he knocked at the panes in a sideways sweep that broke the lower section. Two more blows finished the job.

"Watch the glass," he said automatically.

Gordon put one foot on the rough stone and climbed in the window. Matthew, gritting his teeth, followed suit. There was nothing within save darkness. Gordon took five steps to the door, and Matthew, swaying unsteadily, stood where he was, reaching vainly with one hand for the support of a chair or table. He finally found the window ledge and waited.

The opening of the hall door threw light into the room from the narrow hallway that ran off the main hall twenty feet away. Matthew saw a chair, a high-backed chair. He went to it and sat down. He drifted peacefully into unconsciousness. When next he opened his eyes, there were three people in the room and Gordon was holding out to him a cup of colorless liquid that swirled before his eyes.

Matthew drank it in one gulp. Gordon poured a drink for himself and another for Matthew. A woman was bending over the hearth, and the crackle of flames was already in the room. Two candles had been lighted, the curtains drawn over the broken window. Then the woman straightened and turned. Matthew stared.

She was deathly pale, her white skin like alabaster and her great bluish eyes shadowed. Her hair was gleaming, raven black. Matthew said, low, "Mistress, there is naught to fear!" He set the glass down, and tried to catch his breath and summon more energy. Then he saw Jane Gordon.

"Mary is not fearful," Jane cut in, haughtily. "She has been ill."

"Oh," said Matthew, letting his eyes come back to Mary. "I'm sorry to hear that—"

Jane interrupted. "Who are you, knave? George, what in God's name does he do here? Are you mad to bring him?"

"Hold your tongue," said George. "Mary, you look a fright. Get yourself upstairs to bed."

"Oh, George," said Mary. "Let me stay."

"You look a fright," George repeated. "For God's sake, can't I leave this house for two days without—"

Jane snapped, "Aye, you leave, and come home like a whipped dog! What has happened?"

Mary whispered, "Be quiet, an' it please you both. Must you quarrel now? Must you always—" She too broke off, and steadied herself by the mantel. Matthew saw she was trembling.

Matthew had been looking from George to Jane. He said, surprised, "You two are twins."

Jane paid no attention. "We aren't quarreling, Mary. We—"

"Since no one is going to finish a sentence," Matthew said, feeling the strong liquor and speaking louder, "I will introduce myself. My name is Matthew, and Lord Gordon has employed me for the sum of ten gold pieces a month. In the event of his being made prisoner, I shall stay here, as soldier, secretary, anything you wish."

Jane, looking like Diana, frowned fiercely. "I'll not pay you any such sum, knave. Are you daft, George?"

"Hold your tongue, Jane. Heed her not, Matthew. She's the worst shrew in Scotland." He grinned, but Matthew was not listening. He was looking at Mary Gordon. She was like a fragile white rose, and she was so slender he could have spanned her waist with his hands. Her eyes widened as she heard Jane use a coarse expression in reply to George's remarks.

"Stop, Jane," she whispered. "George is jesting."

George exploded, "I want food! Jane—" All four of them froze into silence. Jane breathed lightly. George stiffened. To Matthew it was expected. From the front of the house came the sound of imperative knocking, and a distant voice could be heard even to this room. "Open! In the king's name!"

No one of them moved. They heard the opening of the

oaken doors; they heard the heavy sound of booted feet. And then suddenly, Jane, like an avenging goddess, crossed the room to face the man she was sure was striding toward her.

This man entered the room. He wore the marks of Jane's whip plainly. The scar crossed his cheek higher than another scar along the jawbone, an old scar. His hands, resting easily on his belt, were powerful, and Matthew noticed that the third finger of the left hand was missing. Matthew in that brief moment memorized the heavily tanned face, the mobile sensuous mouth, and looked right back into the gray eyes. He knew the man instantly. Excitement went through him, for here was a worthy antagonist, and the battle thus joined was going to be a heady one with the stakes as high as kingdoms. But before the man could speak, before Matthew heard his voice, he became conscious of Jane.

She faced the Hepburn. Anger and emotion turned her eyes to gold as she flung out her hand to indicate the stranger.

"This man," said Jane, whose voice shook a little, "is the Hepburn."

Patrick Hepburn bowed.

The tension between them threatened the Hepburn's poise. Taking his eyes from Jane, he looked at the man he sought. "Lord Gordon," he said, "one of my captains reported you were at home. You are under arrest, my lord."

George Gordon had risen to his feet. He stood next to Jane, now, and the resemblance between them was so striking that both Matthew and the Hepburn looked from one to the other. Gordon had a cup in one hand. Jane, insolently challenging the Hepburn, took the cup from Gordon, filled it, and gave it back to him. George drank.

"Your health, my lord," Jane said equably, taking the cup back from her brother, while he lazily drew his sword from its sheath. He proffered it.

"This gave you away to my soldiers," said the Hepburn.

Jane's mouth curled in contempt. "Did you expect Lord Gordon to deny his earldom?" She gave a mocking laugh which the Hepburn interrupted, his voice hard. He pointed to Matthew with his gauntlet. "Who is that fellow?"

Matthew saw with amazement that Jane was going to defend him. Her eyes shone as she continued the fray. But she said only, "That is Matthew." She waited.

The Hepburn had once again torn his eyes from Jane. "Stand, sir," he commanded Matthew.

At this Jane laughed, putting one hand on her hip. "Art a fool, and free with your 'sirs.' "

The Hepburn reddened slightly.

Jane went on. "Matthew is my secretary. More, he is wounded, and needs attention. Go seek it, Matthew."

The Hepburn said stubbornly, "He is English. So it was reported to me."

Jane swaggered over to him, planting herself squarely in front of him. She dug both fists into the bright red satin girdle and looked up. She knew she was winning this battle.

"Matthew is English," she said. "He is also my secretary." She dismissed that subject. "Where are you taking Lord Gordon?"

"To the castle," the Hepburn muttered angrily.

Jane said, "I warrant he'll be allowed a servant, his chamber child." She spoke to one of the Hepburn's men who stood menacingly in the wide open doorway. "You fellow." She raised one finger. "Go tell a retainer to fetch Percy for his lordship."

The Hepburn's man stared and hesitated. But Lord Gordon should be allowed a single servant. The Hepburn growled, "Go fetch"—he paused, searching angrily for the right name —"Percy."

"For his lordship," Jane said.

George Gordon said lazily, "Thank you." He yawned and ambled to the doorway, stepping aside to avoid the Hepburn and Jane and his own sword which the Hepburn held.

Seeing his prisoner leaving, the Hepburn swung around to follow. George was saying goodnight, as though he were about to go upstairs. Jane answered in the same manner. "Goodnight, m'lord."

The Hepburn started out the doorway too. Jane spoke his

name sharply. He stopped, but didn't turn around. His big shoulders seemed braced for the next blow.

"Tonight I shall send Lord Gordon food and clothes. And a feather bed." Her voice gained in intensity as she went on. "And never dream, Hepburn, that we shall not continue to fight to restore our king to his rightful throne!"

The Hepburn turned. His voice was harsh. His words came at Jane like arrows. "Mistress, James the Third is dead. Murdered. We found his body two hours ago near Beaton's mill."

Jane's face went white. She didn't credit what she heard and yet— The Hepburn was still speaking. "A reward of five thousand crowns will be paid for any information which will lead to his murderer or murderers. Goodnight."

He was gone and the doorway was empty. Gordon was gone. In the silent room Jane looked to Mary and to Matthew. There was no doubt about it, then. Young Jamie, the fourth James, was King of Scotland.

6

THE KING IS DEAD. LONG LIVE THE KING.
Fog muffled the words, and the rain came. Rain beat against the walls, dripped off the corners of buildings into the dirty streets, ran down the great hill and lay deep in puddles on the smooth lawns of the fine homes and their gardens. Signs swung disconsolately over closed shops. Tavern doors were barred. The bells tolled, and through the city marched companies of soldiers, heads bent against the driving winds.

When the rains stopped, the fogs drifted in off the sea, enveloping the city and hiding the massive castle that ruled it. Fog swirled over the waters of the deep moat around the castle. For three days the rain and fog continued.

On the first day the cortege bearing the dead king passed through the city to the muffled beat of the drums. The horses walked slowly, armed men protected the few nobility, and no one dared to go out to watch.

There was little ceremony. First came a troop of cavalry. Then came the black-draped litter which bore the coffin. Behind that rode the King of Scotland, James the Fourth.

He rode on a black horse. His clothes were black, and although men said they saw his face, few did, for a flared hat shielded his eyes from the northern winds and only the curve of cheek and jaw were visible. At the Abbey of Cambuskenneth, where the King was buried, only Patrick Hepburn, Lord Fleming, the Earl of Douglass and a very few others were present. Again men said the new king knelt; they said he wept. But no one knew. They only knew that by royal command all shops were closed, gatherings in the street were forbidden, and no man could enter a tavern for even so much as a penny's worth of ale.

In the houses of the wealthy and the noble, fires were lighted against the damp June cold, and women met secretly, and talked. Jane Gordon spent the afternoon of the twentieth of June closeted with the widows of the Lords of Ramsay and Moncrieff, both of whom had died at Sauchieburn. That afternoon David Lindsay's wife came to stay with Jane. Lindsay was a royal prisoner, lodged in the castle. That day Patrick Hepburn quartered two thousand more men on the helpless city.

The third day six more of the greatest lords of the land were brought back to Edinburgh to stand trial at an ominously future date. The fog lifted a little, at sunrise, to let the people see the great castle that crowned the city, and to let them see plainly its ramparts against the skies. Within its walls was an uncrowned king who had begun his reign in bloodshed.

That day at two o'clock, one man rode down the esplanade that connected the castle with the city. Gates opened, soldiers stared and whisked off their caps. The horseman rode off, and the men watched the hooves strike sparks against the cobblestones. The horseman disappeared into the city streets.

Fear held the city. The streets were almost deserted. One company of men at arms passed the horseman just as he drew rein. They watched, but he dismounted and tied his horse to a hitching post outside an ironforger's shop. He banged on the door with a heavy fist.

The soldiers passed out of sight in the narrow street. Three minutes passed before the shop owner came to the door. He had heard the knocks at the very moment he had heard the soldier's tread. His bones turned to jelly; he had fought for his dead king. The ironmonger looked through the bars at the top of the door.

"I be not open," he said.

"You will open to me."

The ironmonger shivered. Slowly he drew back four bolts, two at the top and two at the bottom. The door swung inward, and the man entered. He was of middle height with massive shoulders, dark-faced and clean-shaven. He kicked the door closed with his foot.

The ironmonger whispered, "Who are ye?" He stared at the stranger's face, and then, afraid, he bent down to close one bolt.

The stranger said, "I want to give you an order, and then I shall be gone. This order I shall call for within one day."

The shopman said, "What is it you want?" Then he added, "My lord," for the stranger must be an earl, he must be a lord of the land.

"I want a belt," said the stranger. "I want an iron belt of this thickness." He held up a strong-fingered hand with one heavy gold-crested ring.

"Half an inch?"

"Aye. Half an inch thick. And this wide." Again the stranger used his hands. He held them in front of him, parallel, his white cuffs slipping back from the big wrists.

"Six inches?" asked the ironmonger. "Six inches, my lord? 'Twill be heavy. 'Twill weigh a stone, at least."

The stranger laughed, and the ironmonger caught the smell

of wine on his breath. He stared because he thought his visitor must be drunk or mad. Unaccountably fear seized him and he stepped farther away. "Ha'ye been drinking?" he asked.

"Drinking?" The man looked at the cold forge. "Aye, I've been drinking. There's naught else to do."

"There's not." The agreement was quick. "And but to stay within and not dare the streets. There be soldiers everywhere. And a reign that begins in blood cannot help but end in it!"

The stranger drew down the corners of his mouth. Anger flared in his eyes, bringing momentary brilliance to their darkness. "You think that, fellow? And tell me, what do they say about the king?"

The ironmonger was silent.

"What do they say?" The question was repeated, and the forger could not deny this man. He felt the words coming to his lips, willy-nilly. "They say young Jamie will always suffer."

The stranger laughed. "What do they know of Jamie and what he suffers?"

"They know," whispered the man. "In his place they'd see a priest and pray God for forgiveness."

"Does a man who is guilty of the murder of his father have a right to ask God for anything?"

A gust of rain blew against the door and rattled it. The room was icy. The shopman repeated. "I'd see a priest. I'd pray I didn't burn in hell forever and ever."

The stranger said, quietly, "You craven fool. D'ye dream Jamie is afraid of hellfire? See that you have the belt ready on the morrow. Fire that forge and have it ready."

The stranger turned. With trembling hands the shopman undid the bottom bolt, and the stranger stepped out into the street. But the shopman was too frightened to watch him ride away. He heard only the distant hoofbeats. Only his wife, watching from an upstairs window, saw the man mount. Before he mounted, he patted his horse, and spoke some words to it. That was all she saw.

It was then three o'clock in the afternoon.

At four the horseman returned to Edinburgh castle to the relief of Patrick Hepburn, who saw the familiar figure dismount and stand in the courtyard a moment. It had begun to rain again; the skies had darkened and the wind was rising. While the Hepburn watched, James Stuart crossed the court, passed two gates, and, head bent, entered the small chapel.

Inside it was dim and quiet. James removed his wet hat. At the altar, candles were burning and James could see the figures of two kneeling priests. He strode forward until he was behind the two kneeling men where he stood for a minute before they, deep in their devotions, felt his presence. The dean of the chapel turned his head to find the king's dark eyes fixed on him. The dean struggled to his feet, and composed his robes.

"Your Majesty," he said.

"Send him away," said James, motioning to the other priest.

"Aye, your Grace," the dean said. His mind was already busy with the probable questions James would ask, and what, if any, safe answer could be made.

James waited, and the dean noticed with misgivings the arrogance of James's face, yet he felt in no mood to compromise with the Lord's truths, some of which must come out in the open now. The priest had gone.

"I want your counsel," said James to the dean.

"It is yours," the dean said. Then he added, "My son."

James frowned. "How would you suggest I might be satisfied in my own mind and conscience—" James hesitated over this word, and glanced at the dean's face as he said it—"my conscience," repeated James, "for my part in the cruel act which took my father's life?" Having said this much, James hitched up his belt and dared the dean to speak.

The dean summoned his courage and reminded himself of the presence of God in this tiny chapel.

"Queen Margaret built this church, and the Lord lives here," said the dean.

James looked annoyed. The dean continued hastily.

"I want your Highness to know you are in the presence of God," said the dean somberly. And then he told more of the truth. "I have been praying for your soul."

James's brows drew together. "My soul is my own," said James, drawing out the last word till it sounded like "aw-in."

The dean asked, "Do I dare utter my mind?"

The blunt question brought the smallest ironic smile to James's face. In a brief moment he had a picture of himself in his high black boots with his red velvet doublet, he—James—vain, selfish, worldly and in bitter trouble. Sudden emotion beat through him.

"Speak!" he said.

It was as though he had flung down a gauntlet and declared war. The dean knew he did not dare utter the condemnation that James deserved. At the same time, he saw that James was struggling, that he was in bitter spirits. The dean felt briefly sorry, for he understood the driving forces of ambition and power and lust which had harried James to this pass. Though he was himself removed from life, he felt pity for a man who was thrusting himself into its maelstrom.

"Thou art in deep conflict," the dean said. "Thou art in need of comfort."

"If I suffer," James muttered, " 'tis right I suffer, for I am guilty of a terrible crime."

"Thou art," said the dean, "and that is why I have been praying for your soul."

"I don't want my soul prayed for," growled James. "By God, I shall—" He stopped, for the dean's face was kind and James was abashed, for a moment.

"You shall pray for it yourself?" suggested the priest, as an ending to James's unfinished sentence. "Your Grace, ask the mercy of Jesus Christ and you have good hope of forgiveness."

James sighed, and suddenly he put both hands over his face. The dean laid a hand on his shoulder.

James said, "I don't want forgiveness! It is a coward's thing to beg forgiveness, and God help me, Father, I am no coward. Whatever else I am, I fear no man."

"But you fear God?"

"No!" said James stubbornly. "I fear naught. Only I am sorry because I never meant my father to be hurt; I wanted only to—" He had been about to say rule. "I convict myself out of my own mouth." He turned aside and the priest looked at the back of James's head. He was silent, knowing James would say more.

"I am guilty," said James, "because it was I who set off the train of deeds which ended in a foul and traitorous and bloody murder. Father, I shall have to learn to live with guilt."

The dean said, "But you said you sorrowed, and when a man says that, he wants forgiveness."

"Are you certain?" James asked.

"I am," said the dean.

"Well, I came for counsel and you have given it."

The dean said bluntly, "You came also for comfort and it has been granted you."

James, who had turned away, turned back. He hesitated. "Mayhap you speak the truth," he conceded.

"Kneel," said the dean.

James obeyed, slowly. He didn't like it, and looking down on his dark head, the dean was moved by quick affection. He put his hand on James's head, and then he said something that greatly comforted James.

"In the name of Jesus Christ pray that it is granted you to be a noble king and one who finds favor in the eyes of the Lord."

James, thus recalled to the fact that he was indeed king, felt much better. He rose. The dean's face was placid and kind. The little chapel was sweet with peace and timelessness. James drew a deep breath, as though sucking in its air to help him keep part of the peace he tasted. Outside the world awaited.

"I shall come back, Father," he said.

The dean smiled. "I shall wait."

Outside it was still raining. James had been inside the chapel about twenty minutes. He realized he was walking rapidly, his hands clenched into fists. The hour's gallop had not done much good. He had not slept for three days and three nights, and he was wondering if he would ever again know relaxed, delicious sleep. Straight ahead of him was the tower that housed the noble prisoners, men who had fought against him, the rebels. It imprisoned more than its share. The doors at the bottom of the tower stood open, revealing its guardrooms and armed men.

To James's right, the massive portcullis stood upraised; twelve feet of stone wall guarded the castle from unwelcome intrusions, and down below lay the city. While James gazed down the esplanade up which he had just ridden, the only avenue to the castle, six riders, obviously weary, galloped up the rise and across the moat. Another man, wearing the insignia of the Gordons, followed.

This man dismounted, and spoke a few words to the captain on the gates. James, coming closer, heard the captain say, "Take this fellow to Patrick Hepburn."

James paid no attention. He wanted to speak with the men he had sent north, who were just now returning. He and Matthew passed each other, both walking fast, Matthew following a guard. Neither man gave the other more than a cursory glance.

Matthew found himself after two minutes in a corner room whose windows opened on a wonderful view of the city and of Castle Hill, where he had just been. It was a large anteroom and through the curtained doorway Matthew could hear the voice of Patrick Hepburn. When he was told he could enter, Matthew turned from the windows, and for the second time found himself face to face with the Hepburn. Once again it produced a pleasant kind of excitement. He smiled.

"Good afternoon, sir."

"Good afternoon," said the Hepburn, who was sitting in a carved chair. His red head was bare, and there were comfortable house shoes on his feet. He was wearing a white linen shirt with ruffling at the wrists, which contrasted oddly with his scarred hands. Those hands lay on the table in front of him.

The Hepburn did not ask Matthew to sit; there was no reason why he should. Just the same Matthew was glad he didn't, for Matthew was sure that the Hepburn was suspicious of him.

"My mistress sends her greetings, sir," Matthew said, diffidently.

The Hepburn looked surprised. "Greetings?" he repeated, a bit incredulously. But he was pleased.

"My Lady Gordon wishes me to tell you that she has received the heralds of the Crown concerning the coronation of his Majesty at Scone on the twenty-fourth of this month, three days hence. My mistress would like permission to attend the ceremonies."

The Hepburn raised one eyebrow. "Continue," he said.

"That is all, sir," Matthew said, "except that Lady Gordon would like permission to travel north after the ceremony. She has planned to proceed to Methven."

"I see," said the Hepburn noncommittally. He was silent. This sounded like capitulation on Jane Gordon's part and the Hepburn didn't believe for a moment that Jane was going to surrender so easily. He raised his gray eyes to Matthew, and he said, "I would put it that the most important request came last. Why?"

"Why does Lady Gordon wish to travel north? To the coronation, sir."

Patrick inquired, "Art so stupid, man?" He started to say something else, when the parting of the curtains in the doorway took his attention. When he saw the newcomer he started to rise, but he was waved to his seat. Matthew turned his head a little to see who it was, but he didn't recognize the man at all, so he respectfully looked back at the Hepburn.

"You were saying, sir?"

"Hold a moment," said the Hepburn.

Matthew, who knew he was being appraised from the rear by the newcomer, felt like a pincushion. He turned sideways, and then he realized with a start that he was in the presence of the king. For a moment, taken off guard, he could not think clearly, for the excitement of meeting James so close made his heart beat faster. Fortunately, he didn't have to speak. The three men, all silent, stood for a moment on the edge of a conflict which was going to involve all of them deeply. Behind Matthew stood, invisibly, the craft and power of the English king. Here in this room, James, with only a precarious hold on his kingdom, looked back at Matthew, with a faint frown on his face. He wondered who he was. The Hepburn knew James was wondering, so he explained. "Sir, Lady Gordon wishes permission to attend the coronation, and she wishes to proceed to Methven after the ceremony."

James finally asked, "Which Lady Gordon?"

"Mistress Jane," said Matthew, hesitating to use James's title, for he was afraid to show that he had recognized James. "Mistress Mary has been very ill. If she is well enough to travel, her ladyship would also like to be at Scone."

"But not at Methven?" asked James softly.

Matthew looked at the floor, but not before he had seen the glitter in James's dark eyes, a mocking glitter. Matthew's hands sweated, and he rubbed them on his breeches. Then James said, "Lady Gordon may go where she wishes."

Matthew concealed his surprise and caught the ominous ring behind the few words. He pretended to look to the Hepburn for confirmation.

The Hepburn said crisply, "You heard his Majesty, knave."

This was sudden. Matthew tried to show his amazement at being told he was in the presence of the king, but the Hepburn was watching him closely. Matthew was afraid he had not deceived him, though he kept the look of amazement on his face until it felt ludicrous.

"Oh, your Grace," he said. "I—" He broke off, and he clumsily went down on one knee. "Lady Gordon thanks your Majesty."

Matthew remained in his kneeling position. The Hepburn said from behind him, "If this is a play, it's a bad one."

James grinned. "Rise and get hence," he commanded.

"Aye, your Majesty," muttered Matthew, getting to his feet. He backed to the door with accustomed ease. Patrick Hepburn did not miss that, either. He frowned at the retreating Matthew, who had decided it was best to leave in a hurry, because after all, had he been only a retainer, he would have been frightened and puzzled at the sudden unannounced presence of James himself.

Left by themselves, James walked over to a chair by the

window and sat down. He stretched out his legs and stared at the tips of his boots.

"Although it's difficult to tell the two apart, wasn't that an English Border accent rather than Scot, Patrick?"

"It is, your Grace. The man is named Matthew. He told one of my men that he was born in Dorsetshire, moved to Carlisle as a lad, served Richard the Third and fled England after his defeat. He fought at Sauchieburn under the Gordon banners and is still wearing their livery. I'd like leave to watch him for a while."

James Stuart did not move from his chair. He lounged back, eyes half closed. For all his heavy build he was as graceful as an animal. His body was unmercifully weary, yet he felt no desire for food, for wine or for sleep; he wanted action. On all sides of him pressed the need for action. Matthew had raised the specter of England, and yet, for the moment, he must put it aside. There was nothing to do now save, as the Hepburn had put it, "watch him for a while."

"The couriers from the Highlands have arrived," he said. "What think you of Lord Drummond?"

The Hepburn was used to James's questions being thrust at him. "I think him completely loyal." He tried to soften James's grim mood. "His daughters are good and delightful evidence. One, Eufemia, is wed to Fleming. I've seen her." He grinned.

James was undiverted. The Hepburn he could trust; there were few he could. "A band has been formed against me," he said baldly. "I deem it wise after the coronation to proceed onward, with immediacy. There is open rebellion. Not far from Scone. Not far from the Drummond castle."

The Hepburn asked slowly, although he knew what the answer would be, "Where, your Grace?"

James looked up. "At Methven," he said.

7

MATTHEW REACHED HOME AT FIVE O'CLOCK. IT WAS supper time. He did nothing before he ate, although he knew Jane Gordon would be fuming with impatience. That knowledge served only to increase the gusto with which he savored every morsel of food and good Gordon ale. While he ate, the guards on the house were removed. Matthew permitted himself a few jeering remarks which were taken in good part by the Hepburn men, and he felt sure he had established himself in their eyes as a good fellow. He wiped his mouth finally, finished his ale, and as a sop to Jane, washed his hands. While he did that, he reminded himself ruefully that he was no longer a gentleman, for he had forgotten to wash before he ate. He started upstairs, the back way, a bit cautiously, for no one was supposed to know he was going to meet and talk to Jane.

In this he was forestalled. The steps were narrow and twisting. At the top of them, he opened the door slowly, and bumped into a pretty, buxom girl with an armful of towels for the laundry. She came to a stop and eyed him.

"What are you doing up here?"

"Looking for you," said Matthew easily. He closed the door to the stairway.

"Looking for me?" she repeated. Then she smiled.

Matthew gazed at her with some interest. He took her by the elbows.

"Let me free," she whispered.

He shook his head, and leaned over to kiss her, but before he had time, a door ten feet away opened. Matthew straightened up and swung around. He faced Mary Gordon.

He said nothing. He reached behind him, and opened the

backstair door. "Run, lass," he said, patting the girl on the backside as she fled him. The door, which she left open, Matthew closed.

"Now, Lady Gordon," he said, bowing. "Say on."

Mary was dressed in white. She wore her black hair parted in the middle, and her eyes were so wide spaced beneath level brows that her face was a perfect oval. Matthew felt impelled to say, "Mistress, you have a dimple in your chin."

Mary flushed. She said carefully, as though she were summoning all her courage, "Do you know that you shall be fined a sixpence for toying with the maids?"

Matthew laughed. "It was only one maid," he pointed out.

"That doesn't matter, it's still a sixpence," Mary stammered.

Matthew stepped closer to her, looking down. He reached into his pocket and brought out a small purse. From this he counted out six black pennies. "My fine, your ladyship."

Mary, whose hands had been at her sides, clasped them together firmly. "You may pay Jane," she said. "I mean Lady Jane."

"I knew whom you meant," Matthew said.

Her downcast lashes made a black smudge against her cheeks. For a moment he imagined how her eyes would widen if he were dressed as he should be, and if they had met at Court instead of this way, in a dark hall. For a moment, too, he wondered why he had bothered to kiss the maid when Mary Gordon was in the same house.

"Why don't you take the money from me?" he asked.

As he broke the long silence, Mary looked up. Her eyes were a different blue from his, a deep purplish blue. "I don't like to take it from you, Matthew," she said. Then she asked, "Are you so poor?"

"No!" he frowned.

Now she did look at him in surprise.

"Don't waste your pity on the likes of me," he said roughly. "Don't you remember I'm paid ten gold pieces a month?"

"That isn't very much," said Mary.

"In your eyes, mayhap. But take these."

The black pennies lay in the palm of his big hand as Mary

held out hers. The pieces clinked together as Matthew dropped them into her cupped fingers. "You may need them."

He didn't know that he meant she might need him. "I ought to tell you," he added, "to save every one of those and every penny you can get your little hands around. I ought to warn you not to sell a jewel, or buy a gown, but only to save. Every penny!"

It was almost dark in the hall. He felt her eyes on him, and he could hear her hurried breath.

"Do I frighten you?" he asked. "Well, you underestimate yourself. I credit it to both your sister and your brother, both of whom are selfish, dominating. But you have call to step back. For them."

She answered now, instantly, "I do not!"

"You do. You deny it with too much vehemence. Now your brother can protect you no longer; he's in gaol. Your family is in disfavor. And yet when I tell you to save against disaster, you refuse to believe me."

Her hands had closed tight over the pennies. He added, "And never heed Jane. Counsel yourself." He started to turn away abruptly. Her voice stopped him. "You see Jane now?"

He nodded. "You guessed aright." Once more he started away.

"I go with you." She had slipped the coins into the pocket of her dress and they jingled as she walked ahead of him.

" 'Twill be an honor, Lady Mary," Matthew said, lamely, to her back.

Jane was amazed to see Mary. Her brows drew together, and she burst into speech.

"Why art thou here?" she demanded.

Matthew closed the door while Mary stood her ground, somewhat unsurely.

"Jane," she said, "I should hear what you and Matthew have to say."

Jane's frown deepened. She paced across the room and swung around. Her gaze flicked to Matthew and stayed on him a moment.

"Jane, this concerns me!" Mary said.

"God's love, I warrant it does! But must you know everything when mayhap it might mean danger to know *anything?* Why do you interfere?"

"I shan't interfere."

Jane smiled, a superior smile. "Remember that," she said. "All's well if you do. Now, Matthew, I see no reason why you may not sit."

Like an empress, Jane waved Matthew to a stool. She herself took a chair in front of the empty fireplace and pulled an embroidered cushion into place.

"Now, Matthew," she said.

Matthew had been watching Mary. He turned to Jane. "Your ladyship," he began, slowly, "I saw not only the Hepburn, but I saw Jamie himself."

"God's foot," said Jane. "Well, I've seen the wretch many times. Is that all you have to report?"

"No," said Matthew. "Not quite."

Matthew sat forward on his stool, forgetting for a moment that he was very uncomfortable because he had nowhere to put his long legs. Before he could continue, Jane said, "I see you purchased new boots."

Matthew smiled. He seemed relieved to find that Jane could change the subject as quickly as any woman. "Aye, new boots. I needed them, mistress."

"Humph," said Jane. "You seem to have plenty of gold."

"I've less now," said Matthew, and Mary flushed a little. Jane did not notice.

"Say on," she commanded.

Again Matthew sat forward on his stool. He spoke earnestly. "Mistress, you may attend the coronation. There will be few attending, and James wants as many as will come to see him crowned. You may even go to Methven." He paused. "But I should not advise it."

"When I seek your advice—" Jane began, and then she waved him aside with a gesture. She picked up her embroidery from the table beside her; the needle was already thrust through a stitch which Jane finished.

"Jamie knows," said Matthew.

"Jamie should know the whole country is against him save the Hepburn freebooters!" Viciously Jane plied her needle.

"Let us be practical, mistress. The Border nobility, led by the Hepburn, is good and efficient in the field. I observed it. The Drummonds, the Douglasses stand firm with James. Argyll will swerve and join the camp."

"He will not!" cried Jane.

Matthew said lazily, "The little plot at Methven is known. Do not go there." And since Jane's eyes were resting on him speculatively, he said firmly, "Ask me not to risk my neck. Warn them not. It would be extremely foolish and not worth the hazard. They are a band of silly men, brandishing swords. The royal wrath will descend surely. You cannot warn them now. It is too late."

"I shall!" said Jane. She threw down her embroidery; it spilled to the floor.

"Outright defiance will bring disaster. Sweet treachery is needed." He smiled a little, his blue eyes sleepy. He was talking almost as though he were alone. Then he got to his feet.

"Let me warn you plain," he said.

He knew Mary's eyes were fixed on him. Jane disdained even a glance in his direction; she had walked over to the window and leaned back against the sill.

"Jamie intends to rule. You will be brought under the mailed fist of the Crown, willy-nilly. Concede gracefully."

Matthew didn't know whether he had made an impression or not. Jane's expression was mocking. Angrily he said, "The Hepburn has been made Sheriff of Edinburgh and Warden of the Border. Go to Methven and you will fall into his hands like a trapped doe. Goodnight."

He made for the door. Jane Gordon deserved what folly she sowed. He stopped in front of Mary's chair. Her feet were on a little stool and her head was tilted back against the wooden chair back, so she could look up at him. She would be embroiled in this. He knew it. Still angry, he was surprised to see her smile at him, almost reassuringly, with a flicker of humor at his male outburst of temper. Her voice was soft as velvet.

"Goodnight, Matthew," she said.

8

PATRICK HEPBURN GAZED ABOUT HIMSELF AT THE TINY room in which he stood. Opposite him a narrow door opened into another, equally small cabinet, with an old empty bedstead and a single chest.

Evidently these two small rooms had once been a part of the suite which he himself now occupied, but they had been closed off, for there was a door blocked off between this room and the one he used for his own bedroom. He walked over to the window.

It was high and very small. There was no possible exit from either of these rooms save by the one door to the corridor which ended in his own apartments. He gestured to the bare wooden bedstead.

"You may prepare these rooms for a prisoner," he said.

He envisioned her caught in these two rooms, the burning anger and impatience that would set her walking back and forth across their fifteen feet, past the bed to the single high, grated window. And from this room his mind went to the house whose plans were already drawn, the stone and slate already purchased, the lands staked out and the gardens that would grow around it.

He turned from the room and went down the hall, stopping only to pick up his helmet. He had postponed donning it till the last minute before leaving the castle. It was hot this morning; even in the gray dawn there was the threat of summer heat.

Out in the courtyard his horse waited. Only twenty men were his escort; the rest had gone ahead, taking the narrow byroads through glen and dale, roads hardly used, roads bearing north, past Scone to Methven. Little more than trails, they were, yet time enough had been allowed to let the cannon go through. Time had been allowed for wheels stuck deep in mud; by now, two thousand men, a small force but enough for today, should have been camped for the night in the hills past Scone.

By now too, she would have left the city. If he had judged her well, she would arrive at Scone early, so the horse she intended to use would have had rest and water, and be fresh.

The Hepburn was thirty-four years old. In all his life he had never encountered serious defeat, and it did not occur to him that he might ever suffer it at the hands of a woman. He had carved out his own fortunes: his power was now as firm in his grasp as the reins in his scarred hands.

In twenty minutes he left the city through the north gate with a wave of one gauntleted hand. They were his own men on those gates. It was he who controlled the military power; on his shoulders the security of the nation rested. The wardenship of the whole Border was his, too, and his lands stretched from the sea to Glasgow. The mighty fortress of Dunbar, the town and mains and castle of Bothwell, a few miles from Glasgow on the river Clyde, were all his to command, though he had not yet seen them. But that could wait.

His methods had always been direct. His times suited him, and he had turned them to advantage, although he knew he would have been successful in any age.

The sun had risen. Shimmering waves of heat lay across the green countryside, a haze over the low mountains in the distance. James would already be at Scone, making his devotions, but the Hepburn had no illusions about the coronation.

It should be a day for rejoicing. Wine should be flowing from the fountains in all the city squares. There should be dancing and drunkenness and ribaldry. The churches should be filled with sober Scots praying for the new king, while the nobility should gather at Scone, paying respects to their monarch.

None of this would happen. Although the heralds had been sent forth to summon the lords of the land to see their king crowned, few would come. Only the Lowlands, the Borders and the capital lay subdued; today instead of celebrations, there would be fighting in the north. It would be a grim, quick ceremony which saw James crowned.

Patrick Hepburn did not regret this; neither did James. Both understood the task ahead. Thus far they had succeeded. More could not be asked. Today at least James would cease to be an uncrowned king, which was dangerous; and today would see the first blow struck at recalcitrant nobles. A lesson would be taught.

The pace was set at a hard gallop. Not until the Edinburgh road reached its eminence outside the town of Perth did he rein in. Forty miles had been swallowed up.

Below him the valley of the Tay lay in a lovely giant cradle of hill and mountain. They said the Romans, on approaching here, had cried out with wonder, "Lo, behold the Tiber!" The Hepburn thought this far more beautiful than any river in Italy could possibly be. The water glistened. The church spires of Perth pierced through the trees. From here he could not see Scone. That small town with its coronation abbey was a few miles beyond Perth. He spurred his horse and began the dip down into the river valley.

He passed through Perth. The streets were crowded; everyone was abroad; if not to laugh and sing, at least to watch and look and appraise. They had seen the new king; they had seen a few of his adherents; and as the Hepburn rode slowly through the streets, they called his name. It went like a whisper through the people as they stared.

He cared little, though he was magnificently dressed. His boots were of soft Spanish leather, and somehow they reminded him, as he rode now to the chapel, of the day, seventeen years ago, when he had first ridden out from Hailes, alone, to seek service with the Earl of Argyll. The boots he wore then, he had made and sewed himself, and the horse had been stolen from across the Border. Now he was riding a black stallion bred from the same line. He decided his crest would be a horse's head bridled.

He reached Scone at ten o'clock. He dismounted in front of the chapel. His horse was led away. He removed his helmet; one of the men took it from him. James himself should come soon.

But she came first. He saw her from a distance, and he knew it could be no one else. The surprise at her arrival made as much impression as his had.

He saw that she alone was leader of thirty men, who rode in rows of three behind her. The horses were all caparisoned in gold and white. The Gordon insignia was blazoned on the backs of the men's short cloaks, and the Gordon dragons marched across their chests. Ahead of them rode Jane herself, in gold velvet, trimmed with ermine. Around her neck she wore a chain of diamonds that glittered like fire in the sun.

They cheered her. They cheered the Gordons. Jane acknowledged the shouts and cries with an upraised hand sheathed in a velvet glove. She turned from side to side, sitting easily in the high saddle. The Hepburn's eyes did not leave her. He crossed over to her as she came close.

She pretended not to see him. Her gaze went past him, she reined in, and two of her men leaped forward to help her dismount. But the Hepburn paid no attention to them. Unable to stop him, afraid to interfere with him, they backed away as he approached.

The crowds of people around the chapel now surged back and forth, trying to see. They could see Jane because she was still mounted, and they could see that the Hepburn reached up and took a whip from Lady Gordon's fingers. They could not see the smile that lifted the corners of his mouth nor the glint in the gray eyes as he did it.

"Now, Lady Gordon," said Patrick. He put both hands on her waist, and lifted her down.

She stood in front of him, eyes on his face She was breathing quickly. She ran her tongue over her lips; with a twist of her hips she settled her long gown. But she gave him no greeting.

"Pray, give me my whip, Hepburn," she said crisply.

The whip had a mirrored handle. Jane pretended to study herself as she tucked in an errant lock that had escaped the golden coif she wore. Then she turned the mirror slightly. It caught the sun, sending a blinding flash into the Hepburn's eyes. Jane tilted her head and laughed.

The Hepburn took a purposeful step toward her, remembered where he was, and offered his arm. "Will ye enter?" he muttered.

Jane refused his arm. "I think to tarry awhile, to see Jamie come." Ignoring him, she tucked the whip under her arm. In the distance she heard the sound of bugle and drum and hoofbeat. Her eyes glistened, and she lost some of her calm.

"He comes!" She half turned, to share the excitement with the Hepburn, but thought better of it. Smiling to herself, she motioned him to move aside so she could climb one step to see better. On the next step up she poised. "Look!"

The Hepburn looked down at her head instead. He caught a whiff of perfume. The street seethed with people; the gaily decked horses of the royal heralds and buglers came into view; the ancient pageantry had begun. A new king was riding toward the chapel at Scone.

The crowd caught the fever. The cries, murmurs at first, swelled slowly. Even Jane bit her lip as she saw James come close. Traditionally the king must be the finest horseman in Scotland. His father had failed. But James rode like a centaur.

"Ah," sighed Jane in approbation.

The bells began to toll. A silence fell. Jane entered the chapel.

Her place was far in front because of her rank. Her father had been an earl; her mother, a Stuart princess. Jane was cousin of Jamie Stuart.

Border nobility crammed the chapel. Notoriously absent were the Highlanders, brooding in their fastnesses, ready to fight and plot and band together.

Just before James entered the chapel, Jane gave the Hepburn a sidelong glance to remind him he was out of place. The Hepburn followed Jane.

James, dressed in sables and velvet, was kneeling now, in front of the altar, pledging his troth in low measured tones which Jane could hear. His voice was resonant and compelling and fearless.

It was hot inside these stone walls. Once she closed her eyes, during the prayer. Then she realized the Hepburn must have been watching her, and, thinking she was faint, put his arm around her, steadying her.

She stared straight ahead, seeing the crown and scepter, seeing the crown placed on James's dark head. The gold crown glittered with rubies and emeralds and pearls and diamonds. The scepter was put in his hand as he sat. The priests and bishops in their satins and velvets and furs, with massive chains around their necks, glittered too like birds of paradise, and the sun slanted through the stained-glass windows to make patterns on the stone floors. Over her head the arched and vaulted roof echoed to the ancient ceremony. It made Jane remember that the English had seized the Coronation Stone, an insult and indignity which had not yet been avenged. Was Jamie Stuart, the boy she had known, now thinking of that?

James was king. The coronation was over. Jane hardly realized it. The Hepburn offered his arm; they waited while James, alone, made his way out of the chapel. Jane noticed the Hepburn's hand with its missing finger. Next to the king himself, this man was the most powerful in Scotland, and, it was said, he was as tenderhearted as a tiger. Jane raised her eyes to his face; above his lip was the remnant of a scar, a small white line from the flick of her whip.

She studied him openly. His gray eyes showed only a flicker of interest before they became wary.

"If I should ever ask you a favor, would you grant it?" Jane asked, without preamble.

His quick reply did not quite conceal his surprise. "I cannot answer that till you tell me the favor." Then he asked, "What do you want?"

She seemed to muse. She frowned a little, her slender brows

drawing together. Then her wide mouth curved in a slow smile, "You asked me what I want as though you could give me anything," she said.

"I could. What do you want?"

"Nothing." She laughed, satisfied at having bested him. He had offered her anything, and she had refused. As they emerged into the brilliant sunshine, she let her hand rest on his arm. She was very close. "I want nothing from you, Hepburn," she said idly.

"That's a bargain you yourself will break!"

He would have dropped his arm, but Jane tightened her fingers. "Pray escort me to my mount." This time the smile she gave him was dazzlingly sweet, and the Hepburn realized with a start it was because so many people were watching. Her men were drawn up in front of the chapel, and his were forced to wait. He started forward faster, remembering the pressure of time.

"Do not hasten," complained Jane. She reached down her left hand for her train and swooped it gracefully over her arm. A groom held her horse. Ready to mount, she asked the Hepburn a sudden, direct question. "Are you beset by time?"

He looked down at her, his face unsmiling. He reached out for her with both hands. The action forced her to blurt, "No!"

He lifted her up and set her in the saddle. Then his hand closed over the bridle. "Where are you going?" he asked.

She gestured, vaguely. Then she pointed directly to a mansion he could see in the distance.

"You are lying."

He paid no attention to her denial. Her expression was cool and mocking. He wanted to seize her now and have done with it. But her men were armed, and the hot-blooded Highlanders would resist his own men fiercely, here in the street. Even so, for a moment, he was tempted. His jaw set grimly, he held her horse firmly.

He released the bridle and tried to match her calm. "It would be most wise to return to Edinburgh, Lady Gordon." It was the last time he would be patient. Her answer to the warning floated down to him.

"Perhaps I shall." For just a moment she remembered James taking his vows. On both sides of the road were the already mounted Borderers, their fleet mounts smaller than hers. She was uncertain. Yet her duty was to her clan, and surely she would be in time. She gave spurs to her horse, and started off down the road at a gallop that sent horses and people scrambling to the sides as they made way for Jane Gordon.

9

THE KING AND THE HEPBURN RODE SIDE BY SIDE AT A pounding gallop. Just behind them came a company of spearmen, the flags fluttering from the long lances. Five hundred bowmen rode solidly to the rear.

They were riding north. Yet the distance they had to cover was not great. They took side roads, pounded through villages clustered by the roadside. Not a soul was seen abroad as the king's forces advanced. The king and the Hepburn had both changed their clothes; they wore the new steel armor, plumed helmets, and short riding cloaks which made a splash of color across the gray. They spoke little, for they had to shout to be heard.

At two o'clock they were within sight of their destination. A hill sloped down to a narrow stream that made a natural moat on this side of Methven castle, where its ramparts reared the highest. It was on this hill, in this cover, that the cannon were ready to fire.

James, still ahorse, was considering the position. "I think this is not the correct range," he said. "There is cover there." He pointed. Halfway down the valley was a thick grove of trees. "I remembered them," he said.

Shouted orders rose above the sound of men and horses.

The cannon began to roll once more. One stuck in the mud was pulled out to an accompaniment of oaths and shouts of encouragement. Then it too began to roll on its wooden carriage; at that moment from the castle, for the first time, there was activity. A single arrow heralded the approach of hostilities.

"They're going to fight," James said, pleased.

The cannon had to roll over open sloping meadows, bright with flowers, downhill to the shelter of the trees of Methven wood. In the meantime, the trundling guns presented a good target.

A hail of arrows from the rebels in the castle enveloped the moving cannon; one of them stopped short, with six men wounded.

Both James and the Hepburn spurred their horses forward. James seized the reins of one of the horses pulling the cannon and urged it onward. He reached the trees and so did the Hepburn. Once there, they exchanged a brief smile.

The cannon were loaded hastily. Arrows flew through the leafy cover. James ordered all men to protect themselves by standing behind the trees. With so small a group of men his commands could be heard plainly as he sat astride his big horse.

The gunners were quick and well trained. The powder smelled sharp and acrid. And the sudden bursting of the guns brought shouts and cries of delight from the bowmen and spearmen still under orders to stay at the top of the hill. Their jobs came later.

It took only half an hour to reduce one side of the apron walls of the castle to ruins. Only the left tower and the drawbridge and wall were standing. Showers of stone piled up in high heaps.

"Thirty minutes bombardment," said James thoughtfully, marking the time well.

The bombards trembled, straining at their iron hoops as they fired the heavy balls.

At this moment the drawbridge of the castle was lowered violently and a company of mounted men rode over it. James gave a shout; the trumpets blew to sound the charge. From the hill behind, the lancers pounded down, and at the bottom, in Methven wood, the brief battle took place.

It was swift, decisive and bloody. Outnumbered by the royal forces, the luckless rebels had come out to fight. Most of them were killed. In one hour, a white flag was fluttering from what remained of the castle ramparts, and on the bare woods and ground there was but a handful of men to surrender. Those who had tried to flee had been cut down by the bowmen.

It was a bloody scene. The ruined castle, the cries of the wounded and the shrieking of hurt horses. A headless man was lying almost under the feet of James's horse. Captain Knox was busy rounding up his own men and seeing who was hurt. James himself was looking toward the castle; it was the Hepburn who produced a spokesman from the few live defenders of the castle.

This man shivered as he faced the king. He could not speak for a moment at all and fell on his knees.

James swore, and then, across the drawbridge, two men approached on horseback. They were the lords of Glencairn and Semple. They rode up slowly, and James waited.

They saw his face close. Semple blurted, "Mercy, sire!" He slipped from the saddle and knelt beside the body of the dead man.

James had no intention of dealing out mercy. He was contemptuous of cowards who quit fighting and asked for mercy.

"The charge is treason," he said. Semple whitened, for he knew the penalty. He was seized and taken away; hands pulled Glencairn from his horse.

That done, James wanted to see inside the castle. He spurred forward, with the Hepburn at his side, and fifty horsemen crowded around to protect James from an errant arrow.

"This might be a rat's nest, sire," the Hepburn said.

James said, "I want to inspect the amount of damage."

They clattered over the drawbridge, past a huge pile of stones. In the inner courtyard James and the Hepburn dismounted and looked about.

Most of the damage had been done to the keep and the

whole front wing. One tower still stood, but it had been sheared off from the rest of the castle and the flight of stone steps went up crookedly and exposed, to the second floor. Great piles of rubble and furniture sprawled across the court. Great holes had been blown into rooms, so that both the Hepburn and James could see into the great dining hall: its table had been crushed by the weight of more stones; one cannon ball had plowed through its walls. Both men looked satisfied at the amount of damage. The castle would never be used again; the lands would be confiscated and added to the Crown lands.

"This will be good grazing land for sheep," said James.

The Hepburn's men were disappearing in different directions. The young Border lords, Home and Grey, came riding in, looking about curiously. Lord Fleming followed at a slower pace.

The women and children would be clustered in the kitchens, probably. But the Hepburn was suddenly sure she would not be with them.

James turned to greet the vociferous Lord Grey. Patrick left them with long strides. He had a notion where he would find her.

The flight of stairs carved into the side of the tower was narrow. He ran up the steps quickly; past the second floor he disappeared from sight, for the third story of the tower was still intact, its round walls pierced only by slits.

At the top of the steps was a little hall. The door was closed. He flung it open, unthinking, and he saw Jane. He had been right then, but he had guessed she would be alone. Instead he faced a man with sword already drawn.

There was no time to do anything. He couldn't step back; there was nowhere to step. In desperation he lunged forward, and took the cut of the sword on the side of his arm.

If he hadn't been wearing armor, he would have lost an arm. As it was, his left arm was numbed completely and hung useless. He tried to use it, to wrench the dagger from his belt, even as he drew his own sword with his good right hand. But he wasn't going to need the dagger. The man he was fighting had been taken off guard by his first failure to kill the Hepburn, and Patrick, yanking his sword from its sheath, swung it in a murderous arc that found his opponent's throat.

He was killed instantly. He fell forward and the blood gushed freely. Only the tip of the Hepburn's sword was bloody.

He thrust his sword back into the scabbard, and stepped over the body of the fallen man. By the window, her cloak drawn around her, Jane waited for him silently.

He didn't touch her. He stood over her, conscious of anger. "That man died protecting you!"

There was the smallest shrug for answer. But when she spoke, there was vehemence in her voice. "He was a fool! I told him not to fight!"

There was silence while the Hepburn also dismissed from his mind a man who had tried to put himself between the Borderer and the woman he wanted. Now in this small room in a ruined castle, she waited for his next move, patiently, as though she were studying a chess board; her only movement was to wrap herself closer in the tawny velvet.

"Come with me," he said.

By a barely perceptible nod she acknowledged the words. She went toward the door, assuming to precede him. She stepped around the dead man's feet. The Hepburn watched her. When she got to the narrow door he took two strides to stand beside her. She motioned to the man on the floor, as though she had just thought of something.

"That was John Fleming," she said. Then she went out into the hall.

He caught up to her, and started down the twisting stairs just behind her.

"Was he kin to Fleming that is wed to Eufemia Drummond?"

"Aye," said Jane. "His brother."

They emerged now into sudden daylight. Below them was the castle yard; a waterfall of stones cascaded from their feet to the court. In the court was a melee of men and horses. James had dismounted and was talking to Fleming and Lord

Grey. And every man below was looking up at the figure of Jane silhouetted against the sheared-off tower.

Jane was looking at the destruction. She flung out her hands. "I tried to warn them!" she said.

The Hepburn scowled. He put out his hand and turned her to face him. "I warned you."

At this he saw the familiar mocking smile. "I heeded you not." She shrugged, and made to turn away. But he stopped her. He indicated the steps, carved from the wall, in a sheer drop now where the wall had collapsed.

"Are you afraid?"

She shook her head.

"I go first," he said. He started down, his body turned sideways, so that he could watch her and be ready to catch her if she fell.

But she did not. She came down the perilous flight, sure as a prideful cat. When she got to the bottom, he gave her his arm. That was all the protection he could offer now.

She took it. He felt her lean a little. She went straight to James. She bent her head and curtsied low, as though she were before the throne at Edinburgh castle.

"Your Majesty," she said.

The helmeted courtiers and men-at-arms around James were silent. James himself prolonged the suspense by frowning while he appraised Jane from head to foot as though wondering what in heaven to do with her.

"Lady Gordon," James growled finally. "You could have joined your brother in the castle without coming this far."

To this Jane could only agree. "Aye, your Grace."

James fixed her with his dark eyes. But he said nothing further. He turned away; he was ready to mount, and he wanted to have a look at a bombard that was not firing correctly. He was very interested in the cannon. James had just put his foot in the stirrup when a voice called down, from the tower Jane had just left, to Captain Knox.

"Captain, there's a man up here—dead—mayhap a lord."

James swung up into the saddle and waited. The Hepburn said,

"I killed him, your Grace. 'Twas John Fleming."

James looked at the brother, Lord Fleming, who had involuntarily cried out. Jane found herself forgotten. She looked up at the Hepburn. She whispered, "Did his Grace mean I was to be prisoned in the castle, too?"

"Aye," said the Hepburn.

There was suddenly a loud rumble, terrifying, gaining in intensity. A portion of the undermined wall slipped forward; stones showered down between the court and the drawbridge. It stopped as suddenly as it had started. The man nearest the wall had leaped away in terror. No one had been hurt. The tenseness lessened; the last stone rolled over and was still.

The whole courtyard was in shadow. The sun was behind the hills of Methven wood. Among the silent men Jane stood as though carved in gold, fettered by the stones that had rolled almost to her feet.

Without a word, the Hepburn swung her up into his arms and carried her to his waiting horse.

10

"REMOVE THOSE WEDGES," JAMES SAID. "THEY'RE TOO large for the piece." He looked down at the cannon from the saddle of a fresh horse.

The gunner grinned with pleasure at talking thus with the king. "Aye, your Grace."

"They're like to fly off when it is shot," James said.

"Aye, 'tis true," one of the men said sagely, nodding his head.

Lord Drummond did not like to interrupt. However, when James noticed him, he said quickly, "Your Grace, there is no cemetery at Drummond."

James rested his hands on his high pommel and looked puzzled. "What are you suggesting?"

The men laughed. Then James remembered.

"Oh, I see," he said. "You have no adequate accommodation for John Fleming." He glanced about to see if the live Lord Fleming was within earshot.

Drummond said, "Fleming is there, sire." He pointed to the broken castle. "But I have sent a message ahead to Drummond castle. They will be expecting you. In truth, your Grace, I might arrive before, but I am taking another way, past the wee church." Again he pointed, into the hills. Then he added, "Lord Fleming is wed to my lass, Eufemia."

James had known that, and he also realized that those words were Drummond's way of explaining an interest in Fleming. The live Fleming should not be blamed for the rebellion of his brother. James reserved opinion about Fleming, but he did remark on the bluff Drummond's loyalty to his son-in-law.

"I commend your action, and I look forward to your hospitality."

"Thank you, your Grace," Drummond said, with heartfelt relief. Inwardly Drummond had damned the dead Fleming to hell for getting him and his daughter involved. He had no choice but to stand by Eufemia's husband. He did not realize what a high price James put on loyalty; he needed it so badly himself. Drummond galloped off; the gunners struggled to remove the wedges from the iron rings that bound the cannon; James himself was ready to ride. In less than an hour Captain Knox pointed to Drummond castle.

The castle, very old, was a great square. From its architecture James could picture its inner court with huge flagstones and pillared arches. Then James became conscious of the fact that the gates were closed. He frowned.

But he kept on his steady pace. Ahead of him were two horsemen bearing the royal banners, that flew in the late afternoon sun. He was waiting for the gates to open and for sounds of greeting, when the first hail of arrows came from the castle.

James checked his horse so suddenly that the animal reared high. The horseman ahead of James clutched his shoulder, almost dropping the flag; across the field shouts of defiance and jeers sounded, and for a moment James was so angry he could not think.

If Lord Drummond had been here, James would have hanged him from the nearest tree. But Drummond was not here; Grey and Home were staring at the castle in sheer amazement, and Captain Knox, acting on his own authority, wheeled his men in front of the king.

The crossbows were already fitted. On the castle ramparts the figures of men were plain. The crossbows aimed up, but Knox knew they could do little damage. He had one hundred men, and the safety of the king to insure. James galloped up to him, heedless of the arrows that were flying.

"Send men back to the troops for the cannon!" James ordered.

"Your Majesty," cried Knox, "seek cover, for God's sake!"

At this moment, the unexpected happened again. Suddenly the gates flew wide and fifteen mounted men emerged, shouting and waving.

"Cut them down," said James grimly.

Knox would have waited to see what was going to happen, but James had given a command. He barked an order. The crossbows twanged. Against the rain of arrows the castle horsemen fell or fled in desperation.

Now a silence fell. Between James and the castle was about two hundred feet. No one was visible. The archers lowered their bows and waited. James, quieting his horse, said, "They may try that again with more men."

Knox muttered, "I hardly think so, sire. Jesu—I don't know what to think!"

Behind the square old castle the sun was sinking; the skies were purple and red and black. The gates stood open. It struck James that this was the sign of surrender.

"Follow me!" he cried.

Before the startled Knox could do anything, James had galloped forward alone, dashing down the sloping hillside toward the castle. Knox gave a great shout himself, and raced after his king.

Alone, James Stuart clattered over the drawbridge. The small court was deserted. Still mounted, he entered through the wide doors of the castle itself, his horse's hooves sounding loudly on the square flagstones in the arched, pillared hall. He reined in. Then he saw her.

She was coming toward him, not running, but on light quick feet, her gown held up a little. As she came close, she saw clearly the dark-browed face under the golden-plumed helmet. She picked up her skirt, ran the last few feet, and stood poised in front of him.

In the few seconds it had taken her to cross the hall, his men had entered.

Lancers flanked the doorway. In the court was the sound of horses and the tread of booted men. James's servants had rushed forward. One of them held his horse while another waited for him to dismount. This James did. His horse was led away as his attending lords hurried to him, as the belated buglers blew hard on the horns and a voice announced: "His Majesty the King!"

Margaret Drummond spread her skirts in a graceful curtsey.

She said clearly, "I am Margaret Drummond, if it please your Grace. Welcome to Drummond."

There was a silence while James wrestled with anger and the normal pleasure of a man suddenly beholding a lovely woman. Her full yellow skirt was like the petals of a flower; her eyes were flecked with green and her little satin cap only partially concealed the heavy, shining blond hair.

"Rise," said James.

He was satisfied with the result as she stood before him. It was the fashion to be slender, but the curves of her hips and breast left nothing to be desired. Her waist was tiny and her stomach flat. James said, "Your welcome, mistress, was more full of arrows than a thistle of nettles." But he smiled.

Maggie Drummond drew a deep breath. She put out her hands in an appealing gesture. She did not bother now with explanations. She said simply, "Your Grace, will you forgive me?"

Again James wrestled with two conflicting thoughts. He

was more than ready to bestow royal mercy on such a lass, but—

"Did *you* give the order to shoot arrows at your liege, mistress?"

Her eyes were enormous. "Aye, your Grace."

James grinned at the incongruity. He yanked off his helmet and paid no attention to the man who took it. "Art warlike, mistress?"

"I am alone," Maggie said.

"I cannot understand that," he answered.

Maggie glanced past James to the other men. Then she hurried on. "I meant that my sisters are out visiting near by, and so I was alone here. I received my father's message. It said spears and arrows."

James's face clouded again. "It said what?"

She hesitated only a second. "M'lord, my father writes poorly. He writes little. When guests are coming, he writes spits and ranges, for us to get the birds turning on the spit. When 'tis an enemy, he writes spears and arrows. I misread the note."

James said, "Spits and ranges. Spears and arrows. Where is the note?"

"I was in the kitchens when it came. I burned it."

He imagined her in the dark kitchens. "What were you doing there?"

"Making perfume from the early roses."

He smiled. Involuntarily he sniffed to see if he could smell the scent of roses. She held out a white hand which he raised in his gauntleted one to his lips. That was what Lord Drummond saw as he came stamping into his own castle.

The scent of roses stayed with James Stuart. He was divested of his armor, his boots. The other Drummond sisters arrived home, their pretty faces alive with the excitement of entertaining James himself. Drummond, now relieved after the explanation about the terrible mistake his handwriting had caused, was filling himself and everyone else with wine. In the kitchens, great activity prevailed: cooks moaned over too-hastily rolled pastry and made sure the gravies were not too thick. It was six o'clock and Drummond knew James preferred to eat at five.

"Dinner is not quite ready, your Grace," he said almost mournfully.

"Time was wasted fitting arrows to the bows instead of fowls to the spits," young Lord Grey said. He was quite drunk. He got neither reply nor smile from James, so he backed off. James, who was relaxing in a wide window seat, saw no one near him but Drummond, which was what he wished.

"M'lord," he began. Over by the empty fireplace was Maggie Drummond. James fastened his eyes on her and did not bother to look at her father while he spoke. "Your daughter, the Lady Margaret, finds favor with me."

At this, Drummond looked across to Maggie too. He clasped and unclasped his gnarled hands. "Maggie?" he asked.

"Maggie," repeated James, smiling a little as he said her name.

Drummond was not insensible of the honor this interest bestowed on his house, an honor which might blossom into financial reward and royal grants. But it would have been considerably more of an honor had James been a deal less fickle. Drummond glanced at the king, lounging back on the pillows, at the dark face and the sensual, arrogant mouth. Besides, Maggie was betrothed to a very wealthy and attractive young man.

Drummond said, "Your Grace, Maggie is betrothed."

James's black brows drew together. His voice was like the crack of a whip. "To whom?"

Drummond, taken aback by the anger, was only too aware that his clumsy note and Fleming's brother had neither of them improved his position with James. He reflected with some self-pity that the fates seemed to be conspiring against him and his family. He wished he had never mentioned Maggie's fiancé. But he had to answer James.

"Your Grace, Maggie is betrothed to the Crieff lad."

There was silence as Drummond went clumsily on. "He is a personable lad. Fought well at Sauchie. And today." In his confusion he added, "Your Majesty knows him. He is there. There, with Maggie." He could see the back of Crieff's broad shoulders and his thick, light hair. Crieff's obvious suitability as Maggie's husband was reassuring. Without thinking, he assumed James would perceive that too.

At that moment Crieff turned toward them, and his rugged looks made James say harshly, "We shall find a suitable bride for him."

Drummond saw that the subject was closed. James had never requested, only demanded. There was nothing further to do. " 'Tis an honor, sire," he said.

11

LORD DRUMMOND SAID BLUNTLY, "BECAUSE YOU PLEASE him, Maggie, take him the water and towel. Not that, lass, the silver one."

Maggie laid the linen towel over her arm and picked up the silver basin. She was adept at this service to the men of the house, so her eyes could be busy watching James as she walked toward him.

He sat at the head of the table. She put the bowl in front of him.

He was listening intently to Douglass' description of Roxburgh castle, across the border in England. He washed his hands. Maggie gave him the towel, watching him use it, watching the big, tanned hands as though they were symbolic of his power to seize what he wanted. Then he looked up and handed her the crumpled linen. As he did, his face lighted with a smile. Their eyes held.

She leaned over to pick up the basin. His low-spoken thanks reached her ears. For a moment she felt only pleasure and content in waiting on him; it was a simple, instinctive pleasure, and she did not try to wonder why it was so. Slowly she bore the basin away. She took her place with her sisters at the end of the table.

Maggie was hungry. Dinner was very late. And she had had nothing to eat since eleven in the morning.

A sister sat on either side of her: Sybilla and Eufemia. They were both married. She heard wisps of their conversation as she ate, but she made no attempt to take part or to listen. She ate mechanically, her gaze ahead on James.

She knew that the whole fabric of her life had been suddenly changed. It had been taken out of her hands, and yet she was not ready to relinquish it. Seeing James plainly, from about thirty feet away, she knew well enough he was a formidable adversary, king or not.

It did not occur to her to seek advice from either sister. Anyway, all her life she had heard them talk, at night, in bed, during the day sewing or playing cards or learning their music in their room—in that time she had heard all they knew.

She sighed. Conflicting emotions made her hold her bread halfway to her mouth, stop and put it down again. She looked at it lying there on the side of her plate. She was no longer hungry.

She would never marry Ian Crieff. She looked at him in sudden desperation and knew with fatalism that he could not help her, that she could never ask him for help because it was not only useless but hazardous. The only one who could help was James himself. She began to eat again.

She emptied her plate. The last of the wine was gone and dinner was over. She wiped her mouth and stood up. Across the table James was looking at her; she had no idea how beautiful she was; she did not know that Lord Fleming suddenly stared from her to James and hastily lowered his gaze. Nor did she know how much more time she had before she would face James alone.

She had exactly sixty minutes before Lord Drummond ushered her into a small anteroom on the ground floor. Formerly used as a bedroom, two carved chairs and a table were now its only furniture. The candles had been lighted, the curtains drawn to at the doorway. Maggie was alone with James.

He was standing. His request for her presence had already swept away the need of formality, and Maggie, taking advantage of this, made a small curtsey such as she would to any other man.

"M'lord," she said, and she held out her hand.

He kissed her hand, and Maggie withdrew it. Maggie, who played chess well, went instantly into the offensive.

"M'lord," she said again, "although I am not unknowing of the honor you do me, and regardless of the love and loyalty I bear your Majesty, I would like leave to speak truly."

This was hardly what James expected. The candlelight cast a glow over her face.

"You have my leave, mistress," was all he could say.

Maggie said, "It will not take me long. It is simply that I would decline this favor."

The rebuff hit James squarely. He rose quickly to the battle as he always did.

"You love another man?"

He had taken a step toward her. His dark face was set, angry. But he swept away subterfuge and compelled the truth.

"I have known Ian Crieff all my life and we planned to wed!"

He took her by the shoulders. "You deem that love?"

Wordlessly she looked up at him. Her face was white.

He made no motion to caress her. He held her so she must look at him. He thought he had said enough, yet he could make it plainer. "It is not our will that you should wed with Crieff." Impatiently he dropped his hands from her and paced to the table and back again. "And what is more, mistress, never speak to me again of loving him. It pleasures me not."

He had again come to a stop in front of her. This time she waited for him to speak. The silence deepened while he studied her face. The next words came at her like steel-tipped arrows.

"Do my attentions displease you, mistress?"

Desperately Maggie came back at him with the only hurt she could inflict. "Aye, your Majesty! They do displease me. And trouble me!"

Roughly he took hold of her, encircling her in one arm, and tipping her head back with a hand under her chin.

She tried to twist away, the arm around her tightened.

She could not move. His mouth closed over hers.

Maggie Drummond had been kissed before. But something had happened. This was not the same. She broke away from him, wrenching herself from his arms. She backed off, her lips parted a little, her eyes luminous. Against the panelled walls, her yellow dress pale as a daffodil, she waited.

James walked the ten feet that separated them. In the shadow, in every light in which he saw her face, she seemed more lovely. Here the curve of her cheek was indistinct, there only her mouth and eyes were plain to see. He said low, "You deny me?"

He watched her lips as she answered, "I do."

He sought for a reason. "Are you virgin?"

Her lashes lowered, then raised. He could not see the slight flush of her cheeks. "Aye, my lord."

He was relieved. "So that is your shield and buckler." He smiled a little. This could be dealt with. He delivered his first warning. "Then Crieff was more patient than I shall be."

"He did not demand, your Grace. He was kind, and good."

James frowned.

"That was not intended for a reproof, m'lord. You are different. You are the king."

"Unhappily so," he muttered, "but also a man, mistress. Do not forget. I—" He broke off sharply and turned away, but not before she had seen plain the black mood that suddenly enveloped him. She said softly, "M'lord, how could I possibly forget that you are a man?"

He swung back to her, to make sure whether he had heard a hint of laughter in her voice. When he saw her smile, he grinned boyishly, and a sudden irrational happiness went through him. She was sweet as honey and warm as summer sun. His eyes glowed with pleasure.

He said, "Now, I usually put no price on maidenhood, but it rather pleases me you have known no men."

She made him a quick bow, from the waist, solemnly. "You flatter me. But how fortunate that I am meek and ask you no questions like the ones you do me. Is't not, Jamie Stuart?" She drew out his name.

He laughed. "Cease, mistress."

She shook her head determinedly. "I shall not. You are six and twenty, and—"

"Hush, lass. I ask the questions. How old are you?"

"Nineteen, my lord. And Crieff is twenty."

"God in heaven!" burst out the words and he saw she was laughing.

Now Maggie retreated. "I jest but a wee bit," she said tentatively.

"And I relent a wee bit." He found himself beside a chair. So he sat down. Next to it was a low padded stool. "Will you sit here, Lady Margaret?"

Maggie sat down.

"This will be more comfortable than the other chair." He reached down and with ease turned her and the stool, so her shoulder was against his leg and her head against his knee. He pulled off the little satin cap and laid his hand on her shining hair. The great heavy knot was held with wooden pins.

"You part it in the middle," he said. "Only the bonniest can do thus." Her profile was turned to him. His hand rested on her head, and he sighed.

There was peace in the room. Neither spoke. Maggie closed her eyes. The candlelight was dimmer than the flood of moonlight which made a radiant shimmering path from the long window across the room. When Maggie opened her eyes she saw the moonlight touched her gown and her clasped hands like an ethereal, cloudy mist.

The night air from the plowed fields was sweet and clean. From outside came the hum of the creatures of the night, a singing sound. Maggie bit her lip to keep back the sudden stinging tears because the beauty of the night had indefinably engulfed them.

But she knew that the sudden passions of this man who was James Stuart would be reawakened. He was only a man; she forgave him willingly but that hardly meant she would surrender. She knew too that this moment would end, but while it lasted it was nigh to heaven.

His fingers reached down for her hand. He held it close. "Tomorrow I leave."

"I know," she whispered.

"I ride the ayres in the Border."

"That is well," she said only. It was enough to say. He was referring to the trials of the last week of June and the first weeks of July.

"There is better justice done when I appear," he said, dryly. "We cannot hope for infallibility, but—" He stopped.

"It may be difficult," said Maggie, "for your Grace to realize how much we look to you"—she paused, searching for a word —"for everything."

"Authority is the term you want. Mistress, I should like your company on our progress through the Borders."

Maggie didn't move. Sitting sideways from him, so she didn't have to look at him, she kept her cheek against his knee as she replied. "I cannot, my lord."

Had he heard her? He was continuing: "It is my desire to have part of my Court and a gay company with me."

Maggie stood up. "I am desolate that I shall have to decline." She stood straight as though bracing herself for the next blow.

James looked at her quizzically; then he seemed to realize that he had been rudely refused, and he got to his feet. "Lord God, madam, do I hear aright?"

Maggie said stiffly, "May I have my cap, your Grace?"

"No!" His dark eyes swept her. "You come here to me—"

"You commanded me!" Her eyes blazed at the injustice.

He said grimly, "Aye, mistress. I am accustomed to it. Nor do I like interruptions. You came here and before I had a chance to speak—nay, as if I were a Viking rover, a pirate, you put it bluntly you will have none of me. Even after that I told you I would be patient. I would have given you even a week."

He was frowning, still angry; he had made concessions, he was sure.

Maggie said, "I want no week, no month, no year! May I have your leave to retire, your Grace?"

He took a long step toward her.

"I am weary, my lord." She curtsied.

He looked down at her bent head. "Leave, then!"

She drew a long breath before she rose. "May I have my cap, if you please?"

"No!" He crushed it in his fingers.

From the doorway she looked at him as though she would never see him again. "Goodnight, my lord."

The curtains fell closed. The hall was dark. Yet there was hurry in the air, and Maggie, tense, stood still and strove to hear and to look through the shadows. There was nothing.

Nevertheless, she picked up her skirts and hastened toward the dim lights of the center hall where the main staircase rose. There was no one there either. Maggie started to ascend. Instead she turned on the third step and asked one of the king's men forty feet away at the big doors, "Did anyone pass through here before me?"

"Aye, mistress." His voice echoed over the paved hall. "Lord Fleming."

Maggie glanced up to where the stairway turned. She heard her father's voice saying, "Fleming gave the note to the McAlpin lad."

Irresolutely, Maggie stood on the third step. Then slowly she turned and made her way upstairs to her room.

12

TORCHLIGHT FLARED OVER THE STONE COURT AT EDINburgh castle. A muffled roar from the caged lions showed they had been aroused by the sounds that had heralded the Hepburn and his men.

It had been a six-hour ride. Jane Gordon, her eyes half closed from fatigue, her whole lithe body aching from exhaustion, sat still in the saddle, seizing eagerly the first moment of relaxation. The Hepburn had dismounted and stood by her horse, his hand on the reins.

"Dismount."

He half lifted her down. Within the circle of his arm she watched her horse led away. She said, "I go there." She gestured to the round tower with its barred rooms.

"No," he said.

"No?" she echoed. Then she looked up at him lazily.

"You go with me."

Her soft, short boots were exposed as she gathered up her gown. "Wherever I go, I want water for washing and food for my belly. I starve. And I want a bed for sleeping." She stretched and moved her shoulders. "Which way?"

He did not take his eyes from her. His men had disappeared, the horses had been taken away.

Jane cried, "Must we stand here?"

"If I wish."

"Gape at my back then." She whirled.

She felt his big hand close over her arm. At that she turned and struck out with both fists, the blow catching him on his left and injured arm.

The pain went in waves to his head, and he swayed. But he

didn't loosen his grip on her. He got his balance and jerked her after him.

His apartments were on the first floor. They went up a flight of stairs, through an anteroom, through another smaller room. He half pushed her through a doorway, entered himself and kicked the door shut with his foot. He leaned back against the door.

Jane looked at him and around herself at the massive furniture, the big bed. Then she looked back to the Hepburn and laughed.

"Ah, I fear thee not, man. You're nigh to swooning."

He made a denial deep in his throat.

"Why didn't you stop, on the way?"

He asked, "With you?"

She shrugged.

"You're too big, Hepburn, even to lean on me. I'll push a chair over."

"No." He shook his head, walked over to the chair nearest him and sat down. Jane went to the only other door and flung it open.

As she had suspected it opened onto a long hall. She raised her voice. "Rogues, knaves! To me! To your master!"

She lighted the already laid fire. The Hepburn was sitting close to it, watching her. She found wine and was pouring it when the sound of running feet became plain. A man appeared, and then another.

"Who are you?" Jane asked the first arrival.

"Willie, mistress." His eyes went past her. "M'lord!"

"Aye, he's wounded. Fetch water and linen and food." Jane was leaning over the Hepburn, feeding him wine. Willie rushed out.

The Hepburn was gulping down the wine; some of it ran down his chin.

"I can see you've never fed a baby milk." He took another gulp.

"I never had a baby," said Jane. "And I'd do this for a dog."

Unexpectedly he lurched to his feet. "I tire of impudence!"

He was still wearing light mail and the heavy helmet. A dagger gleamed in his belt. He was breathing hard.

Jane, standing very close to him, knew she had angered him and she was a little afraid. She looked up at him. He was so big. Instinctively she wanted to placate him, and she wanted suddenly to touch him. She reached up and took the helmet off his head.

She dropped it on the floor. Then she lifted her hands again and put them on his head, running her fingers through the thick, red hair.

"The helmet is so heavy," she said softly, her face upturned to his.

He would have reached for her but she said quickly, "I used to do that for my brother. Sit down."

Willie appeared with water and another page with fresh linen. While one page knelt at the Hepburn's feet and drew off the leather boots, Willie divested his master of his mail and with the dagger slit the jacket and shirt to expose the injured arm.

They washed and tended the wound, as well as his face and hands, as though he were a baby. They bound his arm, slipped a clean shirt over his head and gave him more wine.

Jane stood behind his chair, rubbing his head with her long slender fingers. Standing there, saying nothing, looking down on his head and at his face in repose with the eyes almost shut, she knew she was doing exactly what he wished. She dropped her hands.

She still had her cloak on. She took it off and laid it on the bed, aware that the Hepburn was watching her. The pages had brought water for her, but first she undid her coif. Her hair was plaited, and she unwound the long braids and loosened them and let them fall down her back. She washed her face and hands. While she was doing this, food had been brought.

Willie seated Jane at a table which had been carried in. The Hepburn with the loose sleeves of his shirt hiding the bandaged arm looked much as usual except that his face was drawn. His voice sounded strong.

"Leave us," he said.

The door closed; Willie had been the last to leave.

"Mistress, I desire to be served, please."

Jane sat stiff in her chair. "The pages could have done it." Her eyes were narrow and cold.

The Hepburn leaned forward, resting his elbow on the table. "I didn't want them to hear your quarreling."

"I wasn't quarreling!"

"I should be amused by that obvious misstatement, but I am not."

"Be damned to you," cried Jane.

He started to rise, and Jane surrendered.

"I'll serve you, Hepburn, because I don't want you touching me!"

She cut a few thick slices off a joint of meat. She put the plate in front of him.

"Wine or ale?" she asked icily.

"Always ale."

She looked up sharply, spilling the ale. She set the dripping flagon near his right hand, then she poured herself some and drank it off. She put the flagon down, and surveyed him. With her mouth stuffed full of meat she spoke to him.

"Where do you live besides Hailes?"

"I'm building a house in the Cowgate. I have been granted the castle of Bothwell, near Glasgow."

"Why that is the great castle of the Ramsays!" Jane swallowed her meat. "You killed Ramsay?"

"At Sauchie."

"And now Bothwell belongs to you?" She could not believe it. "Have you ever been there?"

He shook his head. "I stayed a night at the Priory on the opposite side of the river." He was on the defensive.

Jane had taken another bite of meat. She spat it out. "I cannot sup with you, Hepburn. You put me off my food."

This time the Hepburn showed no anger at all. He finished chewing his bread. "I favor a slim lass."

Jane jumped to her feet. Leaning on the table she looked across at him, eyes blazing. "Look, Lord Hogface, what are you going to do with me?"

He said lazily, "I'm going to keep you here." He raised his voice. "Will!"

"Wait," cried Jane.

He shook his head. There were steps in the hall.

"Wait," cried Jane again. "You would—you would brand my name!"

There was a knock on the door.

The Hepburn said, "Come in, Will." He rose, walked over to the bed and picked up Jane's cloak. He put it around her. "Take Lady Gordon to her chamber."

For a moment Jane stood with his arm around her. She drew away and walked over to the table, picking up two pieces of meat in her fingers, and a large hunk of bread. She gave him a long insolent stare from the doorway. Then she turned her back.

Willie took her only a few feet. An armed guard opened a door. Within the tiny room was a bed and a crude table. The window was barred. Jane sat down on the bed and began to eat.

13

MATTHEW, BOOTED AND SPURRED, WAITED OUTSIDE A closed door. Behind it he could hear the murmur of Mary's voice, and he waited outside impatiently, his thoughts going from the mission ahead of him to the woman inside.

For ten days now she had avoided him. And yet—he slapped at his boots with his heavy short whip—when she had met him, she had been polite and friendly with just the reserve necessary between mistress and retainer.

The door in front of him opened. "Mistress bids you enter," said Wat.

Mary was sitting in a high chair that necessitated her footstool. "You may close the door, Wat," she said. "Good morning, Matthew."

"Good morning, mistress," said Matthew, his blue eyes lighting at the sight of her. She had a little lacy shawl around her shoulders, for the gray dawn was cold.

Mary said, "Well, Matthew, you look capable of beating off any belligerent Borderers, but I like little to see you leave."

"Will you be afraid?" His voice was suddenly urgent.

"No," said Mary. " 'Tis not that. It is that I truly see no reason for your trip."

Since he could hardly tell her the real reason for the trip, he was baffled for words momentarily, which was odd for Matthew, who was proud of his command of language and his ability to lie.

"I want to see what's happening in the Borders," he said. "I shall be gone only tonight. With Parliament meeting day after tomorrow, it's imperative we have some idea how strong James will be, taking into account the Border force which is of course his greatest strength. Mistress, that is why Jamie is there now, with the Hepburn, holding trials at which he will no doubt pardon or grant clemency to his own followers, be lenient with criminals, free a few murderers, and in general make a fine impression on the fighting Border. That solid strength, if he can produce it, will have a definite effect on Parliament, and it will have a decisive effect on what your brother and sister may expect in royal mercy. The stronger James is, the less mercy we can expect him to deal out."

Mary's face had grown paler.

"I will return in time to advise your brother of the course he should take, when he will have to take the stand before James and answer the charge of treason. Since—" Matthew stopped and swore, and added, "Mistress, for God's sake! Don't look so. Even Jamie can't hang all the lords in Scotland."

"No," said Mary, "but he might."

Matthew grinned. "He'll not," he said. "But we have a battle of words ahead, and it will be best to be prepared, to know how far we may go. For instance, we may have to throw ourselves on the royal mercy, make no attempt to plead the case at all."

Mary said, slowly, "Matthew, how can my brother be tried for treason when he was fighting for the real king?"

Matthew said quickly, "According to law he cannot. However, he fought against the present king, who is now crowned." He lifted his shoulders as if to say it was a most vexing problem, a problem that was probably vexing even James himself. Then he added, "There is another point of Scottish law I want your brother to know. I'll be back tomorrow night. Have a cask of wine ready for me, and I shall need wax." The last words were peremptory; the morning was lightening, and he was losing time. He started for the door.

His hand was on the latch when she asked, "Why?"

"Why what? The wax?" He frowned. There was no reason for her to know. He answered curtly, "To send a message."

"I see." She was distant. "You may leave me now."

He didn't like being dismissed. He said, "Don't you think you should send your knight forth to battle with some kind of token?" He walked toward her.

Her smile began as an impersonal one and then gathered delight as Matthew knelt on one knee. For a minute she could think of nothing to give him. Then she remembered and reached in the bosom of her black morning gown and drew out a black silk square, a little crumpled. She held it out.

"I remembered the perfume." She was pleased with herself. "I so often forget. Matthew, I dub thee Black Knight, and God go with you."

Matthew, kneeling in front of her, took the square from her fingers. "Thou art so fair," he said.

Her eyes were shadowy blue. He got to his feet quickly. "Forgive me, mistress." He was resolving never to repeat such a scene and wondered briefly what had trapped him into it. He went to the door, opened it and left, forgetting again to wait for dismissal. In the hall he tucked the black square into his sleeve.

He took the south road. At eleven he stopped to dine

hastily at a wayside inn; there were few such in the Border. At three in the afternoon he crossed the Border. He was back in England.

At half after four he entered the iron gates of Bewcastle, his English Majesty's garrisoned fort for the protection of the Border. Captain Graham came hurrying to meet him as Matthew swung off his horse. Graham followed him into the room Matthew had set aside for his own use.

"I have not much time, Captain," Matthew said, also greeting his servant, and letting the man remove his old boots.

"Sir Matthew, we are honored," Graham said, eagerly. "I knew not when to expect you. Sir, what news?"

"None now, man. I'll be back later. What is the news here?" He was stripping off his clothes, and a black square of silk fell to the floor. The servant picked it up.

"James is at Jedburgh, holding the last of the trials. Hepburn is with him. The Border has been active, shall we say?" Graham grinned.

"You raided?" Matthew asked, slipping into a fine shirt that the servant was holding.

"Aye, and we expect a reprisal tonight. There's a moon, but not till very late. About three."

Matthew frowned. "I hardly want to run into a raid," he said. "I'll need twenty men, good ones, Captain. Not so much for protection as to impress the arch traitor I shall see tonight."

Graham said, "But you yourself, sir. How have you been?"

"If you mean am I unsuspected, no. The wily Hepburn has his eyes on me. However, I don't matter too much, so long as our traitor keeps himself unknown, and we can continue to deal through him."

"A pity," said Graham thoughtfully, "that we cannot raid Jedburgh and seize James himself."

"Good God," said Matthew, "are ye mad? The Hepburn is with him, and a man called Knox, who is worthy of respect. More than that, Jamie is amply guarded. But why hurry? Jamie will be over the Border himself—that is the way his policies are taking him." Matthew, serious, as he put a sealed paper on the table, said. "Here is the report for his Majesty. See that it is amply guarded. It should be in London tomorrow. It bears all the news that I hope to be able to regale you with later tonight."

"Unless we have a raid," Graham said hopefully.

Matthew stood up, dressed now in black velvet, with shiny black boots and a rakish feathered cap. He buckled his sword belt and looked around to see if he had forgotten anything.

"A touch of jewelry, sir?" the servant suggested, eyeing his master.

Matthew shook his head, then thought better of it. "A bauble to impress my host, perhaps." He yawned and said, "The beryl ring."

The ring was handed to him. It was heavy and carved and supported an enormous beryl, yellow as a cat's eye, the stone itself set on a golden hinge lifted to reveal a tiny hiding place. The servant, watching Matthew slip it on his finger, said to Graham proudly, "That was a token of affection and regard from his Majesty."

Matthew grinned. "For services rendered," he said. He patted the man on the shoulder. "Your romantic notions." He went to the door, and raised his hand in a gesture of farewell.

"I'll be back tonight by that moon," he said.

He started away. He was out of the sprawling stone barracks into the yard where his escort awaited when the servant came running after him, waving a black square.

"D'ye want this, sir?" he asked breathlessly.

Matthew looked down from the fresh horse. He saw the scarf. "Since you've brought it," he said. He wheeled. "Now we'll make the best time we can."

14

IT WAS THEN ALMOST FIVE O'CLOCK OF THE TENTH DAY of July. It was cool, and Matthew congratulated himself on picking good weather for his hard fast ride. He could count on getting almost no sleep tonight; he intended to be back in Edinburgh the next night and already thought with longing of his narrow, hard bed. That made him wonder when he would ever have the luxury of sleeping in a feather bed again.

Trees brushed at his head. Although the foliage was not so full and lush as it would be in August, still it was thick, the trees close set, and Johnnie, ahead of him, was proceeding through what looked to Matthew like an impenetrable forest over angular hills.

"I thought I said I wanted to make good time," Matthew said irritably.

Johnnie said, "Aye, sir, but this is the quickest way. There are no roads, so we should have to pierce through here anyway."

Matthew swore, visions of even an hour's rest were vanishing.

"In fifty feet we come out onto a moor," Johnnie said.

"Thank God," said Matthew. A branch slapped his cheek, and he tried to keep his temper. Ahead he could see the trees were less thick, and with pleasure increased his pace until they emerged onto the level moor. In the distance, steep hills confronted them.

Johnnie spurred his horse, remembering Sir Matthew's quick temper. "But 'tis boggy," he shouted in warning. They had almost crossed the moor when Matthew saw a company of about one hundred horse.

Johnnie saw them, too. Johnnie looked at Matthew, and Matthew, knowing they had been seen and would be certain of pursuit, galloped ahead of Johnnie to take command. In two minutes they had reached the shelter of the trees, and Matthew reckoned it would be about another five before the opposing Scots would be upon them. Matthew dismounted in the center of the ring of twenty apprehensive men. They were hopelessly outnumbered, and the Scots no doubt were anxious to fight his men, these very men who had raided last night on Scottish soil.

Matthew said, "Tether these horses here, take to the trees in a semicircle protecting them, and face the moor." Then he smiled as he said, "Have you ever heard of Robin Hood?"

He was answered with nods and reassuring grins.

"There is nothing better than the English longbow," said Matthew, climbing up a tree.

"Aye, sir," said the man who had climbed the tree nearest him.

Matthew, settling himself comfortably on a broad, low limb, announced, "I have a good view of the plain and the coming horsemen. Have all of you such a view?"

"I haven't," said one voice.

"Climb higher, then," said Matthew.

The horsemen were coming fast. Yet even while Matthew watched and was about to give the signal for the first rain of deadly arrows, the leading horseman of the Scots held up one hand, and the troop slowed, almost to a stop.

"He suspects us rightly," said Matthew. He frowned a little, fitting the arrow carefully, raising it to take good aim, for in a few moments the troop would come into good range, range short enough to allow the well-aimed arrow to pierce a man.

Matthew, squinting through the leaves, with one leaf dangling over his ear, suddenly shouted, "Hold. Don't shoot till I do!"

He peered ahead, the leading horseman had stopped, and Matthew recognized him.

Johnnie said, "Sir, he's tying a handkerchief over his face!"

For a lord to go masked was a rather common procedure on the Border. If he were known, there were likely to be reprisals.

Matthew, turning on his limb, looked around the circle of his men.

"I want no arrow sped," he growled. "That's the Hepburn."

The English knew that if the Hepburn were cut down by an arrow, none of them would escape alive if it took the whole force of the Scot Border.

"He knows what we have done. 'Tis what he *would* have done, and so he's going to be careful," Matthew said. Then he raised his voice in a loud shout. "Come no further!"

Not heeding this, the Hepburn applied spurs to his horse and cantered slowly forward. Matthew, blue eyes grim, thought the Hepburn didn't know he was riding to probable death. Matthew could not shoot the Hepburn, but there was another way. The meeting was a godsend. He felt for the black square of silk to see if it was still in place. He said, in not so great a shout because the distance between them had narrowed, "Hold, sir, or I'll be forced to use you as a target."

The Hepburn reined in. "I wanted to be close enough to parley," he said.

"There's naught to parley about," Matthew said. "Either we go in peace or we fight."

The Hepburn laughed, letting his horse take him a few feet forward, negligently. "Are you going to come down out of those trees?" he asked.

"No," said Matthew. "We are but twenty men, sir, and we fight this way. Come close, and ye will learn about an English longbow."

"By God, he comes from London, my lord," said a Border voice at one side of the Hepburn. "We've treed a Londoner."

Hepburn said, "How much money are you carrying?"

"I pay no ransom," Matthew called back. The time had come. His voice was taut. "Shall we elect single combat to settle this?"

This was usual on the Border. Even so, a silence fell.

The Hepburn never took long to decide anything. "Done," he said.

Matthew said to his men, "Which of you wants the honor?"

The Scots let out loud jeers.

"Why don't you fight yourself?" they shouted, edging closer to the thick trees, and through this came Hepburn's voice, amused.

"I'll fight you, if you consent, sir," he said lazily.

"He's afraid of you, my lord," one of the Borderers said. "He comes from London, he does."

Matthew, thus challenged, had a small smile on his face. The impression of uncertainty, even cowardice, had been given. He took the black silk square from his sleeve. While he tied it on, under his eyes, covering his face completely, he deemed it would be hard for the Hepburn to recognize him. His clothes were in the height of London fashion; his accent was now his own, soft and clipped. He pulled his cap down over one eye. Before he slid down from his perch, he whispered to Johnnie, "Stay behind. Keep the arrow strung."

"Aye, sir," answered Johnnie as Matthew reached the ground and walked out alone onto the plain.

The Hepburn dismounted, motioning to his men to do the same. "Let all the men make a circle and watch," he said.

"Come on out," Matthew called to his men.

The nineteen English did, unafraid. Johnnie remained perched in a tree. Pledges were never broken on the Border; they came out grinning, swaggering a little, looking around at the faces of their foes.

Matthew said, "I am using the new, lighter sword with a steel hilt." He drew it from its sheath and held it out.

Hepburn said approvingly, "Mine is almost identical, sir." He and Matthew stood quite close.

"D'ye want to measure the blades?" the Hepburn asked.

There was scarcely half an inch difference.

By this time the men were sprawled out comfortably on the ground in a big circle.

Matthew, tall and lithe, elegant in his black velvet, was a sober contrast to the Hepburn dressed in a leather riding suit. Both men took off their cloaks. The Hepburn removed his own jacket, but Matthew waved for a man to assist in doffing the black velvet. In their shirtsleeves they faced each other, and the first strikes of steel sounded loud.

The first experimental thrust on Hepburn's part was parried by Matthew just in time. There was an almost holiday air to the scene; the Scots were making wagers though the English seemed tense. Matthew backed away from the Hepburn's whirring blade, wielding his slender sword as though it were merely a clumsy barrier between him and the Hepburn.

Although the Hepburn's face was covered by the mask, his eyes showed his amusement. He feinted and lunged, gracefully, stepping on the boggy ground delicately for all his brawn. The Scots were smiling.

Matthew ineptly moved to one side to avoid a feint. He seemed off balance. The Hepburn drove in, seeking the sword arm.

But the weapon didn't find its mark. Matthew caught its point in a sudden shattering blow that knocked it from the Hepburn's hand. There, before Matthew, the Hepburn stood disarmed, while a great shout rose from the English.

The Hepburn allowed no more than one brief moment to elapse, a moment in which he knew he was near death. He hurled himself shoulder first at Matthew, almost twenty stone of man and muscle. Both men sprawled full length on the ground as the shouts died away.

Why had Matthew not run him through? Every man present had understood the situation. To kill an unarmed man was a breach of Border law, and for the Hepburn's life the Scots would have taken full toll. The pledged truce would have ended in that instant, and all the English would have paid with their lives. Yet for a second, Matthew's eyes had met the Hepburn's, and the Hepburn had understood that he was considering killing him, and paying the price.

Now Matthew was pinned down. But the Hepburn had no hold on him. Matthew twisted his whole body to free himself, and as he twisted, using every muscle, drawing his legs up to facilitate the turn, the Hepburn grasped his sword arm and set his knee on the elbow joint.

Matthew grimaced with pain and dared not move the arm

for fear of breaking it. Now the Hepburn could reach for his own blade. His fingers closed around the hilt, Matthew felt his arm released, and, not daring a moment's loss, rolled away and jumped to his feet. Once more the two men faced each other.

Both were breathing heavily. They were hardly more tense than the circle of watching men. Their sword points were lowered; over their masks their eyes met, their chests rose and fell almost in rhythm while they measured each other in silence.

Now there would be no mercy. This was sport no longer, no Border duel, no ransom paid. The loser would not forfeit monies, but his life.

This was English against Scot, England against Scotland, with all the ancient hatreds fierce and alive.

For the Hepburn enough time had passed, a minute probably, to cool his savage anger at the Englishman.

"En garde," he said, through the mask, the words a muttered warning. Now methodically he set about to kill the Englishman.

Matthew dissembled no longer. The duel which followed was a match, brilliant and cruel and grueling.

The ground was muddy, and the more it was trampled, the more dangerous the footing. Extreme care had to be taken to avoid a fall which would mean sure death.

Not a murmur came from the circle of watching men. In the summer afternoon, with the sun slanting over the steep hills bordering the boggy moor, only the cries of the birds sounded loud, and the breathing of the fighting men was audible.

Sweat poured from them. Their shirts clung to their backs, their shoulders, even to their strong forearms. The clash of steel resounded, heightened by the startling quiet of the light blows that tinkled as they disengaged.

But Matthew was battling under disadvantage, for he was beginning to tire badly. He had ridden eighty miles, while the Hepburn, who had spent the morning sitting in court with James, was fresh and rested. Matthew began to retreat.

Behind him the English scrambled back to give him room. He edged back, his feet testing for good footing. His breathing was short and quick. He could feel his heart thudding against his ribs. He fought with care, sparing himself, to recover breath and strength, retreating, easily, gracefully, always sideways to the Hepburn, dancing back, out of reach.

Then he seized the offensive again. A brilliant riposte slid under the Hepburn's blade and forced him back. Matthew followed, using the last of his strength. Now the Hepburn retreated, easily also; over his forehead the thick red hair was dripping wet. He too was husbanding his endurance, carefully, for the moment he knew would come.

It came, finally. Matthew, struggling to end it before another few minutes could pass, knew he could not last much longer. He was moving more slowly, too slowly. Recklessly, with a feint that did not deceive the Hepburn, he lunged forward with his last ounce of strength.

The Hepburn stepped to one side. Matthew's blade was out of line. The Hepburn's sword drove to Matthew's heart.

Matthew took the steel. He swayed back. A cry went up from the Scots; the English were silent. The Hepburn withdrew his sword sharply. The front of Matthew's shirt was already dyed red with blood.

But Matthew still stood, unsteadily. He put the palm of his left hand flat against the fleshy part of his shoulder; he shifted his weight and essayed a backward step. He slipped and fell.

The Hepburn approached him, as Matthew turned a little on his side, his hand clutched tight against his shoulder, his fingers extended stiffly.

The Hepburn looked down at his fallen foe. He bent over, took the beryl ring off Matthew's finger, and tucked it in the pocket of his jacket. Then he rested the point of his sword exactly below Matthew's hand, on the ribs, over the heart. He had taken the booty he wanted from Matthew before he killed him.

Matthew hardly opened his eyes as he spoke. "Don't move, m'lord."

The words low spoken, reached the Hepburn plainly.

"There is an archer in those trees who will take your life if you take mine," Matthew added, sounding lazy, but he had not much breath. The blood oozed through his fingers and spread down across his whole chest. The Hepburn's sword was pricking his ribs, nicking them. The pain was more irritating than the throbbing wound in his shoulder. Matthew swore a foul oath.

"Skewer me and you'll get air through your guts," he snarled. This left him no breath at all, but his eyes opened wide and flashed with anger.

The Hepburn and Matthew could not be heard by the circle of men, their voices still muffled by their masks. The Hepburn, standing over Matthew, knew he was a perfect target; he believed the Englishman, and his anger rose. He looked toward the trees; he set his jaw and looked once more at Matthew.

Then he stepped back. He made an effort at calmness. "Rise then, fallen one," he said mockingly, sure Matthew could not rise. "Shall I summon aid?"

Matthew struggled to his feet; his chest rose and fell with the exertion, and he was bleeding badly.

"You look like a stuck pig," gibed the Hepburn, who pulled out his dripping shirt tail to wipe off his sword. "You're full of trickery, English."

"Your language is crude and untaught," Matthew said. "I hardly understand you. Are you a Border freebooter?"

Under the masks both men's faces were grim, and their eyes blazed.

"You have need for tricks," Hepburn jeered, trying to keep the passion out of his voice.

"The odds were five to one!"

"Ah," said the Hepburn. "You lie!"

Their swords were sheathed. Matthew half raised his right fist; the Hepburn countered by automatically turning his shoulder toward Matthew as he lifted his left arm and brought the right fist up to his waist. Muddy, sweaty and bloody, they almost forgot where they were, that the duel was over and that encircling them were their men.

The Hepburn took a rein on his anger. He could not strike

the wounded Englishman. He could have killed him before, but not now. He swore.

Matthew bowed. But he could not retain composure either. "We'll meet again!"

"A pleasure," growled the Hepburn.

They exchanged one last look and turned on their heels. Matthew staggered a little; he angrily brushed aside all help. Leading his men, he wove an unsteady course to the trees and the tethered horses. By the time he regained the cover of the trees, the Scots were already mounted, and, with Hepburn at their head, moving away across the moor in the direction from which they had come.

"Mount and get hence!" Matthew ordered.

Johnnie had slid down from his perch, longbow still in hand, Matthew had taken off his improvised mask and was wadding it against his shoulder. He looked around the circle of men. He pointed to one.

"We'll exchange jackets."

The borrowed jacket was smaller than his, so it fitted tightly, pressing the crushed silk hard against the wound. Then Matthew gave his cap to the man who wore the velvet jacket.

"Mount and get hence," he repeated. "You'll fetch Bewcastle within an hour or so. The Hepburn will send men to follow you, to see whence you came. Johnnie and I will seek cover for a bit in one of the caves in which Liddesdale abounds."

Matthew's voice was weary, but his words were unhurried and evenly spoken. He mounted his horse, raised his right hand in a gesture of farewell, and he and Johnnie disappeared.

After less than a mile they drew up sharp before a steep gash in the hill. Inside its blackness, Matthew dismounted, propped himself up against the side of the cave and went to sleep. Johnnie wakened him in what he judged to be a half hour, as he'd been ordered. Their ride was resumed.

Matthew's shoulder ached painfully. He cursed to himself, the image of the Hepburn plain before him. He cursed again aloud.

Johnnie said tentatively, "I shouldna ha' liked to shoot him."

A rush of anger was in Matthew's reply. "You didn't, did you? Well then let it rest, dolt! I'm giving the orders!"

"Aye, sir," said Johnnie. "I just meant—"

"Hold your tongue," snapped Matthew. He sighed, and the action was almost as painful as the jolting ride. "Johnnie, he would have killed me had it not been for you," he said.

"Aye, sir," said Johnnie, "but that was because you didn't let him pick up his sword."

Matthew was thoughtful. The hold the Hepburn had on the lawless Border was part legend, part authority, and part—he frowned—honest affection. Even the English Borderer was drawn to him.

"You love him a little, don't you, Johnnie?"

Johnnie looked embarrassed, and vague. He also had a picture of the Hepburn. "I don't know," he drawled. "There's Hermitage, sir."

Matthew understood. He persisted in his question. "He is what every man jack of you would like to be, is he not, Johnnie?"

This Johnnie was able to answer. "Aye. Aye, that he is." He grinned at the idea. "I'd like that—to be him. There's Hermitage, sir."

"I see it, Johnnie," Matthew said dryly. Indeed he could scarce help it. The great oblong fortress rose out of the vale, formidable, silent, stone upon stone.

The only sound was of the birds and the rushing Hermitage water that foamed at the feet of the Border castle. Stronghold of the Douglasses, its ramparts had guarded the Scottish border for centuries and its walls told tales of siege and bloody raid, of dungeon prisoners, of loyalty and treachery. Yet it had never been in the hands of the English. Unconquered, it stood as a challenge as Matthew rode toward its gates.

The portcullis was up, its chains dangling, and Matthew and Johnnie rode in. After them, the chains clanked as the portcullis was lowered, locking them inside the castle. Johnnie looked about apprehensively, for once inside Hermitage, there was no way out save by this iron gate. He dismounted, and helped Matthew, who stood with some difficulty.

"I am expected. Take me to your lord," he commanded the soldier who had come forward to greet him.

Johnnie was called into the guard room by the lounging men in there; Matthew followed the soldier. Matthew walked unsteadily, but he tried to make the most of what he could see of Hermitage.

He was being taken down a hall that skirted the castle apron. Hidden from him now was the great hall which could and had been used for stabling the mounts in times of war. Above the hall were enormous barracks and dining halls for the men, for Hermitage could accommodate a thousand men and their horses. On this main floor, where there were a few slitted windows to allow air, he supposed the lord of the castle had his chambers; each door through which he passed was studded, so that each part of Hermitage could be separately defended. His guide paused before a corner room. He knocked on the door.

It was opened. Matthew walked in. He bowed briefly, and then sought the nearest chair. As he sank down into it, he said, tiredly, "My apologies, my lords. I'm late."

The Earl of Douglass and Lord Fleming had both risen to their feet as their visitor entered. "My God, sir, you're hurt!" Douglass exclaimed. He flung open the lately closed door and bellowed for aid. Fleming hastened to Matthew's side, unfastened Matthew's jacket and helped him take it off.

"A clean shirt, too, my lord," he said to Douglass, who was ordering what was needed for Matthew's care. Fleming gave Matthew some cold ale, and while he drank it they sat uneasily, waiting for the bandages and hot water Douglass had ordered.

"Who is responsible for your hurt?" Fleming asked, his black eyes resting on Matthew.

"The Hepburn," said Matthew, grudging the breath it took to talk.

Douglass exclaimed again, and there was fear in his tone and on his face. Fleming had rather a look of disappointment that Matthew had been unable to best the Hepburn.

"Did you wound him, sir?" he inquired.

Matthew shook his head. "I disarmed him. Unfortunately —" His voice trailed off. His shirt was being taken off. Under it was a belt of cloth, from which Matthew extracted a leather case, containing a parchment. Unsteadily he walked past the servant and handed it to Douglass.

Douglass' hands shook a little as they took the case. He laid it on the table, whereupon he pulled a chair over, sat down, and put his hand on the case as if to make sure it would not walk away.

Fleming cleared his throat. "Now, Sir Matthew," he said, "there is no need for you to exert yourself in speech. We can wait. While we wait, and while you are made more comfortable, we shall regale you with a little gossip. His Majesty has evidently become involved in an affair of the heart." He smiled, and contemplated his hands.

Douglass made a disclaiming gesture, but Fleming waved a hand at him, smiled again. "This is just a tidbit, sir," he said to Matthew. "But it has possibilities."

Again Douglass demurred. "Jamie at this moment is enjoying the charms of a lass called—" Douglass hesitated, "Sally. I vow, sir, she is the bonniest lass in the Borders. He saw her yesterday."

Fleming said, "Jamie's gallantries are many. But that has naught to do with Maggie Drummond."

Matthew winced as the bandages went on. "Maggie Drummond?" He looked sharply at Fleming.

"Aye. I warrant you know I am wed to Eufemia Drummond. This situation is replete with humor, Sir Matthew. For my sister-in-law, the beauteous Maggie, has refused James. I heard her myself."

Matthew was too tired to be surprised. He grinned ruefully. "Continue," he said.

Fleming put the tips of his fingers together. "First you must know that the Drummond sisters are—" He spread his hands. "What shall I say? I, who am wed to one, can tell you truly she is enough to drive a man to—some lengths. There are times when I would like to strangle her. From jealousy." His black eyes gleamed. "If Jamie feels one quarter of what

Eufemia can do to me, gentlemen, we may have a problem on our hands." He paused, and then he said, almost with stolidity, coming to the point, "The Drummonds have already, in the past, given one queen to Scotland. It is quite imperative that they give no more."

Douglass snorted. "You fear for naught." But he was apprehensive.

Fleming apparently lost his seriousness. "Mayhap. And it is laughable, Sir Matthew. Jamie left his bonnie Margaret, who had repulsed his advances, and came south to ride the ayres. We've been with him. Before three days had elapsed, he'd promised Maggie's betrothed to another lass, and granted Lord Drummond a parcel of land. I"—he pointed to himself—"I am in favor too. I received the royal wine concessions for Edinburgh. I expect to make a deal of monies." He chuckled. "In return for that, I shall try my best to push Maggie into her lover's arms as quickly as possible, for we want no marriage, sirs."

Matthew asked sharply, "There is no question of marriage, is there?"

"No, no," said Fleming smoothly. "Yet it is a possibility we must not overlook. There is one heir to the throne—Jamie's little brother; we want no more."

Matthew drank more ale, felt better now that his shoulder was bandaged and he wore a clean shirt. He said, because this was important, "James till now has spurned all offers of marriage."

"Aye," said Fleming. "Exactly. But this would be different. Jamie's king now, and besides he belongs to the new age. He is romantic, full of passion, hot-headed. More than that, sir, he reads. He can ride, but also he can read. The great deeds of Homeric heroes, the discourses of the philosophers. He knows Froissart, Vergil, reads history, intones the Scripture. He is fascinated by the theories of Columbus—the argument of a new world. He has endowed the printers of Edinburgh. Nevertheless," said Fleming slyly, "his Majesty was almost shot and killed at Drummond. By mistake. He is human.

Mortal." Abruptly he stopped. The servants had left the room. "Now I think it best we consider the business at hand."

Matthew was digesting all this, trying to sort out the facts from innuendo, when Douglass began to speak.

"I am ready to grant you your wishes, Sir Matthew."

Matthew nodded. He looked at the paper Douglass was taking out of the case. Douglass picked up a quill, dipped it, spread out the paper and signed it.

Fleming said smoothly, "Then these walls will be yours, in the event you need them. Hermitage will be yours."

Matthew smiled, still nodding his head. "That is well, my lords. You will be amply repaid. This treaty will go to London tonight."

Douglass looked uncertain, fearful. Suddenly he rose. "I must leave. I am dining with James." There was an ink spot on his finger. He rubbed at it and stared at the stain, as though it must proclaim his guilt and treason.

"Lord Fleming is staying till tomorrow. He will entertain you, sir," he said nervously. "Good-bye, gentlemen."

Fleming waited until the door was closed. Then he resumed his favorite attitude, his head back a bit, his fingers pressed together at the tips.

"He is a wee mite afraid, sir. His is an old quarrel with the Stuarts. Two Douglass heirs were murdered in Edinburgh castle, some years ago, after being served a black bull's head on a great silver platter. Douglass blood ran into the platter, so they say. Then Jamie's grandfather himself killed our Douglass' grandfather whom he had drawn aside to speak with, after supper, and in a rage at some impudence of Douglass', drew his dagger and killed him on the spot. The struggle between the Douglass power and the Crown on the Border has been great, and the Douglass power is waning, with this present struggle. So Hermitage is yours, and 'twill be of enormous use—but secretly. A feather in the cap of England not to be flaunted."

Fleming was pleased with the way he had put that, and Matthew found his dislike of the man rising. He said nothing. Fleming continued.

"Now, certes, Sir Matthew, I know that England is bled worse than you are from your wound. She is bled by the Wars of the Roses, and she is in no condition to fight. Secondly, Henry Tudor is obviously using the old method of spies and hired traitors, such as you and I."

Matthew frowned murderously at being linked with Fleming.

"You need not dissemble with me," said Fleming. "I want no war with England, unless it is necessary to make Jamie uncomfortable, but only for England to maintain the same supremacy she had through the reign of James III."

"Most Scots," said Matthew slowly, "would rather die than bow a neck to England."

"True," said Fleming. "But we do not consider what most Scots want."

There was a knock on the door. Fleming called permission to enter. A man came in with a tray of food. He served the food on wooden trenchers. He was a stout big man, with a long-handled knife in his belt. His face was flushed, its veins prominent.

"The Scottish people," announced Matthew, keeping his eye on the servant, "did not like the foreign policies of James III."

Fleming said, "James III is dead." He glanced at the servant; there was a small smile on his face.

The thrill of a possible discovery made Matthew sit up straight. He tried a direct accusation. "We English do not hire assassins, Lord Fleming!"

Fleming's black eyes drooped. "Do not jest, sir."

"I am not jesting." Matthew turned and stared at the servant, who had stopped serving the food. "Do you listen, knave? What is your name?" he asked.

"Borthwick." The answer was low and surly.

"Leave the room, Borthwick," Fleming commanded harshly.

Borthwick threw his master a look of warning, of threat, but he obeyed this time. Matthew picked up a piece of boiled fowl from the trencher and began to eat. Now he suspected two things: that Fleming, through Borthwick, was responsible for the murder of James III, and that Fleming was also responsible for the attempted murder of Jamie at Drummond. It all fitted together; some day he would be able to use this information.

"Where is Jamie's brother—this next heir to the Scottish throne?" he asked.

Fleming had begun to eat too. He made a friendly face at Matthew. "The next heir, he is only nine, you know, has been given into the custody of one man." He shrugged.

Matthew said, "The Hepburn."

"Aye. It was the first act of James as king. You knew that. James safeguarded his brother's life the best way he knew how by putting it in the hands of the man he could trust utterly. The young duke is now at Hailes, with tutors. He sails the sea every day, but he is more than amply guarded. 'Twould be impossible now to lay a hand on him."

"I see," said Matthew, seeing very well. Fleming wanted no harm to come to the Duke of Ross. He wanted harm to come to James.

It was so simple and standard a plot that Matthew felt cheated. To dominate, to hold a young king, a boy king hostage, was the ambition of unscrupulous men. Through him they'd hold a country in their palm, and—Matthew knew this might come true. He reminded himself that Fleming had probably disposed of one monarch. It occurred to Matthew that he would dispose of Maggie Drummond, if he thought it expedient. He studied Fleming as he spoke.

"Much may happen," he said, "to Jamie. After all, he is reckless. And I hear of the stirring of witches' brews, of bitter revolt, at Dumbarton. Jamie might be killed. Or, for that matter, so might the Hepburn."

"Aye," said Fleming.

Those two stood in Fleming's way.

Matthew stood up. "I, too, must leave."

Fleming said, "I should be honored to have you spend the night here. Besides, you are wounded."

"I should be delighted to stay, m'lord, were it not for the fact that I have promised to be back at Bewcastle this night."

Fleming made no protest. "We can help each other," he

said in farewell. His words and face were pleasant, his eyes, remote and malignant. Matthew shivered; it was the loss of blood, he supposed.

"I am sure we can help each other, in the weeks to come," Fleming repeated.

15

JANE GORDON SAT ON THE FLOOR. LEANING BACK against the bed, her legs stretched out, crossed at the ankles, a pair of dice lying in her palm, she was listening as her guard, sitting cross-legged in front of her, strummed his crude lute and sang:

> "Said John, 'Fight on, my merry men all,
> I am a little wounded but am not slain;
> I will lay me down to bleed a while,
> Then I'll rise and fight with you again.' "

"Stop!" commanded Jane. She threw the dice across the floor and watched them roll. "I don't like it. It's too sad. Sing me a love song. Of the Border."

Elliot, the guard, rested the lute on his knees. Meantime Jane had changed her mind.

"Continue, pray." She scooped up the dice, and leaned back again to listen.

Elliot obeyed. He thought it sad and gallant himself. The ballad ended with the hero's son being told of his father's death. Elliot again rested the lute, and Jane wiped her eyes with the back of her hand. She said abruptly to her other guard, "Hay! You owe me forty crowns."

Hay had been thinking of moonlit nights on the Border, of

a fire burning and men gathered around, listening to ballads, before a raid. He sighed deeply. Then he answered Jane.

"Forty crowns, aye, Lady Jane. But—"

Jane interrupted. "The Hepburn comes tonight. Soon. Is't not so?"

"Aye." Hay was curious.

"If you'll take me to his room so I may wait there for him, you'll owe me naught. Not a penny."

Hay thought this over. He glanced inquiringly at Elliot. Elliot rubbed his head, twanged the lute, and said he saw no harm in the Lady Jane's waiting for m'lord in his own bedroom.

Jane, before Hay could think of an objection, rose, shook out her gown, picked up her thin shimmering veil and went to the open door. There was no one in the corridor. With the veil trailing in a cloud behind her, Hay escorted his prisoner to an oaken door.

He opened it. Inside it was quiet and almost dark. Hay closed the door as Jane took three steps to the center of the room, where she paused.

Over by one window was a high chest with a mirror on top. Jane ran over to it and adjusted her veil, so that it covered her face completely and flowed down around her shoulders.

She started to turn away from the mirror, when she stopped suddenly, on impulse. She opened the top drawer of the chest. She saw a box, and opened the lid. Her eyes sparkled as she took out five gold pieces. She shut the drawer, and with them hot in her hand, went over to the room's other door which she opened very carefully, peering out. She could see nothing, so she opened it wider and prepared to step out. A voice said, "No."

Jane stamped her foot and raised her hand.

"Hay, how dare you, knave? You villain, to suspect me! Out of my way!"

Hay, who was somewhat impervious to insult by this time, considering he had guarded her ladyship for three weeks, grinned. "No," he said again.

Jane held out her hand and dropped her voice to a conspiratorial whisper. "Five gold pieces to you, Hay, if you let me see my brother, Lord Gordon."

Hay wrestled with the thought of the Hepburn as against five gold pieces. The Hepburn won. "No," said Hay for the third time.

Jane threw herself against him, eluded his grab, and flew toward the outer door to freedom. She had time enough to open the door, to gain the next room, which was empty, fly through that and a curtained doorway—into the arms of the Hepburn.

Her face pressed against his leather coat. She didn't dare look up. She heard Hay's pounding steps come to a brief stop behind her; she heard Hay mutter an exclamation and break off as he waited wordlessly for the explosion that was sure to come.

The Hepburn's arms held Jane tight. Over her head his voice came. "How does this happen, Hay?"

Hay mumbled, "We were dicing, and—"

"You and the Lady Gordon?"

"And Elliot," mumbled Jane in the leather.

"And the Lady Jane wanted to wait for you in your room."

"So?" said the Hepburn.

"So, I thought naught of that, thinking mayhap you—and neither did Elliot, m'lord, because after all many's the time—"

"That's enough," growled the Hepburn.

"Well, you'd just come home, and then, m'lord, I thought I ought to still guard her, and she tried to run away. I was on the other side of the door."

"Get hence."

"Aye, my lord," said Hay, grateful that nothing worse had happened to him. By the time Jane raised her head to look at the Hepburn, Hay had gone.

The Hepburn said irritably, "You look like a Moslem woman."

Jane stood up straight. He took her arm and led her to the inner room whence she had come. He closed the door and went over to the mantel to light the candles.

"You would not have got far," he said, as he set the first

candelabrum down. "I've given orders that no woman may go veiled in the castle."

Jane's eyes were fastened on his tall figure. "Why?" was all she could think of to say.

He turned to face her, setting down the other lighted candelabrum. The wax spluttered and hissed a little. "Because it conceals identity."

"Then what will a poor lass do when she goes to meet her lover?" Jane asked. Slowly she unwound her veil, transferring it to the hand that held the gold pieces.

He frowned at this remark. "She'll have to be true to her lord!"

"Oh!" said Jane. "But that would hamper you, would it not? And how if the lass has no lord?" She smiled and drew the veil through her fingers.

He looked hard at her for a moment.

"Where were you going?" he asked.

"To see my brother," she answered truthfully. "Parliament meets tomorrow!"

He nodded. "You sought to free him, perhaps in your clothes, with that veil?"

"Aye!" She threw the veil onto the floor. "I would ha' taken his place!"

"If he is sane, he would not allow it. Or try the deception. You are foolish," the Hepburn said.

Jane started toward him angrily. Suddenly she stopped.

"Were you going to strike me, madam?" He laughed.

"No," cried Jane.

"Your hand was raised." He was hot, and he loosened the fastenings of his leather coat, took it off, and hung it on the back of a chair.

"So you have been playing at dice with your guards?"

"Aye," said Jane.

"Did you win?"

"Aye," said Jane again. "But I ha' never played against the likes of you, my lord. Would you care to play?"

"A wise man would ask the stakes first, Lady Gordon."

"They're simple. I ha' gold." She held out her hand. "You

play with wits. If you win, I pay with gold. If I win, you answer my questions."

He grinned, "I agree."

"Good," said Jane, with some fervor. She dropped to her knees, and rattled the dice, which she had taken from her pocket. The Hepburn sat cross-legged.

"I won these too, from Hay," Jane explained, as she made the first throw.

It was a ten, a bad throw. And almost immediately Jane lost the gold piece she had excitedly pushed forward. The Hepburn took the dice.

He threw a six. Jane, who had risked the two gold pieces, lost them on the next throw.

Jane said, "Can I wager half a gold piece?"

"Don't be a coward."

"A whole one, then," she said, dared into it. She lost.

At this she swore. She reached for the dice. His hand closed over hers. "They're still mine, mistress."

The Hepburn threw a five and then a seven. He sighed, and handed over the dice. "Now what?" he asked.

Jane said, "I've only one gold piece left. You have four."

"So I do. Is that your question?"

"No," cried Jane. "I want to know what you and Jamie intend toward the lords that stand trial tomorrow!"

"I can't answer that," he said.

"You can! You promised!"

"Mistress, I promised to answer, true. But I cannot answer that particular question because I do not know. We do not know what defense they will advance, nor do we know what James intends. Will that do?"

"It will have to," Jane said. "You are winning!"

"Aye," he agreed.

"I warrant you expected to."

He nodded.

She pushed forward her last gold piece, and threw the dice with vigor.

The Hepburn won. Jane glared at him. "I wanted to ask one more question."

He considered this. "What do you have to offer?" He chuckled, scraped up the money, and put it in his pocket.

She didn't quite dare to taunt him by telling him it was his money. He would be angry, she was sure. He probably wouldn't understand at all. Jane swore.

"What if I should offer you one kiss?" Jane asked.

He raised his eyebrow. Then he looked at her carefully. "Mayhap."

"What do you mean, mayhap?"

"I'm wondering. All right, then."

Jane threw an eleven. Her eyes met his.

"I lost." Her voice was soft.

"You owe me a kiss."

"I know." She was lying on her side, her head propped up on one elbow. "Claim it," she said.

She didn't move. The look in his gray eyes was inscrutable. He stretched out beside her, drawing her into his arms. For a moment he looked into her eyes. Her fingers touched the side of his head lightly, caressingly. She turned her head. She spoke in his ear. "M'lord, you will not let them harm my brother, will you?"

Incredibly he said, "I'll forego your kisses. If you are offering yourself in return for your brother's life, I do not bribe so lightly."

Jane could hardly believe the words had been spoken. She struck him, whereupon he seized her hand.

"You would not let them harm my brother, would you?" he mocked. He rolled over on his side and got up, taking her hand and making her stand in front of him. "Go to your chamber now. Tomorrow night I shall tell you what transpired in court. By tomorrow night you will probably be free, never to return to that room again."

Jane stared at him. She turned blindly from him, and went to the hall door that led to her room.

But he followed.

"You are becoming more tame," he said.

Jane turned, and with both hands began to beat him. As

she pounded at his chest, he laughed, and picked her up, a struggling mass of anger. Her hair came loose and fell over his arm, and he carried her down the hall. He tossed her onto her bed and stood looking at her.

"Goodnight, wildcat," he said.

Jane heard the lock turn in the door.

16

MATTHEW REACHED EDINBURGH TWO HOURS AHEAD OF the Hepburn.

The night before he had taken the signed and traitorous treaty back to England from Hermitage; it was now on its way to London. He had had to sleep, but early in the morning he had started back over the byways, getting lost. It was after dark when he reached the Gordon house; he hoped he had come unseen.

The kitchens were dark except for a small fire that always burned for hot water. The windows were shuttered. Only one servant dozed in the kitchen. He awakened as Matthew entered.

He looked at Matthew in the dim light, rose and started away. Matthew called to him, but to no avail; he had disappeared.

Matthew sat his aching body down wearily. He took off his boots and heavy jacket. He wiggled his toes. Tenderly he felt of his swollen and throbbing shoulder. For just a moment he put his head down on the bare wood of the table. That was the way Mary Gordon found him a few minutes later.

The servant had summoned her on her own instructions. She leaned across the table and touched his hand, but neither man saw the expression in her eyes.

"Matthew," she whispered. She thought he was asleep.

He almost was, but raised his head and saw her outlined against the rosy glow from the hearth.

"Direct from heaven," he whispered. "Mistress Mary," he said aloud, and rose.

Mary saw the bulging bandages. "You are hurt!"

"Aye, mistress, but not much."

She remembered how hot his hand had felt. "You are feverish, Matthew."

He shook his head.

"Sit down," she ordered absently. She had everything ready, as he had asked. "Bring the cask of wine, the wax, the quills and paper and ink," she said to the silent servant, "and set them on the table. Bring some ale."

"Aye," said Matthew gratefully, at the mention of ale. "I am not hungry, mistress, but very thirsty."

"It is the fever," Mary said. "You may leave us now, Wat."

When he had gone, she lighted one lamp, poured ale for Matthew and for herself. They both drank. She sat opposite him, resting her chin on her hands, watching Matthew as he spread the thick paper flat, dipped the quill and began to write.

He looked up once, met her eyes, and smiled. The fire gave a little crackle. He had written only two sentences when he rose, and lifted a flat pan from its hook. Into this he put the wax, knelt before the dying fire, holding the pan close over the little tongues of flame.

The wax melted, and smoked. It smelled. Mary wrinkled her nose. Squatting there before the hearth, Matthew turned his head away from the fire and looked at her. She pointed to the paper.

"What did you write, Matthew?"

"I'd rather you did not know," he said slowly. "It is best if you do not."

"My position is precarious now, Matthew," Mary said.

"Aye, that it is. I want to make it no more so." To divert her, he asked, "What do you think of Maggie Drummond?"

The wax was melting faster now. Mary said, "Maggie? She is—charming, bonnie, generous. She is not shy, like me."

The wax was almost melted. Only one piece of it still swam around in the thick hot liquid. "They say Jamie is taken with Maggie Drummond."

Mary nodded. "I know." She smiled, and threw out her hands. "They talk, they talk. Even in the Borders."

Matthew grinned. "Jamie was in the Borders. But Maggie is at Drummond."

He stood up to carry the pan back to the table. He picked up the letter, folded it tight, and then rolled it into a narrow cylinder.

"Have you decided not to read it?" he asked.

"Aye," said Mary.

"Good." He put the cylinder in the wax, rolling it over with a little knife, until it was well coated. As the wax cooled, he lifted it out and set it on the table to harden. She was waiting for him to explain.

"You see, I am sending your brother some information. A point of Scottish law. He may see fit to use it tomorrow in court. If he does, you must be surprised. Tomorrow you shall know what the letter said anyway, if Lord Gordon uses it."

"Do you want him to, Matthew?"

He was inexpressibly weary. It was difficult to think. He met her eyes, but he frowned. The information might be dangerous. To use it might incur the royal anger. It would be a setback for James, and that was what Matthew wanted. Matthew wanted James so embroiled in his own affairs that he would have no time to meddle with England. It was very simple.

Already Jamie's hands were full. Matthew hoped this would make them full to overflowing. But to say it was not dangerous would be to lie, flagrantly.

He said, "According to my lights, this is right." He reminded himself that he was English. He reminded himself that compared to his own danger, which walked close now, Lord Gordon's was laughable. He reminded himself that he would be fully justified in leaving Scotland now. If he were caught, they would undoubtedly torture him.

"I fought the Hepburn," he said aloud. "He may recognize

me. And if he had a look at the wound he gave me, he would."

She breathed lightly. "If he recognizes you, what then?"

"Ah, that is it. What?" He moved the letter with his finger. It was dry. He could hardly tell her that he himself had witnessed the signing of a treaty that opened the gates of Liddesdale to an invader, that now there was a potential arrow aimed at Scotland. Even now, Surrey might be reading that treaty, and calling for a map of Liddesdale, to see where his troops would march.

"The Hepburn might suspect me of machinations and skulduggery," he said lightly, and smiled. But as he said it, he was thinking he must leave Scotland. His work was done. At least it seemed to be.

His fingers were opening the cask of wine. Into the narrow opening he pushed the wax-coated rolled paper, and secured the neck again, tightly. This he would send to Lord Gordon early in the morning.

He glanced for the last time at the barred door and closed shutters. Mary had risen. It might be the last time he would see her. After he slept, he must leave.

But as he went toward the door, as he reached down to open it for her, his hand paused on the knob. He looked at her long, and he had the sure conviction that if he left, he would abandon her.

The very night was silent and they spoke no word. Mary Gordon preceded him through the door. He wanted very much to touch her; instead he steadied himself on the door jamb. Then he turned and made his way to his own quarters.

17

JAMES STUART CONVENED HIS FIRST PARLIAMENT ON the twentieth of July in the Tolbooth, in Edinburgh. Just below him, to his right, sat the Earl of Argyll, the chancellor. To his left was the Hepburn. His Council was full of Border names. Home was chamberlain. The Vicar of Linlithgow, of the Hepburn clan, held the office of clerk of the rolls and council. Whitelaw, subdean of Glasgow, was secretary to the king. His papers were spread in front of him, on his table, and his hands were already ink-stained. The cadets of the Border houses sprinkled in with the Drummonds, the Douglasses, Fleming, young Lord Grey, passionate adherent of the Hepburn.

James wore his sables proudly. Magnificently dressed, only he knew that under the fine linen of his embroidered shirt, a heavy iron belt pained and chafed him. He had donned it this morning, though not for the first time. Now, as he sat here, his guilt seemed to press in on him from all sides, and his face looked somber.

The scene was familiar, except that this time he was king.

The Court criers were garbed in velvet. The halberds of the tall guards gleamed from assiduous polishing. The sword of state had been borne in; the scepter was in James's hand. He looked down at his subjects in the moment of quiet which preceded the chancellor's opening sentence.

"My lords." The words rang out. "My lords, barons, and commissioners of boroughs, today this Parliament considers first the special summons against those who had partaken with the king's father against him—to a number of twenty-eight lords and thirty-seven barons."

Argyll's voice stopped. Facing him, facing James, were the accused men. They had obeyed their summons, those who had not been brought over from the castle. They had obeyed their king, and James was sure it was his swift action against Methven that had brought them here. They might be afraid, but they were more afraid to disobey.

Thirty-seven barons and twenty-eight lords. The red-headed Hepburn heard the numbers with misgiving. The night before he had told Jane the truth. He did not know James's intent. He glanced at James's impassive face as the chancellor continued.

"You are summoned here within the space of eleven days to answer for treasonable conduct. The first lord specified is David Lindsay."

Lord David Lindsay, gray of head, rose to his feet.

"Lord David, you are appearing in this Court, either personally or represented by attorney, for coming against the king at Sauchieburn. Your answer hereto."

Lindsay came forward three paces. He knew everyone was waiting for his answer. Despair clouded his brain. He looked to James's dark face. He burst out. "Ah, you are all false! I dare prove it with my sword or body, on any of you!"

It was a cry of protest against injustice. He had fought *for* his king! Desperately he reached for the truth, to drag it out here, in the open. To shame these former rebels who sat in judgment.

"You!" He pointed to Fleming and Douglass. "You caused the king to rise against his father! You caused that prince's cruel murder! If the king doesn't punish you, you will murder him!"

He stumbled to James's feet. "Sire," he cried. "Beware of them! They can never be true to you! I shall be truer to your Grace then and now, than they shall be!"

Lindsay was trembling. The Hepburn leaned forward. His thick Border accent went through the room.

"Sire, an' it please your Grace, Lord Lindsay is a man of the old school, and has left off reverence. But he is of good will."

James's face, unsmiling, regarded Lindsay, who stood at the

foot of the three steps which went up to James's carved chair. Lindsay dropped to one knee. He could say no more.

Now another man rose to his feet. Gracefully, using his slender height to advantage, he walked to Lindsay's side. In the quiet, believing no one would notice, George Gordon, surreptitiously, kicked Lindsay to warn him to hold his tongue.

But Lindsay was too unnerved by what he had said. Since he had already thrown all caution to the winds, he stood up and said fiercely, aloud, to everyone's complete amazement, "God, Gordon, you're overbrave! To stamp on my foot! Were we not in the king's presence, I'd take you on the mouth!"

At any other time, George Gordon would have laughed. But he was under summons. He stepped in front of Lindsay, forcing him back a pace, and knelt.

"Sire, we are allowed attorneys. But there is no man of law who dares speak for us."

He paused, he raised his head.

"My heart may not suffer me to see my native house perish. To be abolished from memory. I ask from your Grace permission to speak for myself and my cousin, Lord Lindsay."

Lindsay had backed off and resumed his seat, still trembling from his outburst. James looked down at Gordon.

"You may rise." His tone was even. "Your petition is granted, my lord."

A sigh ran around the tiers of seats. The Hepburn drew in his breath sharply, for this might have been Jane. It was as though Jane herself stood there: the eyes, the molding of the face, the thick molasses shade of hair. All made the Hepburn think of Jane.

Yet George Gordon was hardly recalling his sister at that moment. He was recalling the three lines of heavy, firm writing he had read only this morning. He hesitated. He said low, "My lords, I beg you well remember that this is your time, and that we have had our time." Again he hesitated.

James frowned. His voice came laden with impatience. "My lord! We bade you say something in defense!"

Gordon drew a deep breath. His breathing was quick. Again

he saw the writing on a wax-covered paper. Again he tasted the wine, and he had drunk liberally of it. He wet his lips.

"I say now"—but this time he paused only to emphasize his words—"*against* the king's Grace, that he ought *not* to sit in judgment because he made an oath of fidelity when he received the Crown of Scotland! He should never sit in judgment against his lords, on any occasion when he himself has been party to their deed! We desire him in the name of God to rise and depart!"

The boldness of the truth hit hard. There was complete silence. All eyes looked from Gordon to James.

The iron belt pained James. It fretted him when he moved, as he did now, to stand and face his lords.

He put one hand on the hilt of a richly jeweled dagger. He stood proud. And guilty. It was as though he were glad thus to announce his guilt, his part in it. For guilty or not, he was still king. He had taken the oaths. He knew them well. He alone knew why he had seized a throne. His motive was compounded of so many reasons that he himself could hardly separate them.

Lindsay was wrong when he said Douglass and Fleming and the others had seduced him into rebellion. He had done it himself.

"Never, whilst I live, shall I ever be false to my oaths to my native land," James said. He was leaving. He could not sit in judgment. Slowly he went down the steps, brushing by Gordon. To his right was an aisle, leading to a small anteroom, which he took. The king had gone.

Gordon was abashed. Everyone was still waiting. Both the Hepburn and the chancellor were waiting. There was no time to dally. And his respect for James had leaped high.

Gordon's brow was beaded with sweat. He had little more to say. Only the last sentence of a message. He said bluntly, for this was what Matthew had written, "These summonses are invalid. We were to appear before this Court, this Parliament, within the space of eleven days. And now, my lords, it is eleven and one days. The day has expired. Of itself. We should answer nothing till we are re-summoned!"

The Hepburn sat still. This was a point of Scottish law. A small point. Now invoked.

Gordon was right. The chancellor was well aware of it. A great hum filled the room of the Tolbooth. James's secretary leaped to his feet and hurried out. Lindsay ran over and clapped George Gordon on the shoulder.

"Your fine colored words! You'll have the towns of Kirk for this!"

There was uproar now. From the door of an anteroom James Stuart watched for a moment. He handed a piece of paper to his secretary. The Court criers shouted for silence. The secretary came back to his place. He spoke a few low words to the Hepburn and the chancellor. Finally, there was silence.

The chancellor said, "You have proved your loyalty to the king's Grace, by obeying these summonses. His Majesty has left the Parliament."

Smiles and nods came from the accused men. A fine enthusiasm gripped them.

The chancellor continued. "No new summons will be made." Now they grinned. They had won. The next words came like icy water.

"But by royal edict, you shall be deprived of your hereditary rights and offices for the space of three years."

This time the Hepburn had a smile on his face. This was comfortless punishment, not martyrdom but plain poverty. The Hepburn stifled a real grin. The chancellor then said, "His Majesty's secretary will now read to you the points which his Majesty wishes from this Parliament."

Whitelaw rose, papers in hand. It was as though he and James had planned this. It was incredible, because of course Parliament would grant all of this now, and the Hepburn could envision James sitting at ease, probably quaffing down foamy ale. Whitelaw began.

"A new law concerning education. All sons of barons, lords and freeholders, of eight years and not older than nine, to receive elementary schooling in mathematics, languages, including Latin, and then at ages thirteen and fourteen, compulsory attendance at the schools of art and law for a period of no less than three years."

Whitelaw cleared his throat.

"The founding of a University at Aberdeen.

"The founding of a College of Surgeons in Edinburgh, to include the new practice of dentistry.

"Judiciary reform. Judges, appointed by the king, to sit daily in Edinburgh. The whole of the country to be divided into districts, to have courts of law."

Again Whitelaw cleared his throat, shuffled some papers. "The abolishment of the sales tax on articles at market from the towns." This time the borough commissioners frowned.

The list went on. James wanted ships. Each coastal town was to provide twenty-ton fishing boats, manned. Merchants were taxed in pure bullion when their export became too high. Hepburn knew James wanted the Scottish people to buy more of their own products. Then came the appointments.

"The Warden of the Mint, Crichton of Ruthven. The Lord High Admiral of Scotland, Patrick Hepburn."

The Hepburn's gray eyes met those of Sir Andrew Wood. Wood nodded, pleased. The Hepburn, who had served under him, was proud. Sir Andrew was Scotland's greatest seaman; he had been against James, but the Hepburn was suddenly sure Wood would swing over and pledge his allegiance. He certainly would when James and the Hepburn told him they planned five new ships of war, of which the first to be built was to cost forty thousand pounds.

The rest of the list of appointments was formality, and the Hepburn let his mind wander. He knew he held command of Edinburgh castle. The districts that he controlled as sole judge and arbiter had expanded into the Merse, Lothian, Linlithgow, Lauderdale, Kirkcudbright and Wigtown. To this was added the wardenship of the West and Middle Border. He heard Whitelaw say, "And now as to embassies. His Majesty will appoint ambassadors to all courts of Europe, they to be no less than earls, and to be accompanied by no less than four gentlemen and twenty clerks and so forth."

This caused a murmur. Embassies were rather new. The accused nobles wondered if they might have a chance to go abroad in such capacity, or whether their sons might attend the ambassador to France, for instance. The Hepburn smiled openly. Resistance was being swept aside, by various means. He knew that the abolishment of the two taxes would endear James to the people. They hated both taxes which they paid daily.

"The refinement of the currency."

These points would be taken up one by one. It was a beginning. No mention was made of England. The secretary sat down, drawing a long breath. He would get ale as soon as he could. Whitelaw, who had spent hours with James, had come under the Stuart charm. He was intensely proud of the reforms in education, in taxes, of the new embassies. He had ended with the announcement that his Majesty would be pleased to hear Council's own ideas.

Parliament was over for today. The Council would meet again tomorrow, without the accused lords. They'd been disposed of. Patrick Hepburn rose. The reversal he had anticipated had not been reversal. The Hepburn had witnessed James's almost reckless conduct in battle. He now revised his opinion of James as a politician. He was a canny Scot.

18

MAGGIE DRUMMOND LOOKED HESITANTLY AROUND THE room in which she stood. The men were bringing in her boxes. Eufemia, talking fast, was telling them where to put each article, and making sure the feather bed had not been dirtied.

Maggie still studied the room, paying little attention to Eufemia. It was a small room, of uneven shape, about fifteen by thirteen feet. A plaster frieze ran around the cornice; there was a small fireplace and an elaborately carved mantel. The bed took up most of the room, and Eufemia was complaining that there was no room for the chair except on the hearth. Then the men left, and Maggie was alone with her sister.

"I'll call Katie to help you," Eufemia said. She sank into the chair.

"It's such a small room," Maggie said. But somewhere in this vast palace was James Stuart. She went to the window and looked out on the paved court. "Eufemia, what did he say?"

Eufemia knew whom she meant and what she meant. "Yesterday he came back from the Borders. He had been riding the ayres, holding court. He came walking into my room and he said, 'Where is Mistress Drummond?' "

Eufemia dramatized her surprise. "I was amazed, Maggie. I told him you had decided not to come this season, but to stay in the country for the summer." She paused. "He was angry," she said warningly. "He told me to come here and bring you back with me today. Then he left."

"He was angry?" Maggie repeated. He was also very near. This room hemmed her in. And sometime, finally, the door would open, and he would be there. "Holy Mary," she whispered.

At this moment there was a knock. Maggie gave a little gasp. But it was Fleming, and Sybilla was with him. The sisters gave each other quick kisses in greeting. Eufemia turned and went over to the bed. Her only remark to her husband was, "M'lord." Then she curled up on the bed and put her head on the pillow.

"I've come to regale all of you with the facts of what happened this afternoon in Parliament," Fleming announced, his black eyes searching Maggie.

Regardless of her dislike of Fleming, Maggie wanted to hear him. She said stiffly, "Take this chair."

It was the only chair. She stood beside Sybilla. Listening, she almost forgot her aversion in the tale he told. The image of James was very close. She saw the whole scene plainly. Her eyes shone.

Fleming was watching her carefully. She could bring him much in favor; she already had. In the hunt and pursuit of his quarry, James had bestowed a land grant on Maggie's father, and to Fleming had gone the wine concessions for Edinburgh.

"One cannot doubt that you love our Jamie," Fleming said abruptly.

Maggie gave him a level look. "My feeling for his Grace is one of deep respect."

He made a deprecatory gesture, as if he understood.

"Also," said Maggie, "I admire his Grace."

Again he brushed aside her words. He looked at Eufemia to see if she would not back him up, as her father had urged her to do. Instead he saw that she was asleep; she had not been interested in his story. Angrily he rose.

"Would you care to sup with me, Lady Fleming?"

Eufemia wakened. "No, we thank you. We are to help Maggie dress." She smiled and waved him a languid good-bye. Fleming went to the door and banged it shut behind him.

Eufemia then sat up straight. "After a while his way of recounting bores one to death." She yawned deeply.

Sybilla had already opened one of the boxes and was searching for the dress she wanted. She found it; it would have to be pressed, and Sybilla went to the door to call a maid.

Automatically Maggie bathed and did her hair. By the time she had finished the maid was back with the dress; other servants had cleared the room, and put away her things. Sybilla motioned the servants out, and she held up the dress.

It was white. It was thin silk, with long trailing sleeves and a square neck. Maggie, in her shift and petticoat, looked at it. She shook her head.

"It's the prettiest dress you own," Sybilla said.

"You are dressing for the king," Eufemia pointed out, from her vantage point on the bed.

Then Sybilla said, "Don't bother with a busk."

Maggie set her mouth. "Give me that busk!"

Eufemia slid off the bed, and tossed the little corset onto a table. "Foolish lass," she said. "Do you think you're a match for Jamie Stuart?" She put the dress over Maggie's head.

"Only four hooks," she said as she fastened them. She finished her task, and there was envy in her eyes. "You are the bonniest of us," she said honestly. Then, "Sybilla, his Grace won't thank us if we're here when he comes."

Sybilla followed her sister to the door. "Maggie, it is Jamie himself for whom you wait. Don't you realize that? He is the king."

Maggie went to her mirror. Alone she stood before the small square of glass. She wore no headdress. Her white shoulders and the curve of her breast gleamed in the candlelight. She could smell faintly the perfume Sybilla had touched to her hair and throat and wrists.

Going to the bed, she pulled the pillows up behind her back. She spread her dress out carefully so it wouldn't rumple. When he knocked, she would have time to rise and greet him. Now there was nothing to do but wait—wait and listen to the distant, anonymous sounds.

Ten minutes later James entered. Maggie had heard his footsteps in the hall; she had not known it was he. Suddenly he stood in the doorway; he had not knocked, and he closed the door behind himself softly. "Don't rise."

Maggie, sitting on the bed, put her hands to her breast, and then she started to rise. He was standing right over her. It was indeed he.

He was more heavily tanned than when she had seen him last. She knew from Fleming that he had been doing a deal of hunting. His dark eyes were on her; she made another motion to rise.

"No," he said, looking down at her quizzically. "Lass, you forced me to send to Drummond for you."

"I did not *force* you, your Majesty."

He grinned. "There was a compelling force, mistress. I assumed it was you." He sat down on the bed, and Maggie dropped her eyes and looked at the winking jeweled buttons of his doublet. He asked softly, "Aren't you going to answer me?"

He was smiling. He was so assured. She felt a flush rising to her cheeks. "I cannot think!"

He took possession of her hand. His strong fingers curled around hers. "You cannot think? Why not?"

Her red lip was caught between her teeth. She said honestly, "You disturb me. You are too close. Release my hand, please, if you will." She tried to pull her hand away, and she pulled hard. James surprised her by loosing his grip. She slipped off the bed and stood up. There was a flash of temper in her question. "Why do you laugh at me?"

He stood too. "I laugh at your naïveté. 'Tis no way to hold a man off—telling him his nearness is disturbing. Rather it would make him come much closer."

Maggie put out her hands, as if to block him.

"Three times you've refused me, in various ways," he said. "And you are so beautiful, your hair, your eyes."

Maggie said low, "I thank you, your Grace."

"You are most welcome." He laughed. "Mistress Drummond, do I find no favor in your eyes at all?"

"You jest, sire."

"And cannot a man jest a little with you?"

Maggie smiled. Her dimple showed plainly. She fetched a sigh as she looked back at him. For six weeks she had thought of nothing but James Stuart.

"I will cease to jest, then. I am going to make love to you." He took her hand; she stood stiff as a statue; he shook his head sternly. "Your hand's like ice, and 'tis a warm summer night. Let me look at you."

Maggie whispered, "You are looking."

He grinned guiltily. "I warrant I am." He turned her slowly around, till her back was to him. His arms went around her, and he bent his head and kissed the curve of her shoulder. He undid the first hook on her bodice.

She broke away from him then. She whirled and faced him. "Please, your Grace!"

He frowned. "A fractious filly. I'll give you five minutes to accustom yourself to the fact that I am undeterred from my original intention." He took one stride and stood over her. Deliberately he undid the second hook. Then he put his hand under her chin. "I'm falling into love with you, lass. So I give you five minutes." He sat down in the chair and regarded the tips of his slippers.

There was silence in the room. There was the faintest smile on James's face, and when he looked up finally, his eyes were gleaming with humor.

Maggie's hand had been on the hook of her dress.

"Don't hook it," he warned. "I'll beat you."

She paled and he laughed.

"I like delight unconcealed," said James. "Two minutes have passed. What objections can you offer further?"

Maggie said hastily, "We have no clock."

James was grave. "I am expert on judging time. Three minutes have gone now. You are so fair. Cannot I please you? Should I order a moon and write poetry to you?"

"When you give me the moon, I'll consider the poetry." Maggie's eyes flashed. "Would it surprise you to know I could read it?"

He rose. "I detect more temper."

"I don't like to be teased! And there must be a minute left!"

"There is," said James. "But by royal edict I've changed the time." He put both hands on the mantel, imprisoning her, yet not touching her.

Her breath was hurried, through parted lips. He leaned down and brushed his mouth quickly across hers. She drew back.

Slowly his arms closed around her. She stiffened. Her hands pushed against his chest, resisting. He put his lips to her white throat; her head was back over his arm. His arms tightened and she felt his mouth on hers.

Locked in his embrace, it was as though she lost separate identity except with him. She knew she was surrendering. Her eyes closed. Her arms slipped around his neck and held him close. She felt her body yield and mold itself against his. And he did not release her mouth; his kisses deepened. Finally he raised his head. She lay back in his arms; her eyes opened and she looked through her lashes at the face so near hers.

His fingers undid the last hooks and bared her to the waist. She cried out a last low protest, as his hand touched the white breast. James held her tight as she trembled. "No, sweetheart," he whispered. "I love you."

19

THE HEPBURN SAID, "I CANNOT SEE LADY GORDON NOW." He did not look up. "You may tell her to await my—no, send Lady Gordon in."

He rose as Jane entered; the other four men in the room did not notice her. The Hepburn said, "Please sit. In a moment I'll have time for you."

With this she had to be content. She had passed through two doors, flanked with guards, to get here. It was a big room. Over by the great windows two long tables stood end to end. At one of them sat Sir Andrew Wood, and with him the young Lord Grey, whose speech, which she could hear faintly, was even thicker than the Hepburn's. Sir Andrew had not seen her. He was absorbed.

Grey said, "I'm not sure. You'll have to ask m'lord." He turned in his chair, and Sir Andrew, seeing the Hepburn was occupied, shook his head.

"Later," he said. He saw Jane, and nodded. "Lady Gordon." He explained his presence. "I have been asked to read over the specific recommendations to Council tomorrow for new shipping." He looked very happy.

Jane didn't answer. A week ago Sir Andrew had vowed he would never sail a ship for James.

"This must be done tomorrow, if I am to have suggestions," Sir Andrew added, for it was a half after eight, and late for working.

The room was silent. The Hepburn's two secretaries seemed to be compiling lists. A quill broke, and there was a muttered oath. Jane transferred her gaze to the Hepburn.

The table at which he sat, opposite her, was six feet long, heavy and carved, and covered with papers, a couple of ledgers, a letter or two, inkwells, quills, and a brass device which kept the sealing wax hot and sticky. From underneath one of the official seals Jane saw the glitter of a jewel. It was enormous; it was a hinged ring, with a stone of yellow fire. She would have reached for it, to examine it more closely, but the Hepburn suddenly looked up at her. In his hand was a rolled piece of paper to which pieces of wax still clung. He straightened the paper, leaned over the table to show it to her.

"Do you recognize this hand?"

The writing was heavy, with deep downward strokes. "No," said Jane, bewildered. But the words leapt at her. This concerned George.

" 'Tis not your sister's writing?" the Hepburn asked curtly.

"No, m'lord." Jane shook her head.

The Hepburn settled back in his chair. He rubbed his face thoughtfully.

"I've never seen that paper before!"

"I didn't suppose you had. You heard what happened in Parliament today?" He knew she had, so he did not wait for her affirmation. "After Court I had your brother's room searched. I doubted seriously whether he knew enough to question the two points of law he did question. He attended no law college. We found this." He tapped the paper which had rolled itself up again. It had been delivered, cleverly, in a cask of wine. "Now, madam, what is the name of the secretary you call Matthew?"

"That's all the name he has," said Jane.

The Hepburn frowned.

"I'm telling the truth!"

Obviously he didn't believe her. He turned his head to look at one of his secretaries, and the man rose and brought over a flat book. He pointed out something to the Hepburn with his finger, then he straightened up, and he said, "M'lord, if he is quite accomplished, one would have thought he'd given instructions to have that"—he pointed to the paper—"destroyed."

"Ah," said the Hepburn. "True. However, if a man has ridden far, from the Borders, let's say, and if he has suffered a severe wound, he does not think so straight."

The secretary nodded. He could see the edge of the writing. "'Tis an educated hand, m'lord." He held the book, and started away. She made out the gilded letters ENGLISH PEERAGE.

The Hepburn said, "That will be all then, Mistress Gordon. I will attend you later."

Jane's eyes blazed. She jumped to her feet just as one of the guards burst through the doorway. After the guard came a travel-stained gentleman, and after him, another. The guard said, "The Sieur de Montcressault, representing the Duchess of Burgundy!"

Everyone bowed. The Hepburn introduced himself and Jane and the other men. The sieur acknowledged Sir Andrew Wood with pleasure.

"*Mais vous êtes*"—he hesitated—"famous!" The sieur smiled as though he had bestowed a benediction. He kissed Jane's hand, lingeringly, looked slightly surprised to see a woman at all. He had heard that in Scotland women enjoyed great freedom and high respect. Evidently that was true. His gaze came back to the Hepburn, and again he bowed, with a flourish.

After that he introduced his own gentleman. "But we are merely couriers, gentlemen."

The Hepburn knew well enough that the Duchess of Burgundy, in exile in France, was the leader of the Yorkist cause. She hated Henry Tudor. She thought he had her throne. The Hepburn knew that if James weren't told of this arrival immediately, tempers would be more than short tomorrow.

But first he escorted Jane to the hallway.

"We put into Leith an hour ago," the Frenchman was saying.

"His Majesty will want to greet you himself," said the Hepburn.

The audience lasted an hour. It was a private audience. While it went on the Hepburn fretted, trying to keep his mind on the business at hand.

He could not. What the sieur was saying must be vastly important. The letter he carried might dictate a new policy. A new English policy. Yet the Hepburn was sure that it was not yet time to meddle abroad.

He was more than profoundly grateful at the hour's end to hear a request from the king for his presence.

James was alone. To receive the sieur he had donned a satin jacket. This he now took off, and he began to pace the room. He waved the Hepburn to a chair. Then another thought seemed to strike him, an extraneous one, one that had nothing to do with the Duchess of Burgundy.

"Patrick," he said, "I have created an earldom for you. A new one. The Earldom of Bothwell, the castle of which you've already been granted."

The Hepburn, who was still standing despite the fact that he'd been told to sit, looked more shaken than James had ever seen him.

"Hand me that sword off the wall," said James.

The Hepburn reached up, and took it down from the wall by the great hilt. It was the sword of Bruce. He reversed it, and gave it to James. Then he knelt, bowing his red head.

James, feeling the weapon in his fingers, looking down on the red head, remembered.

"If a battlefield were lost and slippery with the blood of men, thou wouldst still pull off thy boots and fight in thy socks." He touched the Hepburn's shoulder. "Rise, my lord."

The Hepburn rose. James gave him the sword. He put it back on the wall, carefully. Its great blade was nicked. Neither man spoke, until, finally, James growled, "Enough," as though many words had passed between them.

"We'll drink a toast." He filled gold cups. The handles were set with jewels. "To Scotland." James drank, set the cup down, and resumed his pacing. Again he waved the Hepburn to a chair, but again the Hepburn stood, waiting. Then James pointed to a letter that lay open on the table. The Hepburn picked it up and started to read.

He read slowly and carefully. While he read, his mind fitted around this letter the big picture, a picture of English history. And more particularly, the history of the English succession.

This letter came from the Duchess of Burgundy, a Yorkist. They called her Henry's Juno. Henry's claim to the throne was Lancastrian, through the blood of John of Gaunt. James said aloud, "The strength of Henry's claim to the English throne lies in the fact that everyone else was either beheaded, murdered, or slain in battle." James grinned. He was in a fine mood. Recounting tales of spilled English blood made relishing talk.

"For instance," James went on, "when Edward, the fourth Edward, a Yorkist, climbed back on the throne, he had two sons, nine and twelve, or thereabouts. Edward also had a brother, Richard, a rather unscrupulous character, and Richard had his nephews murdered, and he succeeded to the throne—Richard the Third, Richard the Usurper, they called him.

"His reign began in terror, and the terror never stopped, so that, because of the holocaust of blood that bathed England, the nearest heirs to the throne were one boy of seven, another nephew, and the Earl of Richmond, whose name was Henry Tudor, and that Henry sits on the English throne today almost securely, for he killed Richard at Bosworth and married the Yorkist heiress, the Princess Elizabeth, daughter to Edward the Fourth, and thus welded in one marriage the houses of Lancaster and York."

"A suggestive tale," the Hepburn said thoughtfully.

"Sinister and most suggestive," said James, "especially since Richard's murder of his nephews is still a mystery—no trace of either prince was ever found. Now, Patrick, if you were Henry the Seventh of England, Henry Tudor, would it trouble you to know that a man who called himself the Prince of York was still alive? And that the Duchess of Burgundy had found him?"

"Aye, my lord," said the Hepburn. "A great deal. But it doesn't matter whether it's true or not."

"It's like a thorn," said James. "It will prick, badly. It may not bleed the victim to death, but it'll sting, and fret."

"It's not possible to put credence in't."

"How do you know?" asked James. "Since the bodies of the two young Yorkist princes, who are—there's no doubt about it—the real heirs to the English throne, since their bodies were never found, how can we say for sure that one of them isn't alive? That Richard, Duke of York, is not now on the Continent, as the Duchess of Burgundy swears he is?"

The Hepburn saw suddenly that the whole Scottish policy toward England had been dictated now. It was going to be an offensive. With a strong weapon, and a worrisome one. The Hepburn briefly considered whether it was wise.

"Your Grace is going to espouse the claim of this—Prince of York? This discovery? This Richard? We bring him to Scotland?"

"Aye," said James.

"Prince or no, we take up his banner?"

"Aye, my lord."

The Hepburn thought of his title, and forgot it again. "Your Grace, Berwick sticks in your craw. The English took it; you want it back. But there are bigger stakes!" He rose to his feet.

"Bah!" James's dark eyes were half closed.

"Give me leave to say it!"

James made a gesture. "I'll have none of't. But say on, if it pleases you."

"It's on the face of it! Tomorrow the Council is going to recommend your marriage. Your Grace, besides Henry the Seventh, there are his sons. One, Arthur, is sickly. The other is—"

"Not sickly," cut in James.

"M'lord, he may not have a son survive him. But there are two princesses of England. Marry with a Tudor lass, and your son may have the whole of it!"

"You see my chance as perfectly as you see your image in a glass," James mocked, but gently. "I recover Berwick first. We bring this Richard, Duke of York, as he calls himself, to Scotland from where he can so easily put his feet on English soil."

"In these Wars of the Roses, we have abetted both sides." The Hepburn tried another tactic.

"We give aid to whom it suits us politically, Patrick, put it out of your head. I do *not* marry."

The Hepburn looked up, surprised. There was vehemence in James's tone.

"Jesus God," said James violently, "I should take a bit of life for mine own!"

The Hepburn said, "Can you?"

"Be damned to you and marriage," James growled, making a turn around the room.

The Hepburn's thoughts went to Maggie Drummond. He frowned a little. James was thinking of Maggie, too. He picked up the chain and heart of precious stones that he was going to send her. The jewels glittered in his palm; his fingers closed over them.

"You cannot break this heart," James said, putting it down again.

The Hepburn knew there was no use pursuing this conversation. "Your Grace, I've a favor to ask," he said.

James's lower lip thrust out.

"For me," the Hepburn said, smiling. "I want to wed."

"You?" asked James. He laughed. "Who is it, Patrick? I wait with bated breath."

"I want to wed one of the Gordons."

"Jane," said James.

"No." The Hepburn shook his head. "I would like a simple contract, my lord. I want whichever of the Gordons should please me best."

"What? Have you the contract with you, by any chance? I, knowing your methods, deem it possible."

The Hepburn reached into an inner pocket and drew it out. James took it, read it through, and sat down at his table. He dipped his quill, scrawled his signature, and handed it back, sand still drifting off it.

"You bear the marks of Jane's whip," he said.

The Hepburn was silent.

James tapped the parchment. "Change the name. When you present this to the Mistress Jane, tell her also that her brother, Lord Gordon, will go into a year's exile. You need not tell her that George will be going to the Continent to find out all he can about the new English pretender, who will soon be under my wing. Do you know, my lord, that this is the first time you have ever asked me a favor? It tells me one thing: that you wanted it pretty badly." James grinned. "Goodnight, Lord Bothwell. I wish you joy of your untamed filly."

The Hepburn unlocked Jane's door, and shut it in the face of the guard in the hall. He came to an abrupt stop.

"My apologies, Lady Gordon," he said stiffly.

Jane raised herself on one elbow. "You apologize?" she said sleepily. "You amaze me." She sat up and slid off the bed, using her hips. She pushed back her tangled hair and yawned.

"My mind was on another—I mean I didn't think that you—"

"How flattering," said Jane. "And why do you stare? Are you shocked, to see me in a blouse and petticoat? Lord, man, I'm more covered than most of the women here at court. Or don't you like the new styles?"

"Aye, but not on a maiden. Not on you—yet."

Jane's eyes opened wide. "You should see my new gown!"

The Hepburn scowled fiercely. "Enough, madam. I have news. When you came earlier this evening, I assumed you wanted to know what was going to happen to your brother. I can tell you in one word. Exile. For a year."

"That was four words," Jane began, when he cut in.

"I'm weary of your carping!"

Jane stamped her foot angrily. Then she turned her back on him. He swung her around to face him, but his hands dropped from her and for a moment they were both silent. Jane broke the tension

"What is that in your hand? Is't something for me?"

He hesitated before answering. "It concerns you, and your sister."

"Give it me, then," she said, in her imperious manner. She took it and went over to the light, moving easily, intent on the parchment. She unfolded it and held it out, her head bent a little. He watched her.

She read quickly. He did not realize it, but she read it twice, because the first time she could hardly believe what she had read. The words, bold and black, leapt up from the heavy paper, and there at the bottom were two signatures. One of them was James, Rex. This then was final. Jane turned.

The parchment rolled up in her hand, crackling a little. She proffered it. She said slowly, her great golden eyes on his, "You are Patrick, Earl of Bothwell."

He took the parchment and laid it down, almost as though to be free for a coming battle. "I am," he said.

She could not realize it. "You needed a title for this," she said, thinking aloud.

"I did not!"

She looked up at him, one eyebrow arched. "This then is the pinnacle you were reaching for? A marriage like this."

She stepped off and measured him. "Well, let us see. You ha' the right to choose which of us pleases you best. Were you ever a stablehand, or a breeder of cattle?" Her eyes glittered with anger and mockery. She burst out, "How did you dare?"

He did not answer. He took three steps toward her and stood over her, his hands in his belt.

Jane met his eyes boldly. She held up her arm. "D'ye want to feel how strong I am? I've a passable limb, two of them, to walk on. And my hips are wide enough, I think." She pulled her skirt tight. "I'd be a good breeder of brats." She flung away to the barred window and whirled to face him again. "Mary would be no match for you, you big ape!"

He grinned lazily. "Do you want me, madam?"

"No!" Jane looked around for a weapon. There was none, no available jar or even a candlestick. There was only one lamp. "I mean," she said coldly, "that I should hate to see Mary sacrificed to you and your ambition."

"You've decided things long enough. From now on I do it."

"Oh, no you won't!"

His voice was slow. "I think I will."

"I'll never stop fighting you! I hate you. I loathe and despise you. I—"

"That's enough!" He went toward her. He put one hand in her hair and tipped her face up to his. His other hand grasped her shoulder. "Persist in this, and by God, you'll drive me to violence!" His fingers loosed her shoulder. "I warn you because I shall not mean to hurt you," he muttered.

"Loose my hair!"

"I like the touch of your hair."

Her mouth was sulky and defiant. His big hand was fastened in her hair, and she turned her face to the side as much as she could and looked down at her shoulder. Her blouse was round-necked and high but she pulled it off her shoulder.

"You have hurt me. The bruise will show tomorrow. I shall wear a low-necked gown and tell everyone those are your marks on me."

He jerked her head back so he could look at her. His voice was cold and expressionless. "Listen to me. Tomorrow you will be moved to apartments on the west side. With your sister. James wishes you and Lady Mary to join his Court. You will be poor. Your brother goes into exile. See if it is possible that you can act like a lady during the next months." He let her go; he went to the door, opened it. For the last time he locked it behind him and put the key in his pocket.

He went to his own room. He flung himself crosswise on the bed and put his head in his arms. He tried to think only of a man called Richard, Duke of York. But he couldn't. Richard of York turned into the face of Jane Gordon, with a mocking mouth. Yet, when he finally slept, it was to dream of a black mask and the blue eyes of an Englishman.

PART 2

20

HE WAS TALL AND SLENDER, OF A WILLOWY ELEGANCE accentuated by his clothes, his broad, high forehead and waving hair. His eyes were serene and humorless: they looked as though they might show hurt easily; his lashes were as long as a woman's.

"I must present my gentlemen," he said, in a voice that was rather free of accent. He spoke English exactly as he would have had he been reared in France. "Master Heron, Master Skelton and Master Astley, my secretary "

The Hepburn thought the designation gentlemen a misnomer. This was the first real clue. Astley had probably been a scrivener. The Hepburn was sure of it. Skelton looked very ill at ease. His hands—the Hepburn deliberately looked carefully as Skelton held his cloak tight against the November winds. The man had been a tailor. In secret he probably still cut Perkin Warbeck's clothes; no doubt he sewed a fine seam.

All three had boldness. Now it was subdued; they hung back with Perkin as their advance guard. Perkin lifted a velvet-gloved hand to brush the drops of water off his shoulders; the fog was so thick that it was almost rain.

Fleming spoke. "I understand there are fogs in your native country." He paused. "England."

Perkin smiled.

"England is not very far away," Fleming continued.

"No," said Perkin uncertainly Were the words a threat? His brown eyes were a little bright with apprehension, just as the Hepburn thought they would be; they were a little hurt too. Perkin wanted to cut a brave caper, not make a picture as grim as these old stone walls of Dunbar castle.

"Of a truth, one cannot see quite to the Tower of London here," Fleming said, stinging deeper.

The Hepburn gestured for him to desist. "Your guard of honor awaits you, your Grace." His voice was stern.

Fleming stepped aside and bowed deeply. "Your Grace," he said with ironic deference.

Perkin approached the guard of honor the Hepburn had promised, fifty strong. From the lance tips flew the taffeta banners, embroidered with the white rose of York. They were wet with mist. Perkin remarked upon it.

"But they bloom well, on foreign soil," he added gravely.

The Hepburn said, "His Majesty is receiving you at Stirling."

The Hepburn mounted with the aid of a man he called Willie. The horns blew, the men tipped their bonnets, the Hepburn and Perkin rode out, flagbearers before them and horses trotting smartly behind. But once on the road, the Hepburn increased the pace. Perkin found himself riding at a hard gallop.

The road followed the Firth. The river was lovely. First it had been gray and silver. Now as they left the coast behind, like a warm promise the sun came out. The Firth turned blue, and waves danced on it. Ships moved lazily up its surface; river craft plied, barges proceeded lazily; from some of them came music and laughter, echoing across the water.

They seemed to be climbing uphill steadily. Perkin knew that Stirling castle was the favorite residence of Scottish kings.

The gates of the castle stood open, like the jaws of a trap. Perkin advanced, a little disconsolately.

"The lions," remarked the Hepburn, from his side.

Perkin started. Almost at his feet was a circular pit. Below, the lions prowled; their yellow eyes gleamed. One great massive beast, tail twitching, raised his head and a low roar reverberated in the pit.

"His Majesty's favorites have been disturbed by the smell of the horses," said the Hepburn. "This way, your Grace." He indicated a narrow curving stair.

Perkin climbed them, the Hepburn behind him. At the head

of the flight, over the castle gates, he stopped. The Hepburn thought he had stopped to look at the view.

The Hepburn said, feelingly, "This is one of the best places to see the Highlands. The towering summits are Ben-Lomond, Penvoirlich, Benvenue, the Trossachs. Those are the rivers Allan, Teith and Forth."

"It is beautiful." Perkin's voice was forced and insincere.

The Hepburn frowned. "Come, your Grace," he said. "His Majesty awaits you."

James Stuart sat in a big tub of soapy water. While one of his gentlemen soaped his back, he reached down and felt gingerly of the blister on his heel. He swore.

Lord Grey, on the other side of the room, winced at the oath. He shot a glance at his inevitable companion, young Lord Home.

"Worse temper than when he left," he whispered, rolling his eyes.

Home shook his head.

Grey disagreed silently. "You didna' see him leave. Fetch the monster, Home. He never bites at the monster."

James had released his foot, and was wiggling his toes. The water stung, but he felt better. He shut his eyes and enjoyed having his back scrubbed.

When his eyes closed he saw plainly the moor and the sea and the abbey. It was his favorite abbey; he did not know why, unless it was its position against the sea, lonely, remote. St. Duthuc's was a royal burgh which one approached across the moor, and he always walked across the moor, to do his penance. This time he had raised a blister, for he was unused to walking in his boots, which was worse than walking barefoot.

This pilgrimage to the shrine had not helped much. The exhaustion, the fatigue, had not yet set in; his mind seemed razor sharp, and it concentrated still only on his guilt. His eyes flew open.

"Stop scrubbing me," he commanded angrily. Then he saw the monster.

"Come over here," he said, and smiled.

It walked toward him. It possessed two legs, but from the hips up, it branched into two sets of narrow shoulders, with two heads and each of its two half-bodies had a pair of arms. It carried two lutes, a sheet of music and a stool, one object in each of its four hands. It bowed, both heads nodding.

James had named it Damon and Pythias. Some months ago he had heard of the freak, and had brought it to court, to be well dressed, fed, and taught.

"How is your Latin?" he asked.

Pythias spoke French. *"Nous chanterons une nouvelle ballade,* sire."

"Bien," James said. He stood up, waved aside the ministrations of two servants, and took hold of the big towel himself, using it vigorously. The thin sound of the lute, and the two-part singing was soothing, but what was more comforting was the thought that if these two boys could bear their cross, certainly he could. Even these periods of deep depression and black guilt didn't last too long. He could bear with them as he had already. He dropped the towel on the floor. His body ached a little. The soft clean shirt he put on felt luxurious after the sweaty, grimy clothes he had worn, and even slept in for the two-hour nap he had snatched at an inn on the way. It was cold today. He donned breeks of the English green, and a short coat, red, and lined with soft lambskin. On his feet went the finest, softest of Cordovan leather.

Servants bore the tub away. James went over to his favorite chair. Damon and Pythias moved their stool nearer. James closed his eyes. The Hepburn and the Pretender would be here soon.

Damon and Pythias sang on. All the woes and all the joys they knew went into their improvisations. They loved James. To them he was father and deliverer. Mockery and horror and scorn followed them no longer. Now, even the women of the Court petted them. Dunbar, the poet, wrote songs for them, to which they put the music. They traveled in a special horse litter. Their tutors were kind, and their tutors opened to them the wonders of the printed word and of the mind.

"He sleeps," whispered Damon.

"Holy Mary, bless and forgive him," prayed Pythias, crossing himself. "Take his troubles, for he is thy son."

"Keep up with thy singing," Damon said, strumming the lute. "Listen. Listen." His eyes lighted, and he nudged his brother with his elbow, as he played five notes, picking lightly at the strings. They were memorizing the new song when the Hepburn and Perkin Warbeck were heard in the outer chamber.

James woke. The chamberlain entered. James rubbed his eyes, patted Damon on the shoulder. "I can't reach you, Pythias," he said. "M'lord, you may ask his lordship to come in. You boys may leave me now. You gave me rest."

Damon and Pythias rose, clutching their lutes. Damon picked up the stool. They started toward the curtained door to James's chamber when Perkin walked in.

Both boys bowed their funny little bow. Perkin's eyes widened in horror. His mouth fell open. Then he recovered and dropped to one knee. "Your Grace," he said. "Your kindness, your hospitality, your immense generosity move my heart. All my life I shall remember this; all my life I shall remember—" He broke off, as if too choked with emotion.

"Rise," said James.

Perkin was taller than James. Perkin looked like a slender gazelle next to a panther; and the Hepburn, standing back, wondered whether he had just imagined, fancifully, that James was going to gobble up his prey in short order.

"Sit down, my lord," said James. Now he looked a little better pleased, and the Hepburn thought he knew why. James had already decided that Perkin's character suited the role he was to play.

Perkin himself looked from the red-headed Borderer to the king. They blocked him in. His three gentlemen were outside. He had to face the king's eyes alone.

There was a tall wide window, mullioned, fifteen feet high and almost twenty feet wide. The afternoon sun streamed through it, lighting the inlaid floors. The chair which Perkin took had a leather seat that gave comfortably with his weight, and he felt on his face the afternoon sun.

James said, "By God, you do resemble the Yorks." He grinned suddenly. "I've made you an allowance of one hundred twelve pounds a month."

Perkin echoed the amount. "One hundred twelve pounds a month?"

James snapped, "Is that less than the Duchess of Burgundy allowed you?"

"Ah, your Grace, no! Indeed. 'Twas that I was only most grateful."

James watched him carefully as he spoke. "Patrick," he announced, "the resemblance to Edward is remarkable!" He was beginning to recover his good humor; his dark eyes glinted with amusement.

"I am assigning you a train of forty," James said. "And I shall pay them, also. As your gentlemen, besides your own, you shall have the Lords Grey and Home and Fleming."

"You are most kind, your Grace," Perkin said, almost in a whisper.

James was blunt. "I would say that you were slow to claim your rights. I would say you have let a good deal of time slip through your fingers. Decisiveness, my lord, is the stuff whereby monarchs prosper. Why did you let so much time go by?"

Perkin hesitated. Then he said, "Your Grace, I was afraid. The horror of the night in the Tower, my captivity in England —then I was shut up in the hold of a vessel and kept secretly in France— Why, until I was taken to Antwerp, I lived each day in terror!" He gestured, and added as excuse: "I was young. But nine, when my brother was murdered, in the same bed with me."

"Continue," was James's only comment.

"I am going to tell the whole story," said Perkin.

James nodded.

There was silence.

"Speak then," said James.

"That night I was asleep," Perkin began. James understood he meant the night in the Tower fourteen years ago, and did not interrupt. "I slept with my brother. He was eleven. I don't know what time it was.

"We always used two pillows, of goose down. The bed was big. We had always shared it, in London. We had one candle burning, as usual. But when I woke up, there was no light.

"I think a cry from Edward had wakened me, but I'm not sure, for the very second that I opened my eyes and saw the blackness of the room. I felt my hands seized, my pillow jerked from under my head and pressed down over my face.

"I struggled wildly. I knew Edward was writhing and twisting. He kicked me. The blankets were all awry; the bottom half of my body was uncovered. I tried to scream but I couldn't breathe."

James's face was somber.

"They killed Edward," said Perkin, low.

James broke in, "Why, my lord, did they murder your brother and let you live?"

"I don't think they meant to murder Edward! But he was stronger than I! Older. He struggled more fiercely. I think in subduing him, they mistakenly throttled him, suffocated him." He put his hands to his face. Then he dropped them and looked squarely at James. "They carried us both off. Edward's body has never been found. I woke in a dark room hours later. I don't know how many hours, your Grace. And I don't remember much of the days that followed."

James continued to study him. "What *do* you remember?"

"Only the dark room. Food thrust in the door by a hand. Sleep, and nightmares, and hours of sobbing, crying out for help, for someone, for Edward, for my mother.

"Then I remember being carried out again, at night, and taken aboard ship. There was another darkened room. And then suddenly, one day, a man came in whose voice I had never heard before. He took me to Antwerp, and left me with a woman called Catherine de Faro.

"She was kind. I grew"—he hesitated, his voice warm—"I grew to love her and to trust her. Some months later, she sent me to stay with a John Steinbeck, to learn the Flemish tongue.

I was not supposed to speak English, so when I spoke Flemish well, I was allowed a little freedom.

"At Easter, three years later, I was sent to Portugal, with the wife of Sir Edward Brampton. A loyal Yorkist family. With them I learned Spanish and Portuguese. Two years later, I went with a knight named de Cogma who took me into his service to learn the ways of a gentleman. With him, I went to Ireland.

"I was seventeen years old. The past was all a memory. De Cogma had furnished me with fine clothes, clothes in which he traded. And, your Grace, it was as though the stage had been set for me! All the Irish nobility, nay even the commoners, did me homage because they thought I was the son of Clarence, who had lately been in Ireland.

"I knew I was not. But it was then that I knew I must claim to be the man I had been born, so I wrote to the Earls of Desmond and Kildare, telling them that I was Richard. This was the first act of my own, your Grace. Previously, as I've said, I let the adherents of my house honor and protect and teach me.

"When I returned to the Continent, the Duchess of Burgundy sent for me. We talked. For hours. I told her all I remembered, and she knew then that I was indeed her nephew, her brother's child, Richard, Duke of York."

James said nothing. The Hepburn, watching him, found the moment awkward. Surely, James, had he believed all this tale, would have given some expression of sympathy. Instead, he said to Perkin, "We have arranged a tournament and supper tomorrow in your honor. I hope, indeed, that you will enjoy our hospitality as much as we enjoy extending it to you. I know you are weary; I know you would like to meet with your gentlemen." He smiled. "Good day, your Grace."

Alone, James paced over to the window, and looked down into the gardens. They were bare, now in November, the walks as they twisted under the trees, the bushes which in spring would burst with flower and fragrance. Then he saw Maggie Drummond.

It had been four days since he had seen her last. She was

entering King's Walk, near the precipitously sloping hill he had known since his boyhood. James shouted for a servant, for a cloak, heedless of the fact that the whole Court was talking about the woman who had held his affection for five months. He snatched the cloak from the servant's hand and made for the door in long and impatient strides.

21

THE GORDON APARTMENTS AT STIRLING WERE ON THE ground floor. Thus young Lord Grey had no difficulty at all in perching on the window sill of Mary Gordon's room. He knocked gently.

It was midmorning. The tournament would begin soon. The sound of the horns was already in the air gaily. Grey pressed his face against the glass. He saw Mary approaching the window. She unlatched it, exclaiming, "Lord, sir, what are you doing here?" She looked very surprised. "It's almost time for the tournament."

Grey disregarded both statements. "May I come in?"

Mary looked even more surprised. "I warrant so. Aye, you had best, before we both freeze."

Grey stepped in, shut the window and latched it. Then he turned to Mary. "Mistress," he sighed.

"What is it, sir?"

"I had to come! There was no other way!"

"No?" Mary's face was upturned to his.

"No." He hurried on, fumbling with his cap. "You ken, mistress, you are not much in favor yet with Jamie. And besides that, you are part betrothed to the Hepburn. I mean—"

"I know quite well what you mean," Mary said steadily, but there was anger in her voice.

"You must not blame the Hepburn," Grey put in.

"I do."

" 'Tis not strange you do. Yet—you do not understand him. He is—"

"I understand him well enough, sir, but I do not understand you." She regarded him from under level brows.

"Oh, mistress, it is simple enough." He smiled a little, gathering courage. "He—the Hepburn—is my lord, and so I come this way, to speak for myself, if m'lord should choose the Lady Jane, then I wanted you to know you have my deep and honorable love."

Mary Gordon looked into his honest young face. She drew a deep breath. "Sir, I am sorry." She said no more.

Grey twisted his cap into a knot.

"I greatly appreciate your love," Mary said. "Believe me, sir, I am—" She bit her lip and turned away.

Over her head Grey said, "Mistress, is there—do you love another? Or might I wear your token today in the tourney, under my coat?"

Mary turned and raised her eyes. This was a relief to say, the words which were coming. It was comforting to say them aloud.

"I love another." She said it proudly.

Grey concealed his disappointment manfully. He did not protest, but straightway put his cap on his head. "I go the way I came," he said. "But, remember, my mistress, love does not alter." He started to take her hand for a farewell kiss, but got no further. The door had been flung open, and Grey found himself seized from behind by murderous hands, and a sledge-hammer blow knocked him across the room. As he fell, he heard Mary cry out, and he saw the man who had struck him coming forward purposefully.

But Grey was a hot-headed Borderer. He brooked no insult from a sober-clothed servant. He scrambled to his feet, drawing his sword as he did. Yet Mary didn't cry his name.

"Matthew!"

Grey, breathing heavily from both the blow and anger,

looked at the man whose name Mary had cried. A moment before he had not been armed. Now, sliding from under his sleeve into his hand, gleamed a short, but long-bladed, knife.

"Matthew!" Mary cried again.

This stopped the Englishman. His blue eyes went to Mary. He remonstrated. " 'Twould enhance your reputation if you let me kill him here, mistress!"

"No!" Mary turned to Grey. "Leave, my lord."

"By the door," growled Matthew, pointing with the knife.

Grey obeyed. He went warily past Matthew, eyes on the thin knife. Grey would not have liked to face the Hepburn, armed only with a knife, and somehow he didn't want to face this man either. He felt very foolish and younger than his twenty-one years.

Matthew shut the door in his face. He slid the knife back under his sleeve into the leather thongs that held it. Neither he nor Mary was conscious of anything but that they were alone together. For a moment neither spoke. Then Matthew said, "I was told there was a man with you!"

He said it angrily, as if no man had a right to be with her, anywhere. He did not disclose that one of Lord Fleming's competent spies had come running to Matthew with a tale that a man had been seen climbing in Mary's window.

"How did he get in? That window was locked!"

"I let him in." Her eyes were deep purple.

"What?"

He felt the tautness in every nerve in his body. Accustomed as he was to living in danger, the last three months had taken their toll of nerves, even of weight. His every move was watched. He could not have escaped from Scotland if he wished, probably, and it was imperative he stay because of the pretender, Warbeck.

"I let him in," Mary repeated. "He came to ask me to wed with him, when I am free."

Matthew clenched his hands. "Do you dream you love that puppy?"

She shook her head. "No," she said only.

He heard her denial, and he heard also the echo of her

former statement: "When I am free." It reminded him anew of the arrogant and infamous contract which would allow the Hepburn to choose her should she best please him. The stabbing jealousy tore down his reserve, and he swore, a ripping resounding oath.

"Matthew," cried Mary, desperately. She loved him; she cared not who he was, but— "Go," she said, pointing to the door.

Matthew seized her hand in his big one. His arms went around her fiercely. He held her tight.

"I go nowhere! Neither do you!"

The reserve of long months was broken now. He found her mouth. He kissed her, a long kiss. He whispered, "I love you, my darling."

Wrapped in his arms, Mary knew only the touch of his mouth, heard again the whispered endearments. She wanted to tell him she loved him too, no matter what. She wanted to say she would go with him, anywhere, now, today.

And then abruptly, he stepped back. Mary caught at him for support. He took her hands down from his arms. He thrust her back, away from him. Mary looked at him wordlessly.

His eyes were remote and calculating. "I am sorry," he said curtly, "forgive me. Forget this, mistress. Forget it!" The last was a command, snapped at her.

He saw plainly the hurt he was inflicting. He hardened his heart. He could not possibly tell her who he was. Nor could he ask her to come away with him. That would be the worst, for the Hepburn, with the resources at his command, would undoubtedly catch them, and she would suffer terribly. He said harshly, "I lost my head. You are too fair." That was true. "I took you from another man, a moment ago. I was once a thief. Old habits cling to one."

She faced him. "Will you leave now? I am dismissing you from our service!"

He shook his head. He smiled. "For what reason? Seduction? Is that what you will tell the Lady Jane?"

Mary's face grew white.

Matthew said, "There is naught you can do, that will not hurt your name. You see I am quite safe. If I were you, mistress, I should obey my dictum. Forget this." He bowed, he went to the door. Mary heard it close after him.

In the hall, Matthew Craddock swore under his breath. He cursed himself. But she was safe. She hated him, but she was safe.

22

JANE GORDON SURVEYED HERSELF IN THE MIRROR AND was satisfied with what she saw. She was wearing what was not only the most daring dress she had ever seen, but the most wickedly expensive.

She had sold almost all her jewels. She had made special trips to Edinburgh, accompanied only by Matthew. She liked to ride with Matthew, because he was an excellent horseman and because she was sure it annoyed the Hepburn.

She had not seen the Hepburn for almost two months. At first she did not know where he had gone. Later she, and everyone else, learned that he had taken four ships of war to the Islands. James thought the appearance of warships might quiet the restless and lawless Orkneys and Shetlands. But, though the Hepburn was absent, she confided to Matthew on one of their frequent trips to the capital that she was certain she was being spied on by the Hepburn's men.

Matthew had replied dryly, "I'm quite sure too, Lady Gordon."

This dress was worth everything. It was made of black, rustling silk, the bodice square and deeply décolleté. Its skirt billowed out, but it was slit to the waist in an inverted V. The scarlet satin underskirt was so tight that Jane had to practice walking, learning to put one foot directly in front of the other. She wore no jewels except one spray of diamonds pinned where the silk was cut away between her breasts. Pins were very new. This one had cost four necklaces and a pendant.

Jane took a last look at herself. She smiled at her image. She pictured the Hepburn when he saw her. Laughing, she flipped her train around with a twist of her hip and leg and proceeded toward the door.

James Stuart's court was gay, immoral and extravagant in true Stuart style. The great room Jane entered was full of people, the jabbering of different tongues, the movement of many servants.

Jewelry gleamed on the bright-gowned women, around the necks of men, and on the fingers of both, even to the thumbs. The use of fur was lavish.

The tables were set in an open rectangle; a great fire burned in the center of the room. Blackamoors stood behind James's table, with ostrich plumes waving from their heads. The court jester, English John, his head shaven, moved around them in his striped green suit.

The Spanish ambassador had arrived four days before. Danish and French could be heard vying with each other. An alliance had just been concluded with the Danes, and their capacity for liquor had amazed even the Scots. The Spanish women flirted from behind fans, their voices soft as the music that came from the players on the balcony. Even so, even with all this, Jane created a diversion as she entered the big doors.

The nearest men swung around to look. The women stared icily, thinking what to say to Jane Gordon when they would have the chance. The Hepburn, across the room, couldn't see her at all for the men who clustered around her. He shouldered his way toward her.

Fleming stepped aside for the Hepburn, a sly smile on his face.

"Lady Gordon, the goddess of love," he said to Jane, and bowed, backing off.

The Hepburn, close now, stared at her in disbelief. Jane offered her hand. He saw the familiar tilt to the corners of her mouth, but he took her hand without a word, and the men around them dropped back a little.

"Your servant, my lord," said Jane, making a curtsey. She had succeeded: for a brief moment she was afraid he would send her to her rooms until she remembered he had not the right. "I know you told me I'd be poor," Jane said, low, "but I wanted it to be merely rumor."

The Hepburn's eyes glittered with anger. But he was prevented from speaking by the arrival of the king.

James entered, walking slowly. He enjoyed his entrances. He spoke to a few people. Jane, beside the Hepburn, made her curtsey. Suddenly James saw her, and he stopped. His eyes went over her. He was amused.

"Well, madam," he said lazily, glancing at the Hepburn. "Of a truth, my dear cousin, your charms are well displayed."

" 'Tis the latest style from Paris, your Grace," Jane said. "Or mayhap Venice," she added, for she had forgotten. Everyone was staring and whispering.

"More like Venice," said James. "Are you vying with your sister for the eyes of his lordship?"

"No, your Majesty!"

James laughed; he went on toward the French ambassador, but as the two men talked together, they both looked at Jane. She flushed a little. She heard the Hepburn say, dangerously low, "Do not call for your cloak, madam."

"I had no such intention!" Jane said.

The Hepburn turned away from her. Over by the fire stood a woman he had met briefly two months ago. He went toward her.

Eufemia Fleming was dressed in pink satin. Over her shoulders was a pink short coat lined in lynx, the short sleeves seamed with tiny strips of fur. Eufemia saw him coming.

He came to a stop directly in front of her. "I had your note, madam," he said without preamble.

Eufemia looked up at him. His voice had been lazy and deliberate.

"Did you, m'lord?" she asked softly. "You fought like a savage today."

In the tournament, James had been the Wild Knight, and the Hepburn, attired as a savage, had been his only attendant. "That was my role, madam," he reminded.

"You were magnificent in costume," said Eufemia, her gaze on the wide shoulders. He looked a little amused. He smiled faintly. His nearness made Eufemia conscious of every pulse of her blood. She wanted to lie with him, and she knew he was well aware of it. "You are so tanned by the weeks at sea." She raised her hands to her cap to adjust the tiny veil through which she looked at him. It was a languorous movement. The Hepburn still looked faintly amused, but Eufemia could anticipate the ruthless passion so lightly concealed.

"Tonight, at eleven," he said.

Eufemia ran her red tongue over her lips. "What of Fleming?"

"I'll send him away."

"Oh," Eufemia murmured. This was more bold and arrogant than she had expected. She smiled, satisfied.

"I may be late," he said. With that he turned away, and Eufemia's mouth was sulky. Her eyes followed him as he went to his place at the dining tables; tonight she would break the thin veneer into a thousand pieces.

Meanwhile he waited at table for Jane. She was walking slowly, of necessity, speaking in French with one of the two ambassador's aides. When she was seated, she turned at last to the Hepburn.

"Look, my lord," she said. "The Duke of York is smitten hard by Mary. Did you note it this afternoon?"

"I couldn't very well, madam," the Hepburn answered.

"Oh, no," said Jane. "I forgot you were on the field. Attired in goat skins. Who was the lass you carried off for James?"

"I don't know her name!"

Enormous platters of meat and fowl were being brought.

"I am going to eat nothing but oysters," announced Jane. She speared the first one and then drank off a goblet of wine. "Tell me," she said, "is Eufemia Fleming your latest whore?"

The Hepburn, angry, annoyed and now guilty, muttered, "Madam, I have scarce met Lady Fleming."

"Well," said Jane, eating two oysters at once, "you are away so much and when you are home you will have, besides your wife, a number of women, no doubt, so I think Mary and I should keep Matthew, don't you?" At this she stopped eating. She leaned her elbow on the table, her eyes met the Hepburn's and he grinned. She must have been watching him closely.

"Are you jealous, madam? You've no need to be."

"How you lie!"

His gaze lingered on her bare shoulders. Jane raised a newly filled goblet to her lips and looked at the Hepburn over the rim. He touched her shoulder with his fingertips.

"The mark is gone," he said.

Jane set the goblet down. "Don't do that!"

He raised one eyebrow. "You invite it. I can scarce resist you."

Jane's hand tightened around the goblet, and it rocked dangerously. The Hepburn laughed. Jane drank the wine.

The Hepburn began to eat too, while Jane stuffed herself with oysters. She drank more wine. Underneath the table her foot tapped. But the wine goblets were big, her foot stopped tapping as she began to feel pleasantly warm. She ate the last oyster, and reached over to the Hepburn's plate for a chicken leg. She put her thumb in the butter and smeared a piece of his white bread, which she also took.

"Thank you," she said. "Your health, my lord." She waved the leg. With her other hand she raised the wine and alternately ate and drank. When she finished, she leaned back in her chair, sighed lustily, and held both hands up in front of her.

A servant set a bowl of water before her in which she washed her hands. The food was being borne away. But it was often James's custom to stay at table for two hours while he drank and watched a wrestling bout, or a dance, or while he gambled or played cards. Fresh logs, black and huge, were thrown in the fire. A fresh hogshead of wine was rolled in. English John, the jester, scampered over to it.

A week ago one of James's sea captains, who had captured

three pirate vessels, had sent the heads of the unlucky sailors to James in a hogshead of wine. Now the jester made a great play of peering into the barrel: he wanted to be sure the wine would not go to his head, he wanted to know what he was drinking.

"I'll taste it first, John," Jane called out.

James looked across at her. The jester brought Jane the first cup. Then he said to the Hepburn, "Does the Lady Jane please you best, my lord?" He pretended to avert a blow, and staggered back.

"Ask my pardon for that impudence," the Hepburn said pleasantly.

"I do beg it, my lord." But John laughed, and went off.

The people nearest, however, watched the Hepburn and Jane. Gossip surrounded them. Which Gordon woman would the Hepburn choose?

Fleming sat back and watched it all, waiting for his chance to stir up trouble tonight by using some information he had. He rose and joined a group of men who were watching the dancing. His chance would come soon, he was sure.

It did. The Hepburn and James were standing together, talking with Maggie Drummond. The Hepburn's shadow, Lord Grey, was just behind the Hepburn. Jane was dancing. Fleming noted with complacency that she was quite obviously drunk; she was clapping her hands, swaying back and forth, and laughing. Fleming went over to her. In a few moments the pattern of the dance would bring her right to the Hepburn. Fleming made certain to get there at the same time.

Jane ended the dance right in front of the king. She made a deep curtsey. Fleming seized her hand and helped her stand again.

James, for all his faults, rarely drank too heavily. If he did, he indulged in private. That was his wish for his Court. He was displeased with Jane. Yet she was not loud; in fact, she looked flushed and extremely alluring. James was inclined to forgive, so he said nothing. He smiled a little. But Fleming was afraid he had not too much time. He spoke up.

"There you are, Grey. I hear you were rudely removed

from a lady's chamber this morning by a servant." Fleming laughed.

Grey, taken completely aback, looked in horror at the Hepburn.

"M'lord," mumbled Grey, his eyes fastened on the Hepburn. "I—" He stopped. He was appalled that Fleming had discovered this. He couldn't imagine where he had learned it.

What Fleming had hoped, was happening. He had indeed stirred up a mare's nest. It seemed quite evident that the Hepburn's mind flew immediately to Jane and the servant would of course be the ubiquitous Matthew.

James, seeing Grey's obvious guilt, looked at Maggie. But before Maggie could speak, Jane started, "Why, be damned to you, Grey, you ass-eared—"

"Lady Gordon!" The Hepburn interrupted savagely.

Now Maggie did take a hand. "Excuse Lord Grey, your Grace."

James nodded, with a good deal of relief. Grey backed off. Then Maggie said, clearly, from James's side, "I think your dress is beautiful, Jane." She turned to give the Hepburn a long stare.

He frowned. "I disagree. Your Majesty, will you excuse Lady Gordon and myself?"

James again looked at Maggie, to see what she thought. He was bewildered, but Maggie seemed to understand. For some reason she was coming to Jane Gordon's defense. Privately James thought the gown much too daring and the Hepburn right. However, Maggie seemed to think it was right for Jane to leave; she made no motion to stop it. He said, "We'll excuse you both." And as they started away, he whispered to Maggie, "But he ought to beat that lass, on her backside."

Maggie pursed her mouth and then grinned. "He deserves her," she said. She tucked her hand in James's arm and watched the Hepburn and Jane walk away.

The Hepburn had offered his arm to Jane.

"Do not lean! Walk straight," she heard him order.

Jane made an effort. She had to traverse the whole length of the room. Carefully she put one foot in front of the other.

Finally they were outside the big doors. Jane put both hands to her temples. Her head had begun to ache, and she swore feelingly. She looked up at the Hepburn, as she stood there unsteadily.

"I warrant I disgraced myself. And you." She smiled mockingly.

He said, "You look like a drunken lady of pleasure. One that I would not bother to lay." He seized her hand and started along the hall.

Jane did not answer. Pain throbbed in her temples. She tried to disengage his grip, but she couldn't, so she rubbed her head with her free hand, and stumbled ahead as she endeavored to keep up with him.

"This is the wrong way. Ha' ye lost your temper?" She laughed.

In his anger he had not noticed. He swung around, seeing he was wrong, and jerked her with him. Jane asked sweetly, "Are ye jealous of Grey?"

The Hepburn came to a stop. Jane continued, "Ask Grey if it was Matthew who put him out."

They were at her door, and the Hepburn pushed it open, dragging her inside. He released her, and she took three backward steps, trying to get her balance. She kept backing up, hands stretched in front of her. Then she laughed at the Hepburn, who stood about ten feet away from her.

"You'll rue me yet, m'lord," she jeered. "I'll sully your new title."

He advanced toward her in four long strides. Her eyes grew wide and pure gold as she stood her ground and looked up at him.

"And if ye wed wi' me, m'lord," she said clearly, "I'll promise all your children will be bastards."

He struck her, then. The flat of his hand caught her squarely across the face and knocked her to the floor. She lay there, in a crumpled heap, at his feet.

23

EUFEMIA FLEMING'S ROOM BOASTED A CORNER FIREplace and walls hung with French tapestries, which went everywhere with Eufemia. So did the thick fur rugs and the feather bed and the white and gold wardrobe and table.

It was ten o'clock. Eufemia sat in front of the table while her woman brushed her hair. Eufemia's hair was a mass of waves and curls.

It was very warm in the room. Eufemia kept her fires burning all day and all night. Stark naked, she stood up and let herself be powdered from head to foot. Then she turned back to the mirror. Her body was perfect. The Hepburn would not find a single flaw.

Her woman said, "I always knew you would find a lover like him."

Eufemia lifted her curls with both hands. "Do my back again. And it's a mercy I couldn't ha' had him first."

Clara was sceptical. "First you wed and ha' a husband."

Eufemia made a face. The door opened without warning.

Eufemia expected one of her maids. But the newcomer was Fleming. Instant rage gripped her.

"How dare you?" she cried.

Clara picked up a big lacy woollen shawl and put it over her mistress, covering her from the eyes of her husband. Clara glared at Fleming, eyes as hostile as Eufemia's. Eufemia was almost speechless.

"Get out!"

Fleming stammered, "I came only to say good-bye. I didn't expect—" Completely taken aback, his black eyes swept his wife, her maid and the room. He trembled with anger, futile anger. His breath came so fast he could hardly control his words. He gestured.

The sight of his hatred and impotent jealousy calmed Eufemia. "Get out," she repeated contemptuously.

He could not. "I came to say good-bye," he repeated. His hands clenched and he turned aside, eyes glistening with tears of anger and self-pity. He brushed at his eyes. "It's the Hepburn," he cried.

Eufemia lifted one shoulder. "You're mad," she said calmly. "Where are you going?"

"To Dunbar. It's going to be destroyed by Jamie's orders." For a moment he wanted to believe he was wrong. "I'm sorry, my dear."

She looked at him as though she had never seen him before. "Good-bye," she said.

Fleming was deceived no longer. It was too plain. He was being sent away, so that Eufemia could spend her nights in the Hepburn's arms. "I'm going to kill you," he said and started toward her.

Clara screamed, then clapped both hands over her lips and backed away. Her eyes searched the room for a weapon.

Eufemia jumped to her feet. A bottle of perfume crashed over. "You don't dare!" Eufemia said. But he was coming toward her slowly, his face contorted with rage. He was very near. Eufemia leaned back against the table "He'll kill you! He will kill you if you touch me!"

Fleming stopped. He stared down at her face.

"You couldn't escape," cried Eufemia.

His hands dropped to his sides. His breath came swiftly.

"Whoreson coward, you don't dare touch me!" Eufemia seized a hairbrush and brandished it. "Get out before I call him," she said, her eyes glittering. "You think you could stand in his way? He'd tear you limb from limb. And I'm mad for him, d'ye understand? Now get out!"

He turned. The door closed after him. Clara gave a deep sigh. Eufemia sank down on her stool again. "Clara, fetch a cloth. He made me spill my best perfume."

"The fat's in the fire now," said Clara. She went for the cloth. It was nearly eleven. Eufemia got into bed, stretching luxuriously between the smooth sheets. The air smelled heavy with perfume. Clara sat on a stool and dozed.

At twelve there was a single knock. Eufemia whispered, "It is he. Let him in."

Clara was waking up. She straightened her white cap. She went to the door. Clara had never seen the Hepburn close before. She smiled in approval and admiration and took the money he gave her.

"Come in, my lord," she whispered.

The Hepburn was looking at the bed. Eufemia sat up. "I had fallen asleep," she lied. "Villain, you are late." She pushed back the sheets and got out of bed, stepping behind an ornamented screen. She put a bare arm over the top of the screen, and yawned. "Clara, hand me my shawl."

Clara did. She took the Hepburn's cloak. "Goodnight, mistress. M'lord." She left them.

Eufemia came out from behind the screen, wrapped in lacy wool. The Hepburn was smiling his lazy smile. He took the hand she extended, and kissed it; the other hand moved lightly up her bare arm to the shoulder.

"You have something to tell me, madam? Your note said such."

Eufemia looked down at the big hand on her shoulder. "Aye, m'lord."

"What?" He drew her a little closer, so she stood in the circle of his arm. He bent over and kissed her white throat. "What, madam?" Then he straightened up, looking down at her.

Eufemia said, "You don't credit my note, do you?"

"No," he said. He touched her hair.

Eufemia pouted. "It is important. And I told Fleming!"

The Hepburn frowned. The hand on her shoulder gripped hard. "Why?"

She didn't answer. He was displeased. She could not control this man the way she could Fleming. She whispered, "Don't be angry with me, my lord."

"God in heaven." He shook his head. "Do you usually inform your husband about your lovers?" But he smiled a little.

"I didn't ask you here to lie with me!"

"No?" He looked very amused.

"I had something important to tell you!"

"Madam, I've never doubted it. I—"

"If you laugh, I shan't tell you!"

"I'm not laughing," he said, and grinned.

"Hepburn, let me go." She whirled away from him. "What I have to say is this. Fleming's a traitor!"

She watched his face change. She was a little frightened. He said, lightly, "I warrant it's a good thing, since I'll probably have to kill him anyway." The Hepburn rubbed his cheek. "Unless he's fond of his horns."

But his gray eyes were intent and narrow. "Madam, suppose you explain that former statement for me."

Eufemia said, "I know he is a traitor! I know it, my lord. And I know he changed my father's note to Maggie. He wrote spears and arrows! He sent that note! My father gave it him to be dispatched, and he must have changed it!"

"Did Maggie say it was plain?" His eyes searched hers. "Did she?"

Eufemia nodded. She was speaking the truth and she was glad she was. It would be hard to lie. "Maggie said she could *never* have mistaken it."

The Hepburn didn't bother to ask why she had not told him before. There were probably numerous reasons why Maggie had kept silence for a while. It was a difficult thing to betray your sister's husband, and it might not be true. The note had been burned. As he was thinking this, Eufemia said, "Maggie tried so hard to remember exactly before she told me. And Maggie didn't know how Fleming is. Was," added Eufemia. "She didn't realize how hateful he had become. She didn't want to accuse my husband without more proof. But she finally told me."

The Hepburn was remembering a scene that had taken place tonight. He remembered Fleming and his gossip about Grey. He asked bluntly, "Was Lord Grey your lover?"

Eufemia shrugged. "He wanted to wed with me, before Fleming."

"And then he was your lover? After you were wed?"

"He was my only lover." Eufemia cast down her long lashes.

"Fleming made trouble for Grey tonight. He must ha' spied on the lad. Tonight he made trouble for a good many people. James wasn't sure that Maggie hadn't entertained Grey. I myself—" He stopped. He recalled Grey's look of guilt. But Eufemia had seen more, he was sure.

"What else do you have to tell me?"

"Little things."

He nodded at her, as though he understood completely.

"Go on."

"Oh, he burns letters. He sees strange people, and pays them. That steward of his—he spies. And that priest."

The Hepburn said, "What do you know about a priest?" He looked down at her, and Eufemia, really frightened, cried, "Nothing, my lord!"

"Describe him," he ordered curtly.

"He's no priest. He's fat, and ugly. He—that's all I know!"

"How many times have you seen him?"

"Twice, only."

"And that's all you know about him?"

"Aye, my lord."

The Hepburn said, with a return to his former manner, "Well, lass, it was important. You see, I'd always wondered why the men who were hired to kill the last king were wearing the livery of Lord Grey. If what you say is true, and I think it is, it was Fleming's jealousy made him try to get Grey into trouble."

Eufemia said, "What will you do with him?"

"He's being watched, now."

"Will you kill him yourself?" whispered Eufemia.

He shrugged. "Mayhap."

She saw that it scarcely mattered to him. He was taking off his doublet.

"I had suspected him before," he said, and evidently that

was an end to the subject. Eufemia thought Fleming might as well be dead now.

She looked across to him. Beyond him was the tumbled bed. The fire spluttered. Eufemia backed away from him. She turned her back as she locked the door. Then she stood against it.

He didn't move. "I don't know much about you," he said. "How long have you been wed?"

"Two years," said Eufemia. She pushed the thick curls off her forehead, her eyes looked sleepy.

"Have you any children?"

"No," said Eufemia. "I'd ha' strangled Fleming's brats."

He smiled, lazily. "What of Grey?"

Eufemia lifted one white shoulder. "I was careful."

He had untied the laces of his shirt and pulled it off. He tossed it onto a chair. "Didn't you ever forget to be careful?"

"No," she answered. She smiled. Out of the fierce Hepburn stock had come a man like this. To carry his son within her, to feel it stirring—Eufemia let the shawl slip down over her high pointed breasts, and over the lovely curve of hip. On her bare feet she walked proudly to him.

24

MATTHEW LEANED BACK AGAINST THE HIGH TRESTLE-seat wearily. He was cold and tired. The high seat-back protected him from some of the drafts. The curtains were drawn across the windows. Outside it looked as though it might snow.

The city, the castle were both tense. Rebellion had flamed in the Highlands, rashly, Matthew thought, led by Lennox, Lyle and Forbes and their clans.

James had laid siege to the castles of Duchal and Crookston, and to the mighty castle of Dumbarton, perched as it was on five hundred and fifty feet of basaltic rock and protected by the rivers of Clyde and Leven.

James had been gone two weeks. This morning at dawn he had ridden back into Edinburgh. At the same time, Lord Drummond had galloped off, and Knox, too—they had gone separate ways. Matthew put his quill down and rose, going to the window to draw back the curtains again. There was an ominous cloud of dust on the horizon, to the south. Matthew was sure that Knox had ridden off to summon men to the Hepburn standard.

He let the curtain fall back. It was now afternoon. Matthew, the Englishman, was afraid this rebellion was going to be quenched as swiftly as James could manage it. And then—his eyes might stray southward to the wavering Border.

Matthew heard voices. He heard the sound of laughter. It brought a light to his blue eyes, and he turned and waited impatiently. The fire was bright; the room was as warm as it could be. He looked toward the door.

Jane opened it. She was dressed in riding clothes, swinging her short whip. A distance behind her came Mary, and with Mary, the Duke of York—only Matthew called him Perkin Warbeck.

Matthew's face changed. Jane had gone over to the fireplace, and put her soft-booted foot on the fender, and her elbow on the mantel. At the doorway, Mary paused, and pulled off her gloves.

The duke bent over her, and said something Matthew could not hear. Mary laughed, she threw back her cloak, and the soft fur framed her face. It slipped off her shoulders and would have fallen to the floor had the duke not caught it and held it over his arm.

Matthew went forward. The duke's high-browed face was smiling and mealy. Matthew wanted to drive his fist into it. Mary went on speaking to the duke. "Your Grace, I should be delighted! To—"

Matthew interrupted. "Mistress Mary, you are in a draft. Enter!"

Mary regarded him, her eyes remote and cool. Matthew muttered, "I am sorry, your ladyship, but—"

Mary cut him short. "Won't you come in, your Grace?"

Matthew turned away. The use of the duke's title from Mary enraged him.

"I cannot, mistress," he heard Warbeck say. "I have an audience with his Majesty."

"Is Jamie back?" Jane asked.

"Aye, mistress," said Matthew, glad to enter the conversation. "He returned this morning, early."

"I have seen him," the duke said importantly.

"Have you truly?" drawled Matthew.

The duke stared at Matthew, then dropped his gaze. He bowed to Mary, kissed her hand. The door closed on his resplendent figure, and Matthew, in his black, was alone with Mary and Jane Gordon.

"I was doing the accounts," he said diffidently, speaking to Mary.

She didn't seem to know he was addressing her. She gave him not even a glance. "Excuse me, Jane," she said.

Matthew's eyes followed her hungrily. He had not noticed that Jane, contrary to her usual way, had kept almost entirely silent. Mary went through this small room, which was also used for dining in winter, and Matthew suddenly looked up to find Jane's golden eyes on him. Those eyes were narrow as she watched him, as she swung her whip back and forth, back and forth. She waited only till Mary was out of earshot before she said, "Weren't you the servant who was like to kill Lord Grey?"

Matthew looked at her, startled. But he had a premonition of what was coming. He went over and closed the door, tightly. Then he faced Jane.

"I was," he said, and waited. He felt drained of emotion.

"Who are you?" asked Jane. She raised the whip. "For the way you look at Lady Mary, I should use this on you!" She started toward him, and suddenly stopped. She threw the whip on the floor. "Matthew," she said softly, "who are you?"

He shook his head. He leaned down and retrieved the whip. "Use it," he said. "Take it."

Jane made a dissenting gesture. "If I did," said Jane, "what should I tell Mary?"

"Anything but the truth." Now Matthew flung the whip to the floor. He looked to Jane and remembered much. He smiled, and she did too.

"Be damned to you," she said suddenly. "Matthew, you and I—we have been much together. I—" She stopped, too.

"I cannot tell you who I am," he said urgently. "Believe me, mistress, it would be dangerous for you."

She shook her head. "Nonsense. Not for me," she added regally.

In spite of himself, Matthew chuckled. Jane frowned at him.

"I know much! You are not an English Borderer, first. You are probably a peer, because I saw the Hepburn secretary point to a name! And they suspect you! Is that why we were always followed? Is it?"

He nodded.

"You might as well tell me who you are."

"Matthew Craddock," he said. It was some relief.

"I warrant I call you Sir Matthew."

"Not here, please," said Matthew.

Jane grinned. "You may call me Jane. Ah, you're a fool. Why haven't you gone? Escaped?"

"I dislike leaving while that puling bastard, Warbeck, is strutting around Scotland."

"Mind your language," said Jane. "I see. Duty comes first. Could you leave?"

"It's always possible to risk escape, but sometimes it is best to brazen out a situation."

"Meanwhile the Hepburn waits like a cat after a mouse—for some overt act of yours."

"That's why I don't want to leave." He was very serious. "Mistress," he said, "Mary must not be permitted to be friendly with Warbeck! He is wanted by us! There's a noose waiting for him at Tyburn!"

Jane said arrogantly, "What makes you think you will ever lay hands on him? He is in Scotland!"

"Forget your nationality," Matthew said. "When Perkin Warbeck sets a foot over that Border—and he will—"

There was a knock on the door. Jane stiffened. Matthew spun around, picked the whip up off the floor, and handed it to Jane. On the way to the door, he dipped the quill in the ink, so that it looked as though he had just laid it down. Then he opened the door.

Framed in the doorway, armed and clad in light mail, was the Hepburn. Matthew stepped to one side.

"My lord," he said. "Would you enter?"

The Hepburn brushed past him. Jane was back by the fireplace, whip in hand, leaning against the mantel. Matthew shut the door.

The Hepburn came to a stop in front of Jane. The heavy cloak swung to his heels, his spurs jingled. Jane tried to meet his eyes but couldn't.

His sudden appearance took her completely by surprise. She glanced guiltily at Matthew, who was standing meekly at his table. Then she brought her eyes back to the Hepburn.

"Excuse my intrusion," he said, his voice harsh.

Jane put her hand to her cheek, as though she could still feel the impact of his hand across her face. She was dressed very plainly; she wore no jewels.

"You find me unfitted to receive you, my lord," she said, very low.

He blotted out the rest of the room. The plumed helmet made him tower over her.

"You look well." He was taking in every detail of her appearance.

She wet her lips. "I'm very strong, my lord. I have not seen you of late, since Stirling, but we have had news of you." She slapped the whip against the stone fireplace, hard. She tilted her head back and her eyes suddenly blazed at him. Then she said, "Matthew and I were discussing my finances. I have sold all my jewels." She put her hand to her throat to indicate its bareness. "I am poor, as you once warned me. Did you not? And how is Lady Fleming?" Jane leaned her chin on her fist.

"Well, I believe," the Hepburn said, impassively. He turned around to Matthew, who was still standing in respect to his betters.

Matthew's easy stance deceived even Jane. He looked just as usual. But he and Hepburn looked at each other too long, each measuring, waiting, and Jane was afraid. She moved between them, with a swirl of her cape. She put her hands on her hips; her back was to Matthew.

"You may continue with your figures," she said to Matthew over her shoulder. "Now, my lord, why are you here?" Defiantly she stared up at his face. "You are dressed for battle, not the boudoir." She drawled the word. Then she said, insolently, "D'ye need armor to call on me?"

"I'm on my way to Dumbarton," he said. "The castles of Duchal and Crookston have capitulated." This last statement was true; the two castles had fallen. But the Hepburn was not on his way to Dumbarton. The night before the rebels had descended from the Highlands into the Low Country, and Lennox's intention had been to cross the bridge at Stirling. The Hepburn and James had anticipated this and occupied Stirling before him.

So Lennox decided to cross the Firth at a ford up the river, not far from its source. It would have been safer had not one of the Macalpin clan deserted and brought to James the information that Lennox and his lords and troops were camped for the night at Talla Moss, about sixteen miles from Stirling.

The Hepburn and James and Lord Drummond, at the head of a hastily composed force, were planning to attack this night.

"Then why are you here?" Jane asked again. "I am busy."

"To bid you a fond farewell," he said mockingly. "Since I intend to wed you in three weeks."

Jane's face went white. She sucked in her breath. Then she turned her back on him, and was silent.

His big hands closed over her upper arms. Over her head

his voice came. "You'll be married at Bothwell. On the fifth of December. You will take up residence there next week."

He had pulled her back against him, her head was on his shoulder. "You arrogant bastard," she said evenly.

He turned her around to face him. She tried to resist. "Oh, no, madam," he said, pinning her arms down at her side with one arm. With his free hand he tipped up her chin. "I have another message," he added, and, bending down, he brushed his mouth across hers as though to have a taste of what he would later take completely. He kept on talking. "Your sister is to wed with the Duke of York. It is a suitable marriage, for he needs a wife with royal blood. This wedding will take place in February. But first, as according to our contract, I chose you. *You* please me."

He held Jane in an immovable position. He looked over her head at Matthew, and he saw in those blue eyes a blazing wrath. Because of that, the Hepburn deliberately, slowly, kissed Jane.

Jane yielded. Not willingly, but because the strength to fight him had gone down before his masculinity. Her slim body was crushed against him; she knew that he was taking, not giving, and that the kiss was ruthlessly lustful.

Jane knew too that she had provoked it. From the very first, when her whip had been swung across his face. She surrendered to her instinct to placate him. She tried to free her hands; they were tight against her.

The Hepburn permitted it. But he didn't release her mouth. Jane touched the side of his face with her long fingers. He opened his eyes and she saw the glittering grayness of them.

Involuntarily she gave a little cry, deep in her throat. He raised his head; one of her hands was fastened in his collar; her breast rose and fell swiftly, she lay back in his arms and slowly her eyes opened and looked up at him.

"I hadn't intended making love to you," he muttered.

"Love?" asked Jane. She shook her head. She turned her head into his shoulder.

He put his lips to her ear; she felt his breath. "What else?" he whispered.

He let her go. He went over to the table where Matthew was bent over the ledger. He walked around behind Matthew and looked over his shoulder at the firm writing. Jane, white, could say nothing.

The Hepburn said casually, "I shall need your services."

Matthew didn't answer. He wrote on.

The Hepburn ripped out an oath. "You may stand when I speak!"

Matthew got to his feet. "Aye, my lord," he said.

Jane moved toward them as though they were a magnet. She reached the table, and put both hands flat on it.

"M'lord," she pleaded.

The two men, standing about three feet apart, were of equal height. The Hepburn was a trifle heavier; Matthew's figure was more loose-limbed and rangy. The Hepburn said, his voice thick with passion, "You now serve me!"

Matthew forced himself to say calmly, "Aye, my lord."

"From now on you wear my livery." The Hepburn smiled a little.

Matthew leaned over and closed the ledger.

"We fight tonight," the Hepburn said contemptuously. "Can you use aught besides a pen?"

"You might find me able with a knife, my lord."

The Hepburn had started toward the door. Matthew went by him to open it. The Hepburn turned.

"Good day, mistress."

Jane didn't answer him. "God speed you, Matthew," she said.

The door closed. In fifteen minutes the great castle gates swung shut. The men had all gone, even the royal household had been armed for the night raid on the rebels at Talla Moss.

But Jane, alone, did not go to the window to watch the men ride out. On the table in front of her lay Matthew's quill. She sank down into the trestle-seat. She opened the ledger.

Matthew's last figure was very plain. She had twenty pounds from the lease of the house. The rents from the great Gordon stronghold of Strathbogie had been paid out to the usurer against George's borrowings for his enforced exile. A hundred pounds of the debt had been paid, too.

Matthew had been so careful. Jane put her fists into her eyes and rubbed them hard. If she herself had not been so reckless and sold every penny's worth of jewelry and gold to buy new clothes! She had only the diamond spray pin. Mayhap she could sell it.

But all avenues were closed against her. She had not yet been received by James after the time he had dismissed her three weeks ago. His mistress was Eufemia's sister.

If a favor was to be granted, one went to the Drummond sisters. Through them both the king and the Hepburn could be reached. Jane pulled her cloak around her. If anything were to be done to help Mary, then Maggie Drummond would have to be asked. Jane Gordon put her hands to her throat and fastened her cloak. She would ask an audience from Lady Margaret Drummond.

And yet even while she walked along the empty halls, from which there had suddenly been taken all sound of masculine voice or tread, she knew it would be useless. There was no hope. There was no one who could help. Except herself and Mary. And Matthew. Somehow, against everything, they would do it.

25

"THIS IS THE FIRST FOOT OF BOTHWELL PARISH," THE rider next to Matthew said.

Matthew's eyes were almost shut. He could feel the dust ingrained on his face; each jolt of his horse jerked him awake, then he settled back into his doze again.

The road was fairly good. This parish was cut out by two

roads, one from Glasgow to Edinburgh, and another from Glasgow to the south, to Carlisle. The parish contained neither moor nor moss; it was rolling rich country, with carefully tilled fields, with vast orchards, threaded with silver river and stream. The Clyde, which had its mysterious birth deep in the frowning hills of Annandale, flowed wide here, between tree-lined banks, and the trout and salmon darted through its waters.

The villages were enclosed; mansion houses abounded. "It reminds me of England," Matthew said. He did not specify that he meant the south of England.

They were going over the North Calder bridge by the iron works. Ahead, the Gothic spires of the church in Bothwell looked tall enough for a cathedral. Matthew dozed again, purposefully.

The Hepburn's treatment of Matthew was diabolically simple. Matthew had served the Hepburn for almost three weeks, and since that first night-battle, he had kept Matthew in attendance on him every minute of the night and day.

The night surprise raid on the rebel forces of Lennox and Lyle had been most successful. Lennox's intrenchments were breached. His whole force had been either slain or taken prisoner. The few fugitives were pursued as far as Gartulunane on either side of the river as the cold dawn came. Almost no king's men had been lost.

The mighty castle of Dumbarton had then surrendered to its king. Matthew had accompanied the Hepburn and James and Lord Drummond to take possession of it. The men said that James was going to garrison it himself, for it was fortress only, surrounded by the rivers at high water and well equipped with guardrooms, officers' quarters and great barracks. Its guns bristled high on its ramparts.

Matthew had been interested in the castle. He had observed the king and the Hepburn carefully in the field. Both were formidable; both were clever; both were antagonists who would bring peace to Scotland and thus, mayhap, war to England.

Matthew shook himself. They were entering the town of

Bothwell. Like an English village, he again reminded himself, it was completely surrounded with gardens and orchards. Footpaths led through hill and dale and over white stiles. If he ever saw England again, Matthew was sure he would be a very fortunate man.

The Hepburn played his game openly; so did his captains. They knew who he was; Matthew did not deceive himself.

Their orders were quick and curt. Their eyes rested on him warily, waiting for the first overt sign that would give him away. They tested him every minute of the day and night, rousing him from sleep which he had more than earned. Matthew was sure that if he had not learned to sleep in the saddle, he would finally have turned on one of them.

But he didn't. He answered their questions, obeyed their orders, kept himself clean and shaven and neat. No matter how tired he was, he never neglected his horse, and no matter what the Hepburn said, Matthew never rose to the bait.

"There's the castle," a voice broke in on Matthew's thoughts. His companion smiled at him; the men had no idea why the Hepburn disliked the English Borderer—they liked him. He was assured and unassuming, dependable, witty.

The troop came to a sudden halt. Matthew heard his name.

"Aye, sir," he answered with just enough pause to show Captain Scott that they were all playing this game.

Scott had been riding off to the side; the Hepburn led with Matthew and his companion at the head of a double line of forty riders. Scott growled, "Dismount!"

Matthew slid to the ground, tossing the reins of his lathered horse to his partner in line. Scott kept him waiting for the next order. But Matthew showed nothing but fatigue. Scott said, "His lordship's horse wants its girth tightened."

Matthew went to the Hepburn. "Which girth, m'lord?" he asked, looking up.

"The left," said the Hepburn.

Matthew reached for the strap. It had loosened. He adjusted it, while the Hepburn watched his hands. Automatically Matthew walked around to the fastenings on the right side, seeing if it was now tight enough on this side and correctly buckled. It was.

"Is that all you're wanting, my lord?" he asked softly, and his blue eyes glistened.

The Hepburn accepted the challenge. "For the moment," he answered.

"Aye, m'lord." Matthew tipped his cap, patted the horse and walked away, taking his time, but not quite enough time to be obviously insolent. He swung into the saddle. Scott glared, and Matthew smiled.

Scott raised his whip, but didn't use it. Matthew, however, was sure that soon he would bedevil the man into outright violence. Although Scott wasn't cruel, he was no match for Matthew. Matthew's smile changed to a grin, and the troop went on. Matthew went to sleep again, jogging along. When he wakened, the castle towers were ahead.

He came instantly, fully awake. He stared ahead hungrily, sitting straight in the saddle. For some reason he had immense energy. Bothwell castle, even in the distance, was as magnificent as a glowing jewel. Its walls were of a deep reddish polished stone. The river here made a sweep around the pile, and its gardens extended in every direction, down to the river banks. Matthew was entering its gardens.

Flowering bush and fruit tree would, in summer, spice the air with fragrance. Above the trees twin towers rose, graceful. The castle's architecture was Gothic; its form, a quadrangle, one hundred feet wide and two hundred and thirty-four feet long.

The entrance toward which Matthew was going was to the north. Hidden from him was the celebrated Bothwell Bank, which sloped from the towers down to the river, and was laced with low, stone walls, secluded walks. Matthew entered the court.

Ivy covered the stone walls. A fountain played. The great flagstones were rosy pink and gray; he saw the beautiful doors to the chapel in the western wing. He reined in his horse.

The Hepburn had ridden almost to the stone steps, under the

shadow of a towering tree whose leafless branches thrust upward against the main wing. Then Matthew saw Mary.

He fetched a deep sigh, quite unknowing. Muffled in her furs, she had a filmy scarf tied around her throat and the ends of it fluttered in the December wind. Her face was touched by the cold lightly, her cheeks glowing, her lips red.

She was only about fifteen feet away. He suddenly was sure she had been waiting there for him. He was sure her eyes had searched each rider in the distance, until she had found him so near.

Matthew Craddock knew then that she loved him, regardless of what he had done. There could be no mistake. He looked back at her.

She had taken only one step toward him. She was carrying a familiar little muff, standing poised on the step as he, ahorse, met her eyes. The December afternoon was sweeter than spring.

Matthew smiled; she looked a little white suddenly, as though she feared greatly for him—feared, and would be too proud to tell even Jane. There had been no possible way to tell her he was safe. For all she had known, he had been killed the night of the battle. For the first time he resented fiercely being a servant—because he could not go to her and take her in his arms.

He was not aware at all that he was being addressed until Captain Scott, infuriated, lifted his riding crop and brought the handle down on Matthew's hands, as they loosely grasped the slackened reins.

The blow numbed his right wrist. He turned to look at Scott, real surprise on his face. Scott said, "Attend his lordship!"

Matthew muttered, "Aye, sir."

For the first time he realized that Jane stood on the bottom step. Beside her, tended by a groom, was one of the biggest and most splendid specimens of horseflesh Matthew had ever seen. It was a great black stallion, and it was restless. The Hepburn himself had ridden almost to the step where Jane stood, so that they were facing each other.

Matthew had no intention of allowing his temper to rise.

There was too much at stake now. Tonight, or this afternoon before dinner, he would try to see Mary. He paid no attention to Scott. He took the reins of the Hepburn's horse, but his eyes went past the Hepburn, even past Mary, to the black stallion. The first warning came immediately, when the black horse reared, front feet pawing the air, lips curled back from its teeth.

The Hepburn had dismounted; Matthew was holding the reins of his horse. But the other groom was not equal to holding the black horse. Matthew was nearest. He said to the Hepburn, "Take these!"

He flung them at the Hepburn, seized the bridle of the rearing horse, brought his hand down on its nose, twisted the reins tight, and pulled hard on the animal's head. Blood showed on the trembling horse's mouth. In the meantime three men had come running. The Hepburn's horse was being led away, hastily. The danger was over. Matthew surrendered the reins to the groom again.

Captain Scott said sulkily, "You cannot obey orders, can you?"

Matthew said, "I meant no disrespect."

Mary Gordon descended the two steps. "How are you, Matthew?" she said, and Matthew noted with delight that she did not look angrily at Scott; she dismissed him. "I hope you have enjoyed his lordship's service," she went on. "You look well."

"I am well, your ladyship." He could feel his heart beating fast. For a single breathless moment, when time halted the December day, he searched her face. "Your ladyship," he said softly, "you look well, too. I am happy—to see that."

It was over then, the few words they could exchange. Jane, who had torn her eyes from the Hepburn, spoke to him.

"What think you of that animal?" She pointed to the horse. The four of them stood close together.

"I think him magnificent, Lady Jane," Matthew said.

The Hepburn interrupted. The big doors were open. "Will you enter, madam?"

Matthew followed the three of them. In the hall the Hepburn sat down on the settle-seat, stretching out his legs. From this position, lounging back, he surveyed all three of them.

"My boots, fellow," he said. He watched Jane.

Matthew knelt on one knee. One of his hands was badly bruised across the knuckles, his right wrist was swollen. Mary, looking down at those hands drawing off the Hepburn's heavy boots, could keep silence no longer.

"What have you done to—" she began. Then, conscious of the pounding of her heart, she stopped short.

Matthew set one boot down. He started to take off the other.

"My south tower rooms are very comfortable, my lord," Jane said.

Matthew knew this was meant for him. He had finished his task. "Will that be all, m'lord?"

The Hepburn looked at him, his face sardonic. Matthew knew Jane's message had not escaped the Hepburn. Perhaps the game was over now.

It was a relief. Matthew reflected that that was what the Hepburn wanted him to feel. He summoned resistance; he was afraid he was more spent than he realized. He looked at Mary. It was possible he might drive a bargain with the Hepburn. And yet—the time was not ripe. England was very far away, and English armies were not marching. Matthew had only a scrap of paper to open the gates of Liddesdale, and he could not use that paper. Its only worth lay in its deep secrecy. Only Douglass and himself and Fleming and Henry Tudor knew of it. Except, for one other man: Lord Surrey, the finest commander England possessed.

Matthew faced the Hepburn, standing. He was a little unsteady, he knew. He heard, "Captain Scott is waiting."

Matthew nodded. He went out the big doors alone, where Scott still waited for him.

There were yet a great many men in the court. Their number quenched his last hopes, and brawny Scott was blocking his way. Scott wore an unpleasant grimace that was meant to be a smile. Without preamble, he said, "English!" Hatred was in the one word. "You're under arrest!"

So Matthew had read the Hepburn aright. The waiting was

over. Scott was swinging his whip, and Matthew let his pent-up anger free. With one hand he seized the whip, the other clenched into a fist, caught Scott under his ribs in the pit of his stomach. Matthew jerked the whip free of Scott's fingers, and brought the handle across Scott's face. A second blow stunned Scott; he swayed and crumpled. Matthew broke the whip over his leg and threw it down beside him.

This action had momentarily stunned the onlookers. It had taken Matthew only sixty seconds to fell Scott. But now he was seized by a man on either side of him. Three others helped Scott rise. The flurry of shouts and cries had brought the Hepburn to the big doors. Scott was on his feet, blood streaming down his face, unable to stand alone.

Matthew, between two men, bowed to the Hepburn. He grinned openly. The Hepburn started toward him, and then halted.

"Take him in at the side," Scott muttered.

These instructions seemed to be enough. Although this beautiful castle was primarily residence, not a fortress, it would have its complement of barred cells beneath the earth. Matthew descended two short flights to where rude torches burned. There were two heavy doors. One, barred and locked, led to the wine cellars, the other stood partially open to reveal a short corridor lighted by a single torch. A tiny guardroom, not eight feet square, contained two armed men, who looked at Scott in surprise.

Matthew was given the first cell. The door shut behind him. They had not used him violently and he had not resisted. His feet touched deep straw. He lay down on it, pillowing his head in his arms, and went to sleep.

26

JANE GORDON WAKENED EARLY ON THE MORNING OF her wedding day.

Around the south tower, the December wind moaned. Occasional flurries of snow blew against the windows.

This room was high in the tower. At its foot was Jane's morning room; on the next flight her servants slept; high above, reached by a tiny, thickly carpeted stair, was her bedroom.

It was paneled. Though the tower walls were more than eight feet thick, the paneling prevented any errant drafts. For greater comfort the Hepburn had installed a fireplace and chimney in every room, and every day an elderly man brought up sandalwood for the fires which burned constantly.

The window, which bowed around the southern side, was seven feet high, tiny-paned. Long curtains fell to the floor. But on fine days, when Jane could step out onto the little stone balcony, she could see to Glasgow. Beneath her windows stretched Bothwell Bank, where the famous gardens sloped down to the shining Clyde.

The whole castle was awake. Huge as it was, it was filled to overflowing: the stables could not accommodate all the horses, and the lesser nobility were sharing rooms, even beds.

James himself had arrived the afternoon before, in time for supper. It had been Jane's privilege not to appear for that meal, to allow the men to sup together.

Jane rolled over on her stomach. In only a few hours, less than four, she would be wed to the Hepburn. She had not dared to seek him out, to ask him about Matthew. Neither she nor Mary had seen Matthew. But certainly she would. She heard her door open quietly.

She buried her head in the soft pillow. More logs were being thrown on the fire; a man's tread went down the steps again, and two maids moved around the room. Jane heard, from below, the chattering voice of the French dressmaker she had brought from Edinburgh. A volley of hot French expletives betokened madame's excitability as she protested about the heat of the iron an underling was using.

"Non, non, nom du chien! You'll ruin eet!"

Jane sat up and pushed back her long hair. She laughed, and got out of bed. Her maid held out a warm mantle to cover her nakedness.

Jane pushed it away, and walked over to the fireplace, holding out one foot to the blaze. "I'll bathe, before. What time is't?"

"You have two hours, madam." The maid was excited. A wedding and feast on the fifth of December, with the feasting and fun of Christmas ahead, was more than one could ordinarily hope for. Not only that, but she had seen his Majesty close. She had seen him smile, nay, even laugh. He was dazzlingly handsome, Jamie Stuart. The little maid sighed from the very tips of her toes.

"Well, fetch the water," said Jane. "Art dreaming?"

"Aye, madam." She added, "I have seen the king."

"I'll slap some sense into you," said Jane.

Her wedding was set for ten. The wedding feast, for eleven. Jane herself had gone over the lists of foodstuffs and wine. The Hepburn had installed one of his kin, an elderly woman, to do that, but Jane had ignored her, and told her she was going to send her home after the wedding. Now Jane, in her mind, ran over the provisions, which had cost the Hepburn close to a thousand pounds. Jane Gordon would show his friends, even the king himself, that no hospitality could be more lavish than hers.

She frowned, remembering the list. Could she have forgotten anything? Three hundred quarters of wheat, for finest bread; three hundred tuns of ale, from the castle brewery; one hundred tuns of wine and a pipe of hippocras, good in winter, hot and strong and spiced; one hundred four oxen, six wild bulls, one thousand sheep, three hundred each porkers and calves; four hundred swans, two thousand geese, one thousand capons, and one hundred peacocks. In addition, stags, bucks and does, for roasting; one thousand five hundred hot pasties of venison; fish and oysters; thirteen thousand dishes of jelly; cold, baked tarts; hot and cold custards; sugared delicacies and wafers.

"Oh, and the wild fowl," said Jane aloud.

The candles to be used were purest wax. Not a rushlight, nor a stinking torch nor quarion would be lighted. Outside the fountain would flow wine. There were morris dances to entertain the guests and the villagers for whom there was feasting too. And as for Jane herself, the Hepburn might gaze with some astonishment at the bills from Edinburgh.

Jane's clothes had cost near two thousand pounds, not including jewelry, like the giant topaz clasp on one cape. She had ordered twelve dozen wine goblets from the silversmiths in Edinburgh, each one more than a foot tall, embossed in gold with the Hepburn lions. Her quick inventory of the castle had disclosed the need for more plate, more candelabra, and smaller platters for whole baked fish, table knives, and linen of all kinds.

Meantime fifteen minutes had gone by. Jane stepped into her wooden tub of hot water. It was in front of the fire and the maid pulled an ornamented screen back of it to shield her. From the tub, Jane gave orders.

The household master came dashing up to say that one of the minstrels was ill.

"Tell him that's impossible," came Jane's voice from behind the screen.

"Aye, madam."

"Impossible," repeated Jane. "He's to get well."

"The dancing girls are here." This was accompanied with a sigh of relief.

"A pity they didn't arrive last night, for the men."

The maids giggled. The dressmaker pushed the household master out of the room. Jane's dress was ready.

The maids looked long. Mary came up. "It's beautiful, Jane."

They couldn't talk much, in front of all these women. Mary pulled a stool over and looked into the flames. "Did you see the duke?"

"Aye," said Mary. "He is most kind, Jane."

Jane sighed. "He loves you."

"I know," said Mary. But her wedding was two months away. Perhaps tomorrow. Perhaps even today—but these were idle dreams, no matter how wonderful.

"Madam, it is nine o'clock!" a voice said.

Jane stepped out of the tub. The maids stripped the bed and were putting on fresh linen sheets, trimmed with lace. Jane was wrapped in a big towel.

When she was dry, a satin petticoat and a low-cut blouse, both white, went on her. She sat down in front of the table to have her hair brushed dry; it shone like the satin undergarments she wore. Her nails were polished; her powder brushed on, her eyebrows and eyelashes darkened just a little, her mouth reddened and her perfume dabbed on.

The clock struck the half hour. Jane stood up. Her dress was slipped over her head.

It was white velvet. Because of her rank, she was entitled to the snowiest of white ermine. More than a foot of the fur swirled at the bottom of the long gown that fitted tightly below her waist and then fell in soft folds of velvet. The sleeves were long, ornamented with bands of fur that partly covered her hands. The bodice was tight, off the shoulders in a square deep neck.

She wore only a pendant, a giant pearl that hung between her breasts. Her hair, unbound as tradition ordered, fell over her shoulders.

"I am ready," she said.

It was like a dream. For the first three flights of stairs the dressmaker came puffing behind, holding her train as the fur fanned it out behind her. Then she was alone. . . .

The chapel was ancient and beautiful. It was hushed. The morning sun, pale and wintry, filtered through the arched windows onto the altar. Beside the Hepburn, Jane knelt.

He had taken her hand. He repeated the vows with her. Jane fastened her eyes on the hand that held hers. His voice was calm and low and assured. What was he thinking?

It took so little time to be married. The priest was blessing them. Then the Hepburn took her lightly in his arms and kissed her, setting her back from him gently. Jane looked up at him; his face was intent and serious. Then he smiled. She put her arm in his, and they left the little chapel.

The dream continued. It didn't seem possible. Yet the dining hall was just as Jane had planned it. The center table was raised slightly, on a dais. Its long cloth fell to the floor. Its silver gleamed as it should. So did the silver on the other tables, which flanked the main one. Up on the balcony the minstrels played. The time had worked out, too. She and the Hepburn, standing side by side, had greeted the villagers outside, and waited while they drank a toast.

Back in the castle the feasting had begun. Jane had delighted her cook when she allowed him the privilege of serving the first dish to the king. The cook carried his great wooden spoon, the badge of his office. This morning he used it not only for stirring and tasting, but for errant blows at miscreants who had not kept the fires hot enough, or who weren't quick enough at turning the spits, or clever with the pastries.

The guests sat on only one side of the long tables, so that each diner had an unobstructed view of the oblong space in the center of the room.

The royal wine cup was filled and presented to James on bended knee. Then the other goblets were filled. A procession of servants began to bring in the food.

Between courses, Jane had arranged entertainments: a juggling act, a group of dancers from the village, and, with the sweets, a Belgian with trained dogs. The Hepburn was amused by them.

Then Jane had ordered in great casks of frozen cider. These

were rolled to the fireplace, where pokers were waiting. The pokers, redhot, were thrust deep into the barrels, and a white liquid was drained off. It was fiery, potent.

After that, the dancing girls. They were most scantily clad. Their specialty seemed to be walking on their hands, but they were lithe, graceful and incredibly competent in their backbends and acrobatics.

Jane had not eaten much, and drunk very little. The hours had passed. The food was served with such ceremony it took a great deal of time. The day had darkened, and the night was coming on quickly. The candles had been lighted for some time.

Jane said to the Hepburn, "I have provided hot, spiced wine to be served at daybreak. They will probably dance till dawn."

He nodded.

Jane motioned to the nearest steward. "Fetch the dancing girls again. His lordship wishes it."

The Hepburn looked at Jane and grinned. "I like them myself," she went on. "I'm going to see if I can walk on my hands, flip over backward and then stand up."

The Hepburn laughed.

"But I don't see why they walk so long on their hands."

The Hepburn said, "Why, to show off their legs." He lifted his cup and drank.

Jane was acutely conscious of him. Her white hand lay on the table alongside his. He was watching the dancing girls, amused.

"Did you ever sleep with one of them?" Jane asked.

"Madam," he said.

She gazed around the long tables. She was the Countess of Bothwell, now. No matter what, she was wed to the most powerful noble in Scotland. And yet—she glanced up at his face. She drew a long breath. She did not dare ask him about Matthew. But Eufemia Fleming could, if she wanted.

"I see your fine hand in Lady Fleming's absence," Jane said. "But I would have preferred her to come. Now—it is quite obvious why she is not here."

The Hepburn once more turned from the dancing girls to look at her. "That is enough," he said.

"Oh, is it? I warrant it's not!" But she didn't say anything further. She didn't hear the laughter and voices around her. She had done her job well, and she wondered suddenly whether she had done it to please him.

For seven months she had fought him, and every step of the way it had been fruitless. For seven months she had battled against his strength.

Today she became another of his possessions, like this castle. Today, tonight . . . her body felt lifeless. She closed her eyes for a moment and then opened them wide. He was leaning back, and she became aware that he was watching her, not the acrobatic dancers. She looked at him steadily, the wide shoulders so correctly covered with velvet, smooth over the heavy chest and arms. His face was tanned, even in winter, the mouth mobile and sensuous, the cheekbones high and the whole face stamped with a ruthless strength.

Yet the gray eyes were honest, and the smile, when it came, could be forthright and full of humor. The gray eyes watched her now, and she put her hand to her throat; the soft fur covered her white breast. She summoned courage.

"Even if I were a dancing girl, my lord," she said, idly, "I should refuse you."

His expression changed. He said lazily, "Would you?" He raised his hand and pushed the long hair back from her face. "Refusal would avail you little."

It had availed nothing so far. The strong finger lay lightly against the curve of her jaw. The palms of her hands were damp. The whole room spun around. "I shall never plead with you," she whispered. But she couldn't stay here any longer. "How long?" she asked. "How long will you give me?"

He said impassively, "An hour, madam. It should be enough."

"Aye, m'lord." She hardly realized she had said the words. She stood up, he stood too, and a sudden cry went up as everyone saw her. James raised his cup for a last toast to the bride.

Jane didn't think she could stand that long. The Hepburn

put his arm around her. She managed a brilliant smile, a curtsey to James. Then she was out the big doors, and Mary was at her side. Next Maggie Drummond came flying out the doors, as though the devil were at her heels; she came to a stop, then she seized Jane's hand.

"Run!"

Amazingly, Jane could. With a swoop of hand they gathered up their long skirts and fled up the stairway. At the curve Jane paused, looking down at the men who pursued them out of the hall. With her long hair streaming behind her, she ran up the rest of the way to the tower rooms.

Once there she stood in the center of the round, warm room and looked helplessly at Mary and Maggie Drummond. Maggie smiled. Mary said to one of the maids, "Fetch her ladyship a cup of frozen cider." She turned to Maggie. "It's strong as the whiskey George makes."

"I'll unhook you," said Maggie. "Turn around."

Jane did. She was divested of the long gown. More of the women came running up the little stairway. Jane downed the fiery liquid; it warmed her comfortingly.

Then the women saw the gown for her wedding night. It lay across the bed. They looked at it, and then at Jane. Maggie held it up.

"It is copied from the wardrobe of the mistress of the King of France," the French dressmaker said.

"Put it on," said Maggie.

The maids took Jane's satin petticoat and blouse. The thin, black silk slipped over Jane's head. Maggie tied the narrow ends of ribbons that held it at the waist and up to the deep V of the neck. In the long mirror Jane caught sight of herself.

"It has a mantle," she said.

Mary put it on her. This had sleeves but again tied at the waist with narrow silk ribbons. It fell straight against her body, but when she walked the women could see it was pleated with a hundred tiny pleats that spread out and fell against her legs with each step.

Jane paced to the window and back again. The maids were scurrying around, taking away Jane's gown and petticoats.

There were four pillows on the deep feather bed, each with an embroidered pillow case. They were plumped up. The sheets were turned down and two long-handled warming pans tucked under them. Two maids struggled with logs for the fire, for no men were allowed in the room yet.

Jane's laver was filled with warm water, and she bathed. Her hair was brushed. Maggie Drummond came close to her.

"Jane," she said low, "you asked me, three weeks ago, a favor. I have not—I don't believe there is any use—protesting."

"Thank you," said Jane. "Say nothing to Mary."

Maggie nodded. "I am sorry."

Maggie moved away. Heedless of the others, Jane looked at herself in the glass, pushing her hair back from her face and framing it in her long fingers. Her mouth, wide and sulky, turned down at the corners; her hair, almost straight, was fine, thick and heavy. Her eyes matched it in tawniness.

Maggie Drummond had said nothing about Eufemia. Of course she hadn't. Yet she knew, well enough. Probably Eufemia got what she wanted from the Hepburn; Eufemia was as luscious as a ripe fruit. Jane made a face at herself in the glass.

"You dried fruit, you," she said to herself. The corners of her mouth lifted, and she laughed at herself. "Bring me some more of that liquor," she said.

She had finished drinking when there was the sound of heavy feet on the stairway.

The little door burst open. A dozen pairs of hands pushed the Hepburn into the room. He was laughing, and James was doubled over with a quip of Grey's. James gave the Hepburn a final shove.

"He is partially undressed, madam," James announced. They had stripped the Hepburn of his doublet and shirt, and he was breathing hard with his exertions; his bare chest rose and fell as he tried to catch his breath.

James looked into the bed. "Empty, by God," he said. His eyes found Jane; then he glanced at the Hepburn and back to Jane.

"Well, madam," he drawled. " 'Tis the custom to await your lord there." He pointed to the bed.

"The Stuarts set fashions, your Grace." Jane gave him a little curtsey.

James raised one eyebrow and chuckled. "However, madam," his voice became soft and slurred, "it is difficult to find a new fashion for a wedding night."

Grey and young Home were both a little drunk. They measured Jane appraisingly.

"I'm in mourning for half the women in the Border, Grey," Jane said, answering his look.

The Hepburn was beside Jane. He put his arm around her, and drew her to his side. He grinned at James. "Goodnight, your Grace."

"His lordship grows impatient," James said.

Jane wanted to turn her head into the Hepburn's shoulder. But she looked back at the men.

James was very amused. But he was leaving. "Get hence, lads," he ordered. He took Maggie's arm. "Goodnight," he said.

The door closed. The room, which had been very full, was empty. The Hepburn dropped his arm from Jane and walked over and locked the door.

"I don't trust Grey," he said, and smiled a little. "Since I've been so abstinent tonight, mistress, with hardly a drop of wine, you might pour me some and bring it to me."

She stiffened. But she poured the wine with unsteady fingers. She set it beside him on a low table.

"Very comfortable arrangement, this," he said, indicating the table. "You didn't want to bring me a little wine, did you? I gather you brought it either because I have already paid three thousand pounds for you, or else because I knocked you down once. Which prompted you, madam?"

Jane's wide mouth drew down.

He took a sip of wine. "I'd like an answer, or I shall be forced to my conclusions."

She faced him. "The money!"

"You have smiled at me seldom, and you have never called me by my name. Would it be so difficult?"

Jane said stiffly, "No, my lord."

He shrugged. "Would it cost me ten pounds to hear you say it? If it should happen that you cannot have children, I would be truly fleeced."

"What did you expect?" Jane asked insolently.

"Exactly what I have," he said. He took the jeweled dagger from his belt and laid it on the table.

Jane pointed at it. "Is that customary?"

"I forgot it, madam. I must have been thinking of you. It's been a long time since I've had to sleep with a weapon handy. And I think it's about time to go to bed."

Jane's eyes were fastened on him. "I warrant so," she said, trying to match his assurance. Then her eyelids fell, and she turned away.

"It's overtime," he said lazily, watching her. He got to his feet. Slowly the space between them narrowed. He stood looking down at her.

Little ribbons held her gown at the waist. He could see the rapid beating of her heart.

"That's very complicated," he said. His fingers went to the ribbon ties.

"No!" cried Jane. She caught at the brown hands.

"Remove it for me, then," he said.

"Is that what you prefer?" she asked, passionately, holding tight to his hands.

He countered with another question. "Why did you wear it?"

She didn't answer. He swung her around.

"Look at yourself, madam." His voice was slow. "It was designed for one reason, of which you're quite well aware. Remove it for me."

Jane's fingers untied the three ribbons. She slipped the gown off one shoulder and then, because it gave her an excuse to move away, she took it off entirely and went over to the chair to lay it down. Slowly she turned to face him.

Her white body gleamed through the thin black silk. Suddenly she said, "Have me, then! I wait!"

Tall as she was, he towered over her. He put one arm around her; her whole body tensed. The first kiss told her what she could expect.

She tried to move her head. She couldn't. She resisted the kiss, but he forced compliance. He lifted her and carried her over to the bed.

He laid her down, and for a moment stood looking down at her, her hair across the white pillow. She put her arm over her eyes. She felt his hands on the single tie at her waist.

He lay down beside her. He took her arm and put it around his neck. He waited no longer.

"But I don't love you," she said desperately. "And I never will!"

27

THE LION WAS THE MOST POPULAR TAVERN AND HOSTELry in Leith.

On the waterfront, it served good food and offered comfortable accommodations to the weary sea voyagers.

This afternoon, the twenty-seventh of January, its common-room was crowded because a small fleet of Spanish ships had put in that morning, bringing with them travelers from Venice. As was usual in the Lion, different tongues vied with one another.

The door opened once more, letting in a blast of north air off the Firth. A man, well protected against the cold by a brilliant red, lambskin-lined cloak, stood on the threshold of the room.

The sailors looked up. Scottish voices were stilled. The babble of Spanish ceased.

"You may show me to Captain Knox's room," the newcomer was heard to say. Then he was gone. But in that moment one of the barmaids had spilled ale all over a bearded Spaniard. When he remonstrated, she whispered, "That was the king!"

The man next nodded. "Ye can never tell when ye'll see Jamie Stuart." He grinned. "Like as not he'll be on deck next you of a sudden."

Upstairs, James flung back his cloak, spoke to Knox, and looked carefully at the man who was neatly trussed and lying on the floor. James bent over and lifted one eyelid gently. Then, satisfied his prisoner was completely unconscious, he said to Knox, "The messages for de Ayala?"

Knox picked up from the table and handed to James a sealed oilskin packet. James broke the first seal, and then the second. He walked over to the window and sat down on a rude bench. He read rapidly.

His face, which had been somber, gradually broke into a sardonic smile. He reread some of the flowing Spanish, storing it in his mind. The Spanish had sent, two months ago, one of their greatest ambassadors, Senor de Ayala. These latest instructions to de Ayala had been neatly intercepted. James rose, and went over to the table. From his pocket he took an imitation of the Spanish seal. It was a matter of moments before the despatches looked as they had before James had read them. James straightened up; the seal would be dry in a minute. He looked at the man on the floor.

"Replace these on him." A money bag also had lain on the table. James picked this up. "Put him in an alley. He will seem to have been waylaid and robbed. Undoubtedly there will be a man arrested tonight for murder, or some foul crime, with this fleet in. Get from him a confession of robbing the Spaniard, and hang him. The Scottish crown will repay this." James weighed the bag. He smiled at Knox. "We shall also apologize profusely for this occurrence."

Outside again, James mounted his horse, tossed a shilling to the boy who had held the reins, and moved slowly down toward the shipyards. By the time he had inspected the newest ship he was building, the three ships that he could see putting into Leith would be docked, and the Hepburn would have returned to Scotland.

James spent more than an hour inspecting the "Great Michael." She was going to be the biggest ship of war in the world. She boasted a keel of two hundred and forty feet. She carried thirty-five heavy guns, and three hundred small shot and culverins. Her complement would be three hundred seamen, a hundred and twenty gunners, and a thousand soldiers. There was nothing so important now, in this age, as power on the seas.

There were smaller ships building also. Nothing made James happier than the activity in the shipyards. He left them at three, and met the Hepburn, with no ceremony at all, as the Hepburn stepped for the first time in seven weeks onto his native soil.

A winter voyage was always hazardous. There was no doubt that James was glad to see the Hepburn. It had been a necessary voyage—to France.

Leith was but a few miles from Edinburgh. Riding side by side into the capital, the Hepburn gave his news to James. He smiled as he did.

"Charles VIII of France is offering your Grace 100,000 crowns for the person of the Duke of York."

James laughed. He was pleased.

"I took the liberty of refusing the offer of his Royal Highness, Charles VIII. With pardonable pride, I reminded his Grace that your Majesty had seen York's value first, and that York belonged to you."

James said, "Meantime, the latest instructions to de Ayala were intercepted by Knox. It seems that the Spanish are worried about York. Briefly, they want England unhampered—they want peace between England and Scotland, so that Henry Tudor can keep the French busy. The Spanish do *not* wish the French to be free to continue their meddling with Italy."

The Hepburn nodded. Charles of France had made it quite plain he wanted the Duke of York in order to hold a club over

England, so the French could be free to meddle in Italy, where they had been fighting for some time.

"Venice is interested for the same reason," James said. "Their envoys arrived early this morning. They had been off the coast for a while, with bad weather."

"The weather has been foul," the Hepburn remarked.

"The Venetians want England free to fight France. Charles VIII has very nearly bottled himself up on the Italian peninsula by the very princes that invited him to help them conquer Naples. The crux of the whole situation is so very simple. But the French alliance, between us and France, is most advantageous to us. We embroil England; and France shall embroil Italy. This the Spanish want to prevent. They want England free to fight France. De Ayala has been instructed to offer me the hand of Catharine of Aragon, as a purchase of peace between us and England."

The Hepburn frowned; he was thinking of the Tudor princess.

"It is not a genuine offer," said James. "Catharine is intended for an English marriage. The English and Spanish are suddenly so friendly it gives one pause." He made a grimace. "I give them a few years before they are at each other's throats again."

They were entering the Netherbow port. Edinburgh had closed its gray stone fronts around them. But they had time merely to skim the surface of the intrigues that were boiling in Europe, and the outcome of the possession of the Duke of York.

"We shall sup privately, my lord," James said. "We can speak further this evening. You had no intention of returning to Bothwell tonight?"

"No, your Grace."

It was almost five. James had been absent from Edinburgh for four days. As always, upon his return, he sought out Maggie Drummond.

She was alone. He walked into her chambers unannounced. She gave a little cry; she had been lying on her favorite daybed.

"M'lord!" she said as she rose.

Four days ago, when he had departed, he had done so alone. She held out her hands to him.

He came over to her and kissed her. "You should not worry." He held her off and looked at her. She looked extremely beautiful to him; her figure was voluptuous. "My absence seems to have done you good, madam."

To his surprise she flushed.

James looked from her face to her portrait over the mantel. It could not do her justice, he decided. "Mayhap it's my lovemaking that accounts for your beauty." He patted her backside.

"You flatter yourself, my lord."

"Have you been ill, sweetheart?" he asked. She was moving away from him, toward the daybed. He had sunk down into his favorite leather chair. Maggie leaned against her pillows and pulled a silken robe over her knees.

"I'm going to have a child, m'lord," she said simply. Lying there, she watched his face, trying to read his expression, trying to think herself all the thoughts that must be plaguing him.

Had they been—had he been commoner instead of king, he would marry her. She knew that. But now—

He didn't rise and come toward her. Whatever thoughts he had of tenderness, of pleasure, of the child, none showed in his actions. He sat quietly, his dark eyes fixed on her.

"When do you expect your child?" he asked.

"Is that important?" Maggie said, her face a little pale.

"Very," he answered.

"In August, then, as I reckon."

"Why didn't you tell me before!"

"I saw no need." She moved restlessly, pushing aside the silken cover.

"I shall judge the need, madam."

Maggie knew that the answer to her own question had been answered. He was king first.

"This raises a problem," he said.

"The wee one doesn't know that," Maggie said, "even if he is part Stuart."

James smiled, and Maggie suddenly rose, one pillow and the cover sliding onto the polished floor. She sat down at James's feet, leaning back against his knees, taking one brown hand in both of hers.

She did not need the physical contact to reassure her. She sat there quietly, holding his hand, taking pleasure in his nearness. Neither did she think much about the child she carried. It was this man, this king, who was her life.

Looking up at his face, dark and lean, she sensed his troubledness, and knew that the English war would occupy all his thoughts. She rose and went over to the couch. Against the dull green satin, with her skirt making a splash of color and the cover lying on the floor in a pool of silk, she presented a picture of lovely disorder.

James rose and went over to Maggie; she moved so that he could sit beside her.

"My lord," she said softly, "in a few days Mary Gordon will wed with York."

"Aye," said James. Mary was to be wed at Bothwell, and James found himself looking forward with pleasure to a wedding day and the prospect of a few hours of vacation and pleasure.

Maggie put her arms around him. "Does she—must she—wed with him?"

The offer of Charles VIII of one hundred thousand crowns for York again made James realize the duke's importance as a political pawn. "For God's sake," he said impatiently.

"I do not like him," Maggie said quickly. "He is vain, and weak."

"All men are vain, and he is most kind and loving with Mary," James contradicted.

"M'lord, if a lion walked in that door, what would you do?" Maggie sat up straight, drawing her legs under her.

"I'd be rather surprised, nay, astonished."

"One might get loose," said Maggie seriously. "And if it did, and we were here, if any woman were here with you, you would draw your dagger and put yourself between the danger and the lass. But he'd run out that door!" Maggie pointed.

James sighed. "I cannot possibly stop the wedding. It would give away my real feeling about York. Politically I cannot do that. We must support him openly, and to the extent to which he has previously been supported by us."

Maggie stayed motionless a minute, sitting there with her legs curled up under her. "Promise me," she began, when she stopped. She had been on the verge of asking him not to let harm come to Mary, when she realized that he might have to break such a promise and then be plagued with his own guilt.

"Loosen the laces, if you please, my lord."

He did so, rather clumsily. Maggie sighed with pleasure at being freed. She leaned back again, the snow-white cones of her breasts swelling against the loose dress.

"You are beautiful," James said.

"I am full of you."

Her half-revealed body was mysterious and fruitful. He drew the pillows from under her head. The couch was wide, and he stretched out beside her, seeking peace.

28

JANE GORDON STOOD ON THE BROAD STONE STEP IN THE court at Bothwell castle. It was four o'clock on the afternoon of January thirtieth. For the first time since her marriage, the Hepburn was riding into his own castle gates. Seven weeks had passed since Jane had seen him. More than seven weeks. He came to a stop right before her.

"Welcome home, m'lord," she said.

She did not remember later what he said in reply. It was a polite answer. But at the sound of his voice, and his gray eyes on her, she felt the warm blood rising to her cheeks. Yet she also felt cold, for it was now clear that what she had grown to believe during the long, long absence must be true. Jane did not need to look at the face of the woman who rode beside him, in her gray velvet and squirrel furs, to know who she was.

"Welcome to Bothwell, Lady Fleming," she said.

"M'lord returned to Edinburgh only last night," Eufemia said. "He most kindly offered to escort me here today."

"Since I was coming anyway," the Hepburn cut in. He jumped down beside Jane.

"It makes me so happy to know you had company, such charming company, m'lord."

He said, "I've been in France! Not—"

"I know, my lord. We have so many visitors, here."

The Hepburn went over and lifted Eufemia from her horse. Jane entered the doors first. In the hall she swung around and regarded Eufemia.

"You're so dusty." She smiled sweetly. "I'll put you in the west wing, Lady Fleming. His lordship's chambers are near. He will be glad to show you."

She gazed up at the Hepburn with her taunting smile. Then she turned on her heel and went down the long hall. She did not look back.

The Hepburn's red head was bent over the accounts. The inkpots were full; the quills were plentiful. Heavy arras hung over the long windows; it was new; she must have just bought it.

Dinner had been marvelous—with great platters of roasted oysters and shrimp boiled in the shell. When he had commented, Jane had replied, "We have too great a tendency to use too much spice when it's not needed."

She was different. He lifted his eyes from the accounts. A new orchard wanted planting; the old stumps would have to be ripped out. The roof of a church in a near village needed repairing. There were so many things. The vast estates he held required constant supervision; not everything, by a half even, could be left to the bailiffs. Tomorrow he must ride out and systematically go over all this long list of needs, and decide which were most important. The church would have to be re-roofed; he wouldn't have to look at that. But some of the others—

He swore, suddenly. His secretary glanced up in surprise. And there was a knock on the door.

"Open it," he snapped, to the bewildered secretary.

The man crossed the room on hasty feet. Mary Gordon stood in the doorway.

"M'lord. Might I speak with you?"

"Certainly," the Hepburn said.

"Alone," said Mary Gordon, as she came into the room.

The Hepburn motioned the secretary out. "That will be all for tonight," he said. It must be late. Mary confirmed this by saying, "I didn't want to disturb you so late, my lord. But the truth of it is I have waited now a long time, very long, longer than I could bear."

He didn't know quite what she meant. He took her hand and led her to the seats which ran almost into the big fire-place. They had high backs; within the alcove it was warm.

"Sit down," he said. He sat opposite. She was intent, and he guessed she had no time for inconsequential preliminaries. "Now, proceed."

She looked beautiful. The firelight played on her face. "I want to know the truth from you." She said it quickly. "What happened to our secretary? What happened to Matthew?"

His gray eyes were a trifle surprised. He frowned a little. But he could tell her the truth, since she asked for it, since it had now been determined exactly what the policy toward England would be.

"Matthew was an English spy," he said baldly.

She didn't say she didn't believe it. But the truth had stunned her; he saw that plainly. "An English spy?" she echoed, as if trying to encompass it.

"Aye, mistress. A knight from Dorsetshire. Sir William Henry Matthew Craddock. He was with Henry Tudor in exile. He preceded Henry to England, as an advance agent. In fact he participated in Henry's first abortive attempt to seize the Crown, was captured and escaped, God knows how, for few men escaped from Richard III. That's all we know."

Her eyes were almost purple. Then her lashes fell. Again he frowned. He did not understand. She was stunned, but there was a kind of pride in hearing what he had said.

"An enviable record, in its way," the Hepburn said, to see if she would respond. "A very clever man. No doubt he deceived you well."

She looked squarely at him. "I don't know, m'lord." There was the faintest hint of a smile. The Hepburn didn't know that Mary was thinking it was no wonder she had depended on Matthew. She still did, no matter where he was. Had he escaped? Now a sudden terrible fear smote her. She didn't dare show it.

"Where is he, then?"

The Hepburn said, "Imprisoned below."

"All this time?" The question was whispered. She caught her lip in her white teeth. But he was alive. And near. She had to get out of this room. She was afraid. But if it were suspected she loved Matthew—she shivered and spoke.

"I am again sorry I disturbed you. But I wanted to know. You can understand, m'lord, he was most kind, and served our interests well." She rose.

He went to the door with her. He could not resist a question. "Did Jane send you?"

Mary said, surprised, "No. No, certainly not. I ask for myself." She extended her hand, and he kissed it.

"Goodnight, my lord."

She was gone. The Hepburn went back to the fire, regarded it for a moment, and then strode over to his table. He opened the drawer, drew out something he had put in it two hours ago, and sat there with the carved box in his hands.

In three minutes there was another knock.

"Come in." He looked up, a little curious. When he saw who it was, he rose.

"Jane," he said involuntarily.

"Aye, m'lord."

She was wearing the same gown she had worn at dinner. It was graceful; her train swept behind her and she looked like a queen. In her arms she carried, as she would have a baby, what looked to the Hepburn like white linen. A sheet, he thought. He wondered vaguely why she was bringing it.

She came to a stop in front of his table. "Please sit down," she said.

"You sit, madam." He seemed awkward.

"No," said Jane. "I would prefer to stand. A long time ago, my lord, you will probably not remember—'twas in the chapel at Scone, I said I would never ask a favor. You replied I would break that bargain."

He said curtly, "I remember. I shouldn't have said it. I apologize."

"No! You were right." She stopped. On his table she lay the linen, which he had not even glanced at since he had first noticed it in her arms. "I brought you a small gift. I come to you a suppliant. For two favors."

He looked down at the pile of shirts she had laid before him. They were carefully folded and embroidered with his initial. He said low, "Why, madam, I thank you very much."

Across the table their eyes met, and Jane had the wildest desire to cry. She blinked rapidly. He was saying, hesitantly, "I brought you a gift from Paris."

He tendered a carved box. She took it, their hands touched. Jane opened the lid, slowly.

"I've never seen anything so beautiful," she said wonderingly. She touched the gleaming collar of emeralds with one finger.

"I wanted you to wear it at Mary's wedding," he said.

"Oh," said Jane.

He looked at her steadily. For the first time he asked her honestly what she was thinking. "Why do you say 'oh' like that? You sound displeased."

Jane Gordon answered, honestly too. "Because it sounds as though you were showing that you were—that I was—I don't know what I mean!" she cried suddenly.

"I don't think you do either. But what you are trying to say is this. That 'tis only my male vanity which prompts me to give you a rather lovely piece of jewelry. But in that, madam, am I Lord Bothwell, the villainous rogue, or am I just like any other man?"

"You are not like any other man," Jane said definitely.

At this he smiled a little. "I fear I am." He sighed. He tapped his fingers on the table. "What favors do you wish from me?"

"Sit down, my lord," said Jane.

He shook his head. "I've a notion I must hear this standing."

"I want a man's life from you," she said.

He drew a long breath. He kept his calm. "I cannot give it. Unless—" He paused. "You are speaking of the man you call Matthew. Sir Matthew Craddock. I might be able to give you his life if he tells me what I want to know, and even then—" He shrugged. "You said you had two favors. What's the other?"

Jane cried, "I want you to stop Mary's wedding!"

Again he shook his head wearily. "You could not ask for anything I could give you, could you? Not a jewel, or a title for someone, or an appointment for one of your kin—" He lifted his hands. "Madam, it is completely impossible to stop Mistress Gordon's wedding. Impossible. Why"—and again he paused, and regarded her long—"why in the name of God didn't you ask me this ten weeks ago?"

Jane's answer came steadily. "Because it took me a long time, and I steeled myself, to ask you for anything!"

Her breathing was quick. Across the table she faced him squarely.

"Well, now it's too late." His voice was curt.

"I disagree," she cried. "I disagree completely!"

He brought his hand down on the table. "Neither I, nor anyone else, can stop that marriage Our whole policy would he invalidated if it were stopped!"

"I'm not speaking of the wedding!"

The Hepburn found himself breathing faster too. "I thought you would return to Craddock!"

"A man's life is more important than Mary's maidenhood!"

"Is it?" He felt the anger beating within him.

"Aye! She'll find love. I hope to God she does. It doesn't matter so much whom she marries. But—"

He interrupted. "Your philosophy is simple indeed. I noticed you were completely unamazed when I spoke Craddock's name. Did you dream that would escape me, madam?"

She remembered. She had given herself away. A few moments ago when he had spoken Matthew's name, and she had evinced no surprise.

"I knew his name," she said.

"I've no doubt you did."

Jane cried, "What have you done to him? What? You—" She broke off. There was no need to ask exactly where Matthew was; she could guess, and she was completely helpless to aid him even though he was so near. The Hepburn was calm, suddenly, sitting in a chair now, not looking up at her at all, but looking down at the writing in front of him. Jane backed away.

But she must ask one more question. "Will he die?"

"Probably. Almost certainly." He gave her only a glance.

"You may keep your gift. I shall never wear it." She was at the door.

"Come here and take it!" His voice snapped across the room at her. She stood still, not moving. "You will wear it," he continued, lower. "I want to see it, around your neck." He did look up to survey her. "Perhaps to satisfy my vanity, perhaps as a badge of ownership. Tomorrow James comes. I want you in your most ravishing gown. Something suitable for the emeralds. Have you any such?"

"I don't know," she said, almost in a whisper. "But I won't—"

"You will," he said. "You will, or I'll have Sir Matthew beaten."

She moved slowly toward his table. Her white hand reached for the carved box. His head was bent over the papers; she saw only the angle of his jaw. Fierce rage gripped her. She wanted to hurl the box at the red head. With an effort of will, she kept her hand clenched on it.

"He has done nothing," she whispered. "Don't kill him. M'lord, have mercy!"

He looked up. Bitter merciless anger was what she saw. She turned the box in her fingers. The door closed after her.

The Hepburn sat for only a moment. Then he got to his feet with a suddenness that crashed his chair over backwards.

He turned back to the table and poured himself a big cup of amber-colored liquor. Made illegally, it was smoky and powerful. He poured a second cup of it, and went over by the fire, nursing the clear whiskey between his hands. When he finished it, he set down the cup and made his way to his own quarters.

He changed to a loose coat and a pair of house slippers. After standing, irresolute, he flung himself out the door and down the hall. He entered a near-by room without knocking. Eufemia was sitting before her mirror, readying herself for bed.

29

MARY GORDON, SILENT AS A WRAITH, SLIPPED DOWN the last flight of twisting stairs. She knocked softly on the big barred door.

After a moment it was opened. By torchlight she saw the startled face of a guard.

"I must enter," she said imperiously. She proffered a gold coin that winked in the light.

The guard stepped away from the door. He took the money with a quick furtive gesture. He knew instantly whom she had come to see.

"Down here," he whispered. He shut the door carefully and bolted it again, first looking up the narrow stairs to be sure they had been unobserved. He hastened ahead of her down the corridor.

A few feet away, lying on his straw, Matthew Craddock heard the approaching footsteps. Instantly he leaped to his feet. He stood by his door, hands hooked around the heavy bars. Accustomed to the half dark, he could see like a cat. What he saw shocked him into a muttered oath. It was not possible.

Mary picked up her skirts and ran toward him. "Matthew!" His name burst from her lips, low, yet compelling. She stood before him, face upturned to his, through the bars. He tore his eyes from her. He growled, to the guard, "Breathe a word of this and her ladyship will have you flogged!"

"Aye." The guard backed up. He was ten feet away. Matthew, hands clenched tight around the bars, kept his fierce frown.

"You should not have come here! You should know better! A good deal better."

Mary touched his fingers with one hand. "Should I, Matthew?"

"You may stay only a moment. It is too dangerous!"

"No, no," she contradicted. Then she cried, "I had to see you!"

Both of her hands were clasped over his. With a movement of his wrists, he took her hands in his. He was conscious now of his appearance; he was unshaven, dirty, a captive in this mean place, a political captive that the Hepburn had not yet acknowledged. Yet he was Matthew Craddock, and there was no need any more for subterfuge.

"My darling," he said softly, "somehow you understood long before you knew. Have you been afraid for me? There is no need."

She cried low, "I cannot aid you."

He smiled reassuringly. All the days had been swept away now, and it was as though they were talking in those lost minutes right after he had first confessed his love.

"I came to help you escape."

"Great God above," he said grimly, "there is no hope of that yet. Oh, sweetheart, it is good that you are here."

Mary's eyes were on the heavy locks. The guard wore the keys on his belt. Eyes wide, she whispered, very low, "How could I get the keys from him?"

Matthew said, "You could not, possibly." He crushed her fingers in his.

"Matthew," she said. Then she stopped. But she must tell him what would be fact tomorrow. And here too there was no escape. She said, "I am to be wed ten hours hence. In the morning."

There was silence. The grip of his hands intensified. "I'll kill him," Matthew said matter-of-factly.

"Oh no," she breathed. "But I want you to know that whatever happens, I love you. I can never marry you—that can never happen but—"

Matthew Craddock, his face bitterly grim, repeated, "I shall kill him." He dropped her hands and paced across his cell. Then he swung back to her. His words rushed out. "Listen! As soon as I can, as soon as I am free, I shall find him. Then I'll have no mercy." He towered over her, looming behind the bars like an angry beast. He took her hands again. His grip was still hard but his voice was more gentle.

"Sweetheart," he said urgently, "is there nothing you can do?"

"There is nothing to do," she said. "You do not understand." She knew that was true. He did not understand that what she was really saying was good-bye. By this time tomorrow she would be wed to another man, and be pledged to him forever, while she lived. "Matthew, I do not love him. I love you. But at least I am here with you. At least we are together for a little while." Bright tears stood in her eyes.

He could get only his hands through the bars. He stroked her head and the side of her face. "I will get free. I promise you. I vow it."

She could say nothing. Suppose she did run away from the impending marriage. Then there would be no one to speak for

Matthew when he needed help. There might be a trial. He said, "Wait for me! I shall not be long."

She clung to his hands. "You must think of me no longer, Matthew."

"What? That whoreson traitor. And I immured like a whipped cur. Jesus God, how can you love me?"

"I cannot help it, sir." She touched the tip of his nose.

"Forgive me," he muttered.

"I love you, and you growl at me." She smiled. In this darkened cell she could see the light in his blue eyes. "I am happy," she said gravely, "because this is true, and no one can ever—touch me, *really* touch me when this is true."

"But I shall be free," he repeated strongly. "Never forget it. In the days to come, be sure that one day I shall be there, with you." He stopped. He had heard the footsteps of the guard. "There is no more time now. But remember that each day that passes will bring me closer to you."

"Matthew," she cried.

"Good-bye, my darling."

"Good-bye." She must go. She turned slowly, feeling her hands leave his. The guard was upon them.

Mary walked away. She remembered to smile at the guard as he let her out. She was out on the steps again. She was leaving Matthew. Step by step she was leaving him, and hours and days and months would elapse before she would ever see him again, and in the meantime, there was nothing to do save one thing. That was to please James Stuart, and to marry as he wished.

30

STRIPPED TO THE WAIST, AND FLANKED BY TWO MEN, Matthew stood in Hepburn's study. His eyes, unaccustomed to light, were half closed for protection against even the late afternoon grayness.

The Hepburn was leaning back on the fireplace seat while the flames roared up the chimney. Matthew had not been able to look at the fire at all. The Hepburn seemed to have been asleep. Matthew did not wonder at this, since even he had caught the noise of gaiety that had continued until dawn. Matthew knew that Mary Gordon had been married the day before.

He was standing only a few feet away from the Hepburn. One of the men had taken off his shirt and livery. He bore the Hepburn's brief scrutiny. The Hepburn looked only at his left shoulder; the scar was very plain.

The Hepburn said, curtly, "Dress."

Matthew did, with a grimace of distaste. He took time because he needed time; he was beginning to see more clearly. The two men were waved out of the room by the Hepburn, who settled back against the seat once more. Matthew finished buckling his belt. Then he raised his eyes and looked steadily at the Hepburn.

The Hepburn was immaculately dressed. Richly dressed. He wore no jewelry, but contented himself with a gold-hilted, jeweled dagger. He was freshly shaven. Matthew felt the contrast to himself. He was wearing the same clothes in which he had been imprisoned; he was unshaven, for he had been allowed water only for his face and hands.

The Hepburn said, mockingly, "Sir Matthew Craddock?"

"Aye, m'lord," said Matthew. He bowed.

"You may sit."

"I prefer to stand." Matthew took a turn around the room. He came back to the fireplace, knowing the Hepburn's eyes had never left him. His eyes were performing their function well now, well enough, he thought. He pushed aside the image of Mary Gordon: there was no use asking a question he knew would be answered affirmatively. Mary was wed to Warbeck. And Matthew, who had escaped from Richard III, continued to cudgel his wits, as indeed he had for eight weeks. Matthew knew his one advantage clearly: the Hepburn's badly controlled temper. It was being held on short rein even now. Matthew tried to plumb the reason for it.

Matthew sank down into a leather chair, facing the fireplace, legs stretched out in front of him.

"Proceed, my lord," he said lazily.

The Hepburn frowned. Matthew rubbed his hand over his bearded chin, his lids lowered over his blue eyes.

The Hepburn was about ten feet away. He was leaning sideways against the fireplace seat, so that he faced Matthew, his back to the chimney. To the left of his big hand, which hung over the seat, rested the blackened heavy iron poker. Matthew felt every nerve in his body tingling. He forced himself to relax. The weapon he wanted was twelve feet away, with the Hepburn between.

"Proceed," repeated Matthew, examining his thumb. He yawned.

The Hepburn's voice cut sharply across to Matthew. "There's no reason why I should not hang you, sir, except that I want information from you."

Matthew opened his eyes. "I have little or none."

The Hepburn rose. "Tomorrow I am sending you to Edinburgh."

The single sentence gave Matthew to understand that he was now to be a political prisoner. It must mean that James Stuart had decided on a course of action, of necessity one that was hostile to England.

"I cannot say that I've enjoyed your hospitality," Matthew offered.

"Edinburgh may not be pleasant," said the Hepburn. "Why don't you tell me now what I wish to know?"

The black poker was behind the Hepburn. Matthew still didn't move.

"Are you threatening me with torment?" he asked directly.

"Aye," said the Hepburn.

"The role seems to suit you," Matthew said. He rose too. But he knew that what he said was not true. He didn't need to bait the Hepburn. The Hepburn wanted nothing more than to get his hands on Matthew's throat. Matthew didn't even try to analyze the reason. It was so.

The luxury of anger had been denied Matthew a long time. The blood pounded in his chest and heart. He didn't need wits; he needed action. He hurled an oath at the Hepburn.

"Whoreson Scot! I—"

"You used to kneel to me!" The Hepburn took a step forward.

Three feet separated them. As if both were anticipating with brutal relish the violence that was sure to come they measured each other. The Hepburn raised one fist. Matthew moved one foot, turned his shoulder to block the blow that was coming, his left arm raised to the waist, the right fist clenched loosely.

The Hepburn moved slowly. He knew he risked being sent backward into the fireplace. He started to move sideways, out of the alcove, and as he moved he lashed out with the left fist in a whistling blow that grazed Matthew's shoulder. Matthew spun with it, to take the force from it, and came up with his right hand.

The blow landed high on the Hepburn's chest. Now they were parallel with the alcove, and the Hepburn was free of the two long benches.

Neither underestimated the other. Both were conscious of the lack of room, of the heavy furniture, which was a hazard.

Matthew ducked the Hepburn's first blow to the jaw. He drove his right fist into the Hepburn's ribs, feeling at the same time the impact of the Hepburn's bare knuckles against his cheekbone. Matthew swayed back, and hit with both fists, one at the Hepburn's eyes, and the other harmlessly high on the chest.

Strategy was forgotten. Both men were already badly cut on the face. Matthew licked blood off his lips, but he didn't even bother to back away from the murderous fists. The Hepburn disdained any evasion of the blows, save for movements of his head. They preferred to take the punishment for the joy of giving it back.

Eyes slitted, teeth bared slightly, they fought with animal anger that lasted until Matthew was driven back by a blow to the jaw. He almost stumbled over a stool, but recovered, he flung himself forward and caught the Hepburn on the side of the face in a crashing right that sent him to the floor.

Matthew stood unmoving, waiting, breathing heavily, blood dripping down his face, from his chin. The Hepburn had been hurled into a heavy chair; he was in a sitting position against it, getting up slowly, his eyes never leaving Matthew's face, fists already knotted to resume battle, when sanity suddenly returned to Matthew.

In one brief moment Matthew realized that he could have leaped on the Hepburn, and seized the dagger which the Hepburn wore. He had not done so. The poker was too far away; he could never reach it now. He had forgotten it completely while he might have succeeded. And now in one clear moment he saw what he deemed his only chance (for he knew that he could not beat the Hepburn into insensibility before he himself succumbed) and seized it. He took the next blow from the Hepburn full on, and fell backward onto the floor.

The blow had been to the mouth. He could feel his lips swelling, and the pain. His whole head pounded. The sudden draining of his anger left him limp. He lay motionless.

The Hepburn walked over to him and looked down. He felt at the dagger in his belt and realized he had not even thought of using it. The Hepburn walked over to the door and opened it.

One eye was almost closed. He touched his cheek with his hand; he looked at the bloody palm and wiped it off on his leg.

The two guards outside had heard the noise but had not dared to interrupt. The Hepburn paid no attention to their stares.

"Fetch me some water," he muttered, and went back into the room, standing over Matthew like a lion over a fallen prey.

The other guard sidled in, his eyes curious. The Englishman seemed completely unconscious. The water arrived, and the Hepburn splashed his face and mopped himself off with a towel, tenderly. There was silence in the room.

After five minutes, while the Hepburn, his face still bloody, paced up and down the room beside the tipped chair, Matthew stirred.

"Fetch more water." The Hepburn paced on.

Two more minutes passed. Matthew sat up. The Hepburn motioned to the big bowl of water.

Unsteadily Matthew rose. He used the water, as the Hepburn had. He finished drying his face and hands, and, as the Scot had, kept hold of the stained pink linen. Deliberately, Matthew swayed. He put his hand to his temple, then he made an effort to open his eyes wide.

The Hepburn's head throbbed with pain. He had had little sleep. And he had drunk a good deal the day before. While he watched, Matthew tried to take a step and stumbled, catching himself on the table, clinging to it.

The Hepburn made a gesture to the guards. "Take him away." He went over to the fireside bench, and sat down wearily.

The guards obeyed. But it was plain the Englishman couldn't walk. One of them slipped an arm around him and laid Matthew's arm across his shoulder. The other guard opened the door. The three of them went out into the wide hall, walking abreast.

Matthew stumbled along, half dragging his booted feet. There was no one in the hall. It lacked an hour to supper, and the whole castle seemed asleep after its strenuous day and night of wedding feast and festivity.

Here the hall was thirty feet long. Matthew managed it

with a few low grunts of pain. Then they neared the turn, where, to go past the kitchens, they must enter a narrow winding hall. Matthew, his arm resting over the guard's shoulder, reeled around the turn.

The action came so swiftly, later neither guard remembered. Matthew's one hand had been resting on the guard's shoulder. The other came suddenly upward, as though to clutch at support, but instead seized the guard's head and knocked it into the stone wall with a vicious strength. The guard slumped to the floor as Matthew turned on the other and drove his fist upward to the jaw.

The second guard had no time to cry out. The Englishman looked as though he would like to kill him. He reached for his knife, and in that split second, Matthew struck him on the temple with a brutal blow that had all his weight behind it.

Both guards lay at his feet. The first guard had a head wound above his ear and was bleeding profusely. Matthew leaned down and took the knife from the fingers of the second. With the hilt, he struck him again, to make sure. It might conceivably be ten minutes, even longer, before anyone would come down this little-used kitchen way. Matthew turned, thrusting the knife through his belt. He was armed, and momentarily free.

He knew the way to the south tower. But he must get there without being seen. Except from the back. He was still wearing livery. Only his unshaven face proclaimed him fugitive. He peered around the turn.

No one was in sight. He started down the hall in long unhurried strides. He went by the Hepburn's closed door. Behind him, he heard a step. He didn't look back; he kept on his even way. Around the next corner lay the door to the south tower—and Jane's apartments. As he opened the door gently, he heard the outside gates of the castle closing. It was exactly four, then. The gates always closed at four. Now Matthew realized that he was trapped inside these rosy stones of the castle walls.

He went up the carpeted stairs. He listened outside the first door. He heard nothing within. He opened the door.

The room was empty. He crossed to the window and looked out. He could escape from this window, which overlooked Bothwell Bank. His hands went to the catch.

They dropped to the sill. Mary had walked in those gardens. He crossed again to the door and stepped out on the small landing. He went on up the stairs.

Then he heard her. The sound of her voice floated down to him. She was singing a favorite song; he heard her steps above him.

Matthew climbed the last flight. He knocked lightly on the door and stood to one side. There might be a servant within. But Jane herself opened the door.

Matthew stepped inside, closed the door and shot the bolt. He looked down at her and smiled, with a grimace, because his face hurt.

"No, no," he said, gently. He put his arms around her. "I'm not bad hurt. We fought a little."

"Oh, Matthew," said Jane.

He released her. "I have but a moment. I have a message. That is why I came. If she is ever in danger, if she needs me ever, you understand, send to me, through Hermitage."

Jane nodded her head.

"I go now," he whispered. "I've not much time, Jane."

"How did you escape him?"

He frowned. "I've no time," he muttered, and started to draw back the bolts of the door.

"No!" she cried.

"Aye," he said. The bolt slid back.

"No," said Jane, flinging herself at him. "There is a better way!" She was trembling, facing him. She bolted the door again. He looked a little angry. "Matthew," she cried, "there is a secret entrance to this tower!"

He could not believe it.

"There is! I've used it! When I was a child. And later!"

His blue eyes shone. She saw his twisted grin. She was standing at the paneling, she was turning a cluster of roses carved into the wood. Then she seized it and pulled hard. A four-foot high section of wall moved outward on a hinge.

"I used it only last week!" She could hardly speak for excitement.

"What a wench you are!" He was at her side, trying to look into the darkness.

"Steps," said Jane. "Hurry." There was a hooded candle in a brass holder. She lighted it at the fire and brought it over. By its light Matthew could see the narrow steps cut into the stone walls. Jane continued rapidly. "This passage goes all the way under the river. It emerges in the priory which you can see from my window. I'll meet you, with a horse."

Matthew took the candle.

"Go carefully."

"I shall."

"You will enter the chapel. There will be no one there, probably. I shall come to the clump of trees you can see from the back door of the chapel. I'll close the panel after you."

He heard the squeak of the hinges as he descended. The air was foul, it would be worse under the river, and now the light from above was gone.

31

JANE REACHED THE STABLES FOUR MINUTES LATER.

"I want my horse!"

Her voice was sharp and taut.

The head groom stared at her. "The gates are closed, your ladyship!"

"I know it, fool. Does the closing of a gate keep me from riding out when I wish it? Bring me my horse!"

He walked away, and returned leading the black stallion.

"He's not been ridden today," Jane said with satisfaction.

"He's been run, this morning," the groom said quickly.

"I meant he was fresh, I want to enjoy my ride." The great horse pawed at the ground with his foreleg. Jane was up and in the saddle; she clattered through the flagged court.

The groom looked after her with apprehension. But it was not his business; the men at the gates could stop her.

At the gates, the four guards were amazed. But Jane rode as though the devil were after her, and she reined in just at the gates.

"Open them," she cried, brandishing her whip.

They obeyed. They obeyed quickly. The iron gates swung open. As soon as there was enough room for her and the horse, Jane spurred forward, cloak flying, almost upsetting the man nearest her. They heard the noise of the flying hooves gradually become a faint beat in the distance.

Jane crossed the river by Bothwell Bridge, old, yet solid, with its stone arches. Then she left the road, picking her way carefully down the sloping ground to the group of pines behind the chapel. From behind one of them Matthew appeared when he saw Jane. Again Jane had difficulty believing that the two of them stood here together. At the same time she realized she might never see him again.

He lifted her down from the saddle, gripped her hands briefly.

The cold wind whistled through the pine branches, sighing with winter cold. The ground was hard and bare beneath their feet. It was half after four, and the day was almost gone.

Jane looked at him. He was strong and tough and reliable. He was leaving her. For a long, long time Jane Gordon had depended on herself—and now, now suddenly she was weak and terrified. She shook her head.

"I keep you, Matthew. Go. God speed you."

He kissed her on the cheek. He swung up into the saddle. He had last instructions. "Tell them you were thrown. Let me see you get down on your hands and knees and crawl. I'll abandon the horse as soon as I can. He'll return. Good-bye,

Jane. God speed you. And remember your promise to me. Good-bye, Jane."

"Good-bye, Matthew," said Jane.

He wheeled; the hooves dug into the hard ground; he raised his hand in farewell.

"Good-bye," Jane repeated. She waved until the trees came between them and she could see him no longer.

She did not forget his instructions. She went down on her knees and started to crawl fast through the trees. Her knees hurt, she got scratched, and then she felt some measure of safety return to her. After she had gone about fifty feet, she deemed she could walk. A long branch pulled her cap loose and with it a strand of hair. She rose thankfully, automatically brushing off some of the dust. She walked rapidly toward the bridge.

The river was quiet. It gleamed like silver in the darkening day. The gray skies were patched with clouds, like badly mended homespun. Wind flew by Jane, cold, moaning.

It was uphill walking. The castle, beautiful always, looked pinkly ephemeral against the cloudy sky. Inside those walls he was waiting.

She was not conscious of cold. In fact the long trudge had warmed her. The wind was like a challenge. She let it blow her cloak away from her body.

She tried to think of him clearly, but she could not. Emotion filled her, and she knew when she faced him she would try only to protect herself and Matthew. The castle towers were now obscured by the gates. Jane walked up to them. Using the handle of her stout whip, she hammered on them fiercely.

The blows resounded. They could be heard inside over the baying of hounds and over the sounds of men and horses. The gates opened, as indeed they were about to anyway; as they swung inward, there stood the disheveled Jane. Swinging her whip she entered the great quadrangle. She saw the Hepburn.

She stood very straight, the wind still blowing her cloak. He turned from the man to whom he'd been giving orders, and saw her. He started toward her in long strides. Jane raised her hand to push back the long lock of thick straight hair that had fallen over her forehead. She looked up at him with the expression he knew so well, a mocking expression that taunted him.

"Was this for me?" She pointed to the pack of hounds, the mounted men.

There was a cut on the side of his face.

"No," he said.

"I was thrown."

"Thrown? Are you—" He broke off, his gray eyes narrow.

"My mount will return—when he runs off his bad temper."

She smiled and drew her cape around her. Instead of looking at him she kept her eyes on the front of his jacket and on his wide shoulders. Her heart was pounding. These men were going after Matthew.

Desperately, to gain time, she leaned down and picked up one of the hounds that were clustered around her. The troop of mounted men waited; in front of her the Hepburn stood, blocking her path. Jane fondled the dog, holding him in her arms like a baby.

"I wanted to ride," she said, calmly. "It was a wild day."

"Set the dog down," he ordered, low.

Jane did. He offered his arm, and she put her hand on his sleeve, lightly. He led her to his study.

Jane sat down quickly in the chair Matthew had sat in. The Hepburn went to the fire, and stood with his back to it.

The room was very still. Only the crackle of the fire broke the silence. Her cloak was thrown back; he looked down at her slim figure, her white face.

"You ride that black stallion?" he said finally. "Suppose you'd been with child. You'd ha' lost your bairn."

Jane pressed her hands across her flat stomach. "I've no bairn. And if I had, I wouldn't lose it. Not by riding. Not my son." Then she said recklessly, "Go to your whey-faced whore. Get your brats from her!"

The Hepburn looked grimly at her. Jane's heart leaped. But she went on, "They won't bear your name!"

He took a step toward her.

She leaned back in her chair, head tipped to look up at him.

He turned and walked back to the fireplace and sat down on the bench.

Jane rose in turn. Her mouth curled. "Go seek Eufemia. Get comfort. Go to your woman who says, 'Aye, Patrick.' " Jane broke off, for, incredibly, he was saying, "Leave me, madam." He did not even look at her.

He knew, then. He did not even bother to ask her if she had helped Matthew. He knew she had.

"M'lord," she said suddenly, holding out her hands. There was a cut on the side of his face, and a black bruise under one eye. The hand that hung down over the bench was split across the knuckles. Jane moved toward him, and looked down at his thick rough head. Jane remembered the night in Edinburgh castle when she had first touched the red hair.

"My lord," she whispered.

He looked up. He said, low, "I've warned you before." He didn't move.

Jane backed away.

Very slowly he rose and walked toward her, and Jane, her legs shaking a little, waited. He came up to her. The hands that seized her were rough.

"There will be a night when I shall treat you as you should be treated!" he said.

She matched his tone. "You'll tire of Eufemia!"

He said nothing.

"You'll tire of every woman save me—and me you'll never have!"

He said two words. "Get out!"

His hands dropped from her.

The gulf between them was very wide, very deep. She swept him a curtsey.

She walked away with her long graceful stride, out of his sight, to her room where she closed the door. She decided against locking it; she left the heavy bolts drawn back. She knew she could neither eat nor sleep.

She, herself, put more logs on the fire, taking pleasure in their weight and in the struggling to pile them evenly and high until the flames roared up the chimney. Then she bathed and changed to a furred and velvet robe.

From the table she took a cup and a jug of wine, and stretched herself full-length on the fur rug in front of the fire. She had eaten almost nothing all day. The fire crackled. Jane finished the jug of wine, put her head on her arms, and fell asleep.

32

"WHAT ARE YOU GOING TO DO WITH ME?" FLEMING asked, trying to keep his voice even. This sight was incredible. The great guns, the swarms of mounted men, the castle of Dunbar already crumpled and broken with the incoming tides sweeping over the piled stones. The air was stinking with the smell of powder.

Incredibly too they were binding his hands like a common criminal. Yet he had done nothing in these past weeks to give himself away, and all the previous evidence had been destroyed. He heard the shouted commands from the Hepburn as the last of the guns were fired.

"What are you going to do?" he repeated, miserably. "Where are you taking me?"

Captain Knox shrugged. He could not answer any question but the last. "Hailes," he said. He was examining Fleming's dagger, a pretty thing. He put it in his belt. "You'll not need this again."

Fleming blanched.

"Hailes?" he whispered. "Then—"

Knox smiled wickedly. "Lord Bothwell wishes to question you. What better place than Hailes? Would you prefer Edinburgh?"

"Aye," said Fleming eagerly. "I'll swear allegiance to the king! I can pay, too!"

"I reckon you'll pay, sir. But at Hailes."

"No!" Fleming cried, his voice drowned out by the sound of the guns. He watched the cannon balls plow into the side of the last standing walls of Dunbar; the wall swayed a moment, and crumpled as though a giant hand had swept it over like a toy. The rumble of stones made speech impossible. Fleming saw the Hepburn wheel his mount; the Hepburn was coming toward him.

Fleming backed up, away from the oncoming horse. The Hepburn reined in, and from the great horse, looked down at the bound man. Fleming felt the black hatred rising in him, along with the terrible fear. He could not speak for the violence of his sudden emotions. Then hatred blotted out fear.

"You son of a whore!"

Knox raised his hand to strike.

"Hold!" snapped the Hepburn.

Fleming's voice came jerkily. "You sent me here, while you take your pleasure with my wife. And now, and now—"

Knox asked, "Shall I unbind his hands, my lord, so you can kill him here and now?"

"Take him to Hailes," the Hepburn said. "Put him in the cell next the oubliette. I shall be there within an hour."

Tears of passionate rage stood in Fleming's eyes. "Why don't you fight me?"

Knox laughed aloud. "I'd kill you with pleasure," the Hepburn said, "but Jamie wants your head as decoration. Take him away, Knox." The Hepburn wheeled and was gone. Through the tears, Fleming saw him disappear, and he saw Knox bring up a mount. Fleming had to be helped into the saddle. He sat unsteadily.

"There is something poisonous about you," Knox said genially. He rode off, guards came in on either side of Fleming: one of them took the bridle of his horse. They started off.

Hailes castle was very old and very small. It was fortress only, round in shape. On one side the Tyne river lapped at its walls, on the other three sides a wide moat protected it.

Fleming knew it well, for Hailes lay directly between Edinburgh and Dunbar, on the road south from the city.

The town looked peaceful as they rode through. The people stared at Fleming, pointing. He lifted his bound hands from the pommel and shook them. A sudden wildness seized him, and he shouted an insult at a woman who waved to Knox.

The man on his left reached out and slapped him across the mouth. It was not a hard blow, but Fleming began to cry quietly, his shoulders shaking. His lip swelled. Thus he entered Hailes.

This was the Hepburn's first stronghold. Against the sky the ancient gibbet flung its arms like a menacing scarecrow, black and grisly. Fleming was pulled out of the saddle.

They took him down three flights of stone steps. Moisture dripped from the walls. The river was above them here. It was black except for the torches. There was a narrow passageway, and three more wide stone steps. Fleming saw a barred door.

Knox stopped in his stride. The two guards stopped with Fleming and watched as a torch in the sconce was lighted. Then Fleming heard the moaning sound that filled the foul air.

"What is it?" He crossed himself.

"A murderer," Knox said. "Would you like to see him?"

Knox walked forward, and Fleming could not help himself. He followed. Knox lifted the torch from the wall and shone it down into the black hole. What was down there looked not like a man but an animal. Fleming screamed.

"He's been there only a week," Knox said. "He'll be hanged tomorrow. He was convicted of murder and sentenced by Bothwell last week. There is another oubliette. Empty. We don't need to wait till tomorrow to put you down there with the hungry rats. You cannot sleep, you know. They'll gnaw at you."

Fleming cried, "He said the cell!"

"Aye, he did. So the cell it is." Knox put the torch back in the wall-bracket and opened the door which the guards had unbolted. Inside there was nothing but some straw in the corner, and a tin cup hanging from a nail in the wall. There was also a quarion.

"I beg you, light it!" Fleming put his hands together in prayer.

Knox hesitated.

The guard said, "His lordship'll want light, Captain."

"Light it, then," Knox commanded.

He was obeyed. "Be careful of the straw, Fleming," he said, "you'll sizzle to death." He grinned, and the heavy door closed. The bolts were shoved into place. Fleming sat down on the straw in the corner and began to weep.

The tears trickled down over his face. The smelly square candle flickered unsteadily and threw a great shadow on the wall. Fleming wept silently.

Finally with an effort of will he got control of himself, wiped his face with his hands and then his sleeve. He sat up straighter.

Opposite him hung a tin cup. Above eye-level was the tiny barred window in the door through which he could see nothing. There would be no use in trying the door. It was locked. No doubt there was a guard lolling outside at the chair and table in the passageway at the foot of the last three wide steps. He began to unfasten his doublet slowly.

Around his waist, under his shirt, he wore a belt. From that belt he drew out a tiny vial.

He studied the liquid in the candle light, holding it close to the flame. The Hepburn would be coming soon, and he had not much time. It was probably good he had provided himself with this; it was providential they had not searched him.

He smiled bitterly. He was guilty of treason, and the Hepburn had told him that James knew it. If he did not take the stuff in the vial, just a little of it was needed, they would—God only knew the kind of death he might be facing.

He tried to screw up his courage. Certainly if he took it at all, he must take it now. The Hepburn would arrive at any moment and might order him searched.

The liquid was clear and frightening in its innocence. Fleming came to the sudden realization that he had not the courage to tip up the tiny vial and drink it. It would sear; he might not even be able to swallow. He replaced it in his belt, leaving his shirt fastened over it, and went to the door.

The narrow window in the door was barred. He put his mouth to it and called.

"I want water," he said, his nervousness making his tone sharp and fretful.

"No," said the voice of the guard, pleasantly enough. Fleming opened his mouth to protest when he heard another voice. He stiffened with terror. He listened. His heart pounded.

"My son, I wish to see Lord Fleming."

It was a husky voice, husky from drinking, Fleming knew. He held his breath, and the voice came again.

"Lord Fleming has not long to live. He should be shriven. I shall be only a minute or two."

The guard was scowling. "How did you know he was here?"

"He sent for me at Dunbar. I rode over on my mule. I told them to give the poor beast water," the priest went on.

The guard smiled. "I warrant his lordship won't mind." He got to his feet and Fleming heard his footsteps coming nearer. He stepped back from the door, wondering wildly what Borthwick wanted, why he was here, and how in the name of God he hoped to rescue him. Perhaps Douglass had men near!

The door opened. The priest, his gray robes swinging, stood framed in the doorway.

"My son, you may close and lock the door," he said to the guard.

He stepped into the cell, and the guard closed the door. Both men heard him lock it. Fleming stared at the newcomer in the uncertain light.

"What do you want?" he whispered.

"To see you," Borthwick said. A smile played over his face, and Fleming then knew why he had come. Borthwick had been sent to kill him.

"I wouldn't have betrayed him!" Fleming cried.

"Quiet," said Borthwick smoothly. "Sit down."

As in a dream Fleming obeyed. He sat cross-legged on the floor.

"They would have persuaded you to speak," Borthwick said. "They have ways." He looked down at the sitting man, his little eyes marking the bared throat. Under his cassock was his long-blade knife. "I have no time to spare."

Fleming started to cry out, and stopped. Borthwick was drunk; he was always drunk. Fleming tried to think. In his belt, under his shirt—

He said, pleadingly, "Borthwick, ha' you got wine?"

Borthwick nodded.

"Gi' me a wee bit. I beg you!"

Borthwick reached within his cassock and drew forth the flagon he always carried.

"There's a cup on the wall," Fleming said. Borthwick took it. He set it down, next to the flagon.

"Only a half cup," he warned.

Fleming hugged himself in pain, taking a chance that Borthwick would not kill him as he bent over to get the vial from his belt, and hide it in his hand. When he looked up, he saw Borthwick had got out his long knife.

"No," he sobbed.

Borthwick smiled. "Pour it," he commanded.

Fleming picked up the cup, then laid it down. He lifted the flagon and poured.

"Half a cup!"

"Aye," Fleming nodded. His hand held the vial. He lifted the cup to his lips and took one swallow, then another. As he set the cup down he tilted the vial. He hoped that the dim light hid his gesture. He hoped also that he had put enough, yet not too much, in the cup. With the other hand he filled the cup with wine and handed it to Borthwick.

Borthwick raised it to his mouth and drank it in a gulp. He hung the cup up. He swayed as he took a step forward, the long knife bare.

Fleming retreated. He said nothing. He could not cry out. He retreated, step by step, with only five feet to go.

His breath came in swift short gasps. Borthwick was following him. Step by step the priest was coming nearer, slowly, deliberately. He raised the blade; Fleming could not suppress a little cry.

Almost as though the cry were a signal, Borthwick doubled over. The knife clattered to the floor. Borthwick sank to his knees, he moaned. Fleming took the knife and hit him on the head.

The blow was not necessary. Borthwick was unconscious, and he was dying. Fleming started to unfasten his clothes.

It took only a minute. The priest's robes were easy to slip off and to don. Fleming replaced the vial in his belt, under the robes. He tipped up the flagon and drank. Then he took a last look at the priest, who lay huddled in the far corner of the cell where the light from the open door would not reach.

He knocked on the door.

"I am ready, my son," he said, trying to imitate Borthwick's husky tones.

He heard the guard in the distance get up. The door opened. Fleming pulled his cassock's hood over his face. The light was so dim.

"He is praying for his soul," he said lugubriously.

The guard banged the door shut. "He had better, Father."

"My son, you must not sit in judgment." Fleming walked along, and started up the steps.

"I think you'll find they watered your mule," the guard said.

"I hope so," Fleming answered, remembering his voice. He went on up the steps. He remembered the way he had come. It was etched on his memory, like a terrible dream. And he was not free, yet. This was some kind of miracle from which he might be rudely shaken any moment. And it was indeed a miracle that he and Borthwick were both short and stout. The priest's robes fit him perfectly.

He went on. He gained the court. There was his mule, waiting.

He mounted the animal. Could it be easy as this? The great drawbridge was open, no doubt because the Hepburn himself was expected. The sun shone. The spring winds blew fitfully. Fleming started over the drawbridge.

He crossed it. It was impossible, but he had crossed it. He

looked back. No one was following. No one was paying attention to a fat priest on an ambling mule. Only a few women by the roadside nodded to him.

"Good afternoon, Father," one said, as he went past.

"Good afternoon, my daughter," Fleming answered unsteadily.

He urged the mule to its fastest pace. An hour went by. He was riding to Edinburgh.

The hour's ride had brought him almost to the capital. He tethered his mule in a deep grove of trees by the roadside and went on foot. Soon he was swallowed up in the city streets.

He had something important to do in Edinburgh. He wound his way through side streets. The afternoon had waned and given way to early evening. The shops were closing. When he came to the shop which was his destination, he saw with satisfaction that it was closed.

He went around to the narrow close at the side. He did not wait for darkness, and even then no one saw him. He knocked out a small windowpane with his elbow, opened the window and climbed in.

Inside it was dim. This was the proper evening too, unless in his fear he had made a mistake. He groped his way through the musty rooms, filled with barrels, with tilted bottles. It smelled of wine, as indeed it should. This was his wine shop.

The front room was vacant and dark, for the shutters were closed. There was little sound from the street, for the dinner hour had claimed most of Edinburgh. Fleming began his search.

It did not take him long to find his cask. Marked as usual with his crest. He opened it.

Then he drew the vial from his belt. He pondered. Would the full vial be too much? He rather thought it would. He would save a little—for the Hepburn, or for Douglass, or for himself.

He poured it carefully into the open cask, reserving only a little. Just enough. He replaced it in his belt, and closed the cask. Then he retraced his steps, until he stood once more on the narrow cobbled close. Now it was almost dark. He would sit here till complete darkness fell. Then he would try to get south, to England.

33

MARY GORDON RODE AT HER HUSBAND'S SIDE. SHE WORE a white headdress which covered her like a nun. She wore flowing white velvet. Only her blue eyes and her red mouth contrasted with her gown and wimple. James had picked a white mare for her to ride.

Before her flew the banners of the house of York. On all sides of her moved companies of pikemen, bowmen, cavalry. The flags that flew were red and blue taffeta, embroidered with the white rose of York. In the faint mists that lay over the Border hills, she saw that ahead of her was England.

They were passing through the first small village. The houses were shut and barred. The duke found himself shivering. Fear swept him like a cold wind, and yet it was a warm day. The trees were green, the fields were green, and behind the distant hills would be fertile farmland and populous towns, rivers, valleys, England. Indeed, this was England.

War had been formally declared at Ellame Kirk. At the same time the duke had made a proclamation, in the name of Richard, Duke of York, true inheritor of the Crown of England. He had branded Henry VII a usurper, and ended by putting a reward of one thousand pounds on Henry's head. Then, with great dignity, he had signed his royal name, while James had watched with hidden amusement.

James had proceeded with his plans. The fortress of Norham came under the first siege guns. In spite of them, it did not surrender for five days. In this time, no adherents to the Yorkist cause had been gained.

If this surprised James, he gave no hint of it. He stormed and razed the Border castles of Etal and Ford. The scouring of the country had begun. At Ford castle, only the round tower had been left standing. Its master, Lord Heron, was sent to Scotland to be held for ransom. Its mistress, the Lady Heron, lovely and artful, surrendered gracefully to her royal captor. From the king's pavilion that night came the sound of music and laughter.

"This is a Border raid," Mary said. "Don't you understand? These are the acts of a royal freebooter, not a war!"

Perkin was staring down at the floor. He raised his head. "Tomorrow we proceed onward."

The walls of the tent rustled in the summer wind, and shimmered in the lamplight. Mary Gordon looked at her husband, her brows puckered a little.

"You do not understand," she said finally.

"What?" he snapped at her.

She was accustomed to his petulance. She paid no attention to that. She was concentrating on what must be his own thoughts. As she met his eyes, he looked away and made a gesture of impatience. It crossed her mind he would have liked to join the men in the royal tent, but didn't dare, either because he was afraid of her displeasure or because he was unsure of his welcome from James and the Hepburn.

But he did try to please her. In every way. He was in love with her—which, for him, meant that he wanted her to protect and comfort him. He was rising to come to her and kiss her.

"No," said Mary, shaking her head. She used a mild little oath. "Richard, you've lived too long abroad!"

"I could scarcely help it."

"It was not your fault. But you are not practical." She was silent. She tried to push away the thought that he had not told her the truth. She said, "We, English and Scot, have fought too long."

She saw again his familiar petulance. "Am I a fool, then?"

"You goad me into saying aye."

The next day the thirty-mile sweep into Northumberland

began. Mary was fifteen miles deeper into England. A camp was thrown up in haste. Provisions arrived, guards and sentries paced.

At five in the afternoon the king returned to camp.

James flung himself off his horse. His men removed the light armor. The Hepburn appeared, grimy and bloodstained, his leather coat open at the neck. Young Scottish lords clustered around both men, talking fast, laughing. Their servants scurried up, and a cask of wine was opened. Mary stared, unbelieving.

"Child's play," Grey said, grinning.

"Quite," said the Hepburn grimly. "However, Grey, 'twill not be easy once the English send an army."

"D'ye think, my lord, that Henry will fight?"

The Hepburn made no answer.

"We are not provisioned for a long march," Grey added.

James tossed off a cup of wine. The circle of men grew quiet. Mary supposed they knew he had orders for them. They listened and so did she, incredulously. James was assigning towns to each man.

" 'Tis now five," James said. "I'm going to eat."

Mary had a vision of these English towns lying helpless and peaceful.

"You may attack now, seize what you can. Delay the fires till nightfall. Fire is more terrifying by night."

Mary was pale and unsteady. Her husband was beside her, his eyes fixed on James's dark face under the helmet.

"Your Majesty," Mary said. "Those towns—they?"

"Are being given over to indiscriminate plunder," James said.

Mary looked about her. The camp stretched in all directions. There were thousands of men, and to them was to be given this part of England—for plunder.

"You cannot!" Mary cried.

Then her husband spoke. "Your Grace, I do not approve!"

James Stuart shoved back his helmet in preparation. He waited.

"I shall renounce my claim! I would rather renounce it than gain aught at the expense of so much misery!"

James spoke then. "My cousin of York," he said. The words were low and mocking. "You are most solicitous." He swept the duke with a long glance, and looked about at the other men. "I would say his Grace was *too* solicitous for the welfare of a nation which hesitates to claim him either as king or subject." James drew out the word "subject." He ordered brusquely, finally, "Seek your tent."

Perkin turned away. Mary stood her ground. White-faced she listened.

"The fool," James said angrily. "Go, sirs, and take your pleasure out of England. The aim is to sweep Northumberland."

Mary heard their various answers as though they could not be true. She saw that the Hepburn was watching her, and while he made no move toward her, she took a little comfort from his presence. She thought he also approved of this, especially when he made a suggestion to young Home to be sure to set the fires to windward, and cautioned him as to rounding up his men, especially, he added, those Borderers of yours.

"They're like to get into trouble in a wine shop, to say naught of the women. Set no fires till your captains have corralled your lads, and peal the church bells as warning. Let them understand that. Also the people will understand and flee in time."

Grey had already moved off and was ahorse. His young captains with him on their beautiful horses made a splendid picture as they galloped off, and Grey turned and waved gaily.

Horns sounded all over camp, rousing the men. The troops moved away, the mounted Borderers first, their voices raised in their own particular Border war cries. The Hepburn said to James, "I'm going to throw special guards around York's tent. I have a notion that Henry's first move will be to try and get possession of his Grace."

"Heaven forbid," James said. He turned and went into his own tent.

Mary still stood, looking at the Hepburn. The camp was emptying swiftly. Blue shadows lay over the English hills. Mary thought with terror of what the night would bring to Northumberland.

"You are cruel. Merciless."

"Go to your husband," the Hepburn said.

"Why?" cried Mary.

"You belong to him," he said.

"I do not mean that. He could not stop you."

"No? He did not try."

She clenched her fists. "We shall never do this again! If we make another claim on England, we shall make it open and plain, land in England, and go forth to London. If they don't want us, we shall bother them not!"

He looked startled and grim and angry.

"That would be the way, Hepburn! That is what you would do, is't not?"

He grunted an aye. Then he said strongly, "Mistress, the situation between us and England demanded drastic action. This is that action. They have done the same to Scotland."

"We have been pitiful pawns," she said. "I am ashamed. And we shall never again allow you to use us in this way." Mary turned, and made her way to her tent.

A faint evening haze lay over the hills of Northumberland. Ten miles south of the Scots camp a troop of but fifteen horse paused for the last time to refresh the horses and drink a little ale. Then they mounted again.

Five miles farther a single rider joined them. He rode up to the leader and told him quickly what was happening.

"For thirty miles in all directions, sir," he ended. "Are they sending men, sir?" The question was put slyly.

"I'm here," said Matthew Craddock.

"There isna' a Border town that won't be put to the torch tonight!"

"Fellow, I can hardly stop that." Matthew looked around at the English Borderers with him, picked men, clever, silent, used to hazard. "Tonight we try to lance this boil. A pinprick suffices, sometimes."

They didn't understand him, but he hardly cared. He had very little time till nightfall, and this job must be done right after dark.

The messenger spoke up again. He said, "Sir Matthew, Lord Dacre has deserted to the Hepburn."

"Christ Almighty!" Matthew stared at the speaker. This shook even his aplomb. He muttered what he was going to do to Dacre when he caught him, as he would, certainly. But it meant that tonight there would be no counting on the English warden here. He was a deserter. "In the name of God, why didn't you tell me that first? You might ha' forgot!"

"No sir, I should not."

"It is time," Matthew said impatiently.

It was almost dark. The troop resumed its steady canter. Matthew thought of the simple plans he had made. They might work. Desperately he wanted them to work.

Matthew Craddock wanted a man's life and he wanted to take it himself.

He carried in his saddle bag a round device of taut sheepskin. When it was shaken it made a terrible noise. An eerie frightening rattling noise that would echo out over the silent hills.

The nearest town was burning brightly. Great pillars of fire stood upright into the black skies. Matthew smelled the smoke. He spoke to the man nearest him.

"You are accustomed to this, are you not?" In the darkness his blue eyes tried to see the face of the man he addressed.

"Aye, sir. We see it often enough."

"The uneasy peace we have had lately lends itself to raids," Matthew said. "Perhaps out of this will come—" He broke off. The roar of the flames was deafening as a sheet of fire shot up the church steeple; it burned and swayed and sparks flew; finally it began to crumple.

"The Scot's camp is there, sir." He pointed. He had slowed his horse.

Matthew reined in. He dismounted. From the saddle bag he

took the noisemaker; there were two more of them. Matthew spoke to the men who were to use them.

"You know this part of the country better than any of your fellows?"

"We all know it, sir."

"Then you know what to do. Give us enough time. John will lead you to the animals. Escape from the scene as soon as you can—to our next meeting place."

"Aye, sir." It was all the answer he needed. The horses were tethered in the thick brush. The night was dark except for the blood-red sky. Matthew and his fifteen men moved off into the blackness.

There were no men better or cleverer than Borderers when it came to night raiding. Born to it, living in it, they moved silently through their own hills and valleys, across the familiar lazy streams. They carried only long knives; they wore white leather jacks and breeks; they looked exactly like the Hepburn's men and were as capable. Nevertheless, if caught, they'd be hanged for spying.

Matthew moved silently from tree to tree. His men were spread out. He could neither hear nor see them. And that was good. His objective lay almost straight ahead. Past two campfires, past two sentries. A tent that flew the white rose of York and housed a man Matthew called Perkin Warbeck.

Patrick Hepburn stretched out flat on his stomach, was dozing. He could hear the shouts and cries from the nearest beleaguered town. He closed his eyes and drifted off into light sleep.

Then the night was shattered by sound.

The Hepburn rolled over and leapt up, dazed, frowning. The noise echoed from every side, as though a giant were shaking a dreadful rattle. Then the air was split with the first trumpet call of terror from a tethered horse.

"The horses," someone shouted. The few men left in the camp started in the direction of the mounts. The awful rattling continued, and the horses were panicking. To the rattling was added the stamp of hooves, the crashing of branches as the animals tried to free themselves.

The Hepburn became suddenly aware that the men he had set to guard this tent were disappearing into the flickering lights of the middle campfires, running to see to the horses and what was making the noise that frightened them.

"Hold!" he shouted. The words had just left his mouth when he whirled to face the possible danger that might be coming on silent feet. He knew without thinking that this ruse was what he had tried to guard against, and that now, this minute, probably an attempt would be made to enter this tent.

He saw nothing around him. He pulled the dagger from his belt. He raised his voice. "To me! Will!" But he didn't have time for more names. He did not know whether he could be heard above the noise that was coming from the horses and the shouts of the men who were trying vainly to calm them. A riderless horse galloped past him as though the devil were after it. Then he saw a figure, shadowy. He went forward, bare knife in hand.

He was instantly engaged. The swordsman he faced in the darkness he could barely see. He made a lunging slash at the figure, and he felt the impact of steel on steel. His dagger slid into human flesh. At the same moment he was seized from behind.

He struggled silently with his two opponents, when, to his surprise, he felt one of them loose his hold and fall to the ground.

"To me!" he shouted again. He saw a figure leave his side, and dart to help another struggling pair of men. In the blackness it was impossible to tell friend from foe, but the Hepburn was sure it had been Will who had come to his rescue.

Utter confusion reigned in the camp. The horses were stampeding; men were trying vainly to catch them, and the air rang with human and animal noise. The Hepburn faced a new opponent, when a blow on the head laid him low.

Then a swift motion of a boot to his temple sent him into blackness. He lay sprawled on the ground.

But he had delayed Matthew Craddock just long enough. Men were coming. Matthew leaned down and took the Hepburn by the heels. He dragged him twenty feet into the shelter of low bushes. A knot of men clustered around him.

"We have failed," Matthew whispered. "The Hepburn gave the alarm in time. Here, help me with him."

They carried him silently through the woods to their own horses.

"We have an extra mount," Matthew said. "I'm sorry we do. We have lost one man. Put him in the saddle."

They hoisted him into the saddle, and roped him securely, his head lying forward. Matthew felt the Hepburn's pulse. It seemed strong enough.

"It would take more than this to kill him," he muttered.

He mounted himself. "They will try to find him," he said, "as soon as Knox returns from Berwick. And there is only one place they will not think of looking. That is Hermitage."

34

MATTHEW SAT UP SUDDENLY ON THIS STRANGE BED and for a moment he wondered where he was. Then he remembered. He was at Hermitage.

He remembered the night ride. He remembered reaching the castle, remembered its great doors lowering so he and his fourteen men and one prisoner could ride in. He remembered unroping the Hepburn and giving him over to other men. Then he had lost consciousness himself.

He sat up and swung his legs over the side of the bed. It was a wide comfortable bed; they must have put him in one of the best rooms, on the ground floor. It was still night, for a candle burned and through the narrow slit that served for a window he saw only blackness. Dawn could not be coming soon. Anyway he reckoned he had slept only about two hours.

The old shoulder wound ached. The Hepburn's dagger had nicked his upper arm this time. He picked up his bloody shirt, but decided against wearing it. The air was warm. Naked to the waist he moved out of the room and down the narrow hall. He heard voices.

He listened a moment. Then he opened the door without knocking and walked into the room. The sight he saw brought him up short.

He said nothing, at first. He flexed his arm a little, and laid his hand on his dagger.

"What goes on here, Fleming?" he asked softly. "Where's Douglass?"

Fleming was standing in the center of the room with three other men whom Matthew catalogued instantly as knaves. He looked them over with ice-blue eyes, which then returned to the Hepburn.

The Hepburn was bound to a heavy chair, both legs and arms tied down securely. There was a black bruise on the right temple, a deep cut on the left cheek that was bleeding. His eyes were closed, and his head was forward almost on the broad chest. The red rumpled hair fell over his forehead. Matthew repeated his soft question.

"Where is Douglass?"

Fleming answered this time, and he was satisfied with the reply he could make. "Douglass is dead."

Matthew kept the look of amazement off his face. "So?" he inquired, wondering whether Fleming had lost his mind. He looked odd. "Dead? How did he die?"

"By poison," Fleming said. "I poisoned him. He would have killed me, or rather he tried."

"What?" asked Matthew, asking the question as his quick mind put together the pieces of this puzzle. The last he had known, Fleming was a prisoner of the Hepburn. Evidently he had escaped, and it was probably before that that Douglass had tried to have Fleming killed, as well he might, for Fleming could have told much.

"I killed Borthwick, too," said Fleming. "That was how I escaped from Hailes. I came here uninvited." He laughed. "I poured a little poison into a glass of wine."

Matthew stared.

"I am not mad," Fleming said. "And now you've brought me my wife's lover."

"Well," said Matthew, "her lover or not, Fleming, I brought him here to ask him a few questions, and I can hardly do it while he's in that state. I suppose you intend to kill him. And what are your plans after that, may I ask?"

"I'm going to England," Fleming said.

"You'll make a charming guest," Matthew murmured, looking closely at the Hepburn. He went over to him, and lifted one eyelid gently with his forefinger. Perhaps the earl was faking this; perhaps he was conscious. Had he been in the Hepburn's place he would have pretended unconsciousness. The Hepburn would be sought for—not a stone on the border would be left untouched by Captain Knox.

"Have you wine?" Matthew asked.

"Aye," said Fleming.

"Pour me a cup. So you're in charge here now, eh, Fleming?" He reached out for the cup of wine, took it from Fleming, tipped back the Hepburn's head, and poured the wine down his throat. He noticed that the Hepburn didn't choke as much as he should. He propped the Hepburn's head back against the chair-back. It stayed there. Then he examined the ropes that bound him.

"You've tied him with enough rope for a horse," he said, conversationally. "And you've bound him too tight, all circulation will stop, and he'll remain in this state." His deft fingers were busy with the cords and knots. "I want this man to talk, Fleming. And you're not going to make him talk by knocking him around this way. You want a slow and exquisite pain. Send one of your men for a couple of mine. And fill that wine glass again."

Fleming filled the glass. He looked at Matthew. "Why do you want your men?" he asked suspiciously.

"Because I'm not going to do the tormenting," said Matthew. "I'll do the questioning." He grinned, and Fleming nodded.

Matthew turned aside and looked down at the Hepburn. He forced open his mouth with two fingers and tipped up the wine glass. This time he was sure the Hepburn drank. He heard one of Fleming's knaves go out the door.

There was silence in the room while Fleming watched both Matthew and the Hepburn. He watched them carefully, with wily eyes. Matthew was thinking that he had but fourteen men inside this fortress. He drew a deep breath. Then the door opened.

He saw with relief the familiar faces of three of his Borderers. At least there were now three men in the room on whom he could rely. And now he would test the Hepburn.

"Come here, John," he said coldly.

Johnnie came. He stood before Matthew, looking a bit bewildered and very sleepy. He had been rudely roused from his cot in the barracks above.

"Aye, sir."

Matthew raised the Hepburn's hand so the fingers were extended. "Run your knife under the thumbnail. Gently."

Johnnie stared in amazement. But he obeyed. He drew his knife, and Matthew saw the muscles in the Hepburn's jaw and neck stiffen for the pain. He was conscious. When the pain came, despite his effort, his eyes opened and his jaw set. His gray eyes gleamed fire at Matthew and Matthew almost gave a sigh of relief. The Hepburn was completely conscious.

"Well," said Matthew heartily. "So you are awake now, my lord."

The Hepburn swore a foul oath. Blood dripped from his thumb.

Matthew pulled forward a chair. "Stand there," he ordered Johnnie. He glanced toward his two men, and with a motion of his head, they gradually sidled over.

"This is what you were planning for me, m'lord," Matthew went on.

The Hepburn didn't answer.

"You might as well save your strength," Matthew said. "Except that it will be no use, in the end, as you warned me." Then he snarled, "Can we not forget our personal animosity for but a moment?"

The Hepburn looked startled that Matthew should put such a question.

Matthew leaned forward and began fiddling with the cords again. "They're tight," he announced to Fleming, over his shoulder. "I'll be through with him soon, and then you can do what you will."

Fleming made a satisfied sound, and leaned back in his chair. "I'm content to wait," he said.

"Try the bonds, my lord," Matthew said mockingly. "You'll see you cannot move. And this man here is adept at making men talk."

Johnnie's face was the picture of amazement. The Hepburn tried his bonds. They gave. Immediately he ceased the movement of the one leg he had tried to move. He did not understand. He tried to frown at Matthew warningly because—he had to have a little time.

Matthew seemed to know what he could not say. He asked the man John to fill the wine cup again. Matthew held it to his lips. And he drank eagerly. His head was clearing a little.

Matthew said, "My lord, I'll introduce myself. At this moment I represent the English Crown. Directly and yet indirectly. Do you understand?"

The Hepburn did. He was being approached by the English. To get through to James. He tried to think of a proper answer.

"What do you want to know, sir?" He forced the words out.

"He is ready to talk," Matthew said to Fleming excitedly.

Fleming got up and came to stand over the Hepburn. He smiled down at him.

"Son of a whore," he said. He laughed silently. "I'm going to kill you."

Matthew said sharply, "Sit down, Fleming. I've told you that you could have him when I finish!"

Fleming said, "Hurry, then." He suddenly became excited

and his voice rose. "Hurry! How much time do you think we have? They may be after him now!"

Matthew nodded. He knew the time to act had come, but he postponed it, for a moment. It was so damned risky. He kept reminding himself he had three men here, and only eleven more, asleep somewhere in this vast fortress.

"Jesus God," he said. "Do not harry and hurry me so. Listen, my lord." He turned his attention back to the Hepburn, standing over him until he looked up. "I seek words," Matthew muttered. "Free of emotion."

"Speak," growled the Hepburn. "You failed tonight. You sought to kill York. You failed."

"Don't fret me further. It's most simple in any event." He paused. "We want peace."

The Hepburn smiled grimly.

"Ah." Matthew made a gesture. "You hold York. You have the die. The stakes are high. M'lord, would Jamie Stuart marry?"

The Hepburn was silent. He looked grave, and he licked his lips while he studied Matthew. Matthew slowly nodded his head. The Hepburn wanted and believed in the marriage Matthew could offer now. But would Jamie marry?

"Will his Majesty take a wife?" Matthew repeated.

"I don't know," answered the Hepburn.

Matthew tried another question. "Will he give up York? If he is offered Berwick?"

The Hepburn answered readily. "No."

Matthew believed this because he knew James Stuart.

"His Grace will never betray York," said the Hepburn. "He may use him, but never abandon him."

"We are at an impasse," said Matthew, "because of a wench named Maggie." He set his mouth and swung away, rubbing his chin, wondering what to do.

The odds were that tomorrow, having completed the despoliation of Northumberland, James would return to Scotland. But the flames of war were not extinguished; they would smoulder and smoke until the conflagration sprang up anew.

"Terms must be made," he said strongly to the Hepburn.

At the least he had made a start. The Hepburn had been approached; James's ear would be reached directly, with an offer of marriage with the English princess, Margaret Tudor. Matthew drove his fist into his open palm.

"Christ, m'lord, we offer much!" he said.

The Hepburn tipped back his red head to look up. While he spoke he was testing his bonds. "It shall probably be refused." And then he added, "Unhappily."

Matthew's eyes glistened. The Hepburn approved and wanted the English marriage for James. So much had been accomplished, but the problem of escaping from Hermitage remained, for Fleming, he was certain, had no notion of allowing either of them to escape his toils. But Matthew had one more remark.

"While we parley, towns are burning!"

The Hepburn said softly, "They are English towns."

"Your reminder angers me slightly." Matthew's tone was silky. Both men had temporarily forgotten Fleming. Matthew suddenly looked around at him.

Fleming was sidling toward the door, and Matthew instantly read his intent.

"Stop him!" Matthew commanded, gesturing to Fleming, and in the same gesture drawing the knife at his side. He flung himself forward on the nearest of Fleming's men, driving the murderous dagger upward in a swift movement that neatly found his quarry's heart. Matthew withdrew the narrow blade and whirled to look at the door and at the Hepburn. The Hepburn was safe, but Fleming was battling at the open door, sword in hand, with Johnnie who had only his knife. Johnnie would be killed in the next seconds. Fleming's sword was heavy bladed.

One of Matthew's men held out a sword he had confiscated. Matthew seized the weapon eagerly; Johnnie jumped back and let Matthew engage Fleming. Then Johnnie tried to get between Fleming and the door. He could not.

Fleming had backed into the doorway, and in another second was out of it. They heard him shouting for aid. Matthew banged the door shut and surveyed the room.

The instant he did so, he regretted it. Nevertheless he bolted the door, since it was too late now to catch Fleming.

"I should have gone after him!" He was breathing rapidly.

The Hepburn said, "You could not have caught him." He had freed one arm and was untying his legs. Matthew noticed that the only one of Fleming's knaves who had not been killed outright was trying to rise and crawl toward a discarded knife. Matthew with an almost reflex action struck him on the head with the heavy sword he carried, and laid down the weapon.

"Drag those knaves out of sight, John," he ordered. "The sight of them makes me sick to my stomach, although they're prettier dead than living."

The Hepburn wriggled free of his entanglements. He stood up gingerly, holding onto the arms of the big chair. He looked at Johnnie and grinned, lopsidedly.

Johnnie said, "I'm—I didn't—I'm sorry I had to hurt you, your lordship."

The Hepburn looked at his thumb; it had stopped bleeding. "Almost healed, lad." His hands left the chair and he stood upright. "My thanks, Sir Matthew," he said, stiffly.

Matthew was pacing the room restlessly, like a caged lion. "I wish to God I were a dwarf, or had one handy," he said, indicating the slitted windows. He glanced back toward the door and its heavy bolts. They would not withstand concerted attack. "We could make a barricade of the furniture to fight behind," he announced. "We could hold them off for a while. Turn that corpse over on its face, Johnnie."

The Hepburn was considering another bracer of wine. As he lifted the cup, he muttered, "D'ye suppose this is safe?"

Matthew laughed. "He said he was temporarily out of poison. I think he's mad."

"No," said the Hepburn. "Canny and cruel. Poisonous." At his inadvertent use of the word he smiled, and tossed off the wine. "I feel better."

"Taste life deep before you leave it," said Matthew. Then he looked at his three men. "Hearken not to me, lads. We'll find a way out." He smiled and sounded most assured.

Of course there was no way out. No way at all. There were

but five men in this room; upstairs, in the big barracks, there were probably at least two hundred. The odds were so weighted that they were laughable. And even Knox, arriving as he might with a hundred, would be unable to breach the walls of Hermitage. Cannon would be needed. He looked at the Hepburn just as, overhead, he heard the stamp of feet, of many feet, as Fleming roused the sleeping garrison.

"We don't have much time," he said unnecessarily, for all had heard the sounds of the fortress wakening. The Hepburn, listening intently, was standing straight, his heavy leather jacket bloodstained and opened almost to the waist, revealing the smooth broad chest and stomach. His face was marked and bloody, the red hair in wild disarray. Matthew was equally rumpled and half naked.

"We're a pretty pair," he said thoughtfully.

The Hepburn nodded. He addressed Johnnie. "Were you in speech with any of those men above?"

"Aye," said Johnnie.

"Are they—where are they from, lad? Most of them?"

"Liddesdale, my lord. Annandale."

"Ah," said Hepburn. He looked squarely at Matthew. He gestured toward the door, toward the heavy table Matthew was maneuvering into place just where the door would open.

"Useless," he said.

"Quite," said Matthew irritably.

"We have one sword?" Hepburn went over and picked it up. He balanced it in his hand. He considered it. "There is only one chance."

They faced each other. Matthew's three men were silent. The English and Scot, together now in danger, remembered fleetingly all that had gone before. Their faces were expressionless.

"Are you able?" asked Matthew.

"Aye," said the Hepburn. He unbolted the heavy door.

"Would you care for company?" asked Matthew.

"You're English. Stay back." The Hepburn looked down the hallway. It was still empty. But from the great hall came the sounds of many men.

Without a word he went forward down the long hall alone, and alone he stood at the entrance to the great straw-covered main hall.

He was not noticed. Torches burned. Men were streaming into the room from above, half dressed. At the guardroom, circular in shape, he saw Fleming, talking fast and gesticulating. Hepburn raised his voice.

"Lord Fleming!" The tones carried out and there was silence. "You wanted me?"

He leaned back against the wall to conserve his strength. Sword in hand, its tip resting lightly on the stone floors, he looked lazy, insolent, proud. And it must be he. The red head, the powerful broad-shouldered body; it was the Hepburn. In the quiet, his Border-laden accents carried plain.

"Would you care to fight me, Fleming?"

Fleming, speechless only momentarily at the audacity, cried out, "Seize him. Seize him!"

At the command, men moved forward slowly toward the Hepburn. There was now a muttering in the room, exclamations, as they realized it was he they had been summoned to lay hands on. But they moved forward, the first five closing in slowly, drawing the swords from their sides.

"You'll have to take me, lads," the Hepburn said softly, rather ruefully. He raised the heavy sword and waited.

They came closer. The first one engaged him. He swung the heavy blade, as the others sought to entangle him. He knew he could hold them off with sweeping cuts for perhaps two minutes. It was time to act. He raised his voice, as now desperately he fought back, the urgency making his face humorless. He needed help from the Borderers. He asked for it.

"To me!" he cried. For the first time he used the words that were to become the byword of the Border. "To me! A Bothwell! A Bothwell!"

Above the clashing of swords the cry to arms rang out. Men glanced at their nearest fellows to see the effect of the war cry on them. The Hepburn needed help from them. He needed it desperately. He asked for it openly and gallantly. A big Borderer suddenly lunged forward and grasped one of the Hepburn's assailants from behind, swinging him around.

"A Bothwell," he shouted as he flung the man backward to the floor. "Knaves, dolts! To him!"

He drew his knife. He seized another man by the arm, while the first started to get to his knees and retrieve his sword. A young boy threw himself on the rising man. In a medley of arms and legs they writhed on the floor. The Borderers of Hermitage had begun to brawl. Into this growing melee, Matthew and his three men threw themselves with vigor.

They fought barehanded, with knives or swords. A great torch toppled from the wall, razed by a sword-cut. The wrestlers, whom it hit, let out a yell of pain; someone stamped out the flame with a heavy boot.

Some men, fallen, crawled on hands and knees to the walls, and crouched there. The big Borderer, the first to respond to the Hepburn's cry, had been felled by a blow. The Hepburn stood over him, protecting him, with long sweeps of his great sword.

"Back! Back!" he shouted. There was a twisted grin on his face as he called, "Hold! Enough!"

He started forward.

With both hands he seized two men, and pushed them apart. "Stop!" he commanded.

Their arms dropped to their sides.

"Sheathe the knives!" He brought the heavy sword between two duelers. They stopped.

He shouldered his way among them almost negligently, barely avoiding the combatants. He looked ahead, his eyes on the circular guardroom, to the figure of one man who saw him coming. He kicked aside a stool someone had thrown, never deviating from his direct course to Fleming.

Fleming had backed into the far corner of the guardroom. Unthinkingly and in fear he had backed away. Anyway, there was no escape, for no one man could operate the portcullis that so effectively sealed Hermitage. Fleming pressed back against the wall, and as the Hepburn entered the round room, he began to work his way around it.

The Hepburn didn't increase his pace. Fleming did. He made a sudden rush for the door; the Hepburn lunged after him. Neither man spoke, but Fleming put up his sword to protect himself.

They fought outside the entrance to the guardroom, on the edge of the stone hall. The men who were still struggling with each other stopped. Knives were sheathed, wrestlers desisted, picking themselves up off the floor. Men edged back, to give the duelists room, and gravitated into a semicircle to watch the fight. The room, only a few minutes before in a state of riot, became still.

Fleming was short and plump but remarkably agile and light on his feet. He fought desperately, with the recklessness born of his fear. The Hepburn fought carefully, husbanding his strength. His reach was longer than Fleming's; gradually he began to force Fleming back.

But Matthew, who had come up behind Fleming, was apprehensive. The Hepburn barely parried some of Fleming's quick thrusts. Matthew had no compunction about killing Fleming; he would have killed him as he would have stepped on a spider. But the Hepburn's life was important. The Hepburn wanted an honourable peace with England. He must not die. Matthew moved to one side to watch better, his eyes fastened on Fleming. Balanced in his right hand was his slender knife which he was ready to throw should that be necessary.

Matthew flicked his hand back and forth from the wrist, readying the knife for a flight to Fleming. The men near him gave him glances as they watched the fight.

Matthew never threw the knife. Suddenly, almost without warning, the Hepburn's sword pierced Fleming's guard, sliding through the ribs like a well-calculated butcher's knife. Fleming fell to the floor.

Matthew gave a sigh of relief, and absently sheathed his knife. Fleming had fallen almost at his feet, and he looked down at him, satisfied. He had been killed instantly.

The Hepburn gave not one glance at his enemy. He looked out over the hall, at the faces of the bearded men, uncouth, rude, men who counted the life of a good horse more important than a man's. He smiled at them.

"My thanks, lads," he said, in a low voice that carried to all of them. "We'll roll out a cask of ale." He raised his hand in a gesture of thanks, handed his sword to one of the nearest men, and walked into the guardroom. Matthew followed.

The Hepburn had expected him to follow. He indicated a stool and himself sat down on a bench behind a crude table which was equipped with quills and ink. Weapons hung from every available hook on the wall; two torches smoked and stank. From all over Hermitage came the smell of horses.

A man brought two tin jugs of ale. The Hepburn and Matthew drank eagerly. The man who waited on them had a swelling lump on his head; he was the big Borderer who had first come to the Hepburn's aid.

"Your name?" asked the Hepburn.

"Garth, my lord." He was both respectful and delighted.

The Hepburn grinned. But Matthew saw he was not going to offer Garth gold. Instead he said, "You may fetch more of this ale, Garth. And two of your fellows for a night ride."

The man disappeared. The Hepburn pulled out a heavy piece of paper, and dipped the quill pen. He wrote only a few words. Matthew guessed that he was penning a brief order for Knox.

Two men appeared with Garth. The Hepburn ordered them to improve their appearance, and polish their boots. They gave him an "Aye, m'lord," and were gone again.

"Sir Matthew, you are free to leave. I will convey to his Majesty your messages. They will bear no fruit," the Hepburn said.

"You are unwarrantedly pessimistic, m'lord." Matthew rose, leaning his hands on the table.

The Hepburn looked up. The pupils of his eyes were large. His head throbbed. "I see no outgate, sir. None."

Matthew smiled a satanic smile. "D'ye credit a myth, m'lord? Is't possible ye dream we will not fight? That your blows will go unanswered?"

"You offer peace. Do you not?" The Hepburn squinted his eyes to see the Englishman's face. It was blurred.

"Aye! On condition."

The Hepburn started to shake his head, but the pain made him forego the gesture. "You offer the Princess Margaret?"

"To Jamie Stuart," said Matthew. "I bid you leave." He turned on his heel, and went to the door. He gave a shout for his horse, and went on down the hall to fetch his coat. By the time he got back the Hepburn was standing unsteadily in the doorway.

He paid no attention to Matthew. The two messengers, looking neat, with boots polished, galloped out with the message for Captain Knox. Garth was holding a piece of linen. As Matthew mounted, he heard the Hepburn say, "Wrap it carefully. His Majesty wants that head."

35

THE GATES OF EDINBURGH CASTLE STOOD OPEN, HOSPITABLY wide. The mist that would lift later in the day swirled around the gray walls and the sharp rise of the esplanade. Below the castle, the city stirred and busied itself; the shop-doors opened, the streets began to fill, butchers sharpened their knives, flames roared in the forges.

From one wine shop a messenger shouldered a crested cask of Marsala and started for the castle. On the south side of the city, up an uneven road, Garth galloped, carrying a linen-wrapped head for the King of Scots. Garth passed a travel-stained courier from England, from Cornwall. Jane Gordon entered the city ahead of both; she had been riding since before dawn.

Within the castle, Maggie Drummond yawned and moved

lazily, careful not to disturb the man who slept so soundly at her side. She lay quiet, listening to the familiar sounds of the castle rousing. She lay content because James Stuart was back. In the next room her three-day-old daughter wailed suddenly, and Maggie tensed and listened. The wail stopped abruptly and Maggie relaxed again.

James did not move. Maggie pulled the light woolen cover up over his shoulder. It was cold this morning for summer. James might sleep later than he did usually, for it had been the middle of the night when he had returned. Usually his tremendous energy roused him from sleep soon after dawn. Maggie slept again.

It was nine when she wakened. There were voices in the next room. James opened his eyes. He saw Maggie. He remembered he had a daughter.

"By sweet St. Ninian, thou'rt the bonniest thing a man could feast his eyes on in the morning. But my apologies, madam," he said. He lifted his hands and contemplated them, frowning. His shirt sleeves were crumpled, his hands were dirty, and he was fully dressed save for his shoes, which lay on the floor. "I didn't mean to fall asleep here."

"I didn't let you in bed," Maggie said. She sighed with pure pleasure at having him with her again.

"I see you didn't," said James, pushing aside the woolen throw with which she had covered him. "How's the bairn this morning?"

At this moment the door opened, and the lady who carried Maggie's daughter let out a little scream when she saw James. She started to back out, but James motioned her to come in. He held out his arms.

"Put her here," he said. "I can't touch her with my hands."

He looked down at the infant. She looked like Maggie. James said so. "I thought so last night," he added.

Maggie said, "I was hoping she would look like you."

"Heaven forbid," he said, and meant it. He scrutinized Maggie. "I wanted her to be exactly like you."

Maggie said, "I love you so much."

The baby slept in his arms. Another woman and the wet-nurse entered. Not knowing James was within the chamber, there was a flurry of jerky curtsies and cries.

James did not heed them. He looked down at the sleeping infant. She was his daughter. She should be a princess, but she was not.

He frowned. "I shall bestow a duchy on her," he said angrily. Maggie crawled across the big bed and curled up beside him. She leaned her head against his shoulder. They were both silent. Finally James said, "In thine own image the bairn is, sweetheart."

She took the child from him. He rose and looked down at the both of them, unaware the other women were in the room, seeing only Maggie and his daughter.

He leaned down and kissed her. "I love you," he whispered. He picked up his discarded boots.

Maggie cradled the child in her arms, rocking it.

"Are you well enough to dress today, madam?" he asked.

Maggie nodded. "I am going to dress for breakfast. Mary Gordon is joining us."

James smiled indulgently. The Drummond sisters ate a light breakfast at eleven, a most unusual meal. It was a meal to which the Court yearned to be invited.

"We are celebrating this morning. Eufemia is opening a new cask of Marsala," Maggie said.

It was then nine-fifteen, and the English messenger had arrived with advices from Cornwall. There was trouble and rebellion in Cornwall, outright rebellion. The army which Henry VII had started north to Scotland had swung around. This news occasioned a pleasant humor in James, who bathed and dressed and joked with his gentlemen until the chamberlain entered with the message that the Duke of York would like permission for a private audience.

"By all the saints," grumbled James, but the chamberlain knew that he could reply in the affirmative to the duke. "I'll see him now," said James.

The duke looked the same as ever as he came into the cleared chamber, so that his first words startled James. The duke said, "Your Grace, I deem it time for the duchess and me to leave Scotland."

Since James had no intention of allowing him to leave, he said nothing and waited. Perkin Warbeck rubbed his hands together hard.

"I feel we have outstayed our welcome."

James's face was inscrutable. "No, indeed, my lord."

Perkin became a trifle excited. "There is rebellion in Cornwall! Against Henry Tudor's new levies!"

"Quite so," James said. "I can allow you two more minutes."

There was a sharp rap on the door, and voices outside. A servant entered. James rose to his feet, forgetting Perkin. He had seen Knox.

"Send him in," he called out, as Perkin rose.

Knox came in on a run, and behind him another bearded man, who laid a linen package on James's table. James watched as it was unwrapped, whereupon Perkin took a step backward and averted his eyes. James then spread out the paper Knox carried and began to read. Fleming's head stood upright on the table. Perkin Warbeck found himself forgotten again, though not dismissed, so he waited patiently, chewing his lip.

James finished reading the Hepburn's message. He put down the letter and looked up at Knox.

"Return when you've refreshed yourself."

Knox bowed. James instructed Garth to be paid a gold piece for his trip to Edinburgh. When they were both gone, James Stuart motioned Perkin Warbeck to sit.

James, his hands resting on the table in front of him, looked across at Warbeck but did not see him. Instead a picture took shape in his mind.

Way to the south, there was disaffection in Cornwall. But Surrey, with an English army of thirty thousand men, would soon be ready to swing north. At Hermitage, the Hepburn waited. The Earl of Douglass had betrayed James, and had signed over Hermitage to the invading English. But no more could the English count on that open gate to Liddesdale. Douglass was dead. James picked up the linen cloth and put it over the head of his father's murderer. He was very dead.

Henry Tudor was suing for peace. He wanted Perkin Warbeck, who now was alive. And breathing. James glanced at him. How much of his story was true? There did not seem much doubt that he was not the Duke of York, yet there were puzzling bits and scraps of truth in the fantastic story. Enough to worry Henry Tudor mightily.

Last night the Spanish ambassador, de Ayala, had offered once more one of Spain's four daughters to James Stuart. In exchange for peace with England. Now England herself offered a princess. James's dark face was somber.

"So you wish to quit Scottish shores—and sail for Cornwall?"

Perkin, suddenly addressed, answered boldly. "Aye, your Grace. There I shall find adherents! They're promised."

"Put no faith in't," James muttered. "No faith." Maggie's clear greenish eyes with their flecks of color were right before him. He wanted no Spanish daughter to wed, no English bride. But now he was getting what he wanted. It was a precious parcel of prestige. It had not been—was not—enough to rule Scotland. He must be strong enough to wield influence other monarchs hearkened to, sued to please, recognized as equal.

This victory was within his hands. One of the pawns he had used was willing to give even more. He would probably go to an ignoble death. James could imagine him in Westminster, exhibited on barrels before they'd hang him.

"You wish to sail for England?" James repeated. The instruments to power were not pretty. But he, with an army already mustered, could seize Berwick while this fool sacrificed himself and was captured. Then peace could come. With all honor accruing to James Stuart. And there would be no need for a foreign marriage.

James said, "I shall have a ship made ready at Ayr. It will be well provisioned. At the time you sail, I shall invade England."

It was said, then, and since said, done. Had only thirty minutes passed?

The second quarter chimed out. Jane Gordon paced back and forth across the room as she listened to her sister.

"Are you mad, Mary?"

"I'm his wife."

"Does that make you party to his follies?" Jane, booted and spurred, stopped her pacing, and the room was still. "The Duchess of Burgundy is a silly old bitch," announced Jane. "Why does the duke heed her? And what is this of revolt in Cornwall? What nonsense?"

Mary laughed. She looked at Jane with affection. "Janie," she said. " 'Tis good to be with thee, like bygone times. It seems much longer than a few months. But listen to me."

Jane threw back her cloak. "Well?" she challenged.

"I am the Princess of York. That is my name, willy-nilly. If it were forced on me, that is still no matter."

Jane muttered, "I might ha' stopped it—if I'd—"

"No." Mary interrupted. "That's useless. My husband claims a throne. So we, he and I, are no longer just a man and woman, but political beings."

"You could renounce your claims!"

"Impossible," said Mary. "D'ye think Henry Tudor would permit us to do that? My husband is a threat. Living, he is always a threat. An attempt was made on his life just hours ago. No, we have taken our stand. Richard wants to go to England to seek openly what is his."

"That is mad," said Jane firmly. "You talk as though he were your child, and you were humoring him!"

Mary said desperately, "At least it is direct and honest."

"And you are not sure if he has been honest with you, are you? Are you? You doubt. Admit it to me."

Jane walked toward her, whereupon Mary cried, "Well then, what am I to do? What is there to do?"

Jane evaded an answer. Suddenly she said, "I was to start my return trip at eleven, and it lacks but a few minutes to the hour. I must go."

The plan forming in her mind was a wild one. "Then if his Majesty allows Richard to sail, you would go?"

"I cannot desert him," Mary said. "I cannot!"

In the distance a clock struck. " 'Tis eleven," said Jane. "Time for your breakfast with Maggie." She was intent only on what she was going to do. Mary sensed it. She ran after her.

"Jane! Never interfere!"

Jane started to say something. She had been about to ask Mary if she loved Matthew Craddock. She did not know why Mary had never confessed it to her. But now was no time to question.

"I won't interfere. I'll be back tomorrow, perhaps. Do not worry, duck."

She was gone with a sweep of her riding cloak. She hurried down the hallway. She would get to Matthew, and warn him that Mary was coming to England, as the consort of the Duke of York. And if this spoiled the plans of the Hepburn, so much the better. She'd keep her promise to Matthew. She'd ride to the Borders, to Hermitage.

Maggie's cook carefully lifted the poached eggs onto a platter. Then he tasted the sauce. He licked his lips and looked to the ceiling for inspiration.

"A little ginger?" asked one helper.

"Dolt." The cook raised the spoon threateningly.

The helper backed away into the still unopened cask of Marsala. The cook decided the sauce was almost perfect. He added a soupçon of saffron and a dusting of blanche powder.

"Instead of ginger," he said grandly, "ginger, cinnamon, *and* nutmeg." He poured the sauce over the eggs. The quinces in compote rested in footed silver dishes, and from the oven were taken sweet buns and planchets of finest white bread.

"The wine," said the cook, as he picked up the platter of eggs and bore it from the room.

He was relieved to see that the Duchess of York, with a servant bearing her train, was entering the room. Had Mary Gordon not been there, he would have had to wait with his serving. Eufemia also was permitted a servant for her train since she was now a countess, not a mere baroness—but she could not be seated in the presence of a standing duchess. And Mary did not sit. Eufemia drew her brows together, tossed her curls.

Maggie was carrying her child. Sybilla's two-year-old tried to stand on tiptoe to see the newest baby, and Maggie leaned down to let her see. The little room was crowded; this cabinet for dining was only about ten feet square. The cook was afraid the eggs would get cold. Because of the importance of his position he was allowed to remonstrate.

"Madam," he said. "Your ladyship."

Maggie smiled, and handed her baby to its nurse, Lady Montford. Montford carried the child out. Sybilla's little girl scampered after them, and Mary advanced toward the table, her personal servant still patiently bearing her train.

At last the duchess was seated. The cook heaved a sigh, waved the big wooden spoon, and began to serve. The cook took great pride in the manners of his four diners. They could be counted on to break only a small piece of bread to put in their mouths, so that what they left was whole and ready to give to the poor. He was proud of the ivory table with its rich white linen, and he saw that the flowers were appropriately strewn across the board to rival in scent and beauty these four women.

"The eggs are delicious," the duchess said.

The cook beamed. He felt so fine that perhaps he would even allow the turnspit to eat what the duchess left of her sugared bun. The cook smiled again, and signaled for the pouring of the wine.

The goblets were gold. They were tall and heavy. The wine gurgled into them. It had been touched with the shark's tooth. Eufemia lifted her goblet in both her white hands. She frowned a little.

"The bouquet is not as fine as it should be."

Maggie lifted her goblet. "I think so, Eufemia."

"Well, a toast to my laddie the Hepburn," Eufemia said, looking insolently at Mary.

The women raised the goblets to their red lips. They drank,

all except Mary, who refused to drink the toast. It was little enough to do for Jane.

The eggs were very rich, sweetened with honey. Mary began to be very thirsty, but she was also hungry, and the goblets were too heavy. She remembered James's remark that if he needed money all he had to do was melt down one of them. Eufemia had just made an incautious remark about a certain Lady Heron, an Englishwoman.

"I'd prefer not to talk on't, Eufemia," Maggie said.

Sybilla, who was nearest Maggie, said, "Thou wert big with child, Maggie."

Nothing could quiet Eufemia when her mind was busy with one subject. "I warrant she wasn't bonnie."

Maggie tilted her head. "Dost insult his Grace?" She flashed an impish look at Mary. But she was flushed. Her curly hair was loose and she wore a flowing gown with half sleeves, which were very new. They fell back as she raised the golden goblet. Mary was struck by the richness of her beauty. She felt a rush of affection for Maggie Drummond. Maggie winked at Mary.

"To Jamie," she said, and Mary reached for her wine. She was tasting it on her lips when Maggie gave a sudden cry, rose unsteadily to her feet, and threw the goblet away from her, onto the table, so that the wine spread in all directions, among the flowers, touching the petals, running freely like spilled blood, seeping into the white cloth. Then Maggie leaned across to Mary and struck the goblet from her.

One of the servants screamed. Eufemia's goblet was empty. It fell from her hands, and she doubled up, striking her forehead on the gold. Sybilla set her wine down. Her hands clenched around it. Her body shuddered. Mary forgot her and Eufemia. Her chair crashed over. She went to Maggie.

"Fetch his Grace!" she cried.

Her hands were trembling. The shark's tooth had been passed over the wine. It could not be poisoned. And Maggie had drunk less than her sisters.

The servants had shrieked for aid. Lady Montford came scurrying.

"A doctor!" Her voice rose in terror. Maggie was still standing, clutching the table, and Mary supported her from the side, with her arms.

"Are you in pain?" Mary cried.

She barely heard the answer. "Aye," said Maggie, as the king came through the curtained doorway.

He knocked a chair out of his way. Eufemia's face was hidden from him, Sybilla was moaning in short quick gasps; the heavy feet of men running sounded from outside. James took Maggie in his arms, he lifted her and carried her from the room where Eufemia already lay dead.

"My darling, my darling," he whispered. He had taken her on his lap, and she was huddled against him, her legs doubled under her. She crouched on his knees, her arms around his neck, fiercely.

She could not speak. She burrowed against him. Mary came running with a bowl. And James forced Maggie's head up. He forced her jaws open. She began to retch.

The doctor stood over her. This was the only thing to do; there was nothing more except to pray. He wiped Maggie's mouth with a towel dipped in rose water.

"Would you lie down?" James asked.

"No."

In the next room they had already covered Eufemia's and Sybilla's bodies. The maids sobbed. James could hear their long gusty outbursts. A little maid rushed past James, her apron over her head. Mary had barely sipped the wine. But she felt the first griping pain knife through her stomach. Now fear touched her.

"I, too," she said.

The doctor led her away. Maggie's eyes had closed. Her face looked sweet and peaceful.

Mary vomited up her breakfast. She told the doctor how much wine she had drunk. He did not seem afraid for her.

"It was very quick, you see, your Grace." But he advised her to go to bed. He seemed stunned. The baby cried in the next room.

"The sisters died almost instantly," he added.

"Is there any hope?" she asked. She trembled.

"None." He lifted the curtain and Mary looked into the next room.

James had lain Maggie on her bed. He was pulling up the white sheet. Mary saw his brown hands on the white linen.

He did not cover her face. Suddenly he tucked the sheet across her breast. He lifted her hands and crossed them. Then he bent down and Mary saw the broad shoulders shaking. Slowly she let the curtain fall back into place.

36

JANE GORDON KNEW EVERY BORDER TRACK. MONTH after month she had ridden out, ofttimes alone, spending hours in the saddle, discovering lazy little towns, the crumbling ruins of old castles, a Roman bridge over a swift river.

She had come to be known, she and her black stallion that was as big as the Hepburn's. Most Border mounts were small and fleet; the people knew Jane from afar as she would come thundering down the valley road and rein up in clouds of dust beside the meager wayside inn, which had no accommodations but merely served to dispense ale and food to occasional travelers.

In this wild Border she rode safe, even a marauding English troop would not dare lay hands on her. Sometimes they watched her from a distance as she galloped across a moor to disappear into the thick forests she knew so well. Often she stayed at the hunting lodge deep in Ettrick Forest, sitting at table with the men there, sharing meals of venison or wild fowl, hardly blooded. Occasionally she dined on English beef.

She did not know whether or not the Hepburn disapproved.

She gave no thought either to whether his people liked her. But the last time she had stayed at the lodge in Ettrick, she had taken part in their dice game. She had stayed up all night. When dawn came, and she had drunk the last of the foamy ale, she had pushed back her loose hair, and tossed her winnings on the table. In the rude rushlight, they had looked up, surprised.

"That's not for you," Jane said. " 'Tis for a new roof." She grinned, "Lord God, I'm sleepy; you knaves have kept me up past my usual bedtime. Any man who makes a noise and wakens me gets a week in the stocks." She moved out of the room and did not see that they watched her with affectionate and admiring eyes.

Now she galloped steadily through the early evening; she was already in Liddesdale. The last town had not been familiar, for she had never ventured this far south before. Still, she should be almost there.

There were no roads. Only tracks through the thick woods, across moss and moor and bog. The sound of water made her slow her pace. That might be Hermitage water. She had timed herself well, for she would reach the great fortress before darkness fell. It was just about dusk when she pushed through a rocky burn and saw Hermitage itself.

The noise of the waterfall drowned out the sound of the birds and wood noises of evening. An animal brushed by her close, on the way to the little pool at the foot of the falls. The air was still, the moon was rising. Jane looked around this valley where she was alone. As she was telling herself there was nothing to fear, she saw with surprise that the great portcullis was drawn up and open. She spurred her mount forward.

The ancient drawbridge over the swift water was made of planks. Her horse's hooves sounded loud as they trotted over it. It occurred to her as she crossed that it was legend that no woman had ever entered the castle.

It was not impressive, outside of its size. The stone hall into which she rode was also equipped as a stable for the mounts. Straw covered the floors, fresh laid and clean. To her right was a guardroom. She reined in.

From overhead the noise and talk of men came clearly. She smelled food cooking. It was the supper hour. She threw back the hood of her cloak, and still astride, looked down at a man who was staring at her with utmost amazement.

"Fellow, your hand," Jane said impatiently.

He stared. He obeyed slowly. He helped her dismount, holding out his hand to her as if he would never get it back.

"His lordship," he muttered weakly.

"A pox on his lordship," said Jane. She looked into the guardroom, from where five men gazed at her in helpless wonder. She beckoned to one. "Come take my mount, dolt."

He didn't move. He shook his head and looked at the man with Jane.

"You'd best go!" that man said suddenly.

Jane leveled him with one look. "Take me to your lord."

He was holding the reins. He made to return them to her, but she disdained them.

"Are you in possession of your wits?" Jane asked. "Take me to your lord." Then it suddenly crossed her mind that he might be afraid to take her to Douglass because she was wed to the Hepburn. "D'ye know who I am?"

He shook his head. "No. But his lordship would not approve."

Then she heard footsteps coming swiftly down the stone steps. She turned and waited for the newcomer who perhaps would have more authority.

The man reached the hall, saw her, and started toward her rapidly. He came to a stop in front of her. His eyes raked her. Jane took refuge in her name.

"I am Lady Bothwell!"

At that his manner changed abruptly. He bowed briefly. "Follow me, then, madam." He started across the wide hall toward a corridor. He called back to the man. "As soon as the captain comes in, close the gates." Then he went on ahead.

"There are his lordship's apartments, madam," he said. "I

shall fetch him from upstairs. In the meantime, you may wait here." He threw open a door.

Jane entered. It was a corner room with an enormous fireplace and a big uncurtained bed. The floors were stone.

Jane waited until his footsteps had retreated. Then she slipped over and opened the door. She looked down the empty hall. There was suddenly a lot of noise of men and horses. In the distance, the chains of the portcullis began to creak; the great door lowered with a resounding clang.

Her heart beat fast. But she had to come. Someone had to warn Matthew that Mary and Richard were going to England. And there was no risk. Everyone was used to seeing her in the Borders. In five minutes she would be riding away.

She was still looking down the narrow hall where men were moving. One of them seemed familiar. He walked and looked like Willie. But that was impossible.

She closed the door hurriedly. She paced across the room. She had taken off her cloak but now she put it on, drawing it around her. She walked over to the chest as she had done so many months ago in Edinburgh castle, opened the drawer and looked in.

It could not be. She lifted out the first white shirt. Her heart pounded. It was a monogrammed shirt, and she had initialed it. There could be no mistake. Jane pushed the drawer closed and fled across to the door.

Once more she opened it. She must get out. She ran down the hall and almost reached the end when she remembered the gates were closed.

"Holy Mary," she whispered. It was then she heard his voice. She turned and ran.

She regained the shelter of the corner room. In the quiet she could plainly hear his deliberate footsteps coming down the hall.

His hand was on the latch. It lifted. Even then she could hardly believe it. The door swung inward. The familiar chamois jacket and breeks he wore were rumpled, the jacket open at the throat. His red head was bare. He filled the doorway.

He did not take his eyes from her. The look in them made her pull her cloak close around her. She stepped back away, while with one hand he pushed the door behind him. His voice was low, but the Border accent was very thick.

"I don't flatter mysel' you came to see me, madam. I gather it was another man."

"I didn't know you were here!" The truth burst from her. "*You* are the master of Hermitage castle?"

He was still in the doorway. "In that capacity, perhaps I can aid you, since you rode so far, and since the man you came to see is not here. Sir Matthew left two nights back."

Jane retreated another step. The Hepburn had not latched the door securely, and it started to swing open. He turned and kicked it shut with a sudden violence that crashed it shuddering against its frame.

The noise died away. "You cannot aid me," Jane said bravely. "I'll go."

"Aye, you'll go." He did not move toward her. "When I've had as much as I want from you, you'll go. Come here."

"No!"

He didn't repeat his command. But his big hands were clenched. Slowly Jane moved toward him. When her steps had brought her right before him, he smiled mockingly.

"It might be best to obey me, madam. Unless you want to provoke the brutality of which I am capable. Remove your cloak."

Jane set her mouth. Then she let the cloak slip off her shoulders onto the floor, where it spilled into a heap of color on the stone. "Aye, m'lord," she said, mockery in her own tones.

He still made no motion to touch her. When he raised his hand, he pointed to the cloak.

"Pick it up. I dislike disorder."

Jane hesitated. Then she leaned down and picked up the cloak, carrying it to a chair and laying it down neatly. She whirled.

"Does that suit you?" she cried. She endeavored to quiet

the trembling in her knees. She rubbed her damp palms on her skirt.

"I told you once," he was saying, "that there would be a night when I would treat you as you should be treated. Return to me." He beckoned to her.

"No!" Across the room she stamped her foot, hard.

In answer he took off the leather jacket and put it on a stool. "Do you want me to force you?" One eyebrow raised, he looked across at her.

She blurted, "I deny nothing! I shall deny nothing." Her heart pounded. He was coming toward her now, and she backed away, eyes fastened on him. "Patrick."

He was very close. His hands reached out for her, taking her by the shoulders. Had he heard what she had said?

"Please," whispered Jane.

His outward calm was almost broken. Still he said, as he prolonged the moment of holding her, "Please what? D'ye want money?"

"No," whispered Jane. "No, m'lord."

"I'll pay you high," he muttered, his hands tightening on her. "But first tell me how you freed the Englishman."

Jane averted her face. One arm went around her. He tipped her head back.

"Answer me!"

She told the truth. "There is a secret passage to my tower rooms."

"Ah." He looked down at the lips that had confessed, the lips that had probably whispered endearments to Matthew Craddock. The Hepburn bent to kiss those lips. They were unresponsive.

He shifted his position, bending her back in his arms, using the strength of arms and legs to weigh heavy against her slim body. Holding her thus, he reached for the pins in her hair, loosing it. He undid the buttons of the high-necked dress she wore. He felt her shiver at his touch, and angrily his mouth closed over hers. Tonight at least, she would belong to him, and to him alone.

The Hepburn lay flat on his stomach, one arm flung over Jane. He did not know how long he had slept, when at last he opened his eyes. He imagined she slept, too. Her eyes were closed. He reached out lazily and fastened his hands in her hair, turning her face toward his. Propped up on one elbow, he watched as her eyes opened.

They met his for just a moment. She sought the sheet, and pulled it to cover herself.

"Modest, my lady?" he gibed. He let go her hair. It swung like a gold curtain between them. The Hepburn yawned. Then she spoke, spacing each word, very low, hesitantly, "May I leave now, then?"

He shook his head. He wrapped his arms around her and put his head down on her breast. "Don't you like to sleep with me?" he murmured.

She did not answer. He could not see her face. He dozed. After a few minutes she spoke again.

"I would like your permission to leave. You said I could leave!"

The Hepburn raised his head. He pulled the sheet away, uncovering her. She made a cry of protest but he stopped her mouth with a long slow kiss. He spoke between kisses. "You must have had inadequate lovers. You may leave in the morning."

Jane said, "Oh, no!"

"Open your eyes. Is it that you do not want to make another confession of love for me?"

Jane looked into his eyes. They were half closed, the gray eyes, narrowed and ironic.

"I'm ashamed of loving you," she said clearly. "I shall never return to Bothwell."

The Hepburn smiled grimly. "When I have a desire for you, I'll find you. You may go in the morning. But now I want to hear you say you love me. It pleases me."

"I'll not say it," Jane whispered.

"You shall," he said. "You shall."

37

ST. MICHAEL'S MOUNT REARS ITS ROCKY PILE OUT OF waves off the Cornish coast. A swift channel separates it from the mainland, and the summit of its jagged stones is crowned by the frowning walls of an ancient monastery.

But the monks have gone. It is a fortress only now, lonely, gaunt. One side of the chapel roof has caved in; the flower-like window over the altar is broken and empty of glass. Far, far below, the churning seas pound and the wind moans over the gray water.

From the main of England proper, across Whitesand Bay lashed by the September gales, a boat pulled. Its tiny sail was furled; unfurled, the boat would tip and founder on the rocks. Its oars flashed, rhythmically; there were two men in it. And on the narrow strip of shingle at the foot of St. Michael's Mount, Mary Gordon waited.

The wind blew. It enveloped her body in ragged gusts. Spray flew; the sound of the surf drowned all other sounds except the shriek of a lonely gull. As the boat came closer to shore, Mary raised her hand and waved. It would have done no good to shout.

Her scarf, seized by the wind, unwound itself and fluttered like a signal. The boat was caught by an incoming breaker. It posed on the foamy crest and then, gathering speed, a minute later it was flung up on the beach, still upright. One man leaped out into knee-high water. He beached the boat, and came running toward her.

But once he stood before her, breathless from the long row, he found no quick words. His companion joined them. The incoming tides forced them all back a few feet, as the water surged over the shingle, spilling from the high gray sea.

Mary had waited alone three long days. She said quietly, "Tell me."

The first man began.

"We—the duke—went first to Bodmin. We were joined by about three thousand Cornish. We were pleased. We then marched on Exeter."

Mary said, "Go on."

"The Cornish were but rudely armed, with bills, and arrows, and old spears. We reached Exeter. The duke made a speech to the people to induce them to open the gates of the city to their rightful and lawful sovereign. They refused." He paused. "We had no artillery, madam. So the duke ordered fires set at the city gates."

Mary Gordon heard him plainly; she heard the sound of the seas and the cries of the sea birds. Could this be she who stood here? He went on.

"Before the fire had burned enough to clear a passage for us, the citizens had piled a great barrier of fagots, which continued to burn, madam, whilst they made ramparts and trenches within. And our efforts to scale the walls were equally unsuccessful. Certainly his Majesty had learned of our coming; we knew he was sending Lord Willoughby and Daubeney and others to succor the town, but meanwhile the Earl of Devonshire and his son were rousing their men and the local gentry. I knew we were cut off, and I so informed his Grace. We went on to Taunton, in Somersetshire, as if we were making to go to London."

Mary knew that she had never truly thought there could be any end but this. She said, low, "What happened, then, to m'lord, my husband?"

The hired German mercenary, his lean face set, smiled grimly. "He fled in the night, madam, leaving his poor rebels to face the loyalists alone. He escaped to Beaulieu Abbey, in Hampshire, and in this sanctuary, which was soon surrounded by a body of horse, he is prisoner till further orders from Harry. King Harry himself is now at Exeter. They are sending for you, madam."

Mary gestured, as if to say that was no matter. "What happened to the Cornish? Who followed you?"

He shrugged. "They were left leaderless. We"—he indicated his companion—"rode through the sleeping men, rousing them, commanding them to surrender to Devonshire, to save their lives. They did."

"There was no battle?"

"No, madam. But you cannot stand here and talk. Out there is a little bark. One of the ones we used to sail here."

Mary shook her head. "Who is with the duke?"

"A handful of attendants, only! Madam, listen to me!"

"I might be able to save his life," she said strongly. "I wait for the English."

"His life is worth nothing," said the German. It was incredible to him that this beautiful woman could love the Duke of York. The German, himself an adventurer, had only the lowest regard for Perkin Warbeck. "Loyalty is out of place now. Pity too. Both are wasted." But even as he spoke it was too late. Mary was looking toward the English coast.

"They come," she said.

The town of Exeter was filled to overflowing. King Harry had marched in that morning, and he had been joyfully received. He had presented his own sword to the mayor of Exeter, to be carried before the town's mayors in future processions as a mark of honor. He had congratulated the citizenry on their brave repulse of Perkin Warbeck. Wine flowed in the fountains. Soldiers thronged the streets, and a holiday had been declared. The hastily dug trenches still remained, the piles of earth were high and dusty. Through the fire-blackened gates, Mary Gordon rode that afternoon.

The king was with the mayor. Way was made slowly because of the throngs in the streets. Crowds of others whom Mary must pass gathered along the way; they hung from the windows to see. They had briefly seen the pretended duke. They had heard his appeal three days before. But this woman was the cousin of James of Scotland. The crowd surged around the flanks of her horse, stared at her and the four serving women who followed her, and at the two men who rode ahead.

In front of the mayor's house, the king's guard of honor stood at attention, their plumed helmets waving, the halberds held straight. Mary passed between their ranks. Lord Daubeney was with the king; Willoughby de Broke, the Earl of Devonshire, and others, attendants and gentlemen. The hall was vibrant with deep voices; frock-coated clergy moved, servants hurried. Slowly, toward the king and his surrounding nobility, Mary Gordon moved.

She was the only woman in the room. Her own women waited at the doorway. The King of England was stooped and gray and thin. He was crafty but given to odd kindnesses; he was avaricious, yet a cool and clever statesman. He was the founder of a dynasty and he knew it; he knew it and relished it as much as he relished the feel of gold between his palms.

But King Harry was also a man. As Mary Gordon came to him, the brawny Earl of Devonshire flashed a knowing look at his tall son. The proof of the pudding might be the way King Harry looked at his feminine prisoner.

The king smiled at Mary, showing his broken teeth. She curtsied deeply; her great eyes were almost purple.

"Your Majesty," said Mary.

Willoughby de Broke sighed at the sound of the soft Scottish voice. The mayor of Exeter thought vaguely he must summon his wife, for this beautiful girl should not be alone here, in a room full of men. He whispered to a servant. In the meantime Henry Tudor had, hours previously, decided on clemency for everyone concerned except two people, and they, both men. Besides that, besides the beauty of this woman who was young enough to be his daughter, she was part Stuart, and at the border, James Stuart had an army. Henry said, "We are glad to greet you."

Her rank and her misfortune made a gallant out of Harry of England. Privately he decided to give her an allowance, which would continue long after his death. The decision did not even amaze him. He continued, "We shall send you to keep company with our queen."

"I thank you, my lord," Mary said.

The mayor's wife bustled toward her. She took Mary in charge, took her from the room, from the eyes of the men. When the doors closed, Willoughby de Broke grew positively poetic.

"The Lady Mary is not a Yorkist at all, sire," he said. "She is a white rose from Scotland."

38

THE ROYAL COURIER JUMPED OFF HIS LATHERED HORSE. He was immediately admitted into Matthew's tent where he found that gentleman waiting impatiently.

"What news?"

The words came few and swiftly. "Warbeck is lodged in the Tower."

"Ah," said Matthew, getting to his feet. That was all he wanted to hear. A page in the tent rushed out. A horse was ready. So was an escort and four wardens of the Border. Matthew picked up his sword belt and buckled it.

He was reading the message.

"How long have you been riding?"

"Three days, sir. The roads."

Outside it was raining as though the clouds had borne their burden so long they would never rid themselves of it. The camp was a sea of mud. Surrey's tent, brave yesterday, waved a disconsolate banner; its sodden walls had lost their shine. Thirty thousand men were encamped here, a few miles away from the Scots.

Undoubtedly James already had the same news Matthew had just received. James had retreated back toward Scotland during the night, and had established himself at Norham castle, which he had taken a month before. It was probably more comfortable.

Matthew rode off at the head of his escort, his cloak fastened tight against the beating rain, his hat pulled over his eyes. The horses slipped and sank into the mud. Across the barren border the winds whistled, tearing the autumn leaves from the few trees. The wind sighed over the moors, which stretched like graveyards. All was desolate.

Matthew and his men struggled onward. The ruts were deep with water. It took an hour and a half to reach Norham.

The great castle, half of the west wing ripped asunder by Scottish artillery, looked unlike a setting for peace. And yet the way had now been cleared.

Perkin Warbeck was a prisoner of the English. The armies, crouched for action, probably would not fight. As Matthew and his men entered the apron of the castle, he saw the Spanish ambassador climb into a shielded litter; the Hepburn himself closed the curtain. Matthew dismounted. The Spaniard had done a good deal for peace; he wanted it badly so England could fight France. Matthew went forward to greet the Hepburn.

The two men bowed. Within the vast hall, servants came running to take the Englishman's cloak. The wind moaned through the stone arches of Norham. Matthew deemed that what he and the Hepburn wanted was now going to be fact. Matthew grinned.

He got no answering smile. A flicker of dismay went through Matthew. The Hepburn had not given his word—he had promised nothing—but still, he had talked frankly and honestly that night at Hermitage.

"M'lord," said Matthew, "I remember well an hour spent with you. Each word is engraved on my memory."

"My memory serves me well." The Hepburn was distant.

"Then it rivals mine, to be sure." Matthew shook out his white cuffs, and his eyes met the Hepburn's. The Hepburn looked away. Suddenly he growled, "I remember you have a powerful right fist!"

With amazement Matthew realized the Hepburn was spoiling for a fight and Matthew's gorge rose. He said softly, "You know I'd be most happy to oblige you, my lord, but 'tis so undignified brawling here. It shall be something to look forward to, in the not so distant future." Matthew continued, his jaw jutting out, "Suppose you compose your foul humor and take me to Jamie."

Evidently the Hepburn did not trust himself to speak. He strode ahead. The tall guards lowered the halberds. The pages withdrew. The Hepburn said, almost in a mutter, "Your Majesty, may I present Sir Matthew Craddock."

James was taking his ease on his daybed. Matthew bowed deeply, and James inclined his head. He did not rise, but he asked Matthew to be seated near him. The Hepburn disdained to sit, and stood over Matthew. Matthew's voice was low.

"Your Grace, I greatly appreciate your receiving me. I bring you regards and greetings from his Majesty, Henry of England."

James said, "How is my dear cousin?"

"Well," said Matthew. "But I bring you news too, your Grace."

James affected surprise. "News, sir?"

There was a small silence. James knew what was coming, so did Matthew and the Hepburn. For a moment their thoughts went to the man who had been used to excuse a war between two nations. Matthew said baldly, "Sire, the man who calls himself the Duke of York landed on English soil three days ago. He was captured and taken prisoner, and he is now lodged in the Tower of London."

James's dark face was inscrutable. His hands were untied now, by Perkin himself, by Perkin who was on his way to heaven or hell, and James had nothing to do with that decision.

"Did the duke fight?" he asked curiously.

"No," said Matthew. "He fled the face of fighting."

After a moment's silence, he continued. "Your Grace, I must speak openly. I am here to offer peace, to begin negotiations for peace."

James Stuart gave no outward signs of a sense of victory. He said, only, "Proceed."

But he was going to hear what he wanted to hear. He leaned back and listened to Matthew's words.

"We offer an honorable peace." Matthew paused. "We are willing first to forget the despoliation of the Border. Further, his Majesty is offering you, as complete proof of his devotion, his first-born daughter, the Princess Margaret."

Matthew kept reminding himself they were able to make these terms because Henry held the nuisance, Perkin Warbeck. It was true that all the glory of this game of war had accrued to James. Matthew saw clearly that glory was necessary to James, more so than it was to Henry, who ruled a nation more stable, wealthier and more advanced. This peace, a victory for James, increased the Stuart stature, and for a young man it was a heady triumph. All Europe would take note. Matthew begrudged it, yet Henry, the wily Henry, had won too. He also needed the Duke of York: to part his head from his rather slender neck.

James Stuart rose and walked over to the window. The day was dying, and miles away at Dumblane Abbey the priests would be chanting a mass.

Under the stone floor of the abbey was interred the body of Maggie Drummond. Hers was the middle grave; her sisters rested on each side of her.

The graves were marked with blue flagstones. Each dawn, each dusk, the masses were sung for her. James Stuart could hear again the thin singing he had heard five days ago, at Maggie's grave. Suddenly he remembered something he knew Maggie would insist on his doing. He said quickly, "My cousin, Lady Mary Gordon." He swung around from the window and looked at Matthew, his somber face intent. "Let harm come to her, and by all the saints, ye'll suffer."

Matthew said, "Your Grace, his Majesty has given her an honorable place beside and in the company of his queen. He has given her an allowance."

"What?" said James. A gleam of humor was in his dark eyes. "Let it continue."

Matthew said, "His Majesty would send Bishop Fox as his emissary and the meeting place should be Berwick."

James's face was again somber. Matthew knew that James Stuart wanted no marriage personally. But politically? A month ago Bishop Fox himself had said to Henry that he was afraid such a marriage might be to the prejudice of England. Suppose young Henry, who would be Henry VIII, had no issue? The king's answer had been astute.

"Scotland in that case would be an accession to England, for the greater would draw the less, and it is a safer union for England than a union with France."

Matthew deemed that true. And yet James Stuart might yet, he or his heirs, rightly claim the English throne. All that was in the future. Now little remained to be done.

"I shall be pleased to greet Bishop Fox," said James. "We have met before."

Matthew bowed. He took leave of James Stuart; he knew he would never forget him. The Hepburn, still silent, followed.

In the hall again, a man brought Matthew's cloak; it had been dried before a fire. He confronted the Hepburn squarely, his brows drawn together, and his own anger caught fire from the Hepburn.

"If I didn't have to return to London as fast as a succession of nags could take me, by God I'd meet you tonight." His hands were clenched and he let his anger loose with pleasure. The two men stood eye to eye. The soldiers near backed away and stared with amazement and expectancy. Were their lords going to fight?

"This is supposed to be a peaceful mission," Matthew muttered. "But I'd meet you tonight if I could!"

"Why can you not?" sneered the Hepburn.

"Because of Mary Gordon," Matthew snarled. "A great deal you've done for her, you whoreson bastard."

The Hepburn stared at him.

Then suddenly Matthew understood. He had no time for words. He crinkled his eyes a little as he looked at the Hepburn and adjusted his cloak.

"You fool," he said. He mounted and spurred his horse.

The Hepburn stood with the rain beating against his whole body, in the gusty wind and the darkness of the deepening night. Matthew was disappearing into that darkness.

"Wait!" cried the Hepburn. He raised his arm.

Matthew did not hear. The wind had torn the single word from the Hepburn's mouth. The wind reminded him of the day when Jane had come walking back to Bothwell, after she had freed Matthew through the secret passage. And so it had been for Mary, for quiet little Mary, all the time. Mary, who had said no, in genuine surprise, "No, Jane did not send me."

"Jane," he said, aloud, to the black night. Where was she? He had a moment's vision of her, riding as only she could ride, on that enormous black beast he feared would some day throw her. Yet she was as good a horseman as he was.

But that was not quite true. She was not as strong. He clenched his hands. She was only a woman and she had fought him as fiercely as a man, using the strength and weapons at her command as he had used his.

"I deny nothing! I am ashamed of loving you." The sentences drove back into his memory as sharply as the beating rain on his face. Where was she?

She had made good her promise—that she would never return to Bothwell. She had not. And she had ridden out of Hermitage before he had awakened, four weeks ago.

"Jane," he said again, low. The guards were only twenty feet away. He shouted suddenly, "Fellow!"

The guard replied.

"Bring me my horse! I'll keep your post till you return."

One guard scurried away. When he returned, the Hepburn seized the reins, and swung up into the saddle. No matter where she was, he would find her.

39

THEY SHOWED MARY GORDON INTO THE SMALL TOWER room. Mary crossed the room. Perkin, who had risen, leaned down and kissed her forehead gently.

He resumed his seat in front of his table. Mary sat opposite him, studying his face. It was as always nobly vapid, with its sweep of forehead crowned by the chestnut curls.

"Was it very bad?" she asked.

"At Cheapside? No." He shook his head. "The people were very kind, and curious. They clustered around me to see if I truly belonged to the Yorks."

They had paraded him through the streets of London on horseback.

Mary asked, "Why did you try to escape?"

He thought of the wild ride through the night. When dawn had broken, he had seen his pursuers. He remembered rushing up to an abbey door and crying to the priest, "Save me, Father!"

The priest had not been able to help, although he probably would have if he could have, Perkin thought. He answered Mary's question.

"Lord Warwick thought I could get safely away."

"You should not have involved him," Mary said. Suddenly she was appalled by the amount of death this man had caused, yet he never seemed aware of it, as though it were not his responsibility. "If you were not sure you *could* escape," she started to speak forcefully but she broke off. It was no use. He would never understand.

"You have no money to give me, have you?" he asked suddenly.

"How can you ask that?" She threw out her hands.

"I need it. I am helpless without money!" His voice rose a little and she saw he was greatly affected by his own plight.

Mary felt the nightmare unreality pressing close around her. She tried to be calm. "What are you writing?"

"I'm writing my mother."

"Your mother?" She stared at him.

"Catherine de Taro," he said. "They have promised to carry the letter to her. Maybe she will send money."

Mary leaned across the table. "Let me look."

He shoved the half-written parchment over to Mary to read.

> *"Ma mère,*
>
> As humbly as I can, I commend myself to you. It may please you to know that by chance certain English and Scottish men have made me do certain things, and undertake to be son of King Edward of England, his second son Richard, Duke of York."

Mary gasped. "Certain men made you do this? What men?"

He said, "They all did."

She read on. "Mother, I pray that you are willing to send me a little money in order to aid me, so that my guards may be made more amiable."

Mary pushed back the sheets. "Your mother?" she repeated. She tried to puzzle this out and could not. This Catherine de Taro, who had taken him to Europe, was she his mother, or was she a woman who had taken care of him? The truth was shrouded in lies.

"You have not even a few shillings?" he asked.

She said, "Where would I obtain money, Richard?"

"They've been kind to you," he said. There was resentment in his tone.

"They have been kind to me, Richard, because I am honest." From her pocket she took a little purse. She laid ten shillings on the table. " 'Tis all I have. I have paid my women. I shan't need more this month."

He picked up the money and smiled. He leaned across the table. "The Earl of Warwick and I are planning!"

Mary's hand grasped the table. "Oh no, Richard!"

He nodded. His face was expectant.

"Richard," she said. She was trying to marshal her thoughts. "Look, you, m'lord, this Warwick is but a boy and—"

"He is two and twenty."

"Aye, two and twenty, but since he was a tender ten he has been kept here. He is a poor thing, Richard. You could sway him. But you would send him to his death!"

Perkin looked away. "Did you come to lecture me?" he asked fretfully.

"No," she said, "but you must see you cannot take this boy's life. He is the unhappy son of the Plantagenets. Let him be."

He shook his head. "We're already as one."

Mary cried, "You cannot do this!" She put her fist down on the table and on the letter. And she said, "And you cannot send that letter. You will break your mother's heart!" Suddenly, as if a rent had torn itself across his face, she saw him clearly. He was saying, "See if you cannot obtain more money. That is what I need."

Mary Gordon rose. Her gown caught in the stool. It tore. She went slowly out the doorway and down the stone steps.

It was the middle of the morning. Dinner was at eleven. At Court she tried to eat but she could not.

The Court was stiff. It was not at all like James's Court. After the meal the queen sat surrounded by her ladies, while the men gathered in another part of the room, usually by the massive fire, and there they talked and laughed. Mary's needle flashed rhythmically. She was embroidering pillow cases for the royal household.

She sat next to Queen Elizabeth, but she felt completely alone as the other women gossiped, sometimes throwing a barbed remark at her.

"Your dress is tattered badly, my dear," one woman said.

"I tore it at the Tower," said Mary. She took a careful stitch.

The women studied her covertly. What was her position?

It was already rumored that the Earl of Warwick and the Warbeck pretender were plotting—their lenient guards, who had allowed them to meet, had overheard them. Rumor said too they were to be tried for treason, by a jury of their peers.

Mary Gordon stood suddenly. She would ask the queen to excuse her. She saw one of the men look over at her with a sidelong glance, and she turned her back on him. She was about to speak when another woman addressed her, low.

"Are you looking for another husband already?"

The queen didn't hear and the woman smiled maliciously. Mary raised one eyebrow. "They say a second husband is like warmed-over fish."

The queen did hear this and she laughed. Mary went on. "Madam, may I ha' your leave to go and mend my gown?"

The queen extended her hand. Mary kissed it. The queen was kind. So were a few of the others. At that moment the doors opened and a lackey called out: "His lordship the Earl of Pembroke."

Mary backed away from the queen, toward the near door. She took only two steps. In long strides the man who had been announced crossed the room, bowed to the queen, who had had his letter for two weeks. From her elevated chair the queen said, "Mistress Gordon, I present the Earl of Pembroke."

He carried his furred hat in his hand. The velvet cloak swept back from the wide shoulders and the rangy tall figure. His eyes were just as blue as they had ever been. Mary extended her hand. She looked up at him. Her lashes were stuck together with quick unshed tears.

"M'lord," she said. His hand was warm around hers. "Matthew," she whispered.

40

THE HALL AT HAILES CASTLE WAS SMALL. IT WAS blackened with smoke from its fireplace, which was but a pit in the center of the stone floor. Handhewn rafters crisscrossed the room at a low height; in them birds nested and twittered and sang. The windows had no glass; wooden shutters barred them.

The floor was laid with straw; the torches smoked evilly. The Hepburn closed the door after himself. It was all the same as it had ever been. The fire was burning brightly, the ends of the logs sticking out of the pit as they had always done. The Hepburn crinkled his eyes against the smoke. He would get used to it, in a few minutes. In the winters he had sat alongside the firepit, mending saddles, learning to read, having his hair cut. A long time had passed since then.

At the far end of the room a crude dais of wood lifted itself above the stone floor. The lord of the castle ate there, and it was there he had eaten, first with his father, then alone. The Hepburn passed the fire and looked across to the table. He walked over to it slowly, and stood over his wife, behind her. He did not know whether she had seen him enter; she gave no sign of it.

Knox was with her. Knox and the bailiff for Hailes, and the castle's captain of the garrison. They were all aware of his standing there; the Hepburn looked down at Jane's cards, held fanwise in her brown hand. She had pushed forward one shilling, and he deemed it not enough, for the others were paying little attention to their cards. He threw down five shillings.

Knox grinned. He tossed in his hand and the others followed suit. Jane didn't move, and the Hepburn scraped in her winnings for her. Then he made an almost imperceptible motion of his head to Knox, who stood. The two others rose also and bowed and said goodnight. Then they were all gone.

The Hepburn still stood behind Jane. Her head was bare. He laid his hand on the shining hair.

She leaned forward to escape his hand, and then pushed at the table and stood, swinging around to face him. She was wearing a shirt and breeches and boots. A leather belt accented her waist. She dug her hands into her hips and said, "You did not ask me if I wanted them to leave, did you?"

The Hepburn muttered, "No. I forgot." He shifted his feet. "Jane—" he began. She was so lovely. "I do not deserve to be heard, lass, but—"

She interrupted. "If you wish to be alone, I do not." She paused, leaning back against the table. "I'll ride on tonight, since you are here."

"The draw is closed, Jane—"

"You ordered it closed? As lord of this stinking pile?"

"Aye, I have searched for you for three weeks. Always you had just gone."

She brushed by him, and walked over toward the door. At the firepit she stopped. She hooked her thumbs in her belt. She was silhouetted by the firelight, proud. "I didn't want you to find me!"

He shook his head. "That's not true!"

"It is true!"

He said, low, "I have always loved you."

Jane did not reply. She turned her back.

The Hepburn said, "I have only four days. Then I go to London to wed the Princess Margaret, in James's place for him. James will not receive her here for a year."

There was still no reply. "Sweetheart," he began.

"Good-bye," said Jane. "God-speed."

The Hepburn frowned. He started toward her, and she whirled. He came to an abrupt stop.

"Jane, I'll let you go! But first, will you spend the four days with me? And I should like to say that I will always love you, and—" He broke off. She faced him, and he continued awkwardly, "I have been so much at fault! I am sorry. You have only my greatest admiration, and—"

"Did you memorize that speech?"

"No. Well, I warrant so. But I mean it, lass." The smoke curled up around her.

"You clumsy knave," said Jane. "You stink of horses." But incredulously he saw her flashing smile. With one swoop he gathered her into his arms.

Her head was buried in his shoulder. "My darling," she whispered.

The Hepburn held her tight. He smoothed her hair with one big hand, gently. The firelight flickered; a sudden trill of sound came from a bird's throat. From Hailes, from this old stone pile of rounded castle, he would set forth in four days for the journey to London. But there were still the four days. And after—there were more days, and years. Years that would see the birth of a new century. What could they not make of it, the two of them? He lifted her in his arms and carried her from the shuttered hall.